HAIL TO THE QUEEN!

MARTHA GRIMES
WINNER OF THE NERO WOLFE AWARD
FOR BEST MYSTERY

"HER WIT SPARKLES, HER PLOTS INTRIGUE, AND HER CHARACTERS ARE ABSOLUTELY UNFORGETTABLE."
—*The Denver Post*

"SHE REALLY HAS NO SUPERIOR IN WHAT SHE DOES. . . . Grimes's books are powerful comedies of no-manners, of the assumed gap between the blue-blooded and the red-blooded people. . . . Her people are delineated in Hogarthian outlines, vitalized by Dickensian gusto, but characterized by a detached humor and understanding that make them distinctly and exclusively Grimesian. . . . Her world is enriched by every new novel and our admiration grows."
—*The Armchair Detective*

"MARTHA GRIMES IS NOT THE NEXT DOROTHY SAYERS, NOT THE NEXT AGATHA CHRISTIE. SHE IS BETTER THAN BOTH."
—*The Atlanta Journal & Constitution*

By Martha Grimes

Scene of the Crime® Mysteries

The Man
with a
Load of Mischief

MARTHA GRIMES

A DELL BOOK

Published by
Dell Publishing
a division of
The Bantam Doubleday Dell Publishing Group, Inc.
666 Fifth Avenue
New York, New York 10103

To June Dunnington Grimes
and Kent Holland

ISBN 0-440-15327-1

Reprinted by arrangement with Little, Brown and Company, Inc.

Printed in the United States of America

Published simultaneously in Canada

Two Previous Dell Editions

September 1988

10 9 8 7 6 5 4 3 2 1

KRI

Come here, my sweet landlady, pray how d'ye do?
Where is Cicely so cleanly, and Prudence, and Sue?
And where is the widow that dwelt here below?
And the ostler that sung about eight years ago?

Why now let me die, Sir, or live upon trust,
If I know to which question to answer you first;
Why things, since I saw you, most strangely have varied,
The ostler is hang'd, and the widow is married.
And Prue left a child for the parish to nurse,
And Cicely went off with a gentleman's purse.

Matthew Prior

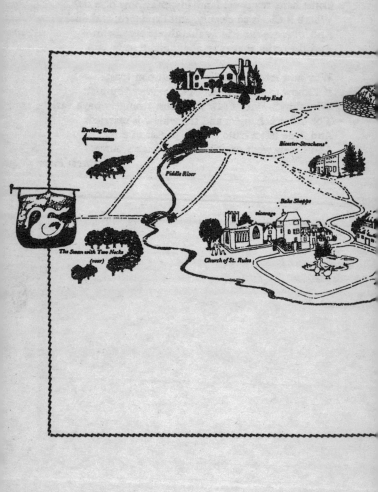

Ardry End

Dorking Dean

Bicester-Strachans'

Piddle River

Bake Shoppe

vicarage

The Swan with Two Necks
(rear)

Church of St. Rules

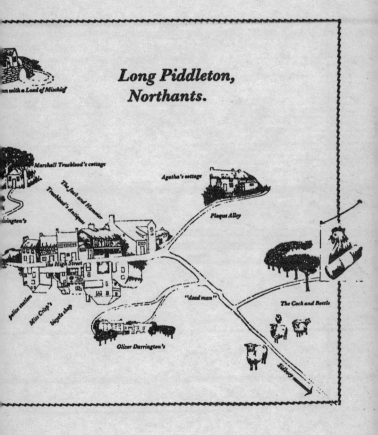

Long Piddleton, Northants.

...n with a Load of Mischief

Marshall Trueblood's cottage

Agatha's cottage

The Jack and Hammer

Trueblood's Antiques

...sington's

Plague Alley

The High Street

police station

Miss Crisp's

bicycle shop

"dead man"

The Cock and Bottle

Oliver Darrington's

Sidbury

CHAPTER 1

Outside the Jack and Hammer, a dog growled.

Inside, his view of the High Street obstructed by the window at his shoulder, Melrose Plant sat in the curve of the bay drinking Old Peculier and reading Rimbaud.

The dog growled deep in its throat and started barking again, something it had been doing intermittently for the last fifteen minutes.

Sun streaming through the cerulean blue and deep green of the tulip-design of the leaded panes threw rainbow colors across his table as Melrose Plant rose up to peer over the reverse letters advertising Hardy's Crown. The dog sitting in the snow outside the public house was a scruffy Jack Russell belonging to Miss Crisp, who ran the secondhand-furniture shop across the street. Usually it launched its barks from a chair set outside her door. Today, however, it had wandered across the street to occupy itself with the Jack and Hammer's frontage. It barked on.

"I direct your attention, Dick," said Melrose Plant, "to the curious incident of the dog in the daytime."

Across the room, Dick Scroggs, the publican, paused in his polishing of the beveled mirror behind the bar. "What's that, my lord?"

"Nothing," said Melrose Plant. "Just paraphrasing Sir Arthur."

"Sir Arthur, my lord?"

"Conan Doyle. Sherlock Holmes. You know." Melrose took a swig of his ale and went back to Rimbaud. But he didn't get very far along before the dog started barking again.

"Actually," said Melrose, snapping shut the book, "I believe it was the dog in the nighttime."

Scroggs applied his cloth to the mirror. "Nighttime, daytime, I only wish the bleedin' dog'd stop it. He be driving me crazy. Ain't it enough me nerves are in a state with this murder over at Matchett's place?" Dick was, for all his height and girth, a very nervous individual. Long Piddleton's murder had him constantly looking over his shoulder and regarding any stranger who walked into the Jack and Hammer with suspicion.

It was the murder, Melrose supposed, that had put him in mind of Conan Doyle. Murder in fact was not nearly so intriguing as murder in fancy. But he did have to admit their own murder had a certain flair: the head of the victim had been shoved down in a keg of beer.

The dog still barked.

It was not the sort of bark one hears when dogs greet each other over fences, nor was it especially loud. It was merely maddeningly persistent, as if this particular dog had chosen this post outside the Jack and Hammer's window to stand sentry and deliver its canine message to the world.

Dick Scroggs threw down his bar towel and went to the row of casement windows just beyond Plant's table, fronting the High Street. Scroggs wound out one of them and a blur of snow flew in around the corners. He shouted at the barking animal: "I be out there to kick your scruffy, bleedin' head off, just see if I don't."

"How awfully un-English of you, Dick," said Plant, adjusting his gold-rimmed spectacles over his fine nose and returning to Rimbaud. It was his fortieth-birthday present to himself: an early edition of *Les Illuminations,* for which he had paid a ridiculous price, telling himself he deserved it, then wondering why.

But Scroggs's shouts had only exacerbated the barking, since the dog now thought it had got some attention and meant to keep it. Dick Scroggs threw open the door and went outside to show the dog he meant business.

Plant had managed to read partway through "Enfance" when he heard Scroggs gasp: "My God, my lord, come quick!"

Plant looked up to see the publican's head framed in the snowy window. The face was gray and ghastly, a blown-up version of the gargoyle heads beneath the beam outside which gave the ancient building a quaint, ecclesiastical air.

Plant made for the door. Outside, he plowed through ankle-deep snow to where Dick Scroggs and the small, brown Jack Russell stood side by side, looking upward.

"Good God," whispered Melrose Plant, as the clock chimed the noon hour and another clump of snow fell from the figure atop the wooden beam that jutted out over the walk. The figure was not the mechanical smith usually located there, whose hammer made simulated strikes at a forge.

"It's that Mr. Ainsley that come in last night, my lord. For a room, he did." Scroggs's voice cracked hoarsely. "How long's he been up there, I wonder?"

Melrose Plant, ordinarily a man of extreme self-possession, was not sure how his own voice would sound. He cleared his throat. "Hard to tell. Could have been there for hours, all night, perhaps."

"And no one seen him?"

"Twenty feet overhead and shrouded in snow, Dick." As he spoke, another chunk fell, molten in the

sun, *plop*, at their feet. "I suggest one of us trot along
to the station and get Constable Pluck."

But it wasn't necessary. The barking of the dog and
Plant's and Scroggs's attendance at this macabre affair
seemed to have waked the High Street from its snowy
sleep and people were appearing out of shops, in windows, down walks and alleyways. Melrose saw that
Constable Pluck had appeared outside the station up
the street and was dragging on his dark blue overcoat.

"And here was the missus," said Dick with a hoarse
whisper, "wondering if he be wanting a bit of breakfast."

Said Melrose Plant, polishing the lenses of his spectacles, "I'd say it makes no odds to Mr. Ainsley."

The Jack and Hammer was wedged between Trueblood's Antiques and a haberdasher's sensibly called
The Shop, which only changed its window display of
bits and pieces of threads, tea cozies, mittens, dribs
and drabs of dry goods, at Christmas and Easter.
Across the street were a small garage with one bay;
Jurvis, the butcher's shop; a dark little cycle shop;
and Miss Crisp's. Farther along, just before the bridge
that spanned the Piddle River, was Long Piddleton's
police station.

The pub had once been painted a rather distinct
ultramarine. But its most unusual feature was the
structure attached to its front and from which it
derived its name: standing atop a sturdy beam was a
mechanical smith, carved out of wood and holding a
copy of a seventeenth-century forge hammer. When
the large clock beneath the beam told the hours,
"Jack" would raise his hammer and strike away at the
invisible iron forge.

The beam was twenty feet off the ground, about
seven feet long and two feet in girth, and it jutted
over the walk below. The carved figure (now re-

moved from the beam), although not life-sized, was not far from it. Originally, he had been painted into a bright blue coat and aquamarine trousers, but the paint was dull now, chipped and peeling. "Jack" was a favorite butt of jokes and horseplay, especially among the village children, who sometimes dressed him up and sometimes took him down. The wooden figure was treated very much like a rugby trophy, something to be carted away by delinquent boys from the nearby market town of Sidbury, and later rescued by equally delinquent boys from Long Piddleton. It was, in a way, the town mascot.

Just this past Guy Fawkes Day, several children had sneaked into the pub while Dick and his missus were fast asleep. They had gone up the back stairs and into the box room just above the beam outside. And they had lifted "Jack" from his supporting pole (from which he had been loosened by much tomfoolery over the years) and carried him off to the graveyard of St. Rules Church and buried him.

"Pore Jack," Mrs. Withersby had lamented from her post by the Jack and Hammer's fire, "not even a Christun burial, buried on the dog's side, he were, not even in confiscated ground. Bad luck it'll be all round, mark me. Pore Jack."

Since Mrs. Withersby's oracular powers were somewhat diminished by gin, not many people listened. But bad luck it was. Just one night before the discovery of Mr. Ainsley's body, another body had been found in an inn less than one mile from Long Piddleton's High Street—the body of one William Small, Esq.

With word that a killer was on the loose, the villagers were sticking to their parlors and fireplaces, something they might have done in any case because of the snow. It had been snowing for two days all over Northamptonshire, all over the north of En-

gland, indeed—lovely, soft stuff, which mounded on
roofs and settled in corners of windows whose leaded
panes were turned to squares of gold and ruby by reflected firelight. With the snow coming down and the
smoke rising up from the chimney pots, Long Piddleton looked like a Christmas card of itself, despite
the recent murder.

On the morning of December 19, the snow had finally stopped, and a bright sun had come out and
melted enough of it so that the cottages could be seen
to be prettily, even lavishly, painted. The High
Street, down to the bridge, was fascinating, or be-
guiling, or weird, depending upon one's tastes. It
looked like ít had been done by a convention of crazy
housepainters. Perhaps bored with the usual
limestone, in this limestone belt of Northamptonshire, they had gone rioting with ice-cream-parlor
colors: a hint of strawberry here, of lemon there, and
farther on, a glimmer of pistachio, and then a sudden
splash of emerald. When the sun was at its highest,
the street fairly glittered. Sunlight dyed the russet
bridge at the end so deep it was almost mahogany.
To a child, it must have been like walking between
big gumdrops down to a chocolate bridge.

An odd place for one murder to occur, much less
two.

"If you could just tell me what happened, sir, the
circumstances in which the body was found," said Superintendent Charles Pratt of the Northamptonshire
constabulary, who had been in Long Piddleton just
yesterday.

Melrose Plant explained, while Constable Pluck
stood by eagerly taking notes. Pluck was thin to the
point of emaciation, but he had a cherubic, rosy face,
made even rosier by winter's bite, so that he looked

like an apple on a stick. But he was a good man, if a bit of a gossip.

"And you say, so far as you know, this Ainsley chap was a stranger hereabouts. Like the other—" Pratt consulted his own notebook, then slapped it shut— "William Small."

"As far as I know, yes," said Melrose Plant.

Superintendent Pratt cocked his head and looked at Plant out of mild, blue eyes that seemed innocent, but that were, Melrose was sure, anything but. "Then you've reason to believe these men weren't strangers, sir?"

Melrose raised an eyebrow. "Well, naturally, Superintendent. Haven't you?"

"I'll have a whisky, Dick—neat, if you please."

Pratt having left and taken his lab crew, Melrose Plant and Dick Scroggs were alone once more in the Jack and Hammer.

"And have one yourself, Dick."

"Don't mind if I do," said Dick Scroggs. "It's a right old mess, init?" Several hours had elapsed, but Dick was still white, having watched closely the examination by the pathologist and the removal of the body, wrapped in a polyethylene sheet. The superintendent had left Pluck to see to the sealing off of the victim's room. There, they had been shocked to discover the murderer had added the further grotesque touch of placing the mechanical figure "Jack" in the victim's bed.

It was no wonder that Dick Scroggs was still trembly as he plucked up the 50p piece Melrose Plant had dropped on the bar. They studied their glasses for a moment, each alone with his thoughts.

Alone, that is, except for Mrs. Withersby, one of the many whom Pratt had questioned, who charred for Scroggs sometimes to get her drinking money. At the moment she was sitting on her favorite stool, spitting into the fire that had not been extinguished in a hundred years.

Now, seeing that the hard stuff was exchanging hands, she hove herself up from her stool and shuffled over, carpet slippers slapping the floor. Cigarette butt and spittle vied for position in the corner of her mouth. She removed the one between thumb and finger and wiped the other with the back of her wrist. She said—or shouted, rather—"His lordship buyin'?"

Dick raised a questioning eyebrow at Melrose Plant.

"Certainly," said Melrose, placing a pound note on the bar. "Nothing is too good for the woman with whom I danced all night in Brighton."

Dick was setting up a half-pint when Mrs. Withersby changed her tune: "Gin! I'll have me a gin, not that cat-lap." Then down she sat at the bar beside her benefactor, her faded yellowish hair standing up all around her head like a fright wig. She watched closely for her full measure as Dick poured. "If'n you'd add a pinch of dried mole's body to that there gin, wouldn't none of us have the ague."

Mole's body? wondered Plant, taking out his slim, gold cigarette case and extracting a cigarette.

"Or mebbe it was the malaria fever. Me mum always kept a bit of dried mole about. Drink it in gin nine mornin's runnin' and you'd be fit as a fiddle."

Or under the table, thought Melrose, offering his case to Mrs. Withersby. "And did you answer Superintendent Pratt's questions truthfully, madam?"

Her arthritic fingers grabbed up two of the cigarettes, one of which she planted in her mouth, the other in her checkered-gingham dress pocket. "Truthful? A'course I answered truthful," she said with a falsetto whine. "It's more'n I can say for the Fairy o' the Glen next door." She hooked her thumb in the direction of

Trueblood's Antiques. The sexual persuasion of its proprietor had long been under discussion in the village.

"Don't go casting irresponsible aspersions about, now," said Plant, who had just purchased the cure for ague and malaria she now raised to her warty lips. He lit her cigarette for her and was rewarded with a stream of smoke blown in his face.

Then she leaned closer, her tobacco-beer-gin breath rolling over him like a sea fret. "Now we got this crazed murderer runnin' about, doin' in us innercent folk." She snorted. "Oney this ain't no human hand. It's the divil hisself, mark me. I knew there'd be a death the day that bird fell down yer chimbley, Dick Scroggs. And we ain't had no watchin' at the porch on St. Mark's Eve for five years. The dead will walk! Mark my words! The dead will walk!" She nearly fell off her stool in her excitement, and Melrose thought the dead might be walking past them right now. But she quieted down when she regarded her now-empty glass, which no one was paying any attention to. Slyly, she said, "And how's yer dear auntie, m'lord? Gen'rous to a fault, is she. Always buys me a drink, friendly-like." Melrose signaled to Scroggs to refill the glass. Having secured her gin, she went on. "Lives simple-like, not givin' herself airs, and comes round every year with them Christmas baskets—"

For which Melrose paid. As she continued to extoll his aunt's virtues, Melrose studied their reflections in the mirror and wondered which was the toad and which the fairy princess. He was about to tuck into his pickled egg when Dick broke into a fit of violent coughing, for which Mrs. Withersby had her remedy ready: "Tell yer missus to fix up a bit of roast mouse. Me mum always had a bit of roast mouse for the whoopin' cough."

Melrose looked at the egg lolling on the plate and

decided he wasn't so hungry, after all. He paid up his bill—their bill—and bade farewell politely to Mrs. Withersby—Long Piddleton's village apothecary, village drunk, and village oracle.

CHAPTER 2

"These murders," said the vicar, "put me in mind of The Ostrich, in Colnbrook." He bit into his fat rascal, and crumbs cascaded down his dark suit-front.

Around a mouthful of fairy cake, Lady Agatha Ardry said, "Far as I'm concerned, we've probably another Ripper amongst us."

"Jack the Ripper, dear Aunt," said Melrose Plant, "only fancied women. Of dubious virtue."

Lady Ardry finished her fairy cake and dusted her hands. "Perhaps this one's queer." She surveyed the tea table. "You've taken the last of the fat rascals, Denzil." She eyed the vicar accusingly.

Outside the mullioned panes of the vicarage, a fine English rain drifted its delicate veil across the churchyard. The Church of St. Rules and its vicarage sat on a hump of earth not quite a hill, directly behind and above the village square. It was on the other side of the bridge which ended the High Street, and a more sedate temperament reigned here. The square was enclosed by Tudor buildings, thatched roofs and pantiled roofs, all snug and wedged together.

Melrose disliked coming to tea at the vicarage, especially when his aunt was invited. The vicar's housekeeper was never at her best in the food department. Her baked goods would have helped in the Battle of Britain had the country run out of bullets and bombs. Melrose scanned the tiered cake plate, looking

for something digestible: the rock cakes lived up to
their name; the Maids of Honor looked left over
from Victoria's wedding; the Bath buns must have
walked. He had been listening to his aunt and the
vicar rehash these two murders for nearly two hours,
and he was horribly hungry. He reached out with
some trepidation for a brandy snap. Politely, he inquired of the vicar, "You mentioned The Ostrich?"

Thus encouraged, Denzil Smith went on eagerly.
"Yes. You see, when the proprietor came across a
traveler with a good bit of money, he would book
him into the room with a bed set over a trapdoor."
The vicar paused to select a stale-looking bun from
the plate. "When the unfortunate and unwary guest
was sleeping soundly the trapdoor sprang open, and
he fell into a cauldron of boiling water."

"Are you suggesting that Matchett and Scroggs are
disposing of their own guests, Vicar?" Lady Ardry sat
there in the library, solid and square and gray as a cement block, her stubby legs crossed and her pudgy
fingers busy with her second Eccles cake.

"No, no," said the vicar.

"It's obviously a psychotic madman," said Lady
Ardry.

Plant let the redundancy pass, but asked, "What
makes you so sure the murderer is psychotic, Agatha?"

"Are you barmy? To shove a body up on that beam
outside the pub? Why, it must be twenty feet up.
Whoever would stick a body up there?"

"King Kong?" suggested Melrose, running the
brandy snap under his nose like the cork of an old
wine.

"You seem to be taking this horrible business
rather lightly, Melrose," said the Reverend Denzil
Smith.

"Don't expect compassion from Melrose," put in

his aunt righteously, as she sank back into the huge Victorian armchair. "Living in that enormous house all alone, no one but that Ruthven person to do for you—it's no wonder you're antisocial."

And yet here he was at tea, being terribly social. Melrose sighed. His aunt always could fly in the teeth of the evidence. Cautiously he bit into the brandy snap and wished he hadn't.

"Well?" said Lady Ardry.

Melrose raised his eyebrows. " 'Well' what?"

She made brief forays toward their cups with the Spode pot, then plunked it down. "I should think you'd have more to say than that about these murders. After all, you were there with Scroggs." This clearly rankled. She added slyly: "It was Dick Scroggs who actually found him, though. So, of course, you didn't get the awful shock *I* did when I went down to that cellar and saw this Small actually *dangling* out of that beer thing—"

"You didn't find him. The Murch girl did." Melrose ran his tongue over the roof of his mouth. The cream had a decidedly metallic taste. But a pellet of poison would be better than listening to Agatha. "Are you sure the cream in these brandy snaps hasn't gone off? They taste strange." He returned the confection to his saucer and wondered how long he had before they sent round the van.

"There was a similar case back in—let's see—was it 1892? Woman named Betty Radcliffe, landlady at The Bell. That's in Norfolk. Murdered by her lover, I believe, the gardener."

Denzil Smith was not a particularly pious man, but he was a curious one, which made him excellent company for Lady Agatha Ardry. They were dependent on one another in the mindless way of two gibbons dedicated to picking fleas off one another's fur. He was the village repository of old scraps of history, both village and extravillage, a walking book of memorabilia.

Looking around, Melrose thought the vicarage the perfect milieu for Denzil Smith. It was dark; it was as dusty as the waxen fruits that sat under glass globes. A stuffed owl, spread-winged, was stuck on the mantel. The thick-armed chairs and couch had incongruous animal feet sticking out from under their chintz dresses, so that Melrose had the feeling he had come to tea with the Three Bears. Clematis and bindweed roved freely along the windows. He wondered how it would feel to be strangled by a bindweed. No worse, surely, than the rock cakes. That reminded him of the murder of William Small: strangled with a length of wire used to wrap around the cork of a champagne bottle.

Lady Ardry was talking about the expected visit from Scotland Yard. "The Northants police are calling in the Yard. Pluck told me. Wonder who they'll put on the case."

Melrose Plant yawned. "Old Swinnerton, probably."

She sat up suddenly, her glasses perched on top of her frizzy gray head like the goggles of a racing driver. "Swinnerton? You know them?"

He was sorry he had made up the name—wasn't there always a Swinnerton?—for now she would worry it like a dog an old rag. Because Melrose had been born to his title (unlike his aunt, who had merely married one), she seemed prepared to believe he knew everyone from the Prime Minister on down. He diverted her attention by saying, "I don't know why they need Scotland Yard here, when they have you, Agatha."

His aunt simpered, and passed him the awful cakes, his reward for recognizing genius. "I do spin intriguing plots, don't I?"

Long Piddleton had lately begun to attract artists and writers, and Lady Ardry, who had lived here for many years, fancied herself a writer of mysteries, having taken up the cudgel after the passing of the great lady of detective fiction. She did nothing with the cudgel, Melrose observed, except wave it. He had never seen any finished product; he assumed she regarded her writing in the light of a well-beloved child, a kind of fairy sprite who darts prettily about the yard but never knocks to have its dinner fixed. Never, to his knowledge, had she finished one of her "intriguing plots."

Hitting her fist into her hand, Agatha said, "Scotland Yard'll want to talk to me straightaway, of course—"

"I'll be off, then," said Plant, dreading the resumption of his aunt's recitation of her role in these murders, which he'd heard several times before. He rose and bowed slightly.

"I should think you'd be a bit more excited," said Agatha. "Of course, it was Scroggs who actually found *your* body." She didn't want to allow Melrose a larger part than she absolutely had to.

"More precisely, it was a Jack Russell. The Yard will question it first, no doubt. Good day, Agatha."

As the vicar walked Plant through the Gothic arch of the library and to the front door, Lady Ardry's voice trailed after him—around corners, down the hall. "Your facetiousness in the face of this terrible business hardly becomes you, Melrose." Then louder: "But it's what I might have expected." Louder, still: "Remember you're taking us to Matchett's for dinner this evening. Pick me up at nine."

Melrose Plant felt slightly doomed himself, as he listened to the vicar relate the grisly murder, some years ago, of a barmaid in Cheapside.

CHAPTER 3

Ardry End was known to the villagers as the Great House. It was a turreted and towered manor house built of sandstone—hues ranging from rose to russet, depending upon the angle of the sun. Its approach was as elegant as the house itself, over a bridge of the same stone, which crossed the Piddle River on a road routed through acres of green land, now patched with snow. Ardry End's situation, amidst the streams and the sheep and the lavender hills, nearly brought Lady Agatha Ardry to tears because she didn't own it. That her own husband had not been the eighth Earl of Caverness and twelfth Viscount Ardry had always been a searing wound. The Honorable Robert Ardry had been, instead, the useless younger brother of Melrose Plant's father. Where her nephew had dropped the title of *Lord Ardry*, Agatha had picked it up and dusted it off, transforming herself overnight into "Lady" Ardry. Melrose's uncle died in a gaming room at the age of fifty-nine, having lost what little money remained to him, so that Lady Ardry was more or less dependent upon the generosity of her brother-in-law—a fact that did not add to Melrose's popularity. His father had been an industrious member of the House of Lords and vice-president of a stock brokerage. Richer when he died than he had allowed when he was living, he had seen to it that his brother's widow had received a comfortable annuity.

Thus, the marble and parqueted halls of Ardry End being forever beyond her grasp, Agatha never ceased in her nudges and hints to Melrose about "needing a woman round the place." He pretended to believe the broad winks and nods were pointers that he should take a wife, knowing full well that a wife was the last thing his aunt wanted him to have, since he assumed she was fervently counting the hours until some rare disease would bring about his premature demise, and she would come into the inheritance she was apparently certain he would be willing to provide, there being no other relatives of whom she was aware. And she was aware of everything that applied to Melrose Plant's estate—or so it seemed.

Melrose Plant regarded his aunt as the albatross which his uncle had shot down and left to hang around his nephew's neck. Lord Robert had shot her down in Milwaukee, Wisconsin, when he had been on a pleasure tour of the United States. Agatha was an American. But she buried this as well as she could under tweed suits, walking sticks, sensible shoes, interminable plates of cucumber sandwiches, and a good ear for the English idiom but a terrible one for proper names.

His aunt used every pretext to appear suddenly at Ardry End to look covetously at the bisque statuary, the portraits, the Chinese and William Morris wall coverings, the Waterford, the pleasaunce, the swans— all of those appointments of the serene, stately home. Lady Ardry would turn up at all hours, and in all weathers, uninvited. It was nerve-racking to go into the study at midnight with the rain slicing through the winter darkness to see a black-caped, white-faced figure outside the French windows, suddenly illuminated in a flash of lightning. It was equally unnerving to have the figure enter, bulky and sopping, puddling the Persian rugs like a big dog and taking the attitude that it was all Melrose's fault—why hadn't that silly twit of a butler, Ruthven (a name she always mispronounced), why hadn't he answered the front door? Then she would sigh and look about with that "no room at the inn" expression, as if her nephew had been the flint-hearted tavernkeeper relegating her to her hayrick back in the village.

Cycling along, Melrose took deep, appreciative gulps of the December air, and thought of these two murders which had been done within twenty-four hours of one another. They had given the village something to speculate about other than his marital status. And had made everyone wary, very wary, of doing what Plant was doing now—traveling down a lonely road by himself. It was not that he was particularly brave, only that he was particularly commonsensical. He had already deduced a pattern into which he, as a victim, did not fit. Both murders had taken place at inns, and both were grotesque almost to the point of absurdity. Whatever the murderer had in mind was something definite, and the criminal seemed to be the sort whose diabolical crimes were planned to please himself. At least, he seemed to be making quite a production of it.

Plant rolled his bike up the last remaining feet to the iron gate of Ardry End. The gate was guarded by two gilt lions set atop high stone pillars. His aunt audibly and frequently wondered why he didn't have a few large, noble dogs to rush forward and greet his visitors: *The Hound of the Baskervilles* had taken its toll in her youth. Melrose unhinged the gate, closed it again, and pushed the bike along up the sweep of drive, looking at the place with his aunt's practiced eye. The hawthorn hedges on either side were high and neat. Melrose had nearly had to beat the gardener back with a hoe to keep him from turning the hedges into a topiary showplace, the sort of thing Lorraine Bicester-Strachan, his nearest neighbor, went in for.

If Ardry End didn't resemble Hampton Court, Mr. Peebles, the gardener, thought its grounds certainly extensive enough to be compared favorably with Hatsfield House. Peebles was applauded in all of his attempts to turn Ardry End into a showplace by Lady Ardry. These two got on like a team of old dray horses, pulling imaginary loads of ornamental and exotic plants through the grounds, to shape, form, and reform these green expanses which Melrose only wanted to leave to the pleasures of wind and weather. His aunt plumped for views and vistas and *coups d'oeil*, perhaps the surprise of a miniature Pantheon across the lake, its Corinthian columns blinding white in the sun. Left to Aunt Agatha and Mr. Peebles, his natural lawns and woods would have been strangled with knot gardens and stylized patterns drawn in clipped dwarf box, privet, thorn, and yew. Peebles, seconded by his aunt, had been victorious in the one lily pond enclosed in a clipped yew hedge, with a small, discreet fountain at the center. The gardener had tried to sneak lead fish into the bottom of the pond, but Melrose made him remove them. To make amends for the lead fish, Melrose had agreed to two real swans and a family of ducks for the lake. But the swans and the pond were his only concession. Lady Ardry and Mr. Peebles would have spelled out the Mountardry-Plant name on the front lawn in flowering plants, like a municipal building.

The door to Ardry End was opened by the butler, Ruthven. To say that Ruthven was of the old school was to put it very mildly. Plant speculated that every other manservant in England might have gone to school to Ruthven. Melrose could remember him

from the time he was a tiny tot; Ruthven could be
anywhere between fifty and a hundred—he had always
looked the same to Melrose.

Plant had inherited Ruthven along with the portraits and stocks and Morris wallpapers, and during
the course of their relationship, the master had done
only one thing to upset the butler. Melrose had given
up his title several years ago, after a few sessions in
the House of Lords. It had nearly brought Ruthven
to his bed. The news had been handed the butler one
morning at breakfast, casually, like someone giving
back the plate for more kippers: *Oh, incidentally,
Ruthven, it won't be "my lord" any longer*. And Ruthven had stood there, carved out of rock, his expression magnificently unchanged. *I thought it inappropriate, you know, holding down a job, at the
same time having that awkward title*. Ruthven had
merely bowed and held out the silver dish of buttered
eggs circumscribed by plump sausages. *And, anyway,
I never have fancied taking my seat in the House of
Lords. What a bloody bore that would be*. As a sau-
sage went *plop* on the plate, Ruthven begged to excuse himself, saying he felt a bit unwell.

Lady Ardry had received the news with far more
ambivalence. On the plus side lay the fact that she
had finally topped Melrose: now *she* had a title, but
he hadn't. For that she was overjoyed. On the minus
side was the terrible un-Englishness of it all. How
could he *dare* throw away something it had taken so
many years and such impeccable breeding to acquire?
And on those rare occasions when distant relatives
trooped in from the States, Lady Ardry had gloried in
showing off her "ancestral home," and Melrose along
with it ("my nephew, the eighth Earl of Caverness
and twelfth Viscount Ardry") and they would all
look him up and down as if he were one of the *objets*

d'art. Agatha was on the real horns of a dilemma: on the one hand, how delightful to tell herself he was "my nephew, the commoner"; on the other, it was like pulling back the pretty pink bunting, with the relatives standing round, only to discover the baby had suddenly grown warts.

Thus the title was now the one department where she had bested him. She had nothing else to offer as competition. He was not terribly rich, but rich enough; not terribly handsome, but handsome enough; not terribly tall, but tall enough. When he removed his sedate gold-rimmed spectacles to polish them, one could see his eyes were an amazing, glittering green. And his referring to "holding down a job" was a bit of an understatement. Melrose held the chair of French Romantic poetry at the University of London where he taught for about four months out of the year, leaving echoes of himself to reverberate for the other eight.

So to top it all, he was Professor Melrose Plant. It made Lady Ardry positively shudder. He was like a cat with nine lives, or the Man in the Iron Mask, or the Scarlet Pimpernel: a man with extra identities he could leave behind him like calling cards on a silver salver.

And he had one other vice which caused her no end of suffering: he was simply too damnably clever.

Plant could do the *Times* crossword in less than fifteen minutes. She had challenged him at one point to a crossword-puzzle duel. Unfortunately, it took Lady Ardry a half-hour just to straighten out the ups and downs, so she had given up in disgust, claiming it was a childish waste of time. But then Melrose didn't really have to work for a living, did he?—implying for herself a wretched Cinderella role of missed balls, doomed to carrying out the ashes of the world so that others (like Melrose) might dance all night, to wake between satin sheets with their breakfast trays and their *Times* crosswords.

Plant sighed as he sat gloomily in front of the fireplace. Now there was this beastly murder business to which his aunt would bring all of her nonexistent deductive skills. And drag him into it, merely by proximity. Well, he supposed he was in it, anyway, by virtue of having been at the Jack and Hammer yesterday morning. But he really did not want to be forever talking about it. He did not want to hear about this Small person, or the other, either, but he would be forced to hear about them, possibly for the rest of his natural life.

For Melrose did not put too much stock in the deductive powers of the nation's police force, either.

CHAPTER 4

Shielding his eyes with his hand like a man facing into the full glare of the sun, Detective Chief Inspector Richard Jury squinted suspiciously at Chief Superintendent Racer, who was sitting on the other side of his immaculate desk—he was always quick to get the work off it and onto somebody else's—calmly smoking one of his hand-rolled cigars. Superintendent Racer's other hand toyed with a gold chain running from one vest pocket to the other. His French-cuffed shirt was powder blue and his Donegal tweed suit from his bespoke tailor. Inspector Jury regarded his superior as a bit of a dandy, a bit of a dilettante, and a bit—a very little bit—of a detective.

It was not that Inspector Jury suffered under the illusion that his colleagues in New Scotland Yard were all solid with integrity and full of the milk of human kindness—the London bobby in domed hat and short cape happily directing tourists all over town. Or the higher-ups such as himself appearing in neat, shiny suits, under the fanlights of dark doorways, saying to the bathrobed mistress, "Merely a routine inquiry, madam." No, they were not all cool-headed, diamond-witted upholders of law and order. But Racer contributed so little to that pleasant old stereotype. He sat there now, looking terribly county, and thinking, probably, about his dinner or the latest conquest with whom he would share it, leaving the Jurys of the world to sort out the mess.

Jury looked out from under the tent of his hand. "A man with his head shoved in a beer keg?" He still hoped Racer would tell him it was all a bad joke.

Racer only smiled sourly. "Never heard of the Duke of Clarence, eh?" The superintendent was fond of matching wits with Jury, and in the way of true masochists and gamblers, kept it up, though he never won.

"He was drowned—or so the story goes—in a butt of Malmsey," said Jury, stealing Racer's little bit of erudition.

Annoyed, Racer snapped his fingers as if he were calling a dog. "The facts, let's hear the facts."

Jury sighed. Having been given a rundown on the murders in Northamptonshire, he was now expected to give it back, like a stenographer. Racer always listened carefully for errors.

"The first victim, William Small, found in the wine cellar of the Man with a Load of Mischief. Choked with a length of wire, his head shoved in a beer keg. The proprietor brews his own occasionally—"

Racer interrupted: "Too many brewers taking over all these old inns. Give me a free house every time. . . ." He took out his little gold toothpick and, while starting in on his rear molars, motioned for Jury to continue.

"The second victim, Rufus Ainsley, found at the Jack and Hammer, on the wooden support beam above the clock, the one the carved figure of the smith stands on. . . ." Once again, Jury looked at Racer, hoping he would tell him it was a joke. But the chief superintendent merely sat there, having removed the toothpick and looking as if the elves had come in the night to stitch together his leathery lips along with the shoes. What unnerved Jury was that

Racer found nothing at all odd in this lot. Apparently, since the Duke of Clarence had got his, heads in kegs of beer were not to be wondered at.

Jury went on: "A waitress at the inn—Daphne Murch—was the first one to come on the body of William Small, and she called the proprietor, Simon Matchett. There were a number of people in the bar, and all claimed not to know the deceased. Small had appeared, according to the proprietor, only that day, desiring lodgings. That was the first crime. The second occurred twenty-four hours later. The body of Ainsley had been put up on the beam in place of the mechanical figure. . . ." Jury's voice trailed off. The murderer as Guy Fawkes prankster made his blood run cold.

"Continue."

"The body of Ainsley was apparently lowered out the window of a box room directly above the beam. The height of the beam and the snow would account for no one's noticing it for hours. . . ." He wondered if he were dreaming. "The victims were both strangers to Long Piddleton, having arrived within a day or two of one another—"

"Day or *two?* What sort of gibberish is that, lad? What do you think you're doing, Jury? Guessing long shots? Mucking about in the football pools? A policeman's job is to be exact!" And he plugged his mouth again with the thick cigar, staring at Jury while the intercom buzzed. Racer flipped the switch. "Yes?"

It was one of the girls who worked in C-4. She had brought round the file on the Northamptonshire murders.

"Bring it in, then; bring it in," said Racer irritably.

Fiona Clingmore entered and, getting her priorities straight, smiled warmly at Jury before handing over the manila folder to Racer. She was wearing one of those 1940 outfits she seemed to like: black, high-

heeled shoes with a button strap across the instep,
tight black skirt, black nylon blouse with long, full
sleeves which always made her look *en négligée*. As
usual, her neckline was down and her skirt was up.
Fiona always seemed to wear her clothes at half-mast;
perhaps she was mourning chastity, thought Jury.

Jury watched the superintendent's eye peeling the
clothes from her like an onion, layer after filmy layer.
"That'll be all," Racer said, and shooed her off with
a flap of his hand.

With another smile and a wink at Jury, she left.
Racer saw that and said with sarcasm, "Quite the
ladies' man, aren't you, Jury?" Then he snapped,
"D'ya think we could get back to business, now?" He
spread out some photos that he had taken from the
folder and tapped the first with his finger: "Small,
William. Killed between nine and eleven on Thursday night, December seventeenth, as nearly as the
Northants boys can fix it. Ainsley, killed sometime after seven on December eighteenth. Twenty-four hours
apart. No identification. We only know their names
because they signed the registers. Small got off a train
in Sidbury, but we don't know where he boarded.
Nothing to connect either one of them with anyone
in the village. That's the lot. Some lunatic loose, no
doubt." Racer started to clean his nails with a
penknife.

"I only wish they'd called us in immediately; it's a
cold trail—"

"Well, they didn't, then, did they, lad? So get down
there and pick up the cold trail. You expect things to
be easy for you, Jury? A policeman's life is full of
grief. Time you learned it." He snapped the penknife
shut, and began cleaning his ear with his little finger.
Jury only wished he would complete his toilette at
home.

Jury knew it infuriated Racer to have to put him

on the case. Everyone in the division felt that it was Jury who should be chief superintendent. For his part, Jury did not really care. He didn't want to be in charge of a division, and God knows he didn't want to spend his time investigating complaints against other policemen. Having no wife and no children dependent upon him, he could afford the lesser salary, which was ample for his modest needs. What did all this superstructure matter, anyway? Jury had known PCs who were as invaluable in their expertise and knowledge as were the men on the Olympian heights of the commissioner.

"When did you want me to leave, sir?"

"Yesterday," snapped Racer.

"I've still got this Soho murder—"

"You mean that Chink restaurant business?"

The phone interrupted them and Racer yanked it up. "Yes?" He listened a moment, flicking glances at Jury. "Yes, he's here." He listened a moment longer, a mean smile playing on his thin lips. " 'Over six feet, chestnut hair, dark gray eyes, good teeth, and a ravishing smile'?" his voice fluted. "That's our Jury, all right." The smile vanished. "Tell her he'll call her back. We're busy." Racer slammed down the receiver, bouncing several ball-point pens. "Except for the 'ravishing smile' bit, that description could fit a horse."

Jury asked patiently, "May I inquire what that was all about?"

"One of the waitresses down at that Soho restaurant." Racer looked at his watch. The call must have reminded him of his own engagement. "Got a dinner date." He tossed the folder across the desk to Jury. "Get down to this godforsaken village. Take Wiggins with you. He's not doing anything except blowing his goddamned nose."

Jury sighed. As usual, Racer hadn't even asked him

to choose his own detective sergeant. Wiggins was a
young man made old through hypochondria. Likable
enough, and efficient, but always on the verge of
keeling over. "I'll gather up Wiggins and leave early
in the morning," said Jury.

Racer was out of his chair and pulling on his beautifully tailored overcoat. Jury wondered where his
chief superintendent got his money. Taking bribes?
Jury didn't care.

"Well, gather him up, then." The superintendent
flicked his thin, gold wristwatch. "Dinner at the Savoy. Got a gal waiting." His smile was lascivious as he
drew a shape in air. At the door he turned and said,
"And for God's sake, Jury, remember you work here,
will you? When you get to that one-eyed village, report in for a change."

Jury walked down the hall—and what lackluster
halls they were, now, compared with the Victorian
elegance of the old building. No marble and mahogany here, certainly. Crammed and jammed as old
Scotland Yard might have been, he preferred it.
When he got to the door of his own office, he found
Fiona Clingmore hovering nearby, as if she had hit
the spot purely by accident. She was buttoning up a
black overcoat.

"Well, Inspector Jury, off duty at last?" Her voice
sounded hopeful.

Jury smiled, reached inside the door, and grabbed
his coat from the tree. His mates had left, so he
switched off the light and shut the door. Looking
down at her face, less young than one might have
supposed at a distance, and at the high-piled yellow
hair on which perched a kind of pillbox hat, Jury
said, "Fiona, you know what you make me think of?"
She shook her head, but looked at him expectantly.
"All of those old wartime movies where the Yanks

stream into London and fall in love with the local girls."

Fiona giggled. "A bit before my time, that is."

That was true. But she still looked out of another era. She might not be pushing forty, but she was close enough to give it a nudge.

"I don't think my Joe'd like you talking this way to me, Inspector Jury," she said coyly.

She was always talking about her Joe. No one had ever seen him. Jury had guessed some time ago that there was no Joe. There may have been once, but no more. He looked at Fiona smiling at him, saw how empty her eyes were, and felt a sudden rush of empathy, of kinship, even. "Listen," said Jury, looking at his watch, "I've got to go down to Soho on a bit of business. Since it's a restaurant, and I've not eaten . . . how about it? Want a bit of supper? I'm certainly due for a break."

Her face was flooded with what looked very much like a dawning day. Then she lowered her mascaraed lashes and said, "Oh, I don't know if my Joe'd go for that, but . . ."

"Joe doesn't have to know, now does he?" She looked up, and Jury winked at her.

It was nearly midnight by the time Jury had finished with his Soho restaurateur and Fiona's incessant chatter. When he emerged at the Angel tube stop, he was extremely tired and did not relish the idea of an early train to Northamptonshire. He consoled himself by thinking that getting out of London for a few days—or weeks, even—might be pleasant. He had nowhere to go for Christmas, anyway, except to his cousin's miserable house in the Potteries, to be pulled about by her two kids.

Jury yanked a leftover *Times* from under the brick

by the tube exit, tossed some coins on the rest of the skinny pile, and walked off toward home.

It had started snowing—a thin, powdery snow, not the kind of wet, fat flakes that stuck on your lashes and stayed on your tongue. Jury liked the snow, but not the London kind, which only served to muck up traffic in its gray and slushy runoff. It was coming down heavier now, grainy as sugar, and pricked his face as he walked along Islington High Street toward Upper. He swerved off into Camden Passage, which he liked at this time of night, eerily silent as the little shops were, the night disturbed only by the tinny sound of bits of paper being bounced by the wind. The Camden Head was closed up and the little stalls set up by the antiques people all taken down. When they were doing business out here in the open the place was fairly jammed, and Jury liked to hang about sometimes and watch the shoplifters work. His favorite dip, Jimmy Pink, was fond of Camden Passage—Jimmy could take your pocket along with what was in it without your knowing. Jury had nicked him so many times here that he had suggested to Jimmy he might as well set up a stall himself.

He walked out of the passage into Charlton Place, thence to Colebrook Row, a lovely little crescent of houses where he wouldn't have minded living himself, then on for a couple of streets to his own row of houses. Most of them had been converted into flats. It was a bit seedier, but not unpleasant, for it fronted a little park across the way, to which each occupant had a key.

Jury's own flat was on the second floor. There were five others, and he scarcely saw his neighbors because of his weird hours. But he did know the woman who lived in the basement rooms—Mrs. Wasserman. He saw there was a light glowing there, behind heavily grilled and draped windows. Two geraniums flanked the steps, summer and winter. Mrs. Wasserman was up, as usual.

He let himself in and switched on the overhead. The room sprang up in the light and left him, as always, dismayed by the mess, as if thieves had just ransacked his rooms and made a fast exit. It was the books, mostly. They spilled from the cases and tables. In the bay window, which overlooked the park, was his desk. He lay the folder down there and took off his coat. Then he sat down and went through the photographs once more. Incredible.

The first was taken in the wine cellar of the Man with a Load of Mischief and was dark and grainy, but one could still see with startling clarity the almost torsoless body. The victim had been lifted over the waist-high keg used for home brewing, so that his head and shoulders were in the keg and the rest of the body dangling down the side.

Jury wondered why. Why, that is, given that William Small had been garroted with a length of wire, had the murderer bothered with this grotesque embellishment?

The photograph of the Jack and Hammer was even more bizarre. The body of Rufus Ainsley, limp as it was after the rigor had passed off, had been supported by the narrow metal bar that had secured the carved figure to the beam. This tube had been run up inside the victim's shirt, a rope lashed around his midsection, and all then covered by his buttoned-up suit jacket. There were still clumps of unmelted snow on his shoulders. There it was, then, the body hidden in plain sight, the best place to hide anything— beneath your feet or over your head. The victim was a smallish man, five feet five or six, so he made a good stand-in for the carved figure. Hard to say how long it would have been before someone had looked up; anyway, people see what they expect to see.

But again, Why? What purpose was served by this elaborate ruse?

He gathered up the photos, opened the shallow desk drawer, and slid the folder in beside a small, framed photograph. It was lying in the drawer, face down. Jury had taken it off the desk, but couldn't bring himself to throw it away. When he was younger, Jury hadn't given much thought to marriage. He thought about it now, though. In forty years, rarely had a special woman come along. Maggie had been one.

Jury put her picture back, face down, closed the drawer, and was locking it with a little key when he heard a rap at the door.

"Inspector Jury," said the woman outside when he opened the door, clasping and unclasping her hands, "he's out there again. I don't know what to do. Why don't he leave me alone?"

"I've just got in, Mrs. Wasserman—"

"I know, I know, and I hate to trouble you. But . . ." She spread her hands in a helpless gesture. She was a heavy woman, dressed in a black dress pinned at the bosom with a filigree brooch. Her black hair was pulled back smooth and tight into a bun coiled up like a spring. She made him think of a tightly wound spring herself, as she kneaded her hands and pushed her sweater sleeve up to the elbow in a nervous gesture.

"I'll go down with you," said Jury.

"It's the same shoes, Inspector. You know, I can always tell by the shoes. What's he want? . . . Why don't he leave me alone? . . . Is that grill strong enough, do you think? . . . Why does he keep coming back and back? . . ." Her questions floated back to Jury as they descended the flights of stairs to her rooms.

"I'll just have a look."

"Yes, do." Her hands went up to her face, as if even Jury's glancing out of the tiny front window might endanger them both. Opposite her door was a window, level with the top step and the pavement. "There's nobody there, Mrs. Wasserman." Jury knew there wouldn't be.

It happened about every two months. At first Jury had tried to convince her of the truth: there was nobody there. Mrs. Wasserman spent a lot of time watching the feet on the pavement, the bodiless feet and legs passing by her window. It was the one pair of feet, of shoes, she had fixed on and claimed came back and back again to harass her. Stopping. Waiting. She was terrified of The Feet.

Jury had tried to convince her The Feet weren't there, that He wasn't there, until it had at last come home to him that he was upsetting her more. She needed to believe it. So over the past year, Jury had helped her make her flat as impregnable as a fortress: heavier grillwork, deadbolt locks, chains, burglar alarms. But still, without fail, she'd be up at his door. Each time he did something—another lock, another alarm, maybe—and each time she was flooded with relief. He assured her that someone could ransack New Scotland Yard before they could get into the Wasserman flat, and she thought that funny. He had run out of ideas by now, though.

He looked out the window, saw nothing, tested the grillwork as a matter of form. She was watching him anxiously. He knew that if he hesitated too long, she would lose faith. Out of his pocket he took a tiny, round piece of metal and held it up. "Mrs. Wasserman, I really shouldn't do this, it's not legal"—and he grinned and so did she, sharing the secret—"but I'm putting this on your telephone." He picked up the base of the phone and attached the disc to the metal plate underneath. "There. Now, if anyone should

bother you, just lift the receiver and push this metal
disc to the side. It'll ring my phone upstairs." Her
face brightened. "But, look, only use it if you absolutely *have* to—an emergency—because it buzzes Central and I'd be in one hell of a jam."

Relief flooded her face and it was pathetic to see.
He knew she wouldn't use it; it was only the reassur-
ance she wanted, and he was safe for another two
months. Then the tension would build again and she
would see The Feet. It was almost like the tension of
a sexual deviant or a drug addict. And there was so
little to distract her from her obsession. He often
wondered about the emptiness of her life. He would
look in her dark little eyes sometimes and see himself
reflected there.

"Oh, Inspector Jury, what would I do without you?
It's such a relief you living here, a real Scotland Yard
policeman." Quickly, she walked over to the fireplace,
where an electric log burned, and took down a package from the white plaster mantel. She held it out to
him. "For Christmas. Go on, go, open it." She made a
pushing motion with her hands.

"I don't know what to say. Thank you." He undid
the bit of ribbon and flimsy tissue. It was a book.
Quite beautiful, leather with gold tooling and a
black, silk marker. Virgil's *Aeneid.*

"I saw you reading it one day, at the Angel,
remember? I know you love to read. Me, I don't understand that deep stuff. It's all Greek to me." (Jury
smiled.) "I read film magazines, romances, trash, ah,
you know. Is it all right?" She seemed truly anxious
about whether she had got the right book.

"It's wonderful, Mrs. Wasserman. Really. Merry
Christmas to you. You'll be okay now?"

As he climbed the stairs with his book, Jury
thought, Poor woman. That particular He who terri-

fied her, from what vantage point had she seen His feet? Ground-level? Mat-level? Bed-level? Had she had to look down in order to avoid looking up? It was better for Mrs. Wasserman that The Feet stopped just beyond her grilled windows than that they should kick down the doors of memory.

CHAPTER 5

The English inn stands permanently planted at the confluence of the roads of history, memory, and romance. Who has not, in his imagination, leaned from its timbered galleries over the cobbled courtyard to watch the coaches pull in, the horses' breath fogging the air as they stamp on dark winter evenings? Who has not read of these long, squat buildings with mullioned windows; sunken, uneven floors; massive beams and walls hung round with copper; kitchens where joints once turned on spits, and hams hung from ceilings. There by the fireplace the travelers of lesser quality might sit on wood stools or settles with cups of ale. There the bustling landlady sent the housemaids scurrying like mice to their duties. Battalions of chambermaids with lavendered sheets, scullions, footmen, drawers, stage-coachmen, and that Jack-of-all trades called Boots waited to assist the traveler to and from the heavy oaken doors. Often he could not be sure whether the floor would be covered with hay, or what bodies might have to be stepped over or crept past on his way to breakfast, if he slept in an inner room. But the breakfast more than made up for the discomfort of the night, with kidney pies and pigeon pies, hot mutton pasties, tankards of ale, and muffins and tea, poached eggs and thick rashers of bacon.

Who has not alighted with Mr. Pickwick in the

courtyard square of The Blue Lion at Muggleton; or eaten oysters with Tom Jones at The Bell in Gloucestershire; or suffered with Keats at the inn at Burford Bridge? Or, hungry and thirsty, who has not paused for a half-pint of bitter and a cut of blue-veined Stilton, flakey Cheshire, or a knob of cheddar; or known that he would always find the brass gleaming, the wood polished, the fire enormous, the beer dark, the host tweeded, and, upstairs, the halls dark and narrow, the snug room nearly impossible to find—up two stairs, down three, turn right, up five, walk ten paces, like a child playing hide and seek or a counting game? If the streamers have gone from the white caps, and the host is there more in spirit than in fact, like a smile hovering in air—still, with all of this wealth in the vaults of memory, one could almost forget that the pound had dropped.

The Man with a Load of Mischief was no exception—a half-timbered, sixteenth-century coaching inn through the archway of which Melrose Plant now drove his Bentley, parking it in the unused stableyard. Here the stagecoach from Barnet might have clattered in and pulled up in the cobbled court, ringed round with galleries, over which Molly Mog waved and flirted with the footmen. To Lady Ardry, it was the quintessential English inn. In summer, clematis spread its long tendrils over the face of the building, competing with the climbing roses. The inn sat on a hill facing south, a long building which looked as if it had been put together in sections, in a drunken wave. Its thatched roof fitted its windows like a collar. Amid the green and glowing fields of summer, the silver, misty fields of winter, its diamond-paned windows looked off toward the village of Long Piddleton.

When Melrose Plant and Lady Ardry arrived, it

was dark, and this made the lighted inside of the inn
that much more inviting. The inn was a free house
and its proprietor had every intention of keeping it
from being swallowed up by the breweries.

That proprietor, Simon Matchett, greeted them
now at the front door, making a good deal over Agatha but less over Melrose Plant, whom he afforded a
nod and a smile, but the smile was not very broad.
Melrose disliked him; he sensed in Matchett a
climber after both wealth and position, a man of surface polish but underlying vulgarity. To be fair, he
wondered if he might not simply be jealous.
Matchett's popularity with women could hardly be
overstated. All he needed to do to enhance a door
was walk through it. Matchett's apparent attachment
to Vivian Rivington disturbed Melrose.

Perhaps even the tragedy in Matchett's past—something involving his deceased wife and another
woman—might have added to the man's romantic
image, like a scar on the face of a duelist. This had
all happened so long ago that not even Lady Ardry
had been able to dig out all the details.

They stood now in the low, dimly lit hall, hung
about with sporting prints and stuffed birds, his aunt
and Simon Matchett making small talk smaller. Melrose simply leaned against the wall, the top of his
head just grazing a rather tatty-looking brace of
stuffed pheasant. He studied the dusty coaching
prints on the other side. There were the passengers
being deposited in a snowy bank as the coach gaily
overturned. And now here they were whooping into
the cobbled courtyard as Betsy Bunt waved from the
upper gallery. Melrose wondered why coaching
seemed to be regarded back then as a sport, something like rugby or bowls. He watched as his aunt
and Matchett sauntered down the hall toward the
saloon bar, ignoring him. Melrose started up the hall,

where a narrow staircase lined with more pictures—
these of grouse and pheasant hung upside down by
their spindly feet—led to the long corridor of small,
gabled bedrooms on the upper floor. On the right was
the dining room. It had a low-beamed ceiling, with
several stone monoliths as the chief support. They
also served to section off alcoves, wherein sat tables.
The stone was rough hewn, and the slabs looked too
delicately poised between ceiling and floor to offer
comfort. His aunt thought the room quaint, something like the refectory of an old monastery, which it
probably was. Melrose always felt he was eating at
Stonehenge. But the overall chilly effect was broken
by Oriental rugs, fresh flowers, red-globed lamps on
the tables, and polished brass plates lining the walls.
Twig, the elderly waiter, was doing his best to look
overworked by fussing red napkins into empty water
goblets. The waitress, Daphne Murch, did the heavy
stuff. She was inching along now with a laden tray,
moving toward two prim old ladies seated in one of
the alcoves. There was not much custom tonight; perhaps some were put off by the recent murder.

Twig was mumbling reprimands to Daphne Murch.
Poor Murch could never do anything right, and that
extended to finding dead bodies in the cellar.

"Melrose!" It was his aunt's voice, from the saloon
bar. "Will you be forever mooning about the dining-
room door? Come along, come along!"

Should he have answered *Yes, Auntie* and skipped
along with his stick and ball?

Agatha had seated herself at the little table in the
bay window, on the one comfortable, cushioned chair,
leaving the hard bench for Melrose. Matchett was
lounging to her right. The diamond panes gave back
the flickering lights of the monstrous stone fireplace
across the room. Enormous logs spilled helter-skelter
across its stone floor, unscreened. The flames surged

and subsided and surged again as if entertaining ugly thoughts of their own. Unaware of its proximity to the gates of hell, a large dog of uncertain credentials was flopped on the hearth, dozing. When it saw Melrose come in, it opened one eye and watched his progress across the room. After he was seated the dog lumbered up, making its long-haired, clumsy progress to their table. Its liking for Melrose he could never understand, for he did not return the admiration and tried to ignore the dog. Since it stood waist high it was like trying to ignore a woolly mammoth. The dog shoved its nose under Melrose's armpit.

"Mindy, down," said Matchett without much conviction.

In the meantime, Twig had shuffled in and taken their order for drinks. A pink gin for Agatha, a martini for Melrose. She leaned her ample bosom on folded arms and said, "Now, my dear Matchett, let's have Murch in here. She may've remembered something else." His aunt had acquired this silly habit of addressing men by their last names (My dear Plant, my dear Matchett), which Melrose found affected. No one talked like that anymore, except in the sanctum sanctorum of dusty men's clubs, where rigor mortis seemed a cause rather than an effect of death.

Melrose knew his aunt only wanted the opportunity of putting questions to Daphne Murch in her best New Scotland Yard manner. "Why don't you leave that poor girl alone?" he asked, striking a match against a small holder on the table and lighting a cigar.

"Because I've an interest in this whole, grisly business, even if you don't! And the girl might have remembered something odd."

"I should imagine that finding one of the paying guests with his head in a beer keg was distinctly odd. One can't get much odder."

"Let's let her be," agreed Matchett. "It's all made her horribly upset, Agatha."

Agatha was not happy. It was clear she wanted an entrée into the recounting of her own part in the finding of the body, which she managed to make a bit handsomer every time she told it. At least, thought Melrose, the Murch child stuck to the same story every time, afraid, perhaps, that any change in her account would see her in the dock of the Old Bailey.

As Twig sat their drinks before them, Matchett said, "What do you think, Plant, about this business?" He always managed to bring Melrose into conversations as if he had found him, like an old suit of clothes, on an Oxfam rack.

Melrose studied his cigar. "I suppose I agree with Wilde. Murder's a mistake. You shouldn't do anything you can't talk about after dinner."

"How cold-blooded of you—" Agatha began, but was interrupted by Matchett's rising to greet two people who had walked into the bar. "Here's Oliver and Sheila."

Melrose watched his aunt try on several smiles to see which one fit. She loathed both Oliver and Sheila, but couldn't let it show. Although Melrose shared her dislike of Oliver Darrington, he thought Sheila a pretty good sport. She was euphemistically described as Darrington's "secretary," but all knew she was his mistress. And although she appeared to be little more than a hanger-on, like a starlet on the arm of a producer, Melrose suspected she had twice the brains Darrington had—not much of a compliment, since he had none. What she concentrated largely on showing was her body, which, together with her face, made a very pleasant package. Melrose did not really go for the type, though he could understand how many men would. He liked a woman to look at him out of clear and honest eyes—Vivian Rivington's eyes, perhaps.

Sheila's were so heavily outlined that he often got the impression, close up, of looking at a very pretty seal.

Sheila and Oliver drew up chairs, slung their coats across them, and seemed prepared to talk about the one subject Melrose was sick of.

"Oliver's got a theory," said Sheila.

"Only one?" asked Melrose, staring at a moose above the bar, whose cracked white plaster lips were in need of seeing-to by a taxidermist.

"It's horribly clever," said Sheila. "Just you listen."

Melrose preferred to study the moose.

"Don't you think so, Mel?" Sheila was nudging him.

"Think? About what?" Melrose yawned. His stomach rumbled.

Sheila pouted. "Oliver's *theory*, About the murders. Haven't you been listening?"

"Pay no attention to Melrose," said Lady Ardry, adjusting her fox-fur neck piece. "He never listens." Melrose thought the little glass eyes of the fox were imploring him. From the moose to the fox. Had he become a lover of the wild?

Whether Melrose wanted to know or not, Sheila was leaning across the table toward him, pouring out Oliver's theory: "That it's someone with a grudge against Long Piddleton. Someone that was wronged by the town, and the wound festered and festered, and he's seen a way to get his revenge."

"Why didn't he just toss his badge in the dirt?" asked Melrose, discarding the long ash from his cigar. "Gary Cooper did." He was very fond of old westerns.

Sheila looked perplexed and Oliver stopped smiling cleverly.

"I told you, Sheila. Pay no attention to him. Pretend he's not here," said Agatha, who then asked for another pink gin.

But Sheila persisted. "Oliver's writing a book, you

know. A kind of fictionalized documentary about this sort of thing—"

"*This* sort of thing?" inquired Melrose, politely.

"*You* know, about especially weird sorts of murders—"

"Come on, Sheila, don't give it all away," said Darrington. "You know I don't talk about works in progress."

Agatha was looking grim. In Long Piddleton, he was her chief competition, having enjoyed a modest fame for several years as a writer of detective novels. The fame (much to her delight) was racing downhill after his last effort.

Oliver now asked, with a deprecating laugh, "Who was it said, 'If I want to read a good book, I'll write one'?"

Probably you, thought Melrose, turning his attention back to the moose.

Simon Matchett tried to act the part of the perfect host, though Melrose knew he held Darrington in comtempt. "That's an interesting theory, Oliver. Someone with a grudge—but, surely, he would have to be psychotic."

"Well, good God, he must be in any event to go drowning people in beer and stuffing them up on wooden beams. The point is, these two men were perfect strangers to Long Pidd; now what *possible* motive—"

"You mean, we've been *saying* they're strangers," put in Melrose, a little fed up with their assumptions masquerading as facts.

They all looked at him as if he'd just pulled out a snake from under the table.

"Whatever in the world do you mean, Mel?" asked Sheila. Melrose watched as she put her hand over Matchett's. Even old one-track mind Sheila, who would gladly kill half the village to keep Oliver, could not resist this gesture.

"I think he's saying that someone in Long Pidd must have known them," said Simon, lighting a cigar. He got it going and then said, smiling, "So who do you think did it, then?"

"Did what?"

Simon laughed. "The *murders,* old chap. Since you seem to think it was someone in our fair village."

Why hadn't he kept his mouth shut? Now he would have to go along with the little game. "You, probably."

They made, the group at the table, a rather nice little frieze: hands stopped in midair, mouths dropped open, as if the hinges had stuck; drinks paused at lips, cigarettes dangled. Indeed, the only one not locked into the still was Simon himself, who was laughing. "Marvelous! I could have been upholding the honor of my female guests, protecting them from the vile advances of Small."

Melrose wondered at Matchett's facility for driving an insult round the bend and having it come back a compliment.

"I find your sense of humor revolting, Melrose," said Agatha.

"It's always worse on an empty stomach, dear Aunt."

CHAPTER 6

Detective Chief Inspector Richard Jury and his companion, Detective Sergeant Alfred Wiggins, alighted from the 2:05 from London into a cloud of steam, on the other side of which came forth a figure, spectre-like. When the steam cleared, the figure formed itself into Constable Pluck of the Northamptonshire constabulary.

As he stowed Jury's scarred valise in the rear of the bright blue Morris, Pluck said, "Superintendent Pratt's waiting for you in Long Piddleton. He asked me to apologize for not meeting you personal, sir."

"Quite all right, Constable." As they drove out of the station and into Sidbury, Jury asked, "Have you come up with any ideas as to why the body of Ainsley was stuck up there over the clock?"

"Oh, indeed, sir. It's obviously a maniac doing these murders."

"A maniac, is that it?"

Wiggins sat like a stone in the rear seat, his nose-blowing testifying to his still being among the living, for the time being.

They came to a roundabout clogged with traffic, but this didn't deter Pluck, who scooted right in, nearly sending a Morris Mini to an early death in the rear of a Ford Cortina. Seeing the blue cone on top of the police car, the horns pulled their punches. "Near miss, that was," said Pluck, implying it was ev-

eryone's fault but his own. Then he took the Sidbury-Dorking Dean Road. Once beyond the
twenty-five-mile-an-hour limit, Pluck hunched over
the wheel, drove the speedometer up to fifty, and
passed a lorry rounding a curve. He barely missed a
black Mercedes coming from the other direction. As
Jury brought his white-knuckled hand back from the
dashboard, Pluck beamed and patted the instrument
panel. "Nice little bugger, isn't she, sir? Just got her
last month."

"You might not have her next month, Constable, at
the rate you're going." Jury lit a cigarette. "I suppose
the reporters have been thick on the ground over
this."

"Oh, God, yes. The 'inn murders,' they've been
calling them. And don't think people ain't half-wor-
ried, afraid they'll all be dead in their beds."

"As long as they stay out of inn beds, perhaps
they'll be all right."

"True enough, sir. I wish they'd pick that bleedin'
Vauxhall up and walk with it." This was addressed to
the old, green car before them, whose two ancient,
chicken-necked occupants were driving at twenty
miles per and making Pluck's life hell. He fumed and
hunched down in the seat, apparently afraid to per-
form one more death-defying feat in the presence of
his superior.

Long Piddleton took the shape of a mounded row
of limestone cottages to Jury's left, a field full of cows
to his right, then another row of cottages, these with
thatch, and across the road a water splash through
which one solitary duck meandered. Jury noticed, as
they turned left, a woman coming hurriedly out of a
small gate overgrown with creepers, shoving her arm
into a Burberry. So intently was she watching their
car, he half-expected her to thumb a lift.

•   •   •

"Must have thought, in London, we were going bonkers up here when you learned the circumstances," said Superintendent Pratt.

"Quite honestly, I thought someone was kidding us." Jury continued reading the statement made by the vicar, Denzil Smith. "What's this about a girl named Ruby Judd?" According to the vicar, his housemaid had not returned from a visit to Weatherington, where her parents lived.

"Ruby Judd. Ah, yes. I don't think it's anything to do with these murders. The thing is, Miss Judd is given to these, ah, extended vacations. Men, you know."

"I see. Only it says here her parents haven't seen her at all. Is she still missing?" Pratt nodded.

"I suppose," he said, "she'd got to tell the vicar some place respectable she's going. I don't know the girl, but—"

"Cor! I do!" said Pluck, with a lewd smile. "I think the superintendent's right there, Inspector."

"I see." But Jury didn't. The girl had been gone for nearly a week. "Now, what about the identification of this man Small?"

Pratt shook his head. "Nothing, yet. Small came in by train, got off at Sidbury, took the Sidbury-Dorking Dean bus. The stationmaster remembered him, but only vaguely, when we showed him Small's picture, and could only tell us that he got off the eleven A.M. from London. But that makes stops everywhere along the way, and we've not been able to get any leads as to where he got on. But if the man comes from London, Inspector—" and the superintendent spread his arms rather hopelessly.

"And the other one, Ainsley?"

"Came in by car. We traced the car back to a lot in Birmingham. You know the story. Buy the car, you've got the plates. The dealer was playing terribly, terribly dumb. 'Ah, come on, guv, what's a businessman loike me to do? This chappie walks in with two hundred quid and wants the old banger . . .' et cetera, et cetera. Anyway, we're nowhere with the car and nowhere with the name. I assume it's not his own. Certainly no Ainsley at whatever bogus address he gave the dealer."

"So you've got nothing there, either?"

Pratt blew his nose. "That's right. You know, of course, the Home Office has one of its labs set up in Weatherington. Everything there in case you need it."

Jury found it hard to believe that with the expertise and scientific methods of the lab, they'd come up with nothing. They didn't need footprints in the sand or blood drops on the sill. "There must have been something—fiber, hair—the killer must have left something behind."

Pratt shook his head. "Oh, there were hairs, for instance, those of the waitress and the fellow Small was having drinks with—Marshall Trueblood, I think—if you can tie them in. But no motive seems evident, none at all. We picked up marks, yes. But all elimination prints. People who had legitimate access to Small's and Ainsley's rooms, like the landlords and maids. As to the people there at the inn for dinner the night Small was killed, the bureau turned up prints of two already on file." Pratt took back the folder he'd given Jury and adjusted his glasses. "This Marshall Trueblood and a woman named Sheila Hogg." Pratt looked at Jury with a smile: "Pouf and a prostitute. Not prostitute, exactly. 'Actress' might be more the way to put it. Blue movies, that sort of thing. Darling of the Dirty Squad."

"Trueblood?"

"A bit of drugs here and there. But nothing big. Just supplied his friends. His digs got raided in Belgravia."

Pratt was looking so tired that Jury suggested he go home to bed.

"Thanks, Inspector. I could use a bit of a rest." He was still shuffling through the folder. "We know the signature on the register was Small's because he signed his dinner check, so we could compare. Someone could have written in Ainsley's name on the Jack and Hammer's register, though."

"I assume not. That was the same name he used to rent the car, wasn't it?"

"True. I was just thinking that the murderer didn't want us to identify the two."

"He hadn't time to do anything about the car, apparently." Jury lit up a cigarette from his crumpled pack of Players. "What do you think?"

Pratt put his feet up on the desk and leaned back. "Look at it this way. Say this man Small comes in from London; maybe he's got himself a spot of bother there. Chummy follows him, arranges to meet him in this godforsaken village, sees his opportunity when Small is stopping at the inn—"

"Did anyone else get off the train at Sidbury?"

"Several people. We're following that up."

"So he follows Small and then kills Small *and* Ainsley?"

Pratt held up his hand. "I know. I know. Okay. Then Chummy lives here in Long Pidd, or close by. The two of them—Small and Ainsley—converge upon Long Pidd for the purpose of . . . well, we know not what. Some danger to Chummy, who gets wind of them and quickly dispatches them."

Jury nodded. "That certainly makes more sense. It's conceivable that Ainsley was a stranger who happened through, since he was in a car. But Small? No one takes a bus from Sidbury to Long Piddleton who just happens to be 'passing through.' " Pratt agreed. "So Small knew someone round about here, he must

have. Or, at the very least, he must have *meant* to
come here. Would it be jumping the gun to say they
had a connection with one another?"

"I shouldn't think so. They both got themselves
killed, now didn't they?"

After Pratt left, Jury sat at the desk studying the
statements of the witnesses who had been present that
evening at the Man with a Load of Mischief. His
concentration was broken abruptly by the door to the
small antechamber swinging open and the appearance of Pluck and an elderly woman. She wore a Burberry, and he recognized her as the woman he had
seen as they were coming into Long Piddleton. There
appeared to have been a brief scuffle with Pluck, who
thought, rightly, that the villagers oughtn't to be allowed to burst into the inspector's office.

"Sorry, sir—" Pluck began. "It's Lady Ardry, sir."

"You needn't apologize, Sergeant," said Agatha.
"The inspector will want to talk with me." And she
turned to Jury. "Inspector Swinnerton, is it?"

Swinnerton? "No madam, Inspector Richard Jury.
You wished to speak with me?"

Her face fell when he told her his name, but she
quickly recovered. "Obviously, Inspector, I haven't
been wrestling with your dogsbody here for the fun of
it. Certainly I wished to speak with you. Or, rather,
it's you who should wish to speak with *me*. Who's taking notes? No need to sigh, Sergeant Pluck. If you
and that Chief Constable what's-his-name in Northampton had your wits about you, there might have
been no need to call in the Yard. The inspector here
wants to hear my testimony, I'll wager."

Jury instructed Pluck to ask Wiggins to come in
and take notes, feeling a bit as if he'd received a
reprimand from a rather severe old auntie. "Do go
on, Lady Ardry."

She sat down, smoothed her skirt, and cleared her throat. "I was the one to discover the body. Along with that girl, Murch," she added, as if it were of no consequence, as if "that girl" were deaf, dumb, and blind. "I was on my way to the, ah, conveniences, when Matchett's girl, this Murch, burst from the cellar looking as chalky as the Seven Sisters and making noises and pointing downstairs—absolutely beside herself—and then she collapsed on a chair and moaned into her apron and I had to take matters into my own hands, while the others were rushing about, doing nothing but trying to cheer up Murch. I trooped downstairs and there he was, this Small person, and the absolute *reek* of beer everywhere—"

"Did you recognize him, Lady Ardry?"

"Recognize? Certainly not. His head was in the beer keg. I didn't pull it out to have a look at his face, dear man. Didn't touch anything at all. I know one isn't supposed to. I've some knowledge of these matters, after all—"

Jury noticed that Wiggins, who had come in and seated himself, was washing down two-toned pills with tea. He smiled and said, "Go on, madam." Jury already had the details supplied by Lady Ardry from Pratt's report—except for the embroidery of the waitress's hysterics and Lady Ardry's lack of them, neither of which he believed. "What did you do then?"

She squared her shoulders and leaned her chin on her walking stick. "Took in every detail I could, because I thought it might be important later." Then, silkily, she said, "Being a writer, I've quite good powers of observation. The man was not large, but then it *is* difficult to judge sizes when a body's dangling that way. He was strangled, wasn't he?" She clasped her own neck in her hands as if to wrench it from her body. "Wearing a houndstooth-checked suit, a bit racetrack-toutish, and a bit the worse for beer." She

smiled broadly at her little joke. "After observing the
room and making my mental notes, I returned to the
others."

"That would be the people in the dining room and
bar? There were quite a few there, I understand.
Would you like to give me a kind of sketch of those
people who were present?"

She would like nothing better. Hitching her chair
closer to the desk, she drew from her leather shopping bag a sheaf of foolscap. "I've just made a few
notes." She adjusted her glasses. "Now, besides myself
and the servants—that'd be Murch and Twig—silly
young girl and the old waiter, quite palsied, senile,
not a proper suspect, I shouldn't think. Then there's
my nephew, Melrose Plant. He lives at Ardry End.
You may have heard of my family. Descended from
Baron Mountardry of Swaledale—that would be about
sixteen hundred or thereabouts—and Ardry-Plant
(family name shortened to 'Plant'), Marquess of
Ayreshire and Blythedale, Viscount of Nithorwold,
Ross and Cromarty; Melrose's father was the eighth
Earl of Caverness, married to Lady Patricia-Marjorie
Mountardry, second daughter of the third Earl of
Farquhar. Father was Squadron Leader Clive D'ardry
De Knopf, fourth Viscount of—"

Jury interrupted. "I'm getting lost, Lady Ardry.
My, that is an impressive lineage, madam, it really is.
Makes my head spin."

She nodded curtly. "I know. And all handed to my
nephew straight on a silver platter. Lord Ardry,
eighth Earl of Caverness, and all the rest. A title
given him without his so much as lifting a finger.
And then the silly man gave it back."

"Gave it back?"

"Turned in his ticket, or however you do things
like that over here."

"Well, one seldom hears of anyone's doing that—even here. What reason did he give?"

"Reason? Oh, he said he didn't want always to be going down to London to sit in the House of Lords as he should have done—leaving Ardry End there for vandals and squatters and the like to be getting into. I offered to look after it for him and he said . . . oh, I don't know what he said . . . something silly. One never knows what Melrose is talking about." She lowered her voice. "I think he's quite mad, sometimes." She gripped her walking stick as if she might thrash Plant's image, risen before her. "Anyway, now he's just plain Melrose Plant. Family name."

"And the rest of the guests?"

"There's Oliver Darrington and Sheila Hogg—"

"Darrington. The name sounds familiar. Isn't that the chap who writes mystery books?"

"Rubbishy thrillers, yes. Sheila's his secretary—another one of those artsy-tartsy types, you know, blood-red fingernails and necklines down to there. Or I should say she *calls* herself his secretary; I believe we know just about how often she sits down to a typewriter. Lives right in the house with him." Agatha sniffed. "Then Vivian Rivington. A poet. Bit of a stick. Subdued, and long brown sweaters with pockets she's always got her fists in. Probably sexually repressed. That quiet type is always suspicious, don't you think? I know she's sweet on Melrose, though they say she's going to marry Simon Matchett. He's the owner of the Man with a Load of Mischief, and a dear boy. They're supposed to be nearly engaged, but I can't credit that. Vivian's not Simon's type at all. Nor is she Melrose's, if it comes to that. She's nobody's, far as I can see."

"Where was Mr. Matchett when you found the body?"

"Upstairs with the others. When the Murch girl set

up such a howl, of course Simon was the first downstairs. After me, that is. You can imagine his reaction
to find one of his own guests murdered."

"Yes. Now, were there any other guests?"

"Isabel Rivington, Vivian's step-sister. Older than
Vivian, by fifteen or more years, but looks as young.
Or maybe it's that Vivian looks old. Pale, Mousy.
That sort. You'll see. Isabel's been taking care of
Vivian ever since she was small. She's trustee of
Vivian's estate. But it's Vivian who's got the money,
or will do when she's thirty or when she gets married.
I'm not sure *exactly* how much—" She paused here as
if hoping the chief inspector might be able to fill her
in. "Well, anyway, she's an heiress . . . if she
means to marry, I'd say she'd better be getting on
with it, wouldn't you? But that sort, well, men don't
take much notice of. Except, of course, for the
money. Her father died in an accident. Vivian's father, that is. She doesn't like to talk about it. I think
it rather unhinged Vivian's mind."

"Any others?"

"Lorraine and Willie Bicester-Strachan. Not the
most devoted couple in Long Pidd. Willie must be a
century older than Lorraine, and rather dull. Pots
around with the vicar a lot, reading old books and
talking local history. Oh, yes, the vicar was dining
there too that night. Frankly, I think men of the
cloth should go a bit easier on the wine, even if it is
the holidays, don't you? The vicar is our local mole,
burrowing into everything. Hobby is local history.
Well, that's the lot. . . ." She paused and slapped
her knee. "Oh, dear me, no. How could I forget our
antiques dealer, Marshall Trueblood. Dear Marsha,
as we call him. You know what I mean. Pink shirts
and tinted glasses."

"Hmm. Now, according to my information, there

was a broken lock on the cellar door. Did you notice it by any chance?"

She paused. "I ought to have done," was her ambiguous reply.

Jury let that go. "William Small came into the dining room while your party was in progress, didn't he?"

"I think I remember seeing him. Wasn't someone standing drinks for him? Marshall Trueblood?"

"Umm. Do you remember what time that was?"

She hesitated, seeming to search Jury's face for a time—*any* time—to which she might pin Small's appearance. "Not . . . precisely. Before dinner, certainly. And that was nine-ish. I remember feeling fiendishly hungry. Had prawn cocktail for starters, not really fresh—"

"You didn't see Small again until you went to the cellar?"

"No." She was quick to add, "*No* one did. Must have gone up to his room . . . ah, yes! Didn't Marshall Trueblood mention he'd—Small, that is—got a bit tiddly—"

"Perhaps Mr. Trueblood can fill me in on that." Jury doubted very much she remembered with more than fleeting accuracy anything that transpired before her grisly discovery of the body. Jury changed the subject. "About this man Ainsley—"

"Oh, him." She shrugged. Jury assumed that since she hadn't been personally involved with its discovery, that particular corpse needn't be accounted for.

"Were you in the Jack and Hammer that evening?"

"No. But I did pop in for a word with Scroggs in the afternoon—"

"So there's nothing, really, you can add . . . ?"

"No." Her tone was grudging.

"Thank you, Lady Ardry." Jury rose, and Wiggins

snapped shut his notebook and requested a cup of
tea. Pluck honored him with the leavings of the pot.

"I'm sorry, Lady Ardry. It was remiss of us not to
offer you tea," said Jury.

She dusted her skirts and planted her stick squarely
in front of her. "Quite all right. I haven't time to be
lollygagging about over tea, not with all this business
going on. And where are you staying, Inspector?"

Sergeant Pluck, who was unwrapping a package of
digestive biscuits, put in, "I got you digs at the Load
of Mischief, sir. Thought you'd like to be right on the
spot."

As Jury was steering Lady Ardry to the door, she
plucked at his sleeve and whispered, "If I could have
just one word with you in private—"

"Yes, of course." They stepped into the small cham-
ber that debouched onto the street.

"Inspector, will you be talking to my nephew, Melrose Plant, about this business?"

"I shall want to question anyone who was there."

"Thought so. The thing is—I might as well say it
straight out—there's a bit of bad blood between us."

"You mean he might try to implicate you?"

Agatha crushed her walking stick to her bosom.
"Me? *Me*? How could he possibly?"

"I merely thought—"

"If he *dares* do a thing like that, if he in any way
tries to twist the facts—" Her right hand strangled her
cane as her left grappled with Jury's lapel. Then, nervously, she whispered: "Everyone in Long Pidd will
tell you how horribly 'clever' he is. Clever, my foot!
He fools around at University teaching one course.
Couldn't land a full-time job. And just because
he can do the *Times* crossword in under fifteen
minutes—"

"Fifteen minutes!"

"Well, good Lord, man, if you had nothing to do

but sit in front of your fireplace with a bottle of port, you could get a lot of practice in, too. But you and I, we have to *work* for our living. We don't wait for the world to come knocking on our door. The thing is, you see, there's much of Ardry End that's mine by rights. My husband, Melrose's uncle, would certainly have expected Melrose to do better by me." When Jury didn't respond to this, she shook his sleeve as if she'd bring him back to his senses. "The point is—"

"I understand. That your nephew might have some unkind things to say about you."

"Precisely. So now you'll know to pay no attention to him."

"I shall certainly keep that in mind."

Agatha tapped him with her walking stick. "You've a good head on your shoulders, Inspector. Knew it the moment I saw you." And she sailed out the door Jury held wide for her.

Leaving Wiggins to partake of tea with Constable Pluck, Jury walked out through the door over which was the bright blue sign POLICE. He looked up and down the High Street, fascinated by the collection of brightly painted shops whose colors were now muted by the winter dusk.

Since it was early closing, the Jack and Hammer was locked up tight. Jury made a tent of his hands and peered in the windows, but saw only shadowy shapes of tables and chairs. They were probably out for the afternoon. He moved back from the window and looked up at the wooden beam overhead, on which the body had been found.

As Jury stared upward, a youngish man came to lounge in the doorway of the antiques shop next to the pub. He assumed this to be its owner and walked over.

The shop was an attractive little building with Regency bowfront windows. It had escaped the painter's brush, unlike most of the shops and cottages.

Jury produced his identification. "Inspector Jury, C.I.D. Are you Mr. Trueblood?"

"Indeed I am. I thought you were the one from Scotland Yard. Isn't it all too hideous?"

"I wonder if I could ask you a few questions, Mr. Trueblood?"

"Come in, come in. I've just put the kettle on. Have a seat, do." Trueblood indicated a settee that looked much too delicate for the likes of Jury. The legs were cabriole, with finely carved acanthus leaves on the knees.

"Georgian," said Trueblood, as if Jury had come to buy. "An exquisite piece—don't worry, it's stronger than it looks."

Trueblood arranged himself in a fauteuil, his hands lightly folded on his knees. His shirt was sea green and the glasses were tinted, as Lady Ardry had said. Jury glanced over the room as he took out his packet of cigarettes. However questionable Trueblood's taste in lovers might be, his taste in furniture was impeccable. He must have a hundred thousand quid's worth of stuff in here.

"Mr. Trueblood, you were at the Man with a Load of Mischief the night the first of these murders occurred?"

Trueblood gasped. "Indeed I was, Inspector. And do you know, I actually bought the man a *drink*—" He let his forehead fall into his well-manicured hand, as if the drink in question might have been hemlock.

"So I understand. What did you talk about?"

There was a sharp intake of breath as Trueblood apparently gasped for more oxygen before busying his mind. His wide eyes, behind the tinted glasses, roamed the room. "Do you know, we only talked about the weather—it had been snowing for two days, and then pouring with rain that night—well, the usual chitchat."

"This Small didn't seem anxious, worried, anything like that?"

"On the contrary, he seemed quite elated."

"Elated?"

"Yes. As if he'd just got good news, or won the pools. 'Lemme tell you, mate, it ain't orfen a chap 'as a runna luck loike I done.' The man was jubilant. But he wouldn't tell me what his run of luck was."

"This was before dinner, was it?"

"Yes. About eight, eight-thirty. He'd already had his dinner. Yes, I remember Lorraine—that's Lorraine Bicester-Strachan—nearly dragged me off the stool and into dinner."

"And you didn't see him after that? No one seems to have seen him for over two hours."

"I think the poor dear must have been under the weather. He told me he was going up to his room. Been drinking for two or three hours straight." From a room beyond came the whistle of a teakettle. "Now, you really must join me. I've some marvelous Darjeeling, and some delicious petits fours a friend of mine gave me for Christmas." Not staying for an answer, he was up and mincing his way to the kitchen. "Won't be a tic, now." He disappeared into the inner regions.

Jury surveyed Trueblood's stock. Hepplewhite and Sheraton chairs; secretaries, commodes, satinwood tea caddies; Waterford glass in a breakfront. An ormolu clock with porcelain panels was ticking softly at his elbow. Probably cost Jury six months' salary.

Trueblood was back with a silver tray and delicate china. Jury wasn't used to such etherealized cups and saucers. His cup was shaped like a conch shell, the handle an airy spindril of green. He was almost afraid to pick it up. On a plate were tiny cakes, prettily iced.

"And were you in the Jack and Hammer on that Friday evening?"

"I popped in about six-ish for a Campari and lime, yes."

"You didn't see this man Ainsley? I mean later? He supposedly arrived around seven, maybe seven-thirty."

"No, I didn't."

"There's a back entrance to the Jack and Hammer which is usually unlocked."

"Yes, I use it myself, sometimes." Trueblood gasped slightly. "Ah! I see what you're getting at. Like the Small business. Coming in the back?"

That was not what Jury meant; he attached quite a different meaning to the cellar door of the Man with a Load of Mischief. Jury looked ceilingward. "Do you keep rooms above the shop?"

"No, Inspector. I used to do, but what with the noise from the pub—"

"So you saw and heard nothing?"

With his cup at his lips, Trueblood shook his head.

"And you live—where?"

"Have a cottage off the square, beyond the bridge. You can't mistake it; it's the cruck-ended one."

"You lived in London—Chelsea, to be exact—didn't you?" Jury mentally scanned Pratt's report. "And kept a shop in Jermyn Street?"

"Good Lord! You policemen!" Trueblood clapped his forehead in mock wonder. "It's rather like having one's past come up to meet one."

"Northamptonshire seems a bit out of the mainstream," Jury said.

Trueblood looked at him shrewdly. "For someone like me, you mean?"

Jury noticed the pitch of the voice had dropped a bit with this statement, and the man seemed anxious,

or irritated, or both. But Trueblood resumed his
former manner, saying, "I was getting fed up with the
city. And I'd heard this was quite a popular place for
the better sort: the well-heeled, and artists, writers,
that sort."

"I imagine, being in the trade, you've got to know
people hereabout pretty well? The gentleman who
runs The Man with a Load of Mischief . . . ?"

"Simon Matchett? Lovely person, but all that old
English oak is going to fall apart from woodworm
some day. Well, I daresay inns must look inn-ish. Isabel Rivington simply adores it. Or him." Trueblood
winked. "I can't imagine anything *less* rustic than Isabel." As he rose to pass Jury the cake plate, he
glanced out of the bay window. "Well, there she goes,
all got up like a dog's dinner."

"Who's that?"

"Lorraine Bicester-Strachan." He made a face.
"Louis Quinze."

"Is that her companion? Or a period?" asked Jury,
dryly.

Trueblood laughed. "That's rich. The period, Inspector. She couldn't tell the difference between an
original and a copy if she had to. She's a proper little
bitch. I wouldn't be old Willie—that's her husband—
even if you offered me an Oeben original. She's another one after Matchett. Gets her knickers in a twist
every time Simon so much as glances at Viv Rivington. After anything in pants, Lorraine is. Except
yours truly." He adjusted his glasses. "Nearly killed
old Lorraine, I'm sure, when Melrose Plant told her
to scarper. Now, that Plant has good taste. One of my
best customers. Queen Anne, he goes in for. It nearly
kills that crazy aunt of his; she's Victorian. Been in
her cottage? All those awful humps and lumps, the
place writhes with ugliness!"

"Her nephew, I understand, is—was, rather—Lord Ardry."

"Can you credit that, Inspector? Just giving up being a lord as easy as kiss your hand? I mean, people just don't *do* that sort of thing, do they? But then, Melrose isn't just anyone."

"Can you tell me more about Small?"

"No, not really. I asked him where he was bound for, and he just laughed and said, 'I've arrived.' He struck me as the sort one always sees coming out of the turf accountant's."

"Interesting." Jury set down his cup. "Thank you for letting me take up your time this way, Mr. Trueblood." Jury stood. "Incidentally, you wouldn't know the vicar's housemaid, Ruby Judd, would you?"

Trueblood shifted uneasily in his chair, then he, too, stood. "I know her, yes. Doesn't everyone? Perhaps the closest thing we have to a Lady of the Evening. If one doesn't count Sheila. Well, mustn't be catty, must I?" Trueblood smiled. "What about Ruby?"

"Just that she's been gone for nearly a week now, from what I hear."

"I shouldn't wonder. Rumor has it that Ruby's got men here and there, you see."

"Yes, well, thank you again." Jury looked over the room once more. "You've got some beautiful stuff here. I'm pretty stupid about antiques."

"Oh, I doubt you're really stupid about anything, Inspector."

The compliment seemed not insincere, but quite studied. Jury felt an odd moment of empathy for Trueblood. There was something about Trueblood that might have attracted both men *and* women. He might be a homosexual, yes, but was he *this* kind—the silk scarves, the tinted glasses, the swishings and mincings?

Jury stopped at the front door and said, "I wonder
if he meant it literally."

Trueblood looked puzzled. "Who meant what?"

"Small. 'I've arrived.' He must have meant to come
to Long Piddleton."

Trueblood laughed. "Who could possibly mean to
come here in dead winter? And a perfect *stranger*?"

"Perhaps he wasn't a perfect stranger. Good-bye,
Mr. Trueblood."

When Jury and Wiggins were shown into the
saloon bar of the Man with a Load of Mischief by the
elderly waiter, Simon Matchett was in close colloquy
with a dark-haired, handsomely dressed woman, one
of those whose age is always a mystery. She could
have been anywhere between thirty-five and fifty-five.

In the simple process of the proprietor's introduc-
ing himself, Jury understood easily how much Simon
Matchett might appeal to women. Had Jury not
known from Pratt's report that the man was forty-
three, he would have put him at ten years younger.
Light brown hair, close curling, a squarish face, thin
mouth, but amiable. Indeed, the overall impression
was one of amiability, but of a rather studied sort.
The whole face seemed an aristocratically chiseled
mask. The eyes were a brilliant blue, like chips from
a frozen sky, and it was his ability to concentrate
their expression which must have suggested to each
woman that she was the sole object of his interest and
perhaps the single repository of his affections. Today,
the color of Matchett's eyes was enhanced by the
open-necked blue wool shirt he wore, the long sleeves
rolled above the wrist.

This Miss Rivington was certainly not mousy and
subdued; she wore a stylish dress of blue wool, which
looked as if it had been chosen to set off Matchett's
eyes, perhaps to underscore how well they suited one

another. A waterfall of Russian amber beads hung
nearly to her waist. A mink wrap was draped over the
stool in front of the bar.

Matchett introduced her as Isabel Rivington, and
then pulled out two of the oak stools and said, "Let
me get you and the sergeant a drink."

Wiggins, who had been standing about like a
lamppost, asked if he might just have something hot,
a cup of tea perhaps. He felt he was coming down
with a cold. Matchett excused himself to fetch it.

"I'd like to call on you, if I may," said Jury to Isabel Rivington. "I've a few questions."

"Well, I can't see what else there is to tell. I've
gone over everything for that superintendent who was
here."

"I appreciate that. But there might be one or two
small points you've forgotten or overlooked."

"Why not ask me now?" She looked at the door
through which Matchett had exited, as if she needed
moral support. Over the rim of her small glass of
some deadly looking potion, she appraised Jury. Her
eyes were dark, heavily done up with lavender shadow
and mascara that beaded the tips of her lashes.

"Right now, I have a few questions to put to Mr.
Matchett," said Jury.

She put down her glass and picked up the mink. "I
take it that's an invitation to leave."

Matchett was back, telling Wiggins that the cook
had the kettle on.

"Well, I'm off," said Isabel Rivingon, sliding down
from the stool. "I'll see you later, Simon. Notwith-
standing any more murders," she added with icy
sweetness.

When she had gone, Jury asked Matchett to get the
register. He found December 17 and the name of
William T. Small, Esq., written in a rough hand.

"He came in that afternoon, around three I think it was. I was just going over to Sidbury to pick up a wheel of Stilton, and since it's early closing on Thursday, I wanted to be sure I got there whilst the shops were still open."

"And he didn't mention any particular reason for stopping here?"

"No, he didn't."

Jury repeated the names of those who had been at the inn the evening of the seventeenth. "Is that everyone?"

"Yes. Oh, there was Betty Ball, too. Came to bring the sweet for dinner, oh, around six or seven. She keeps the bakery in the village. I mention it because she came around back, and might have noticed the cellar door. Of course, it was earlier when she was here . . ."

"Yes. I'll speak to her. Wiggins," Jury called. The sergeant appeared to be dozing off, in company with a large dog, also sitting by the fire. Wiggins looked up sharply, and the three of them went to the rear of the inn and down a short hall. On right and left of the doorway leading to the cellar were the toilets, with little black silhouettes coyly differentiating the sexes.

"Is the cellar door kept locked?"

"No. We're always going down; you see, half of it's the wine cellar."

"Then anyone has access to the cellar through this door?"

"Yes, I suppose they do." Matchett looked puzzled. "But the back cellar door—as I told the local police—had been forced."

Jury made no comment. The cellar was large, the half on the left taken up with crates and junk. The right side was filled with shelves, tiered in sections on which rested rows of bottles, slightly inclined, necks down. The outside door was in the wall facing the

bottom of the staircase. Jury and Wiggins inspected
it. It was a small door, very old, hinges rusted, and
the part of the bolt which had been nailed to the
jamb still hung by one of its 10d nails. Jury opened
the door, and he and Wiggins looked out on narrow
cement steps, thick with November's rotted leaves.
Jury looked from the door to the cement floor inside.
It would have been easy for someone of even moder-
ate strength to force the door. But why everyone
seemed to believe someone *had*, Jury couldn't imagine.

"So you see, Inspector, since the door was perfectly
all right earlier on in the day, the murderer must
have broken in this way."

Jury walked over to the wine racks. Between the
tiers stood large, wooden kegs. "This was the one, Inspector," said Matchett. "I've been experimenting in
the last year with brewing up some of my own. Not
had much success, though. This is where Daphne
found the body—dangling . . ." Matchett's voice
trailed off. "Was he followed to Long Piddleton?
Hadn't a criminal record, had he?"

"The check on Mr. Small isn't completed yet.
We're just in the process of gathering the facts."
What few facts had been found.

"Yes, of course." Matchett returned the round
wooden top to the now-empty keg. "Is there anything
else you'd like to see down here, Inspector?"

"No, I think not. I'd like to speak to the waitress, if
I may." The three of them trooped upstairs.

Twig was arranging the condiment table while
Daphne Murch was laying out silver when Matchett
led Jury into the dining room.

"Twig, Daphne—this is Chief Inspector Jury, who's
come up from London and would like to ask you a

few questions. I'll just be off, Inspector, but I'll be in the bar if you need me."

The girl went rather pale, plucking at her white apron. Nervous, as might be expected, thought Jury.

"It's Mr. Twig, isn't it?"

"Just Twig, sir." He was standing at attention.

"And Miss Murch? May I call you Daphne?" Jury smiled one of his most heartwarming smiles; this one he meant, since the poor girl looked as if she might drop. She nodded almost imperceptibly.

"I'm sure you've told the superintendent what you know, but would you mind very much going over some of the details?—Perhaps we could sit down."

Both Twig and Daphne looked at the table as if sitting there were quite beyond them. Jury pulled out a chair for Daphne, and she slid herself into it rather tentatively.

"Twig, you went down to the cellar somewhere between eight-thirty and nine that evening. Everything was as usual?"

"Eight forty-five is my guess, sir. Nothing at all out of place. Like I told that Mr. Pratt."

"The bolt and lock on the back door were all right?"

Twig scratched his wispy gray head. "The door was certainly closed, sir. Not like it was later. But I can't swear the lock wasn't broke. I been rackin' me brain tryin' to remember."

"That's all right. Now, Daphne—"

There was a sharp intake of breath, as if it were her turn to recite for some termagant of a teacher.

"You handled yourself very well, Daphne. Not many people could have kept such a cool head." That was not in Lady Ardry's accounting, but then he didn't believe her, anyway. Twig gave a little supercilious snort.

The color had crept back into her cheeks, and she turned to Twig, now with somewhat more spirit:

"You needn't sneer, Mr. Twig. It wasn't you as walked down them steps all unsuspecting-like and found the poor soul—" She clapped her hand over her mouth, and her eyes began to fill with tears.

"It must have been an awful experience for you."

"Oh, horrible, sir. Half in and half out of that keg, he was. I couldn't hardly believe it. Thought some-one was playing a kind of joke. Like Guy Fawkes night, or something. Then I recognized it was Mr. Small, from the suit."

"And what did you do?"

"Went running up them stairs again. And just as I got through the door, here came Lady Ardry out of the loo—excuse me, sir—" and she blushed. "I could hardly talk for my heart going like a hammer. She asked what was wrong, and I just kept pointing down them stairs, and then she went down and pretty soon I heard this screech, and up she come like a herd of elephants, shouting at the top of her lungs. Then everybody just kind of went crazy. I run into the kitchen and put me head in me hands."

Jury put his hand on her arm. "Thank you, Daphne. I don't have any more questions." As they all rose, he reflected that Daphne Murch was probably the only one who had told him the plain, unvarnished truth so far.

Matchett appeared in the doorway of the dining room. "Inspector, if you and your sergeant would like an early dinner, it will be ready shortly."

Saying he felt a chill coming on from the cellar damp, Wiggins had gone to sit by the fire, together with the dog. "We would," said Jury. "And I'd like a word with your cook."

The cook's information was predictably negligible. Mrs. Noyes hadn't seen this Mr. Small. She was so frightened by his death, it was all Mr. Matchett could do to get her to stay on. Jury thanked her and went back to the bar, where Matchett was rearranging bottles, discarding empties.

"As well as you can remember, what were Small's movements on that evening?"

Matchett poured them both a whiskey, and reflected. "He dined about seven, before the others came. Then he disappeared—probably went back to his room—then reappeared around eight or eight-thirty. Had a drink in the bar. I don't remember seeing him after that."

"That was with Mr. Trueblood?"

"Yes. I think Willie Bicester-Strachan was in there, too."

"So everyone saw him, or could have done."

"Yes, I expect so. I was kept busy myself, so I didn't notice who was where, when."

"And not everyone was stone-cold sober? Which would only add to the difficulty of remembering?"

"I admit having a few myself. The holidays, you know."

"But you can't say definitely that anyone had gone down the cellar stairs between the time your man Twig brought up more wine at eight forty-five and Miss Murch went down sometime round eleven?"

"No." Matchett shook his head. "There's something I just can't understand, Inspector—"

"What's that?"

"Your questions. You seem to think someone here, inside the inn was . . . did this murder. No one here even *knew* this Small."

"No one *said* he knew Small, you mean."

Dick Scroggs was wiping down the bar when Jury walked into the Jack and Hammer later that evening, introduced himself, and showed his identification.

This set up some low mutterings from the half-dozen regulars, who seemed to separate like two waves of the sea, three on each side of Jury. They pulled their caps down or merely lowered their noses into their pints of Bass and Ind Coope. One would have thought Jury was going to arrest them all on the spot.

"Yes, sir," said Scroggs with excited flicks of the bar towel. "Heard you was in town. I expect you'll be wantin' me to answer questions."

"I would, Mr. Scroggs. Could we go up to the room Mr. Ainsley occupied?" Jury felt the eyes of the men in the room burning into his back as Scroggs led him up the rickety steps, explaining that he didn't often have a call for one of his three rooms, as his was really more of a public house than Matchett's place. This Ainsley had just popped in several days ago asking for a room. Didn't say where he came from, nor where he was going.

The room was a square, ill-lit box with the standard furniture: bed, bureau, a rather tatty-looking armchair. Its closet gave up no secrets; its dormer window was the third in the row of five that ran along the front of the Jack and Hammer.

Scroggs had moved to a door in the wall at right angles to the window. "Now this door leads to the next room. All of these rooms join one another; as there wasn't no other guests, this Ainsley says not to worry about locking up the other doors."

"In other words, one could go from this room into the box room without even going into the hall?"

"He could have done, yes."

"Convenient for the murderer."

They walked through the door into the next room, identical with the first except for the differently arranged furniture, then into the box room, which was filled with odds and ends of furniture, old lamps, suitcases, papers, magazines.

The casement window was low in the wall, partially obscured by thatch, and, when Jury pushed at it, easily opened. Directly below, not more than a foot down, was the wooden beam on which had stood the carved figure "Jack." The murderer had simply lifted the mechanical smith from the supporting pole and stuck his victim out on the beam.

"You told Superintendent Pratt this Ainsley came in about seven, is that right?"

"Yes, sir."

"And did what?"

Scroggs scratched his head, then remembered. "He asked for his evening meal—that is, after I showed him the room. He had that around eight and then sat about for a bit and went up to his room, oh, I think it'd just gone nine." Dick Scroggs reflected a moment, and then added: "I mean, I *guessed* he was going up to his room."

Jury looked at him. "That's an interesting distinction, Mr. Scroggs. What you mean is, he could have gone out? By a back door?"

"Well, yes, he could have done. Not by the front, no, because I'd have seen him. But that back door"—Scroggs hooked his thumb downward—"it's nearly always open."

"He could have met someone outside, then?"

Scroggs nodded. "Or someone could've gone up to his room, too, I didn't see."

"Who else was in the Jack and Hammer?"

"Near everyone, that evening." He screwed up his face in an effort of remembering, and ticked off the names of the same people who had been at the Man with a Load of Mischief, with the exception of Trueblood and Lady Ardry. Not, thought Jury, that that accounted for much. As Scroggs had said, anyone could have walked in the rear door and up the stairs.

Scroggs looked out of the window. "It's something,

init? Just sticks him out here for all the world to see. Don't make sense."

"It wouldn't, I guess, Mr. Scroggs. Except all the world didn't see Ainsley for some time, did they?"

CHAPTER 7

When Richard Jury awoke next morning in his comfortable four-poster, it was to the sight of new-falling snow. The latticed window was the first thing he saw as he propped himself up in bed to fumble for his alarm and note the time: 8:15. He lay back against the pillows and watched the snow drifting past in wet, fat flakes, and closed his eyes again, feeling rather sanguine. Anyone else, he supposed, would be thinking, What a hell of a way to spend my Christmas holiday. But Jury thought it rather perfect: a postcard village filling up with snow.

He got out of bed and walked over to the casement window, which he threw open and gave himself a rousing chill. He thought of Keats in the inn at Burford Bridge, writing: "Charm'd magic casements, opening on the foam / Of perilous seas, in faery lands forlorn." And Jury was hit with a wave of nostalgia. Before it could overcome him, he dressed quickly and went down the hall to Sergeant Wiggins's room.

Unlike Jury, Wiggins did not seem at all eager to be pulling on macintosh and Wellingtons for a tramp around the village.

"I feel awful feverish, sir. I was just wondering, sir, if perhaps I could lie in a bit and join you later, maybe?"

Jury sighed. Poor Wiggins. But since he was a hindrance knocking about with his pockets full of drops and pills, Jury readily agreed. "Of course. You do that. Maybe a hot buttered rum would fix you up." Piteously grateful, Wiggins sighed his relief, looking a bit like a snowman under his mound of white sheets and counterpane.

It might stave off some terminal respiratory ailment if Wiggins could be made to concentrate on the case instead of the bottles on the nightstand, so Jury drew over a chair, straddled it, and said, "What do you think, Wiggins?"

Wiggins's handkerchief was up to his nose. "Bah wha sah?"

"The case, Wiggins. The condition of the cellar."

Wiggins looked thoughtful and swiped the handkerchief under his nose once or twice. Then he carefully folded it and held it in an almost holy way, as if it were a fragment of Veronica's veil. "The lock being broken? Is that what you mean?"

Jury nodded, waiting patiently. When Wiggins did not continue, Jury said, "It's not likely anyone came in that way, is it? Pratt said there'd been a heavy rain the night of the seventeenth."

Wiggins brightened and sat up a bit. "And the stairs looked like they'd got years of dirt and muck on them. But the inside was clean."

"Precisely," said Jury, smiling. Wiggins looked pleased. "Besides, think a moment." Jury lit up a cigarette. "Why in God's name would anyone coming from *outside* want to meet Small in the cellar? And then have to break down the door? It won't do, will it?"

"But if they didn't come from outside, they must've come from inside." He pointed ceilingward. "It must've been one of them upstairs."

Jury swung his legs off the chair. "Dead right, Wiggins. Get better now, for I'll need your help."

Wiggins was already looking better as Jury turned at the door to say good-bye.

After breakfast—an ample one of eggs, sausages, and kippers, served up by Daphne Murch—Jury crossed the courtyard to the police car parked there. The snow layered the thatch and the cobbled yard, rimmed the bird bath in which wrens were even now leaving their tiny prints. He would first have to deliver Pluck's precious Morris to him; then he could have his tramp in the snow while making his official inquiries. Leaning against the car, he let the wet snow fly in his face while the engine warmed, and he studied the small map Pluck had made for him, indicating the houses of those people he would have to see. He decided to start with Darrington, at the other end of the village. Jury licked the snow from his lips and got in the car. He loved winter above all seasons, even spring. He also liked rain over sunshine, mist over a clear view. A bloody melancholic, he thought, as he drove out of the courtyard.

Oliver Darrington lived on the other side of Long Piddleton, toward Sidbury. As the Dorking Dean Road became Long Piddleton's High Street of rainbow shops and houses, Jury passed the Church of St. Rules and the vicarage on his right, then drove to the square. There was the tea room and bakery, where he supposed Miss Ball was up to her elbows in flour. After he drove over the bridge, Jury saw Marshall Trueblood standing behind his fancy window, and returned a brief salute when Trueblood waved. The Jack and Hammer was closed like a clam, with that air of desolation some pubs have prior to their 11:00 A.M. opening.

Jury parked the car in front of the police station
and turned the keys over to Pluck after the sergeant
had come running out, apparently in a great state of
nerves over the welfare of the Morris.

"I'll be at Darrington's house if you need me, Sergeant."

"You're walking, sir?" asked Pluck, with mild
amazement.

"Um. I've been too long in city pent."

But Pluck apparently didn't care how pent Jury
had been; he was busily inspecting the car for
scratches.

Jury set off down the High Street, admiring the
gemstone colors of cottages that glimmered in the
bright sun, and when he had come to the end of
these, started singing some song he dredged up about
the Coldstream Guards. Singing, apparently, rather
loudly, for a window flashed up in a thatched cottage
near the Sidbury Road and a head popped out for a
brief moment. He stopped singing, and watched
while a curtain was drawn slowly back. He looked at
his map. Lady Ardry lived in that cottage.

Darrington's house looked just the sort of thing a
moneyed writer might choose—secluded and Elizabe-
than. It was barricaded by ash, tall hedgerows, wil-
lows, and elms and sat rather back from the road.

The creator of the Superintendent Bent series must
have found it financially rewarding, given that house.
Jury had read the first, *Bent on Murder*. Clever
enough, he guessed, if you liked fictional detectives
who were cool, strong, and iron-nerved. As Jury
pushed the bell and heard its silver echoes in the
hall, he only hoped the writer did not identify with
his detective, to be forever propounding his own theories.

The woman who opened the door was, by anyone's

standards, dishy. A bit tartish, perhaps, the way she lounged there in the doorway in such fabulous disarray, her burgundy-red housecoat nearly falling off her shoulder. Wanting only to see her reaction, Jury said: "Mrs. Darrington?" and then watched her face register, in rapid succession, embarrassment, irritation, and sadness. In Jury's experience, the Darringtons of this world seldom married ladies with "modeling" jobs in London. Even if you met this one inside 10 Downing Street you might still think you were slumming.

"I'm Sheila Hogg. Long *o*, please. Oliver Darrington's secretary. You're the police, aren't you? Come in." And she held the door wide, but not happily. Her manner was just a shade too bored to be convincing. In the circumstances, no one could be that offhand about a visit from the police.

He followed her through to the living room, divesting himself of his raincoat as he went. It was a handsome room into which she led him, with scrolled and pointed paneling around the door. On either side of the fireplace was a very comfortable looking couch, and it was onto one of these that Sheila Hogg more or less dropped, before she remembered that Scotland Yard would also want to see Oliver. She excused herself, went to the bottom of the staircase in the hall, and called up that the police had come. When she came back, she pushed some newspapers and magazines from the couch and invited Jury to sit. On the butler's table in front of the couch were the leavings of a toast-and-coffee repast, and she offered coffee to Jury, though without much enthusiasm. He declined, and got to the point before she struck up a conversation about the weather, for lack of something better.

"What time did you and Mr. Darrington arrive at the Man with a Load of Mischief the evening Mr. Small was killed?"

She had taken a cigarette from a packet on the table and was waiting for Jury to give her a light. She screwed up her face at this question. "Nine, I think, perhaps nine-thirty. We came in on the heels of Marshall Trueblood." As she leaned over to accept Jury's light, her robe fell open slightly; as he had suspected, there was nothing underneath. "Let's see: Agatha and Melrose Plant were already there. But then, Agatha's always first everywhere. Afraid she'll miss something. How Melrose stands her is beyond me. He's got the patience of a saint. Wonder how he's managed to stay single."

Jury imagined Sheila probably thought of most men in terms of coupling. If not with her, at least with someone.

"Are you?" she asked, looking him up and down.

"Am I what?"

"Single." Her glance was appreciative.

Jury was spared answering by a voice behind him: "Oh, for God's sake, Sheila. Whether the inspector's married is none of your damned business. Oliver Darrington, Inspector." He held out a deeply tanned and well-tended hand, which Jury rose to shake. Turning once more to Sheila—Darrington seemed embarrassed by her very presence—he said, "And we usually dress for Scotland Yard, Sheila."

Her robe showed a good deal of leg, curled up as she was on the couch. She stubbed out her cigarette and swung her legs down. "For heaven's sake, Oliver, he's the *police*. Nothing bothers them, they're like doctors. Seen everything, haven't you, love?" And she turned on Jury a sultry and winning smile.

Jury simply smiled at her in answer. She might be a trollop, but Darrington was a prig, and he preferred trollops to prigs. Jury felt the same antipathy toward Darrington as he had toward Isabel Rivington.

Darrington was wearing a fawn-colored jacket, exactly the shade of his hair, an expensive silk shirt, open at the neck, into which was stuffed an equally expensive ascot. It made Jury slightly self-conscious of his own blue necktie, slightly askew. The man was handsome, but with a profile a little too Greek, features a bit too chiseled; and, like a statue, he seemed chilly and unbending.

Darrington poured himself some coffee and told Jury the same story the others had told—or hadn't, since they were all looking at it through wine-starred eyes. The only thing he added was that Matchett had supplied the champagne. "Holidays, and all that. He can be very generous at times." The implication was that at other times he couldn't.

"Talking about Simon, are you?" said Sheila, who had come back into the room in about the same condition she had left, having merely exchanged the revealing robe for an equally revealing one-piece, green velvet lounging-pajama thing, the long zipper of which still dipped below breast level. The secretive smile that played on her lips suggested to Jury that Matchett might have been generous in more ways than one. However, this did not dispel Jury's impression that Sheila's main mission in life was Oliver Darrington.

Oliver said he had not talked to Small and had not noticed anyone going down to the cellar except the old waiter at one point.

"Drunk as lords, we both were," put in Sheila, winking at Jury through a cloud of cigarette smoke. He noticed the hand holding the cigarette had very long fingernails. Secretary, my eye.

"So you neither of you saw this William Small after you went into dinner?" They shook their heads.

"I can't recall seeing him either after *or* before," said Darrington.

"And Ainsley—?" They both shook their heads. "But you were there the night Ainsley was murdered?"

"Yes. Sheila left a bit before I did. We had a . . . misunderstanding. Over my buying Vivian Rivington a drink." A smile played on Darrington's face, as if such misunderstandings were a source of constant amusement to him.

A coal fell in the grate and lay smoldering. It had nothing on Sheila. "Don't be silly," was her weak response.

Jury remembered Lady Ardry's account—albeit undependable—of the various relationships between these people. "I understand Mr. Matchett is engaged to Miss Rivington. Vivian." Simultaneously, there came an angry *no* from Darrington and a *yes* from Sheila.

Oliver blustered. "Well, there's been some talk of it. But Vivian would never throw herself away on someone like Matchett."

"Who would she throw herself away on, love?" Icicles hung from every word.

Jury felt almost sorry for Sheila. She was shallow but not, he thought, brainless. Whereas, he suspected Darrington was a bit of both. He couldn't quite square this with the crisp style of the Bent mysteries, and said, "I've read your book, Mr. Darrington. Only the first one, I must admit."

"Bent on Murder?" Oliver preened. "Yes, that was probably the best."

Sheila looked away, as if she were uneasy. Jury wondered why she should be disturbed by the mention of Darrington's books. It was a point worth pursuing, thought Jury, who often annoyed his colleagues by not sticking to the facts. But what were "the facts," strained through the grid of the individual perception, assuming even that one wanted to tell

the truth? And most people didn't because most
people had something to hide. He was almost glad
this lot had been drunk—or were said to have been—it
made them realize that the picture was blurred. He
could always tell when something had shifted center,
and something had definitely shifted with Sheila. It
wasn't the mention of Vivian Rivington, either; that
had been pure, straightforward jealousy. Whatever
this was, it was not straightforward. She was staring at
the air over his head.

"I wonder if you might have a copy of your second
book?"

Darrington's eyes flicked toward the bookcase
beside the door and then quickly away. Sheila got up
from the couch and walked over to the fireplace,
avoiding Jury's eyes. She threw the stub of her cigarette into the fire and then started, yes, washing her
hands together. The Lady Macbeth syndrome. Jury
had seen it often enough.

"The second one wasn't too well received," said
Darrington, making no move toward the bookcase.

Jury did it for him. There they were, the colorfully
dust-jacketed Bent mysteries, all in a row. "Isn't this
it?" Jury pulled it from the bookcase and watched
Darrington dart a quick glance at Sheila. "Would you
mind if I borrowed it? And the third also? Your Superintendent Bent might give me an idea or two."

Darrington recovered himself, and said, "If you
want to bore yourself, go right ahead." His laugh was
unconvincing.

They were both relieved to see Jury out.

Jury glanced at the map Pluck had made for him
as he walked down the High Street, at the X showing
the Rivingtons' house. Why couldn't these people
have been gathered together for him fifteen minutes
after the murder, the family all grouped in the

drawing room, choking on their tea, the servants all cringing in the kitchen of some arcane country house? All there nice and neat. Here he had to go mucking about over half of Northants, and the trail days old, so cold that a trained bloodhound couldn't snuffle it out. For a moment, looking down the High Street where the winter light glittered on the gum-drop houses and danced off the snowy roofs, he wondered if he had landed bangup in a fairy-tale town on this Christmas Eve.

The Rivingtons' house was the large Tudor structure just on the other side of the bridge, in the square. When he got closer to it, from the vantage point of the humpbacked bridge, he could see it was two houses together really, quite large.

This morning Isabel Rivington was dressed in a camel's hair suit and a white silk blouse, looking just as elegant as she had yesterday. Although, frankly, Jury would have preferred Sheila Hogg, who was a bit steamier. This one came on as a kind of piranha. Jury wouldn't have been surprised to see a finger or two missing when he left.

"I was hoping to see your sister—Vivian, is it?—today, too."

"She's up at the vicarage."

"I see."

"The night of the seventeenth, the night Small was murdered, do you recall seeing him in the bar before dinner?"

Having invited Jury to sit down, she plucked a cigarette from a china holder and leaned toward the match he held out. She seemed in no hurry to get down to answers. "If he was the one sitting with Marshall Trueblood, well, yes, I saw him I suppose. But I didn't take much notice. There were several people in the saloon bar."

"And you didn't go down to the wine cellar after his body had been found?"

"No." She crossed silky legs, down one of which the firelight made a band of gold. "I'm a bit of a coward about that sort of thing."

Jury smiled. "Aren't we all? Your sister did though."

"Vivian? Well, Vivian's—" She shrugged, as if discounting Vivian's predilection to look at dead bodies. "And she's not my sister, exactly. We're stepsisters."

"You're the trustee of your sister's estate?"

"Barclay's and I, Inspector. What's that to do with the murders of two strangers?" She seemed to expect him to answer.

He didn't. "Then you don't have complete freedom in deciding how the money will be spent." Her expression shifted from bored acquiescence to irritation. "When does she come into the money herself?" Jury asked.

Her heavy gold bracelet clanged against the ashtray as she tapped her cigarette. "When she's thirty."

"Rather late, isn't it?"

"Her father—my stepfather—was a bit of a chauvinist. Women can't handle money—that sort of thing. Actually, she could have got it any time she married, by the terms of the will. Otherwise, when she's thirty."

"And when will that be?" From the way she was looking everywhere except at him, Jury concluded he had found a sore spot. There was something about Isabel Rivington to which he took an instinctive and near-immediate dislike, something dissolute. She was beautiful in a sluggish sort of way that bespoke overindulgence in syrupy liqueurs and two-martini lunches. But her skin was still very good, the pores tight and fine, and her hands well kept. The nails were lacquered in a modish brown-rose shade and so

long that the tips were beginning to curl in at the
ends. It might be difficult to strangle a man and avoid
scratching him with nails like that. He wondered
sometimes if that part of his mind which registered
such details even as he was talking about other things
might not simply have frozen over, impervious to the
human tragedy, catching up facts like flies in amber.

"Vivian'll be thirty in about six months."

"Then she'll have control of her money?"

Angrily, Isabel stubbed out her cigarette, the end
fragmenting like a shell. "Why do you make it sound
as if I'm juggling the books?"

All innocence, Jury said, "Was I? All I'm attempt-
ing to do is gather the facts."

"I still don't see what this has to do with two men
coming here and getting killed."

"How long have you lived in Long Piddleton?"

"Six years," she answered and glumly drew another
cigarette from a silver case.

"And where before?"

"London," was her unembellished answer.

London, thought Jury, had certainly discovered
Long Piddleton. "A bit different, isn't it?"

"I've noticed," she said.

"Vivian's—your   stepsister's—father   was   quite
wealthy, wasn't he?"

The subject of money having arisen again, she
turned her head sharply away, and did not answer.

"There was some sort of accident, wasn't there?
Miss Rivington's father?"

"Yes. When she was about seven or eight. He was
killed by a horse kicking him. He died instantly."

Jury noticed this brief recital was not very remorse-
ful. "And her mother?"

"Died right after Vivian was born. My own mother
died about three years after marrying James Rivington."

"I see." Jury watched her as she crossed and recrossed her legs, nervously making little jabs toward the ashtray with a fresh cigarette. He thought he'd take a shot in the dark. "Your stepsister is going to marry Mr. Matchett, is she?" Not precisely true, but it riveted her attention on him. Her fingers were poised over the ashtray, her head snapped around, her feet were planted firmly on the floor. Then she smoothed out her expression, and bland indifference reasserted itself. Jury wondered if her interest in Simon Matchett were more than merely friendly.

"Where did you hear that?" she asked, casually.

Jury immediately switched the subject. "Tell me about this accident to James Rivington."

She sighed, a woman whose patience was wearing thin. "It was in Scotland one summer. When I was down from school. God, I hated it—the north of Scotland. Sutherland. An isolated, windy place—nothing to do but count the rocks and trees and heather. No-man's-land, as far as I was concerned. We couldn't even keep servants, except for one old cook. *They* loved it—Vivian and James. Well, Vivian had this horse she specially liked, stabled with the others out back. One evening Vivian and her father had an awful row, and she got so furious she just rushed right out in the dark and jumped up on that horse and he—James, I mean—came out after her. They were yelling at one another, and the horse shied and kicked her father in the head."

"It must have been very traumatic for your sister—being so young, to have that happen, and herself up on the horse at the time. Was your sister very spoiled? Did she get much supervision?"

"Spoiled? No, not really. She had a lot of fights with James. As to supervision, I suppose she had her complement of nannies and so forth. And James was pretty strict, certainly. As I said, a bit of a chauvinist.

Of course, Vivian was quite sick about the accident. I even think it might have . . ." She paused and picked up the smoldering cigarette, which had turned half to ash in the glass ashtray.

" 'Might have—'?"

Isabel blew out a narrow stream of smoke. "Unhinged her mind a bit."

Strange that these were Lady Ardry's very words. "You think your sister is psychotic?"

"No. I didn't mean that. But she's certainly a recluse. You wonder why we left London. It wasn't my choice, certainly. All she does is sit and write poetry."

"That's not so odd that one would call it 'unhinged,' is it?"

"Why must people feel they've got to protect Vivian even before they've met her?" Her smile was tight.

Jury didn't answer. "Did you benefit by your stepfather's will?"

A shadow brushed her face, as if a raven had flown past. "What you are working up to—isn't it?—is what will happen to me when Vivian gets her money. You're dead wrong if you think she's going to throw me out in the snow."

Jury studied her for a moment, pocketed his notebook, and rose. "Thank you Miss Rivington. I'll be leaving now."

As he followed her to the front door, Jury pondered on the geography of Scotland, and something an artist friend of his had said about the quality of the light there. There was something in her story of the death of James Rivington that sounded very fishy.

Jury took a deep breath of fresh air and observed the imprint of his boots in the fine crust of new snow; he looked longingly at the sparkling expanse of whiteness which was the village square. As he crossed the road, he saw two children on the bridge. They looked about eight or nine, and were rolling the fresh snow into balls along the gray stone balustrade. It was an odd little bridge with two semicircular arches. As he passed the bridge, he solemnly bade the children good-day and wondered what it was like to be that age again, and have your cheeks turn pink in the cold and your hair stand up in wet spikes. It wasn't until he'd gone another fifty feet and turned to look back that he realized they were following him. They stopped suddenly and pretended to be inspecting one of the pollarded limes along the High Street.

He started back toward them, and they were set to cut and run, when he called out. Clearly, they knew who he was. Trying to keep a straight face, he drew out his badge in the worn leather folder and displayed it. "Here, now. Were you following me?"

Their eyes widened into plates, the girl pinched her lips together, and they both shook their heads violently.

Jury cleared his throat, and in very official-sounding tones said, "I'm about to go into that tearoom just there"—and he pointed across to the bakery—"and have my morning coffee. Probably they serve chocolate, and I'd like to put a few questions to you, if you wouldn't mind coming along."

The boy and girl stared at each other, trying to read permission in one another's faces, then back at Jury's, their expressions mingling fear, puzzlement, and temptation. Temptation, of course, won out. They nodded, and one on each side of him, the three of them tramped along to the square.

The Gate House Tearoom and Bakery was a stone building that had once served the purpose from which it took its name: a little house above a lych-gate, through whose narrow arch one could go up the walk to the Church of St. Rules. It was up a very short lane that led directly off the square, with the church beyond it. The tearoom was on the level above the narrow passageway, and the bakery was below.

Around one half of the square were tile-hung and half-timbered cottages whose upper stories jutted out over the narrow walk that ran as a perimeter around the square. On the west side of the square, there were other cottages, interspersed with a sweet shop, a narrow little dry goods store, and a post office. Most of the shops were back beyond the bridge, but these had smuggled their way into these quieter surroundings. They were all mixed higgledy-piggledy, as if glued together by some child.

Jury imagined the square leafy and green in summer. In the middle was a duck pond, and from this distance he could see the ducks bunched up on one side, bobbing within the reedy marsh grasses like buoys. The snow was coming down a little more now, and the square was the most tempting length of shiny, crusty, unbroken snow Jury had ever seen. Not a track on it, not a print. He stopped as they reached the edge of the square, and reflected that it was not really a good example for the children to have their man from New Scotland Yard, that bastion of Law and Order, go cutting across the park when there were perfectly good paths meant for going around it. Out of the corner of his eye he noticed they were both looking up at him, waiting for him to make his move. The ways of the Yard were, and would ever be, inscrutable.

Jury coughed, blew his nose, and then said sternly: "What do you two know about identifying prints? Footprints? You don't happen to remember seeing any about the Jack and Hammer? Any strange ones? About this size?" Jury planted his outsized Wellington firmly in the fresh snow layering the green. It made a delicious scrunch.

They looked from his large print to him and both, again, shook their heads. He thought he might as well make it edifying. "Do you know the difference between the prints of a man running and a man walking?" Mystified, their small heads flicked back and forth. "Are you willing to help out the Yard in this matter, then?"

Now their heads were bobbing up and down just as furiously.

"Very well. What's your name?" he asked the boy.

"James." The boy spat it out, then clamped his lips tightly, as if he might have given away secret information.

"Good. Now then, what's yours?"

But the girl only lowered her head and plucked at the hem of her coat.

"Hmmm. Then it must be James, too. Very well, James and James." He waited for her to mumble some correction, but she merely kept her head down, though he thought he saw a smile, like a mouse, creep across her downturned mouth.

"Listen carefully, now. It might be most important in our investigations. You, James, I want you to *run*, fast as you can, up to that duck-pond, and wait. And you, James"—and he put his hand on the girl's shoulder—"I want you to *walk* to the pond, making circles as you go. Every once in a while, walk around in a circle."

Both of them looked at him as if they were waiting for a gun to go off, and when he nodded, the boy took off with something equivalent to the speed of light, sending up clouds of snow behind him. The girl started walking very slowly and carefully, planting her feet firmly, and every now and again making an ever-widening circle. Jury himself chose a smooth,

unbroken expanse of snow and crunched over it as
noisily as he could. When he reached the pond, the
boy was puffing from the exertion and the girl was
still out there making circles. Finally, she circled her
way to where they were standing.

All three of them then stood looking back at their
handiwork.

"Excellent," said Jury. "Notice, now, these tracks
where you were running, and how only the first part
of the boot, the ball of the foot, hits the snow. And
notice how"—he crouched down and ran his gloved
finger around the girl's print—"one tends to lean to
the outside when one goes around in a circle."

Both of them nodded vigorously.

"And now, perhaps I can set you a riddle." Jury
and the children walked round to the other side of
the duck pond. The ducks remained undisturbed,
their heads still tucked beneath their wings. He
looked across the remaining expanse of nice, crusty,
unbroken snow, and said, "All three of us will walk
about five feet apart so our tracks are completely separate, to the edge of the road. Let's go."

It took them only two or three minutes and then
they turned and looked back. Jury felt wonderful,
like a man with an addiction who had just had a
fix. He tried to wipe the smile from his face as he
looked over the ransacked greensward, all that fine,
clear glittering, unbroken white, now a crisscross of
black marks and potholes.

For a moment as they stared at him, he forgot what
lesson they were supposed to be learning. Oh, yes, the
riddle. "Now suppose right here, right in front of us,
there was a body." The girl slid behind him and
grabbed on to his coat. "And *suppose* the three
people who had made these prints were back there
now at the duck pond. How did they get back without there being footprints going in that direction?" It

was the old Reichenbach Falls gambit, but he doubted they had read "The Final Problem." He didn't think he'd put it quite sensibly, anyway. Jury scratched his head. Why would the suspect go *back* to the duck pond?

No one answered his riddle. He turned and started to walk backward. "Like this!"

The boy grinned all over his face and showed a large gap of missing teeth. The girl giggled, but quickly clapped her mittened hand over her mouth.

Jury held up a finger like a teacher gathering the attention of his class. "Always remember: when a murder's been done"—they gasped at the words— "there'll always be something odd, something funny, something that oughtn't to be there." How he wished it were true; it sounded bookish, though. "I appreciate your help. Let's go in. Here's the tearoom." A small, white sign, neatly lettered in italics, was stuck in one corner of the upstairs bay window and announced: *Morning Coffee Now Being Served*. They walked up a dark enclosed staircase to the floor above, the redolent bakery-aroma perfuming the passageway. As they removed their wet outer garments, an elderly woman, pleasant-looking like a pudding, came forth from a curtained alcove at the rear. Jury ordered up coffee and hot chocolate and a plate of biscuits, then added to that cakes, scones, jam, and cream.

"Well, now!" said Jury heartily, and rubbed his hands toward the fireplace before which the lady had kindly seated them. The boy gaped and grinned, his hair sticky with snow standing up in even pointier points. The girl turned her face down to the tabletop as if she were studying her reflection. Narcissuswise, in its polished top. Jury did not mind their lack of response. He had not supposed that once inside they would hold forth on the molecular structure of the universe.

The coffee and cakes finally arrived, with fresh cream and jam and buttered scones, enough to feed several times their party. The two Jameses didn't need to be invited to tuck in. The boy held a scone in one hand and a fairy cake in the other and took turns biting. The girl pinched up a fruit scone with her little mouse fingers and nibbled away as if she might scurry back to her hole if Jury so much as peeped.

Before the elderly waitress left, Jury showed his identification, and asked if he might speak with the proprietress, Miss Ball.

The effect was dramatic. The poor woman's cheeks flamed and her hand flew to her face. The guilty flee, thought Jury, sighing, when no man pursueth, and so do the innocent.

"Just you wait, sir," she said, retreating by walking backward to the door.

The children had nearly cleaned the cake plate, and Jury thought they would probably be ill, but after all it was Christmas, and they didn't look well off enough to expect many sugarplums. He was pouring himself some coffee from the pot, when a woman in an apron (Miss Ball, he presumed) walked in—though that was a sedate way of putting it. He thought she might have trounced anything—cats, dogs, muffins—in her path to him, as if he were someone long overdue from her past.

"*You're* Chief Inspector Jury, from New Scotland Yard."

He rose and extended a hand. "Yes, I am. Miss Ball?"

Miss Ball nodded as if she were ecstatic to be Miss Ball. She took a seat. "I was just down in the bakery making up the Christmas stollen—there's such a lot of orders for it, and the day after tomorrow being

Christmas, and . . ." She paused, noticing Jury's morning-coffee companions. "If it isn't the Double children. Wherever did you meet up with them?" She did not wait for Jury's answer. "You're here, I know, about these awful murders—"

As if they had suddenly concluded they had been lured here by cocoa and cakes, the Doubles exchanged glances and jumped up. "We got to go, we do. Me Mum'll be mad as hoppers—" And he was backing away from the table. For James, it was quite a lengthy speech. The girl still kept her eyes fastened on the cake plate. Just before she turned to run, she crept back to Jury and gave him a little pinch on the arm, probably as close she could come to a kiss. Then she whipped the last fairy cake from the plate and cut for the door.

Betty Ball, pursing up her small mouth, said, "They never so much as thanked you! Kids these days!"

Jury smiled, wondering at the oddity of adult concepts of justice. Then he said, "Miss Ball, I understand you made a delivery to Mr. Matchett's inn on the night the, ah, murdered man was found. Or rather, you were there in the afternoon?" She nodded. "And you went around to the back?"

"Yes. That's what I always do there. The kitchen's in back."

"Did you notice anything at all out of place, or different?"

She shook her head.

"The cellar door was just as usual?"

"It's like I told the superintendent: I didn't see lights in the cellar, nor anything like that." Suddenly she turned and called to "Beatrice," who appeared from behind the flowered curtain as a gangly teenage girl, chewing gum ruminatively, like a cow its cud. "Get on with it, my girl! Get the Inspector some more coffee! I'm not paying you to sit back there and read those film magazines!"

Beatrice slopped over, looking ever-so-slightly in the family way. Jury allowed her to take the pot, but refused Betty Ball's offer of fresh scones. From eyes the color of a citrus peel, she looked sorrowfully at Jury, as if her baked goods were her only hedge against spinsterhood.

"Was it raining hard, Miss Ball? I understand a storm had come up."

"That's right. I was nearly drenched just going from the car to the kitchen and back. Have you talked with Melrose Plant yet? He's terribly clever, really." Jury listened as she sang Melrose Plant's praises, and in the way her eyes lit up, he wondered if she had Cinderella designs on the lord of the manor.

By the time Jury left the Gate House Tearoom, the snow had resettled itself in a clean, unbroken sweep all across the square. Only if he looked hard could he see the tracks made by himself and the children, and even as he looked the nearer ones were closing up like dents in dough. The winds had died down and stopped driving the snow at a hard slant, so once again it was falling at a slow and steady pace, the same wet, fat flakes of the morning. Looking at the spire of the Church of St. Rules, he decided to see the vicar later. A long walk in the snow—the mile or so to the Bicester-Strachans and Ardry End—was what he needed. Think of all the fresh tracks he could make.

Shortly beyond the village limits, it was pure country. Snow and ice hung in tatters from hedgerows. Had he been a writer, he thought he could have done no better than to attempt to eulogize the English hedgerow, long and limitless stretches of yew, thorn, or copper beech, low sanctuaries for every kind of flower pushed from the field by the plow, and for so many kinds of birds. Jury sighed as he clumped on with wet black boots, at one point startling a cock pheasant into flashing upward in a flurry of green and chestnut. Jury's face was stiff with the cold, and he could think of worse things than to be greeted at the end with a crackling fire and a glass of vintage port.

Instead, he was greeted by the voice of Lorraine Bicester-Strachan, addressing him from the queenly perch of her chestnut mare: "If you've come about the washing-up machine, would you mind going round back?"

Jury had just applied his hand to the large brass door-knocker, when he heard a sound of something raking around the corner of the house, and looked up to see horse and rider pushing through the trees. It was perfectly clear to him, standing on the Bicester-Strachans' front step, that Mrs. Bicester-Strachan did not think he was a repairman. He was hardly dressed for the part, nor was there a van in sight. She probably made a habit of putting people down.

He touched his hat in a polite salute. "Inspector Richard Jury, New Scotland Yard, madam. I'd like to speak with you and your husband, if I may."

She dismounted but did not apologize for her error. At that moment, the front door swung back and Jury found himself looking into the eyes of an elderly man as tall as himself, and who would have been taller, except for his stoop.

"Oh, do forgive me for keeping you standing here. Ah, but I see my wife has found you—" He fitted a pince-nez, which had been dangling on a grosgrain ribbon, onto his nose.

As Lorraine introduced them, a boy, scarved and

muffled up, came around the corner of the house to
lead the horse away.

"There was a Superintendent Pratt here just yesterday. He was from the police in Northampton," said
Bicester-Strachan, as Jury was taking off his coat.

"Yes, well, I've a few questions I'd like to ask also,
Mr. Bicester-Strachan." They went into the lounge,
which Jury thought rather coldly formal. The furniture ran to the rich but not the comfortable, and as
Lorraine Bicester-Strachan turned to face him, it occurred to him that she ran very much the same. She
was dressed in her riding habit—black Melton coat,
stock perfectly done up, boots lustrous. When she removed her velvet hat, he observed that her hair was
arranged in a rather affectedly outmoded style of the
twenties. It ballooned round her face and was wound
into a kind of bun on top. Her skin was ivory, her
eyes onyx-black. Altogether she gave the impression
of a tabloid fashion-model, coldly, if attractively,
severe.

"Could we not offer the inspector a drink, my
dear?" said Willie Bicester-Strachan.

"Does Scotland Yard drink?" she asked with mock
wonder, as she poured herself a sherry from a cut-
glass decanter.

Exasperated by this collective reference to him,
Jury felt like belting back a double, but remembered
who he was, and put on his bland face. Still he knew
his irritation showed in his face, in his eyes. It had
been something he could never quite master in Detective Training School, that expressionless face. Now,
however, he declined Bicester-Strachan's politer offer
of a drink, while Lorraine stoppered up the decanter
and brought her glass over to a rose velvet armchair.
She slouched there, her legs straight out in front of
her, crossed at the ankles, boyishly adolescent. "But

it's really *Chief* Inspector Jury, isn't it? Why be modest?" She raised her glass an inch in salute.

"You knew I wasn't the dishwasher man, then, didn't you?"

She looked slightly embarrassed, but regained her arrogance quickly. "Oh, I suppose I guessed who you were. News travels fast here. It's just one gets tired of the police wandering over one's place as if they owned it. That Superintendent Pratt was tiresome, to say the least."

"You seem more annoyed by all of this than upset."

She shrugged. "Am I supposed to gush tears?"

"Really, Lorraine—" said her husband, settling himself in a velvet wing chair by the fire, before which sat a small table holding a chessboard. He bent his head as if studying a problem.

"I wanted to ask you about the nights in question—the seventeenth and eighteenth."

"I may as well tell you," said Lorraine, "I was too damned drunk for my recollection to be anything but fuzzy at best."

"Then you wouldn't remember who was in the dining room between nine and eleven, say, and who was absent?"

"I'm not even sure if *I* was in the dining room," said Lorraine.

Bicester-Strachan raised his white head. "I was having a game of draughts with the vicar—Mr. Smith. I don't know what my wife was doing," he added, drily.

"I sat with Oliver—that's Oliver Darrington—for a longish while and then with Melrose Plant, until I could bear his snobbery no longer—"

"That's quite unfair, Lorraine. If you think Plant's a snob, you don't understand the man at all."

She had gone to stand beside the fireplace after refilling her glass. One hand was upraised on the mantel and her boot was on the fender. She was every inch an add for *Country Living*. "Plant is an English anachronism. If he only had a monocle, he'd be perfect."

"It seems rather inconsistent," said Jury, "for someone that conscious of his social position to give up his most enviable possession, doesn't it? I'm talking about his title."

Bicester-Strachan chuckled. "He's got you there, Lorraine."

But she merely grew more obdurate. "Melrose Plant is the sort who would do that to show how much better he was than all of his sword-bearing, ruffle-shirted, belted-earl ancestors."

"Well, I rather admired that move," said Bicester-Strachan, smiling down at the chessboard as if Plant were seated across from him. "He's original, is Plant. D'you know the reason he gave me, Inspector? He said that whenever the House sat, he always had the feeling he'd walked in on a colony of penguins."

Jury smiled, but Lorraine didn't seem to find it amusing. "Merely proves my point," she said.

Jury noticed how flushed her face was. When a woman belittled a man, it was generally one she couldn't get her hooks into. "Do you remember what time you were sitting with Mr. Plant?"

"I couldn't possibly fix the time. Everybody was table-hopping, you see, so I could hardly keep track of anyone's movements. The only two stationary objects were my husband and the vicar. The Reverend Denzil Smith! There's a treat, a walking compendium of trivia, knows every little detail about Long Piddleton and all the inns dotting the country-side, and is forever filling one's ears with their history, how many ghosts they have, or priests' holes in chimneys—"

"Denzil is a friend of mine, Lorraine," said Bicester-Strachan mildly, his eyes fixed on the chessboard. Meditatively, he moved a bishop.

"You were in the Jack and Hammer the evening of the second murder?"

"For a bit, yes. Only a half hour or so," said Lorraine.

"And you didn't speak to the victim?"

"No, of course not," she said. "Someone about has rather a black sense of humor, haven't they?"

"People don't generally kill for the fun of it. So you had never seen either of these men before, Mr. Bicester-Strachan?"

He shook his head. "No one in Long Piddleton had seen them before, to my knowledge. They were total strangers."

"You used to live in London, didn't you?" Jury mentally ran down the statement Pratt had taken. "In Hampstead, I believe?"

"You certainly know a lot about us, Inspector," said Lorraine.

Something in her tone made him hesitate. To her the pause must have been suggestive, for she said, "Should I have a solicitor here?"

"Do you think you need one?"

Lorraine Bicester-Strachan set down her glass with more force than seemed necessary and folded her arms tightly across her breast, as if protecting herself from some invasion of honor or privacy. Her lustrously booted right leg swung back and forth nervously.

"We came here because it's a quaint village that's just becoming stylish—you know, for writers, artists, and so forth. No one goes to the Cotswolds anymore, do they? Isn't all that elfin beauty just a bit démodé? I ride and I paint." She waved her arm about the room, taking in four walls of bad work. They were poorly executed seascapes of boiling waves and cast up, twisted branches. She hadn't even the imagination to see the beauty of the countryside right beyond

her door. The village itself must have been an artist's
dream.

"A bit boring after London, isn't it?"

"We were getting fed up with London. Really, it
isn't at all the same anymore. I mean, one can't walk
down Oxford Street without running into all of Arabia and Pakistan—"

"Why don't you tell the truth, Lorraine?" said
Willie Bicester-Strachan from under the tent of his
hand where his head was bent over the chessboard.

"What on earth are you talking about, Willie?" But
the cool, white mask had slipped, and the voice was
unnaturally high.

"The reason we came here." Bicester-Strachan did
not even look up from the chessboard as he said this.
"We—I—went through rather a bad patch in London,
Inspector. Or perhaps you have ferreted that out already." He looked up then and smiled, but the smile
was not a happy one.

Lorraine rose suddenly like a cat jumping out of a
chair. "I thought we were rid of that—the newspapers, reporters, all that, when we left London. Now
here they come rummaging round again because of
these goddamned murders."

She seemed to think the murders had been done
merely to discommode her. Bicester-Strachan paid no
attention to her outburst, and Jury realized that for
all of her hauteur and her husband's own dotty, ab-
sent-minded act, it was he who was the stronger of the
two.

"Several years ago I was in Whitehall. With the
War Ministry, Inspector. I rather hope you'll forgive
me for not going into details—"

"For God's sake, Willie! This is ridiculous. Why
bring it up?"

Bicester-Strachan waved her words aside with an

impatient flick of his hand. "This is Scotland Yard, Lorraine. Use your brains."

Brains were not the most obvious of Lorraine's commodities, thought Jury. "Something happened, did it?"

"Indeed it did. It never came out because I chose to resign—to avoid any more unsavory publicity. I committed—I'm ashamed to say it—an . . . offense to do with some information that should not have got out. Fortunately, it was the wrong secret; even I was unaware it was misinformation." He smiled wryly. "So I wasn't prosecuted."

"Gave it away—to whom?"

"It doesn't matter, does it, Inspector?"

Jury didn't like badgering him; it had been painful for Bicester-Strachan to admit even this much. "I don't know, Mr. Bicester-Strachan." Secrets from the past had certainly supplied more than one murderer with a motive. Jury rose. "I'll be leaving now. Thank you. I may have some more questions later on."

Bicester-Strachan stood and shook hands with Jury. "It's really a rotten business. I simply can't imagine this quiet village—well, good-bye."

"Good-bye."

"I'll just see you out," said Lorraine.

At the door she asked, "Where are you off to?"

"Ardry End."

"Well, good luck with *him*. Where are you staying?"

"At the Man with a Load of Mischief." He wanted to see the effect of his next words. "I understand Miss Rivington—Vivian—is engaged to the proprietor."

She stiffened, as if struck by a whip. "Simon Matchett? And Vivian? That's rot." She relaxed a little. "You've been talking to Agatha, haven't you? Her chief aim in life is to keep Vivian away from

Melrose Plant. Protecting her so-called inheritance, I imagine. Vivian's one of those terribly shy creatures. I find it tiresome, that sort of awkwardness."

"Well, thank you again, Mrs. Bicester-Strachan."

"Lorraine."

Jury only smiled and turned with relief toward the freshly fallen snow.

CHAPTER 8

As Inspector Jury was questioning the Bicester-Strachans, Lady Ardry was blowing on a cup of tea, grudgingly brought in by Ruthven. The kitchen of Ardry End had even supplied some of the little cakes she was so fond of.

"I only hope he knows his business," she said, speaking of Inspector Jury. She was watching Melrose pour himself a glass of Cockburn's Very Dark Brown port. "Isn't it a bit early for spirits, Melrose?"

"It's a bit early for *anything*," said Melrose, yawning, and corking up the bottle.

"Anyway, I gave Jury all of the interesting details on everyone who was at Matchett's Thursday night."

"That must have taken all of half a minute." He glared at his aunt, who had come up his drive this morning at 8:30. He could barely keep his eyes propped open, having been up half the night reading. But if he had been lending only half an ear, she had been supplying only half a conversation, so it evened out. He watched the fairy cakes disappearing from the silver tray: ghastly little things with currants in their tops like dead flies. But he had Ruthven keep them on hand for Agatha, who doted on them. Already she had devoured three and was just tucking number four into her mouth, which she then wiped daintily with a napkin.

"Whom did you accuse, Agatha? I mean besides me?" Melrose stared absently into the fire, and hoped this policeman would clear things up, and quickly.

"Accuse *you*? Good heavens, Melrose, I should think I've more honor than to go about naming my own flesh and blood—"

"Oliver Darrington, then? Get rid of the competition? It must be hard having another mystery writer around. Though I must say his books certainly don't make for much of a read." He watched her get up and go to the mantel, where she inspected an early Derby plate, looking for the patches on the bottom.

Agatha replaced the plate. "You were always jealous of him, weren't you, my dear Plant?"

"Jealous of Darrington?" What little mental compost pile was she rooting around in now?

"Because of Sheila Hogg. Don't think I don't know all about that." Now she was handling a vase of latticino Nailsea glass. Was her purse big enough to hold it? And where had she got the idea he had the least interest in Sheila?

When he didn't answer, she turned quickly, as if to catch him out. "Vivian Rivington, then?" Agatha didn't care whether the arrow fell wide or not. To her, a miss was as good as a mile. She would run down the list of women until she hit on the right one.

Melrose yawned again. "You've been studying my dance programme, dear Aunt."

When she had reseated herself, making small adjustments to the various silver and gilt ornaments on the table in front of her, Melrose said, "And had the inspector any theories? I mean other than which of these charmers I was planning on marrying?"

"Don't be conceited, my dear Plant. Not *everyone* is interested in your personal affairs." She passed a Murano ashtray from hand to hand, as if estimating its weight for customs. "For some reason, Inspector Jury is asking all kinds of questions about the people who were there—*us*, I mean. Why, I can't imagine.

Not when what he should be doing is looking for some maniac, before we're all dead in our beds."

"So our maniac nipped into the cellar, strangled the Small person, shoved his head in a keg of beer, and nipped out again?"

"Naturally." She regarded him with wonder. "You don't honestly think it was someone who was already *there*?"

"Certainly."

"Good Lord! That's absurd. I assumed you were jesting the other evening." With her astonishment upon her, she went for another fairy cake, one with coconut waving all over its top like cilia.

Revolting things, thought Melrose, sliding down in his wing chair. He heard the long-case clock in the hall drone the half hour. Lord, it was nearly lunchtime and she was still here. He was drawing the line at inviting her to lunch.

"Well?"

Through his half-closed eyes he could see she was waiting for him to retract his assertion that one of her dear neighbors might be responsible for the present horrors. He would not be drawn into theorizing, so he said evasively, "I expect the police will clear it up." They'd better, or she'd be over here every morning at first light, issuing bulletins.

"There is another possibility, of course." She smiled her cat-and-canary smile.

"And what's that?" he asked without interest.

"That this Small person was not killed in the inn. The murderer killed him *outside* and brought him in by that back door. He must have been looking for a place to dispose of the body. Small could have been killed anywhere!"

"Why?"

She looked at him suspiciously. "What do you mean, 'why'?"

"Why would someone have brought him to the Man with a Load of Mischief? Why not just leave the Small person outside in the wild, draped over a tree or something?"

Agatha studied a fruit scone. "Because he knew that the police would think just what you and the police *do* think! That one of us is guilty." Her eyes glittered with triumph, and she munched the scone.

Melrose poured himself another tot of port, and said, "Which makes the murderer, once again, someone from Long Piddleton, doesn't it? I don't imagine every murderer in the British Isles knew that our happy little band was going to be dining at the inn and that he could just bring along his old, dead body to our cellar and let one of us take—as they say—the 'rap' for it." He sipped the port; round his glass he saw her eyes narrow meanly. He had shot another of her clay ducks out of the reeds and she meant to have it back.

"What about the *second* murder, then? This Ainsley person? My dear Plant, someone must be deranged to go stuffing a body up there on the Jack—"

Melrose slid down in his brown leather wing chair and closed his eyes, hoping his aunt would take the hint. But no, she would go on spinning her sticky little theories like some old, senile spider . . .

"Melrose!"

His eyes snapped open.

"Gone to sleep on me again, haven't you? And here's Ruthven wants you for something."

The butler closed his eyes in pain. For years Agatha had been mispronouncing his name. On purpose?—no, thought Melrose, she just couldn't get the hang of English names.

"Your lordship," said Ruthven, "I was just wondering about the Christmas goose. Martha's in need of chestnuts for the stuffing, sir, and it seems we haven't any."

Hell, thought Melrose, wishing Ruthven hadn't brought up the goose in front of Agatha. "Perhaps you could send down to Miss Ball's. She always got things like that when no one else does."

Ruthven nodded and slipped out of the room.

"Goose? We're having goose? How jolly!" And Agatha rubbed her hands together in anticipation of the Christmas feast.

Of course, he had always had her to Christmas dinner. But he had thought to trot out some old turkey for her and save the goose for himself for a midnight snack with a bottle of Château Haut-Brion. "Would you know the difference between a goose and a turkey? I mean if it were all plucked and lying on a plate?"

"Whatever are you babbling about Melrose? Of course I'd know the difference." She was inspecting a Limoges ashtray.

"Even if it were a very *thin* turkey?"

"I think you're having a nervous breakdown, Melrose. Your eyes have a feverish cast. Now, if Ruthven—"

"Will you *please* learn to say his name properly. *Rivv'n*, not *Ruth-ven*. *Rivv'n*."

"Then why does he spell ir *Ruth-ven*? *Rivv'n* hasn't a *th*."

"And while we're on it, you pronounce *Bicester-Strachan* as if it had twenty syllables. It's *Bister Strawn*."

Before she could answer this charge, Ruthven was back in the room. "There's the gentleman from Scotland Yard to see you, sir, in the hall. Chief Inspector Richard Jury, his name is." Ruthven's normally impeccable syntax got a bit tangled, a normal reaction,

Melrose supposed, to Scotland Yard waiting in the wings.

Reprieve. "For heaven's sake, don't keep him standing out there, as Lady Ardry is just going—" Melrose could manage quite a viselike grip when he wanted to. He got his aunt up and out of her chair, holding her purse in his other hand, and had escorted her nearly to the door when she bellowed, "My watch! My watch! I've lost my watch!" And she pulled her arm free to go and search among the cushions.

Melrose sighed, having lost another round.

As Agatha was tossing the cushions in the drawing room, Jury was standing in the hall, which seemed too pedestrian a designation for the magnificent room and its hypnotic arrangement of every kind of medieval weaponry. Swords, rifles, pikes, lances—all were used as decorative displays in the semicircular arches above the doorways, brilliantly polished, the swords and pikes, like shafts of sun. The butler returned and ushered Jury through carved wooden doors.

Jury was surprised to see Lady Ardry rummaging through the furniture, but the moment he appeared she shot forward, her hand out. "Inspector Jury! We meet again!" As she pumped his hand, Jury observed the man standing in the middle of the room. He was tall and pleasant-looking, dressed rather informally in a Liberty silk robe, and tousled, as if he had been pulled out of bed. What Jury noticed most, though, was the expression in the astonishing, emerald eyes over which Plant was now settling gold-rimmed spectacles. Sharp, very sharp.

"My aunt was just leaving, Inspector. I'm Melrose Plant."

Jury grasped his hand, and noticed that Lady

Ardry hadn't the look of a person just leaving. Her legs seemed rooted, treelike, to the floor.

"The inspector might want some corroboration of your testimony," she said.

"First, Agatha, he has to *get* the testimony. And for that, he probably wants to speak to me privately."

Her eyes narrowed. "Privately? Why? What have you to say that I mayn't hear?"

Melrose gripped her arm firmly, planted her handbag under it, and steered her to the door. "I'll see you tomorrow. But not, please, at dawn. Unless there's a duel on my front lawn."

Agatha was still barking out instructions as the door was firmly closed in her face.

Then Plant turned to Jury and said, "Excuse me, Inspector, but my aunt's been here for three hours and I haven't yet had breakfast. If you'd care to join me, we could talk while we ate."

"I've had mine, sir, but I'd be happy to sit with you."

Ruthven appeared, took the order, and padded off to fill it.

Melrose Plant indicated a chair, the one his aunt had just vacated. "You're staying at the Man with a Load of Mischief?"

Jury nodded, accepting a cigarette from the lacquered box which Plant extended.

"You want to ask me about Thursday and Friday evenings, yes? Would you like straight facts? Or my impressions?"

Jury smiled. "Let's get the facts out of the way first, if you don't mind, sir."

"Inspector, I don't think I'm any older, certainly no wiser than you, that you should call me 'sir.' "

Jury reddened. He just couldn't get around all of that Marquess of Ayreshire, Earl of Caverness stuff. "Yes, ah—Mr. Plant. Now, if you'd just make any corrections in the facts I've already gathered." Jury reviewed the people present, the situation of the diners at dinner, the appearance and disappearance of Small.

"Yes, that's all as I remember it. It must have been near eight or eight-thirty when Small was in the bar with Trueblood."

"And you didn't see him after that?"

Melrose shook his head firmly. "No. Not until my aunt came yelling—"

"Your aunt? Yelling?" Jury tried not to smile.

"Lord, yes. You could have heard her all the way to Sidbury." Plant was regarding Jury intently through half-shut eyes. "Did she tell you she was in total command of herself, then? Don't bother to answer. I can see she did. The whole world in tatters, and Agatha like a rock."

"She did indicate the servant girl—Miss Murch—was rather beside herself."

"Oh, Murch was, I suppose. The reactions of everyone were pretty standard—throat grabbings, eye-ball poppings, upstartings from chairs—"

"You make it sound a bit of play-acting, Mr. Plant."

Plant smiled. "Well, I admit I was wondering which one of them did it."

Jury's cigarette stopped halfway to his mouth. "Then you did assume it was someone in the inn?"

Melrose Plant looked surprised. "I thought it was obvious. Unless you share my aunt's Ripper theory, or someone wandering about Long Piddleton who has a grudge against inn guests? Everyone at the Load of Mischief seemed to think he'd come in by that cellar door."

"And you don't?"

Melrose looked as if he'd expected more than this of Scotland Yard but was too polite to say so. "Everyone refers to the Small person as a 'perfect stranger' just happening into Long Piddleton, which is in itself unlikely."

"How so, Mr. Plant?"

"Because he came by train and bus. How could he have been just 'passing through'?" At the butler's entrance, Plant said, "Ah, breakfast."

"I've laid it for you in the dining room, sir."

Melrose rubbed his hands. "Thank you, Ruthven. Come along, Inspector Jury."

Beneath the fan-vaulted ceiling of the dining room hung enormous, rich portraits of the Ardry-Plant line. One, the smallest of them, against the end wall, was of Melrose Plant himself, seated at a table, a book open before him.

"Conceited, isn't it? To have a portrait of oneself hanging about? But my mother, before she died, insisted. That's she. The one in black."

The portrait was of a lovely woman in black velvet, posed in a simple, dignified way. Hanging beside that was one of a squat, friendly faced man, surrounded by hunting dogs. Plant looked like his mother.

As Plant filled his plate he said, "I see Martha assumed my aunt would be staying, since she prepared enough for twelve. Please have some, Inspector Jury." He lifted the silver domes from the dishes: deviled kidneys, buttered eggs like satin, Dover sole, hot scones.

Jury could hardly fault these villagers on their offers of food and drink, but he turned down this elegant second breakfast. "No thanks, Mr. Plant. Just coffee would be fine."

"Mr. Plant, you were saying that you didn't agree with the idea that Small's murderer forced his way in through the cellar door."

"Inspector—I'm quite sure you don't think so either, but I'll give you my reasons if you like. Had the murderer been someone from *outside,* is it within the realm of reason that he would have chosen that public place for a meeting with his victim? But let's suppose, even, that he had made this curious arrangement. Having fixed to meet Small in the cellar, he then has to break the door to get *into* it? Wouldn't Small have just let him in? One can hardly take the view that the killer just happened by chance to walk round to the rear of the inn, spied Small through the dusty cellar window, said to himself, 'Good Lord! If it isn't Small, my arch enemy!' then battered down the door." Melrose Plant shook his head and poured the coffee.

Jury smiled, since Plant had just outlined his own thoughts regarding the murder. He pulled out his packet of Players and offered one to Plant, who accepted. They lit up.

"What *do* you think, Mr. Plant?"

Plant studied the pictures on the wall for a moment, and then said: "Given the meeting place, I'd say it was a spur-of-the-moment thing. Someone there was surprised by the appearance of Small, and during the course of the evening arranged to meet him in the wine cellar. That improvisational method of murder would testify to that, wouldn't it? The murderer choking him with a piece of wire from a wine bottle and then shoving his head into that keg of beer. You know how I see it?"

"How?"

"Our murderer is having some sort of conversation with Small, and all the while untwisting the wire and then—" Plant raised his hands and pulled an imaginary length of wire around his own neck. "Pulls on the larynx long enough to knock him out and then holds his head in the butt. That makes it look rather spontaneous. Or . . ."

"What?"

"Well, there is the possibility it was premeditated and made to look as if it weren't. And the grotesque detail of shoving Small's head in a keg of beer, and stuffing Ainsley up there on the beam—" Plant's green eyes glittered. "Why? The weird touches are, well, *too* weird."

"You mean because they direct our attention to the method, and away from something else—such as the motive? Window-dressing, that sort of thing?"

"Or could one murder have been done to draw your attention from the other?" suggested Melrose. "Ainsley might have been killed to divert attention from Small, or vice versa."

"Something done so the police end up not being able to see the forest for the trees?" Jury accepted another cup of coffee from the silver pot, thinking that Plant was an exceptionally clever man. He only hoped he wasn't the murderer.

"Funny," said Melrose. "Small and Ainsley appeared to be total strangers. No one knew them, and they didn't know one another—or so it would seem. Dear me. Well, Inspector, you're faced with everyone there having an opportunity, but no one seeming to have a motive. It would be so much easier if the victim had been one of us."

"Why is that?"

"Because there are so many motives. Had it been Willie Bicester-Strachan, for example, there's Lorraine to pin it on. Had it been me killed, good heavens, the possibilities are endless—beginning with my aunt. Had it been Sheila Hogg as victim, there's Oliver Darrington—"

"Darrington wanting to murder Miss Hogg? Why?"

"Because then he'd be free to marry Vivian Rivington. The money, you see. And Sheila no doubt has her blackmail all ready in case Oliver strays too far from her side. Had it been Aunt Agatha murdered, the entire village would be under suspicion."

"And had it been Vivian Rivington?"

Melrose gave him a long look. "What about Vivian?"

"Isn't it rather significant that Miss Rivington will inherit a good deal of money in six months' time? Who will lose and gain thereby?"

"Look, I'm playing games. What has Viv's fortune to do with Ainsley and Small?"

"Nothing I know of. Only it wouldn't be the first time several people were killed in order to mask the real motive."

"I don't understand, Inspector."

Jury dropped it. "Mrs. Bicester-Strachan tells me she shared your table for part of the evening. The night Small was murdered."

"Not 'shared' exactly. I managed to hold on to my half through strategy that would have been the envy of Rommel." Melrose helped himself to a piece of toast from the silver rack, bit into it, and said, "Why do the English have a reputation for enjoying cold toast?" He put the remainder on his plate.

"Mrs. Bicester-Strachan seemed to have ambivalent feelings toward you."

"What a very polite way of putting it." Then Melrose sighed, and added, "No, Inspector. There has never been anything on between Lorraine and me."

"Nor Miss Rivington and you?"

"You're beginning to sound like my aunt. I don't see what connection there is between my private life and the business at hand."

"Oh, come on, now, Mr. Plant. If we ignored private lives we'd never be catching criminals, would we?"

Plant held up his hand. "All right, all right. Look, Inspector, contrary to my aunt's belief that half the women in the country want to marry me and thereby deprive her of her 'rightful inheritance,' let me assure you that very few women have ever had designs on me. I have had my perfectly ordinary attachments with ordinarily beautiful women. I have been engaged, broken off by the lady in question because she thought me a snob and lazy, both of which I probably am. My aunt is terrified that some woman is going to 'land' me (to use her quaint Americanism). No one, however, is really interested."

Jury seriously doubted that, but changed the subject again. "According to Mr. Scroggs, several of you came to the Jack and Hammer the next evening, Friday, when Ainsley was murdered."

"Yes. I was there about eight or eight-thirty. Most of the rest of them were there, too. Vivian was sitting with me; Matchett came in for a bar meal. Even he couldn't stomach his own place, I suppose. Anyway, there's Scroggs's back door. Anyone in Long Piddleton could have come and gone that way—"

"You know about that, then?"

"Of course; everyone does. So it doesn't pin things down much for you to know who was *inside*."

"What about this rumor of an engagement between Mr. Matchett and Vivian Rivington?"

"I can't say. But I hope it's not true."

"Why?"

"Because I don't like Matchett. She's too good for him. You said something about masking the 'real' motive. You don't think there'll be more murders?"

"I wouldn't want to make such a prediction. You yourself suggested there were several motives for murder in Long Piddleton."

"Ah, but I wasn't really serious." Melrose swung around toward the dining room door, on the other side of which was a great clattering and raising of voices.

Ruthven entered. "I'm sorry, sir. It's Lady Ardry. Insists—"

"My *aunt*? Twice in one day—?"

But before he could finish, or Ruthven get out of her way, Agatha pushed through the door, shoving Ruthven with it, and sailed in, cape flying. "Well! I see you two are sitting here calmly eating kidney and bacon with the whole village in an uproar!"

"The village has been in an uproar for days, Agatha. Whatever brings you back?"

Lady Ardry planted her cane squarely in front of her and could not have kept the triumph from her voice had she wanted to. "What brings me back? To see if I can drag Chief Inspector Jury from his lunch. There's been another!"

"Another?"

"Murder. At the Swan."

CHAPTER 9

"The moment I heard I came straight away!" said Lady Ardry from the back seat of Plant's Bentley. It had taken Melrose five minutes to warm up the cold engine, and the three of them were now speeding along the main road, which connected Sidbury on the one end with Dorking Dean on the other.

Jury was trying to keep his temper under control. "Why didn't Wiggins simply call me? It would have saved the half hour it must have taken you on your bike."

She was humming and staring out as the fields of melting snow flew by. "I expect he didn't know where you were."

Jury turned in his seat and, with iron self-control, said, "*You* did, Lady Ardry."

She smoothed her ample skirts. "I'd no idea you were still at Plant's, lingering over your coffee."

The Swan was a country inn less than a mile from Ardry End and several miles from Dorking Dean. When they got there, three police cars were drawn up in the small parking lot that fronted the inn. A number of thrill seekers were also parked higgledy-piggledy along the road. As soon as Plant's Bentley pulled up, spitting slush, Wiggins ran over.

"I'm most dreadfully sorry, sir. I called all round, I did—"

Jury assured him it was not his fault. "I was at Ardry End—"

"Having breakfast," put in Agatha, heaving herself from the car.

Pratt came up. "The crew's been over the place, so you can move about freely. I've got to get to Northampton. The Chief Constable is . . . well, you can imagine. Wiggins here can fill you in." Pratt sketched a salute as he got into the car which had pulled up.

Melrose Plant had melted into the small crowd, dragging an irate Lady Ardry with him. The investigation, she seemed to think, had been hampered by her absence, and could now proceed.

"Pluck," Jury called, "get those people back. The police surgeon will have to get his car in here." There were quite a few children there, too, waiting for blood and gore. He recognized the Doubles among them and waved. They waved back, hectically.

"Where's the body, Wiggins? And who found it?"

"In the garden, sir. It was Mrs. Willypoole, the owner, found him."

Several reporters pushed their way in. "Is it a psychopath, Inspector?"

"I don't know. That is apparently what *you* think, from what I read in the papers."

"But it's a *pattern*. Another murder done at an inn, Inspector."

"Yes, well, let me know what the pattern means when you find out." Jury shoved past them.

Before he went in the door, Jury paused to look up at the inn sign, creaking slightly on its ironwork rod. The sign was faded, but it was still clearly a painting of a double-necked swan, each head gaggling off in a different direction. The swan was floating serenely down what was once a green river, and seemed altogether unaware of its strange deformity. Across the top of the sign in graceful cursive lettering was the legend *Swan with Two Necks.*

"How on earth do they ever think of them?" Jury said to Wiggins.

"Ah wha, sah?" asked Wiggins, his voice lost in the folds of his handkerchief.

"The names, Wiggins, the names."

Jury shoved open the inner frosted-glass door to the saloon bar. A woman (whom he presumed to be Mrs. Willypoole) was downing a shot glass of gin at the bar. When she saw Jury, she smiled tightly and brandished the gin bottle like a victory sign.

"This is Mrs. Willypoole," said Wiggins. "She's the one who found him."

"Inspector Jury, madam, New Scotland Yard." He showed her his ID, on which she had trouble focusing. A ginger cat, curled up on the bar, opened one untroubled eye. Apparently satisfied with Jury's credentials, it yawned and went back to sleep.

"A drink, then, love?" Jury shook his head. "Well, you'll have to excuse me, love. It's not often I get a shock like this. Let me tell you, when I went out there—" and her head fell in her hands.

"Of course. I understand, Mrs. Willypoole. I'd like a look first at the garden, and then to ask you a few questions." She didn't seem to hear him, and he decided that unless he wanted an unconscious witness, he'd better not come on quite so pompously with her. He leaned on the bar and tried to match her tone. "Can't say I blame you. But listen, love, go easy on that," and he flicked his nail against the bottle. "I'm going to need your help." He winked.

She looked up at him and set down the glass. "Hetta's the name." Although in the very stronghold of middle age, there still clung to Hetta remnants of an old glamour. Plump now, and hennaed, it was

clear it wasn't always so. Even now there were ripples
of posture and rustles of unseen silk, which suggested
better days. She corked up the bottle and said,
"Garden's just through that door."

And it was very cold.

"Why'd he come out here in the cold to have his
pint?" asked Wiggins as they stood looking down at
the body sprawled across the white metal table.
Beside the body was a half-drunk pint of lager.

"Because he was supposed to meet someone, I
imagine."

"Oh. Who, sir?"

Jury just looked at Wiggins, who seemed to be expecting an answer. "I wish I knew, Sergeant. Look at
this." Jury pointed to a book lying beneath the hand
of the murdered man. Since Pratt said the lab crew
had been over the place, he didn't have to worry
about prints, and he gently pulled the book away.
"Well, well. *Bent on Murder.* By our own Mr. Darrington."

Wiggins said, "That's something, that is. A red herring, do you think, sir?"

Sometimes Wiggins amazed Jury. He could ask perfectly inane questions, as he had done a minute ago,
and at other times he could do a fair job of deduc-
tion. Perhaps it had something to do with his nose
being stuffed or unstuffed. "I wouldn't be surprised,
Sergeant. Now, fill me in."

Wiggins took out his cellophane-wrapped box of
drops, and Jury waited patiently while he undid them
and popped one in his mouth. "Name's Jubal Creed,
sir. From his driver's license we got that he lives in a
town in East Anglia called Wigglesworth. That's in
Cambridgeshire. The Weatherington men are trying
to get hold of his family. We found his car parked
out in the lot. They've driven that along to Weather-

ington, too. He stopped here last night, had his evening meal and then breakfast this morning, and Mrs.
Willypoole said he came out here around ten-thirty,
or a bit later."

Jury nodded and went down on one knee to exam-
ine Creed further. A red indentation around his neck,
the slightly blued complexion, and the eyes told the
story. Wiggins had closed them, but they bulged
beneath the lids. The mark around the neck had
probably been made with a wire, as in the case of
Small. It had cut into the skin. There could not have
been much of a struggle.

"Neat, clean, and quiet. Just get behind your victim for a few seconds and—" Jury rose.

"I called Superintendent Racer, sir. Hope that was
right."

"Thank you. I'm sure he was thrilled."

Wiggins allowed himself a smile. "He wondered
why it wasn't you making the call. I told him you
were busy, sir."

"If Lady Ardry had not been so eager to tell me
about this herself, you would have got hold of me
earlier. Perhaps we should reinstitute the policy of
killing the messenger who brings the bad news."

"She was on the road, bicycling, and some passing
motorist told her about the murder. That's what she
said, anyway."

Jury snorted. "We can break *that* alibi, Wiggins."

Wiggins actually laughed so that he had to get out
his inhaler. He was a martyr to asthma.

"Find out when and why Creed left Cambridgeshire—"

Jury looked closer at Creed, whose face was turned
a fraction upward from his arm, on which the head
was lying. "Wiggins, what the devil's this?" Jury
pointed to what appeared to be a cut on the nose. It
had recently bled. Jury reached down and pulled the

man's face around. Not one cut, two. As if a hand
holding a razor had whipped twice across the bridge
of the nose. Most of the blood had drained down the
other side. The cuts were not deep, but still they sent
a chill up Jury's spine. The practical joker, again?
But what was the joke?

Before Wiggins could comment on the cuts, the
door to the garden was opened by a brisk little man
who introduced himself as Dr. Appleby, and apologized for not getting there sooner. He had had, he
said, rather waspishly, the living to see to, also. After
examining the victim quickly and efficiently, he said,
"Well, there it is again. Strangulation by someone
standing behind him. It's the larynx got most of the
pressure. The skin's cut up a bit. Probably some sort
of wire—like the others. Quick, neat, and, I might
add"—and Appleby observed Jury over rimless spectacles, brows raised—"the third one around here."

"Is that a fact, then?" said Jury. "Why doesn't London tell me these things?"

Appleby grunted. "After the postmortem I may be
able to say more, but not much. Not if it's like the
other two. Can place the time of death right now at,
say between nine and whenever the body was discovered—noon, was it?"

"We can narrow it more than that. He was still
alive at ten-thirty." Jury offered Appleby a cigarette,
which the doctor accepted. "I assume there's no reason to believe this couldn't have been done by a
woman as well as a man."

"None. They've all been very small men—light-
weights. And anyway, haven't we got over the idea
that women are weaklings? It's certainly not a
woman's method, though: poisons, pistols, that sort of
thing—they're more what women choose."

"How chauvinistic of you, Dr. Appleby." said Jury,

with a smile. "What do you make of the cuts across the bridge of the nose?"

"That *is* odd." Appleby raised the face to take another look, then let it loll back again on the arm. "I honestly can't say. Certainly recent. The murderer?"

"Not while shaving, that's for sure."

"Well, I'll be off, then." Appleby looked down at the corpse and said, "Rubber sheet and stretcher'll be coming for that in a bit. See you, Inspector." And he was gone.

Jury turned up his coat collar and shoved his hands in his pockets. He looked at the scene of the crime. It was a walled-in garden, a courtyard perhaps about fifty feet square, partly cobbled where the tables were set up, with the rest laid to lawn. To the left was an old stable block, part of which had been modernized and converted to the inn's toilets. The wall on the other three sides was very high. "Any outlets in that wall, Wiggins?"

"No, sir."

Jury turned and looked at the rear of The Swan. Inside the wall were two truncated wings that enclosed part of the cobbled terrace, that part where the tables were spotted here and there, and where Creed had been sitting. At ground level were two windows, one in each end of these wings, but even if someone had been looking out, he could not have seen the murdered man, since the table was in the nook made by the wings. There were no windows in the midsection, and over the terraced section was one of those cheap plexiglass roofs that kept off the elements. Handy for the murderer, who would leave no tracks in snow. Also, the roof effectively cut off the vision of anyone looking out the rear windows above, on the first or second levels. In such a public place it was an oddly secluded spot. The rear door was the

only danger point, since someone might have opened
it.

"Have the men been over the outside of the wall,
Wiggins?"

"Yes, sir. Pratt had his men go over the ground. No
tracks, though. Anyway, no one could have climbed
that wall in a hurry. It's too high."

"Hmm," said Jury. "Well, let's talk with Mrs. Willypoole. Were there any other guests?"

"Not overnight, sir. But there were two from Long
Piddleton stopped in around eleven when the bar
opened. Miss Rivington and Mr. Matchett."

Jury raised his eyebrows. "Did they now? And
which Rivington?"

"Vivian Rivington."

"Why?"

"She says they had lunch."

"Have you talked with them?"

"No sir. They were gone when we got here."

"Did you get hold of them?"

"I sent Pluck to have them stand by for questioning. He says they're in Long Piddleton, sir."

Jury was silent for a moment, still studying the
garden.

"Are you thinking what I'm thinking, sir?"

Jury was a bit surprised to hear that Wiggins had
been thinking at all. He usually left that to Jury.
"What's that, Sergeant?"

"That it's a regular locked-room mystery, sir."

"How so?"

"Well, whoever did it must have come from *inside*
the inn. But Mrs. Willypoole says that Mr. Matchett
and Miss Rivington never left their table. And she
could only know that if she was in the room, too,
seeing they didn't. So they all three have alibis."

"Very good, Wiggins. And since no one could have

climbed that wall, nobody could have done this murder, by your reckoning."

Wiggins smiled broadly. "Right, sir."

Jury smiled too. "Only somebody did, now, didn't they? Go check the outside of that wall."

"You say you found the deceased when you got curious about his being out there so long?"

"That's right," said Mrs. Willypoole. "Couldn't imagine why he'd want to go out in the first place. There he was sprawled over one of the tables. At first I thought maybe he'd come over sick. But something told me not to touch him." She shuddered and asked Jury for a cigarette.

"He was a guest here?"

She nodded. "I don't keep all that many sleeping rooms and sure not in winter. But he called up here a couple days ago—"

"Called? From where?"

She shrugged. "Don't know. Said he needed a room just for the night, and that's all. Surprised, I was. I mean, that anyone's heard of the place outside of Dorking Dean or Long Pidd."

"So you knew he was a stranger."

"Well, he was to me, wasn't he? He could have come from Dorking Dean, but why'd he want to book a room, then?"

Jury had the register open before him. "Jubal Creed. He didn't mention what his business was?" She shook her head. "Did he say why he wanted to take his drink outside?"

"Just that he wanted a breath of air."

"Do many people from Long Piddleton visit The Swan?"

"A fair amount. Mostly on their way to Dorking Dean, or further. There were two here this morning, I was telling your sergeant—"

"That would be Simon Matchett and Miss Riving-ton?" She nodded. "Do you know them?"

"Him I do. He owns the Man with a Load of Mis-chief." Her eye softened. "Ever so nice, is Mr. Matchett. Simon. She's been here several times, too, but I don't know her all that well."

"Why were they here?"

"Why? Well, to have a bar meal—ploughman's lunch—bread, cheese, you know."

"And what time was that?"

"About eleven. Early for lunch."

"Did they come together?"

"Well, they came *in* together. But I took it they came in different cars, and met here."

"You say it was near eleven?"

"Right after. I can't say to the minute, but I know I'd only just opened up the bar for him."

"Did they sit up at the bar and talk, or what?"

"Oh, no. I served them their lunch at that table back there." She pointed to the farthest of one of a dozen tables in the saloon bar. "So you didn't over-hear anything they were saying?"

"No."

"Did either of them leave the table?"

"No. And I was in here all the time, so I'm sure of that."

"The only way to the garden is through that back door or the gate in the wall?" She nodded. "I noticed the terrace is partly enclosed between the wings of the building." Jury picked up Wiggins's box of cough drops and set it between and slightly to the rear of a bottle of catsup and some Branston pickle. "There are windows at the rear of these wings, but you can't see into this part of the garden." He put his hand on the cough drop box. "So, in effect, the only way any-one can see what's going on in the garden where the tables are is through the door. Which was closed, it being winter." She nodded again.

"Do you know any of these people, Hetta?" Jury rattled off the names of all the others who had been at the Man with a Load of Mischief the night Small was murdered.

"They've all been in one time or another. Even the vicar. I don't know as I could tell you what they look like, but the names are familiar."

"How long did Mr. Matchett and Miss Rivington stay?"

She ran a peeling red nail over her brow. "Umm. Maybe an hour, maybe forty-five minutes."

At that moment, Wiggins came through the front door of the Swan, looking pleased with himself. "I found it, sir. A window. Come outside, will you?" As Jury rose, Wiggins looked down at the condiment-and-cough-drop arrangement and rescued his box from the table.

"Thanks very much, Hetta." Jury smiled. "You've been a great help."

Hetta apparently remembered it was never too late. She straightened her jumper to its best advantage and smoothed back her red curls. "Well, I always say, if you can't keep your head in a crisis, you'd best not go into trade. Bounced a few in my day, Mr. Jury. Men got to learn where to keep their hands, I always say." She looked at Jury's with a smile.

"Absolutely. If we have more questions, you'll be available?"

"Yes, indeed." The smile grew more roguish still.

"It's the toilet, sir," said Wiggins, pointing upward. They were standing on the outside of the wall, that part comprised of the converted stable block. "It's not too hard; I just shoved the window in, crammed

through it and came out the door into the courtyard."

Jury looked from the window down at the ground.
The snow had nearly melted and the ground was
hard. Not likely to take much of an impression. Jury
hunkered down. "Pratt's men must have been back
here. I wonder if—"

He heard a *pssst* from behind. He looked all
around to determine the direction and then saw a
small head dart back behind an oak.

"What was that, sir?" asked Wiggins, looking about
rather desperately and turning up his coat collar as if
it were proof against strange woodland creatures.

"I think I know," said Jury, watching the tree. The
head darted out again, and another just above it.

Pssst. Pssst.

"Come out of there," called Jury, marshaling his
most authoritative voice.

It worked, perhaps a little too well, for the Double
children appeared, their heads even lower than usual.
The girl's small hand gathered in the hem of her
coat.

Jury softened up his tone a bit. "Now, what are
you doing out here James? And James?"

The boy, ever the braver of the two, looked from
Jury to Wiggins, studying the latter carefully and
looking back at Jury, the message clearly inscribed in
his expression. *Get rid of that one. Or we ain't
talkin'.*

"Wiggins, go on inside and see if our Hetta has
come up with anything else after several drinks,
okay?"

As soon as the sergeant had gone, the little girl
started jumping up and down, bearly able to contain
her excitement, and the boy said, in a near-rever-
ential tone: "Tracks!" He jabbed his finger back

toward the woods. Just beyond the wall was a stand of oak thickening into woodland beyond.

The little girl had her platelike blue eyes clamped on Jury's face, apparently thrilled to see their lesson would come in handy so soon.

James whispered excitedly as he tugged Jury along: "We done just what you said, Mr. Jury. We looked for anything funny. You said wherever there's a murder there's bound to be something funny."

Had he said that? wondered Jury, as they pulled him along between them like a wagon. They let him go finally, and made a dash ahead of him through the trees. In the woods the snow hadn't melted as much as it had near the wall of the Swan, and when he came up to them, James was pointing down at the imprint of a shoe or a boot. A few feet farther on there was another, again where the snow hadn't melted. In another twenty feet they had reached a small clearing where the ground was hard and rutted.

James pointed back toward the Sidbury-Dorking Dean Road, screened by trees, and said, "Used to be an old road back here. Ain't no one uses it no more. Used to go round to Dorking."

There were old tire tracks and, when Jury got down and looked more closely, at least parts of one that did not look so old. A car could have pulled off the Sidbury-Dorking Dean Road and stopped here.

Jury got up. "James," he said, "and James." He laid his hand on the girl's knitted cap. "You're brilliant." Open-mouthed, they stared at one another, astonished to hear that word reserved for stars and sunlight applied to them. He took out his wallet and said, "The Yard customarily gives rewards for this sort of thing." He handed each of them a pound note, which they accepted amid a peal of giggles. "This discovery is, of course, not to be mentioned." The giggles stopped, heads nodded, and a new solemnity reigned. "You get along home now. And be careful. I'll need you later." The Doubles took off through the trees, but in a minute the boy was back, shoving something into Jury's hand.

"It's for you, sir. I whittled it myself." Then the boy danced off through the trees, and they both turned and waved frantically, and were gone.

Jury looked at the present. It was a catapult, a very rough hewn one, with a rubber band for the sling. He smiled. Then he scuffed around through the snow looking for stones, turned up a few pebbles, and took some practice shots at the trees. When he was James's age he had broken a whole line of school windows from a hundred feet away.

Then, sheepishly, he looked over his shoulder to see if anyone might possibly have seen him. He shoved the catapult in his inside coat pocket and tramped back toward the Swan.

CHAPTER 10

"The ground was awfully hard, but we managed to get a bit of an impression of the tire marks," said Superintendent Pratt, his feet firmly planted on Constable Pluck's desk.

"I don't expect it's going to do us much more good than the footprints. No one around here wears that size Wellington. If he's smart enough to change his shoes, he's certainly smart enough to change the tires on his car."

"Umm. Well, we're checking them all, anyway. It was a fairly safe place to pull off and park, though." Pratt closed his eyes as if envisioning the car in the woods again. "Screened from the main road by the trees and that small rise of hill." He opened his eyes and looked at Jury. "Those cuts on the nose, now—"

But Pratt was interrupted by Sergeant Pluck, who announced Lady Ardry's arrival. "You sent for her, sir? That's what she says." Pluck was aghast, as if Jury must have taken leave of his senses.

"I did," said Jury. "And when Miss Rivington gets here, and Mr. Matchett, have them wait a bit, will you."

But Lady Ardry was already in the room, happily brushing past Pluck by laying her walking stick squarely against his chest. Pratt drank up the rest of his tea and he said he had to be going. He nodded and left.

Agatha sat there with her enormous cape making a great drift around her chair, gripping her walking stick with both hands. Jury especially liked the mittens, dark brown knitted ones, all ten fingers cut out just above the knuckles. Probably one finger had frayed, and she hadn't bothered mending it. She looked pleased as punch that he had called her in. "You wanted to see me about this man Creed?"

Jury was surprised. "How did you know his name, Lady Ardry?"

"From the Town Crier," she said, smiling meanly. "Sergeant Pluck. Warned you about him, didn't I? He's out there telling the world." Then she puffed out her cheeks and offered her conclusion. "So Inspector, it seems this lunatic is still lurking in Long Pidd!"

"You don't really believe it's some stranger hanging about the village, waiting to pounce?"

"Good Lord, you aren't suggesting it's actually someone who *lives* here?" She snorted. "You've been talking to crazy Melrose." She made it sound as if the Yard took all of its cues from crazy Melrose.

"I'm afraid the lunatic, if he is one, is among you, Lady Ardry." She reared back at that. "Now, you say you were riding your bicycle along the Dorking Dean road. About what time was that?

"After I left you gabbing with Melrose, of course."

Idiot, Jury could just hear her adding mentally. "Yes. But could you be a bit more precise? How long did it take you to reach the Dorking Dean road from Ardry End?"

Her brow creased in an effort of remembrance. "Fifteen minutes."

"And it was then that the car passed you."

"Car? What car?"

Jury prayed for patience. "The car, which, I understand, stopped to tell you about what had happened at the Swan."

"Oh, *that* car? Why didn't you say so? I was on the Dorking road by then. It was Jurvis, the butcher, who saw the lot outside the Swan, and stopped to tell me."

"And it would be about a half mile to the inn from that point." Jury calculated. "You could make it in another few minutes or so."

"I could do. Had I wanted to. Can't stand the Willypoole woman, all tarted up, that one. No better'n she should be."

Jury interrupted. "I merely meant you could have bicycled from here somewhere around eleven-thirty and got to the Swan before twelve." Jury waited for her to make the connection.

She didn't. "Why should I want to do that?"

Jury hid a smile. "Well, there's one piece of good news I have for you." He looked down at the scrap of paper on which he'd been calculating times. "I wouldn't tell this to anyone else," he whispered.

She was nearly lying all over the desk in her eagerness to hear the secret. "My lips are sealed." She lay a cutoff-mittened finger to her mouth.

"One person has an airtight alibi. Unbreakable." He smiled.

Agatha cocked her head like a large bird, simpering, "Me, of course."

Jury feigned astonishment. "Oh, no, madam. That's just what I've been talking about. The times. No, it's Melrose Plant." He smiled his winning smile. "I knew it would make you feel better."

Her mouth opened and closed. Her face was beet red. "But—"

"You see, between about eleven-thirty and the time you returned to Ardry End, Mr. Plant was with me. Up until that time, he was with *you*."

She sat fiddling with her stick, plucking the ends of

her mittens, and looking rather wildly about her.
Then she brightened. "But that also supplies *me* with
an alibi!" Looking as if she'd been quite clever, she
leaned her chin on her hand, her elbows on the desk.

"But it's as we've been saying. Creed was murdered
somewhere between ten-thirty and noon. We've es-
tablished the time you left Ardry End and the
amount of time it'd take to bicycle to the Swan—"

Finally, it hit her. He watched the flush spreading
across her throat and rising to her face. She rose like
a mountain. "Will that be *all*, Inspector?" Her voice
trembled mightily and he knew where she would
have liked to deposit that stick.

'"For now. But make yourself available for further
questions, if you don't mind." Jury smiled brightly.

As soon as her vast form disappeared through the
door, he turned to the window behind him, rested his
head on his arms, and laughed.

He only half-heard the door open and close behind
him, because he was still laughing. It was the voice
that made him turn.

"Inspector Jury?"

Without thinking, he wheeled around, still with
the grin stamped all over his face.

"I'm Vivian Rivington. Your sergeant said that I
should just come in." She was looking at him with a
puzzled frown.

Jury stood there, idiotically smiling, and unable to
move. He had taken one look at Vivian Rivington
and promptly fallen in love.

It was true, as Lady Ardry had said, she was wearing a dark brown sweater, belted, but her fists were
not stuffed in the pockets. The hands were, at that
moment, nervously plucking the hem of the sweater,
as the little Double girl's had plucked at her skirt.

Her coloring was the coloring of an autumn day, one of those tawny-brown, deep-gold landscapes touched with russet. The hair was satiny, like taffy; the face was triangular, devoid of makeup; the eyes were amber, with little flecks, bits and pieces of what looked like semiprecious stones. But it was her aura which reminded Jury of Maggie; a mournful, sad quality, which came through paradoxically as a kind of radiance. For him, it was charismatic.

Her small, embarrassed cough called him from great distances. Jury pushed himself around the desk and held out his hand, drew it back, then outreached it again. She looked at the hand dubiously, carefully, as if it might disappear once more, leaving her grasping at air.

Jury was trying to force himself to begin this interview, to say something, when Wiggins stuck his head in the door to tell Jury that Mr. Matchett was here. Jury said, "Thanks. I'll see him in a moment. Would you please stay and take notes, Sergeant Wiggins." He paid no attention to Wiggins's rather surprised glance.

Jury's tone was so serious that he might have been asking the sergeant to finish up the Lindisfarne Gospels. "Miss Rivington," he said, running his hand through his hair as if her face were his mirror. "I'm Inspector Jury. Richard Jury. Please sit down."

"Thank you."

He looked down at the torn sheet of paper on which he'd doodled various times, along with objects that looked like fat ladies in big capes. Then he folded his hands on the desk and tried to look deadly serious. Too deadly, apparently, for she looked away over to Wiggins in the corner. Wiggins smiled and she seemed to relax a little.

Jury tried to soften up his expression. "Miss Rivington, you were in the Swan during the time, ah, just before . . ." He wanted to put it gently; he didn't know how.

"This man was killed, yes." She lowered her gaze.

"Could you please state your business there?"

"Of course. I was having lunch. I met Simon Matchett there."

Matchett. Jury had momentarily forgotten that Matchett was rumored to be going to marry this woman. He could ask her. No, he wouldn't; not just yet.

"Did I say something wrong, Inspector?"

"Wrong? No, no, of course not." He must have been frowning dreadfully, she looked that worried. So he turned the frown on Wiggins to suggest the source of the trouble lay there. "You getting this—all of it, Sergeant Wiggins?"

Wiggins's head snapped up. "I beg your pardon . . . ? 'Getting it,' sir? Why, yes, of course."

Jury nodded at his sergeant, and then turned to Vivian Rivington. "Just go on, Miss Rivington."

"There's nothing to tell, really. Simon had to go to Dorking Dean, and we decided to meet for lunch at the Swan at eleven."

"Do you go there often?"

"No, but I like it sometimes. It gets me out of Long Piddleton; and as he had to go to Dorking . . ." Her voice trailed off.

Jury was tearing up little bits of Pluck's blotter. He cleared his throat. "You didn't see this man?" She shook her head. "You didn't leave the table whilst you were at the Swan?" Again, she shook her head. "And this Mrs. Willypoole—was she in the saloon bar all the time?"

Vivian creased her brow in thought. "I honestly can't say. I think she was."

"And you and Mr. Matchett left at around noon?"

"Yes." She had inched up to the desk, and put her

fingers along its edge, saying, "What's going on, Inspector Jury?" Jury looked at her fingers—unvarnished
nails like a little chain of opals—and drew his own
hand away from the blotter. "That's what we're at-
tempting to discover." Never had a reply sounded so
weak.

"You arrived after Mr. Matchett? Together?"

"We drove our separate cars. Got there at the same
time, really. I couldn't believe—" She dropped her
head in her hand, but quickly rescued it, as if the gesture had been overly dramatic. Then she sat straight,
like a reprimanded child. Jury got the impression
that Vivian Rivington held constant, chiding talks
with herself. "The thing is: this man must have been
murdered when I was right there. I can't get over
that, I really can't."

Neither could Jury.

"Inspector? Are you quite all right?" She was leaning toward him, looking concerned. "You must've
been working too hard, that's all."

"I'm all right. Look, there are a number of questions I need to ask you, but right now I'd like to see
Mr. Matchett." He was really dying to ask her about
Matchett. He wet his mouth, but held his tongue. He
turned to Wiggins: "Show Miss Rivington out, Sergeant. Then tell Mr. Matchett I'll be with him in a
moment."

"Yes, sir." Wiggins rose, handkerchief and notebook
in hand, and opened the door for Vivian, who, after
looking at the chief inspector uncertainly, turned and
walked out.

Jury sank back into his chair and took several deep
breaths. *You great nit,* he said to himself. *You clod.*

Jury was still upbraiding himself when Matchett
walked in, and took a seat.

After offering him a cigarette, Jury asked him the same questions he had asked Vivian Rivington.

"I have the most uncomfortable feeling," said Matchett, "that I'm going to be It."

" 'It'?"

"Oh, don't come the innocent over me, Inspector. I know the superintendent must have passed along the information to you about my wife. How many other suspects have you with a murder in their past." He tried to smile, but didn't make a very convincing job of it. Jury could understand why.

"I suppose everyone has something he'd rather not have hung out with the Monday wash, Mr. Matchett."

Simon Matchett grimly studied his cigarette. "But not the murder of a wife, I daresay."

Jury observed him closely. Unlike Oliver Darrington, Matchett did not incline toward Italian silk suits and Savile Row tailors. Jury thought he had expensive tastes, only he was not quite so flashy in displaying them. Matchett's image was a kind of careless understatement of dress, speech, and mannerism. He was wearing a cotton shirt, sleeves rolled just above the wrists, and blue jeans. Simple enough. It would have taken someone with Jury's powers of observation to see the shirt was expensive Liberty lawn, and that the same store had supplied the pants. You didn't get them cut like that off the peg at Marks and Sparks. No, he was much more subtle than Darrington. Darrington made of himself a kind of handsome window display. Matchett, however, had a shuttered look—a kind of shadow moving behind the blind. He would convey to any woman he wanted that the power to raise that blind was hers alone.

"Let's talk about this particular murder, Mr. Matchett. Was there any special reason you chose the Swan for lunch?"

"Only that it was on the way back from Dorking."

Jury looked at him. Coincidences did happen, of course. But he wasn't getting paid to believe in coincidences, was he?

Matchett went on: "I find it strange the man would have stayed out in that garden all that time in the cold."

"Well, he wasn't necessarily *alive* all that time, was he?"

Matchett winced. "Am I attracting murderers?"

"I don't know. Are you?"

"This is the second time I seem to have been there when one was done."

At least he was gallant enough not to include Vivian Rivington.

"Was Mrs. Willypoole in the saloon bar all the while you were there?"

Matchett thought a moment, then nodded. "Yes. She was having a drink and reading the paper, there behind the bar."

"And you saw no one else? No one went through that door to the court?"

"No. I'm sure of that. We were sitting there facing the door."

"Tell me about your wife, Mr. Matchett. I've read the report, yes, but you might clear up a point or two."

"Yes, of course. Well, we lived in Devon. We owned—she owned—several inns. The Goat and Compasses was one, that's where we lived. I'm just putting you in the picture, Inspector. You see, the Goat and Compasses was one of those old galleried inns. I thought it would be rather fun to put on the odd play or two in the inn yard. We had the necessary construction done: the stage, some benches done up for the audience. We used the gallery to seat people too, when there were a lot, and there were a surpris-

ing number, after that first summer. It was no
Chichester Festival, but it was successful. We had
floodlights for light after dark.

"I did mention, didn't I, that I was an actor? Not a
very good one, perhaps, but I had my share of small
parts in the West End. It's how I met Celia, my wife.
She fancied herself an actress, and turned up in some
summer production in Kent. Probably her father
bought her the role. He had a lot of money, mostly in
property. All of those inns, you see. Two others in
Devon, the Iron Devil and the Bag o' Nails. When
Celia took them over, she kept a very tight rein on
the purse strings, believe me. I'm not going to gloss
over the fact that there were many reasons for my dis-
satisfaction with the marriage. I hated her after five
years of it. She was so horribly possessive. I wanted
out. We had some awful rows, I can tell you. And so,"
he added acidly, "could the servants. And did tell the
police."

"Why didn't you leave her?"

"I was going to. That was when Harriet Gethvyn-
Owen came along. She was lovely, really lovely. And
another amateur actress. Only she had talent, quite a
bit of it. One thing led to another—the old story. We
fell in love. Which gave me even more reason to
leave Celia.

"During this one summer we were doing *Othello*.
Ambitious of me, but I'd always wanted to try the
part. Harriet played Desdemona. Celia suspected
something between us and took to keeping a little office in a room just across the corridor from the stage.
The rear of the courtyard, with that second level, the
gallery running all the way round—you know such
inns were the precursors of the theaters? That's what
gave me the idea in the first place. Well, Celia's office
was just a few feet from the stage, as I said. That's
how possessive she was. On the night she was killed,

the maid—Daisy something—had brought Celia her usual hot drink. Not more than a half an hour later, the cook, Rose Smollett, came to retrieve the tray and found Celia slumped over her desk. She was dead." Matchett took a long draw on his cigarette. "The desk was gone through, the safe open. It was finally put down to 'person or persons unknown.'"

"But not immediately."

Matchett laughed with some bitterness. "Oh, certainly not immediately. As you can well imagine. I was the prime suspect, wasn't I? Good Lord, look at the motive I had. If I hadn't been on stage when Celia was killed, I'm quite sure I'd have been in the dock. And Harriet, too, perhaps. It would have been the obvious solution—husband and mistress murdering jealous wife—but it wouldn't do. The play was going on at the time."

"I assume there were plenty of people to swear it was you?"

"Thirty or forty. If that's enough witnesses." It was Matchett who smiled now.

"The perfect alibi."

Matchett crushed out his cigarette and leaned forward. "Inspector, in all of Darrington's imbecile mysteries, people are always talking about 'perfect' alibis, or 'unbreakable' alibis, or 'airtight' alibis. Always with that same sardonic tone you just used. It seems to me, though, that if an alibi isn't perfect it's hardly an alibi. So aren't you being a bit redundant? A redundancy I rather resent."

"You certainly have a point there. Mr. Matchett."

"And furthermore, innocent men do have your 'perfect' alibis, precisely because they *are* innocent."

"Another point I'll admit. But I wasn't really implying anything."

"The hell you weren't."

Jury let that pass. "Had your wife no enemies?"

Matchett shrugged. "I suppose so. She wasn't popular, that's certain. But no one, surely, with motive enough to kill her." Matchett wiped his hands over his face in a gesture of extreme weariness. "Afterwards, Harriett just left. Went to the States."

"Why would she do that? The way was finally clear. You could have been together, then, despite the unhappy circumstances. Why would she leave?"

"Guilt, I suppose. The publicity. She was a very sensitive person. Rather retiring."

Jury doubted that.

"And she just decided to pack it in. Said she couldn't live with me, not with the cloud of Celia's death hanging over us . . ." Matchett shook his head as if trying to clear away memories. "Well, it's sixteen years ago. Sleeping dogs, and all that." He looked at Jury. "At least I hope it will lie still, but somehow I doubt it."

"Nothing ever really does, does it?" Jury smiled, making a note to tell Wiggins to get the file of the Celia Matchett murder sent to Weatherington. "Now," he said, trying for as casual a tone as possible, "what about these rumors you're engaged to Miss Rivington? Vivian, that is."

Matchett was surprised by the question. "What's that to do with anything?"

Jury smiled bleakly. "I've no idea. That's why I'm asking."

"Well, I can't deny that there is something between Vivian and me."

" 'Something' can mean a lot of things."

"Let's say I have asked her to marry me, yes. But that's far from her accepting."

"Why?"

Matchett shrugged and smiled. "Who knows what goes on in women's minds, Inspector?" He lit a cigar.

It was not the chauvinism of the comment that was

so irritating; it was the lumping of Vivian Rivington with Women in general. "I should think you'd need to know what's going on in Miss Rivington's mind, if you intend to marry her." It was absurd to be defending a woman he'd met less than an hour before. But Matchett's banal remark grated on him because his work brought him too close to the heart of things to suffer such suave generalizations as Matchett had uttered.

Matchett merely inhaled on his cigar and regarded Jury from half-closed eyes. "Yes, I suppose so."

Picking up a pencil and doodling to distract himself, Jury asked, "Are you in love with her, Mr. Matchett?"

Matchett rolled the cigar in his mouth and studied Jury's face. "What a very cynical question, Inspector. I've just said I'd proposed marriage to her."

How about a direct answer, mate? Jury wanted to say, but said, instead: "Her sister, I take it, knows of this liaison?"

"I should think so. I'd say she approves."

Jury knew the man was neither stupid nor that insensitive, so why was he pretending? "It would be hard on the elder sister if Vivian were to marry. That is, as it stands now, Isabel more or less had the say-so over all of this money."

"Out in the streets, that sort of thing? Vivian would never do that to Isabel. And Isabel is absolutely devoted to Vivian."

Again, Jury was sure he didn't believe that, not for a minute. He returned to his original line of questioning: "So you got to the Swan with Two Necks about eleven—?"

"That's right. It opens then."

"Where were you around ten? Or between ten and eleven?" There was still about a half an hour unaccounted for in Matchett's alibi.

"In Dorking Dean. Doing a bit of shopping."

"And what time did you leave?"

"Oh, about a quarter to. I was stuck in traffic moving round the circle, I remember, for a good fifteen minutes. Christmas shoppers."

"I see. Well, I suppose that's all for now, Mr. Matchett. I'll be in touch."

As Matchett was leaving, Pluck popped his head in the door and told Jury that Mr. Plant was outside, wanting to speak to him. Jury said to show him in.

Refusing a chair, Melrose Plant said, with some urgency, "I think you should come along to the vicarage, Inspector. The vicar has some information that might be relevant. He was outside the Swan for some little time before we got there and he heard those policemen say something about the condition of the body."

Jury was up and putting on his coat. "What about the body, Mr. Plant?"

"The vicar says he'd heard the man's face was cut up a bit. Cuts on the nose? Very odd."

Jury wished the police around here could keep their information—a little of it, at least—to themselves. "Yes, that's right. I agree, it's most puzzling."

"Well, the vicar knows what it means, or so he says."

CHAPTER 11

"It's a corruption of the real meaning, you see." The Reverend Denzil Smith was pointing at a picture in a book of inn signs. The book lay open on the small table between Jury and Plant, next to a plate of sandwiches and the beer the vicar's housekeeper had provided for them. Looking at the book, Jury marveled at the inventiveness of the signpainter, or whoever had thought up the double-necked swans.

"It used to be," continued the vicar, "that the royal birds were marked by cutting small notches into their bills. And the vintners did that sort of thing too, I understand, so that ownership of the swans could be distinguished by the nicks. So, you see, it would really have been a 'swan with two *nicks*.' But what you see here is the work of some illiterate signpainter, who either couldn't read or couldn't spell." The vicar sat back complacently, after selecting a half of a cheese and pickle sandwich for himself.

"Good Lord," said Jury, still looking at the picture. "So the murderer 'nicked' Creed—"

"I would presume so, yes," said the vicar. "It was done on the nose, wasn't it?"

"But why on earth—?" said Plant. "Having his little joke?"

Jury lit a cigarette. " 'Having his little joke?' I don't imagine so, not exactly. Probably another red herring."

The vicar, having got the stage for the moment, was not about to relinquish it. "There are other examples of this sort of thing—I mean, corruptions of the original meaning. Just outside Weatherington there's the Bull and Mouth. Never guess where that comes from, would you?" Without waiting for them to guess, he went on: "It was a sign made up to commemorate the taking of Boulogne Harbor by Henry the Eighth. You see? The mouth of the harbor. Boulogne mouth." The vicar shoved his glasses back on his nose. "One of my favorites is the Elephant and Castle. A lot of theories are tossed about on that one, all the way from finding elephant bones on the spot to Eleanor of Aquitaine. But I imagine the 'castle' was merely meant to represent the howdah on the back of the elephant. Do you know, an officer was once actually appointed to roam the City and check the signs? It was his duty to rid the place of blue boars and flying pigs and hogs wearing armor." The vicar laughed, and went on. "Yes, that was reported in the *Spectator* back in seventeen-something."

Jury, who wanted to get out of the seventeenth and into the present century, still felt that, since the vicar had supplied him with information he would never have got elsewhere, he should indulge him a bit.

"Did you know Hogarth painted the original sign for the Man with a Load of Mischief? There are a few inns by that name. Some called just the Load of Mischief, or the Man Loaded with Mischief. Not so many as there are Bells, of course. Must be five hundred of those in England. The inns around here are all popular names. There's the Bull and Mouth, that I was just talking about. Not too many Swan with Two Necks, though there's one in Cheapside that's got a gallows sign. Like the White Hart in Scole. Cost over a thousand pounds, that sign did and that was back in 1655, if you can believe it. Those

signs stretch clear across the road, and were always
falling and killing people. Outside Dorking there's
the Bag o' Nails, that's a popular name. But I think
it was originally the Devil and the Bag o' Nails. Now
that's an interesting—"

Jury could stand it no longer and tried to divert
the vicar's attention from etymological absurdities
and signs falling on people to their own more
pressing murders. "I certainly do thank you for this
bit of information, Vicar. I can't imagine anyone of
us—the police—would have hit on it." The vicar
beamed. "You were at the Man with a Load of Mischief on the Thursday night, and I just wanted to ask
you a question or two about that."

"Terrible, thing, terrible." His recounting of the
dinner the night Small was killed was even less
promising in detail than the accounts of the other
guests. The vicar had been with Willie Bicester-
Strachan playing draughts between nine and ten, he
said. "I can't imagine this happening in Long Piddleton. Been here forty-five years. Came originally as
curate. My wife died nine years ago, God rest her.
But Mrs. Gaunt has been doing for me very nicely together with whatever housemaids we've had, like
Ruby." He looked puzzled. "Ruby's been gone longer
than usual, this time."

"About this Ruby Judd. I understand she was due
back but hasn't turned up. When did she leave, exactly?"

"It was Wednesday, I believe—good heavens, a
week ago. How time does fly. She asked my permission to leave for a few days to visit her people in
Weatherington."

"I see. Is there a picture of Ruby somewhere? In
her room, perhaps?"

The vicar looked puzzled at this request. "I don't
know. Mrs. Gaunt might." He called in Mrs. Gaunt,

skeletal and unhappy looking, every inch her name, to go up to Ruby's room and fetch down a picture if there were one.

Mrs. Gaunt made some sound deep in her throat which might have been directed at any one of them, and took her leave.

Lowering his voice to a whisper, as if he might be a little afraid of her, Mr. Smith said, "Mrs. Gaunt isn't too pleased with Ruby. Says she's always sitting about reading film magazines and such, or even when she's supposed to be sweeping down the church, Mrs. Gaunt has once or twice caught her sitting down on the job—quite literally—in a pew."

"A religious girl, was she?" asked Jury.

The vicar chuckled. "Hardly. She was putting lacquer on her fingernails."

At least the old man wasn't overly pious, thought Jury. He seemed to think Ruby's behavior rather rich.

Mrs. Gaunt was back in double-time, tight-lipped, with two snapshots. "Stuck in the mirror, they was." She made the snaps sound like naughty calendar poses. She sniffed and left.

The vicar passed them over to Jury. "But you're not thinking something's happened to Ruby, are you? You might ask Daphne Murch about her. She and Ruby were quite thick, being about the same age. Indeed it was the Murch girl who suggested Ruby to me."

Jury put the snaps in his wallet. "You don't seem worried, yourself, Vicar. Does Ruby do this sort of thing often?"

"Well, she's gone off once or twice before. My guess is a boy friend—in London, perhaps. Ruby's not a bad girl. But like so many of these young people, she's a bit flighty."

Jury changed the subject. "You're a good friend of

Mr. Bicester-Strachan. I know that you wouldn't want
to break any confidences, but if you could just fill me
in on the details of that business in London . . . ?"
Jury did not add that he knew nothing about "that
business" at all. And he counted on the vicar's taste
for gossip to override his finer feelings and wasn't disappointed, though certainly Smith made quite a show
of protesting. He sputtered a bit, then settled down to
telling what he knew. "Bicester-Strachan was a minor
official in the War Ministry, and there was an, ah, 'incident': apparently, information was falling into the
wrong hands, information that only Bicester-Strachan
and a few others had access to. He was never prosecuted; no one could ever really prove anything, as far
as I know. He doesn't like to talk about it, as you can
well imagine. But it explains his early retirement.
Bicester-Strachan isn't as old as he looks. Not much
over sixty but he looks eighty and I know it's all from
the shock of that ugly business." The Reverend Smith
sat back and announced pontifically: "Agatha thinks
it's the Communists who are behind all this, and she
could be right."

Melrose Plant, who had been patiently silent
throughout the visit, had to ask, "And just how does
my aunt manage to work them in?"

The vicar thought for a moment. "I can't honestly
say. You know Agatha is so close."

"Close?" It was the first time Melrose had ever
heard secrecy listed among his aunt's traits.

"Hmmm. We were just batting about theories, and
she thought, what with Bicester-Strachan's history
. . . well, it's possible, isn't it? They could be after
him?"

"How well do you know Mr. Darrington, Vicar?"
asked Jury, trying to divert his attention from double
agents.

"Not well, really. Not much of a churchgoer, is

Darrington. Used to work in publishing in London. You know he wrote those mystery stories." He seemed to enjoy his next observation: "There are times when I rather doubt that Miss Hogg is, as he says, his 'secretary.' "

"There are times when all of us doubt it," said Melrose.

The vicar, according to Pratt's report, was not present at the Jack and Hammer the night Ainsley was killed. Still, Jury asked him, "Did you happen to be in the vicinity of the Jack and Hammer on the Friday night, Vicar?"

The vicar looked almost disappointed that he had to answer, "No, afraid I can't help you out there. Unusual, that Jack-arm. You know, there's only one other like it, it's in Abinger Hammer—"

Jury interrupted. "This business about the 'nicks.' That sort of thing is hardly common knowledge. Have you mentioned it to anyone else around here?"

The vicar turned a bit red. "I must admit, I do rather enjoy talking about the histories of these old places. Yes, I'm sure I've mentioned it to this or that person. I can't remember, really." Sitting in his comfortable chintz-covered chair, staring up at the ceiling, the vicar said, "There's more than one murder been done in an inn. There was The Ostrich in Colnbrook—"

Melrose Plant hastily interrupted. He had no intention of sitting through the trapdoor adventures of the guests of the Ostrich again. "I daresay Inspector Jury is thinking of this pattern in a somewhat less literal way, Vicar."

"Well, I certainly don't think Matchett or Scroggs had anything to do with these awful deaths . . . though there *is* that unsavory business about Matchett's former wife. Pity the past must rise to plague the present." His eye flicked toward Jury, apparently in hopes of lighting a fire in that quarter. *"Crime passionnel,* something like that. Matchett had a lady friend—"

Jury smiled. "The police were satisfied at the time that Mr. Matchett had nothing to do with it."

"Never found out who did, though," said Smith, hating to see such a tasty morsel so summarily swallowed without being chewed over.

"You'd be surprised at the number of murders we have to put *Paid* to, Vicar. A bit of a disappointment to see how incompetent the police really are." As the vicar blushed, Jury got up. "Thank you for your help, sir. Now, I must be going."

Outside once again with Plant, Jury paused to look up at the beautiful east window of the church, seven lights of reticulated tracery in the head.

"If you'd like to go in . . ." said Plant.

Jury shook his head. " 'A serious place on serious earth it is.' "

They were both looking up at the bell tower, its windows louvered to let the sound drift up to the highest point. Plant said, "You like poetry, Inspector?"

Jury nodded.

"I saw Vivian going into the station to talk to you. Tell me, what did you think of her?"

Jury's eyes moved from the bell tower to focus on a fascinating twig on the ground at his feet. "Oh," he shrugged, "she seemed . . . pleasant enough."

Mrs. Jubal Creed arrived at the Weatherington police station shortly after four and was taken off to the county hospital morgue to identify the mortal remains of her husband. When she returned, her color was not necessarily worse than when she had left, for Mrs. Creed possessed one of those impoverished complexions that suggested Nature had skimped on paints, settling upon a shade of dingy ocher. Mrs. Creed was no more fortunate in her figure than in her face: she was a scarecrow draped in outmoded and ill-fitting clothes.

Only when she gave her husband's full name, did she refer to him as "Jubal" (which she rhymed with "rubble"); thereafter, he was "Mr. Creed."

Holding a handkerchief to her mouth, which was flat and wide—more like a cutout of a mouth—she looked at Chief Inspector Jury with bleary eyes, and answered his question about Creed's employment: "Mr. Creed's been retired from the Cambridgeshire police for near five years. And no love lost, neither."

"He felt he had been ill-treated?"

"Indeed he was. Passed over for promotion, ended up as detective sergeant in Wigglesworth. Bitter, he was. Can't say as I blame him." She sniffed her disapprobation of the police in general, and Jury and Wiggins in particular, as they sat in the stark, bare room in the Weatherington station.

"Mrs. Creed, can you imagine anyone at all who might, ah, wish to harm him?"

All she did was shake her head vigorously, bowed as it was in the cupped palm of her hand. Jury did not really think she was overcome by emotion, and rather imagined the Creeds' marriage had been, at best, merely a civil one. Mrs. Creed, though unobjectionable, did not strike Jury as a woman of particularly deep feelings.

"He had no enemies you know of?"

"No. We led a quiet life, Mr. Creed and me."

"In the course of his work, could he have made any?"

"If he done, I never did hear of it."

Jury asked these questions more or less by rote, instinctively feeling that the line of questioning was fruitless. He doubted that Creed's death had anything materially to do with dark patches in Creed's own past. Jury opened a manila folder and took out a picture of William Small, one which showed him after he had been cleaned up a bit. Still it wasn't pleasant. "Mrs. Creed, do you recognize this man?"

She looked at it, looked away quickly, and shook her head.

"Does the name 'William Small' mean anything to you?"

Her eyes were hazed over with unshed tears, and despite the lengthy silence, Jury doubted she was thinking very carefully. "No, the name don't mean a thing to me." To the picture of Ainsley, the one which had appeared in the newspapers, her response was the same. Then she looked again. "Wait a minute, here. Ain't this a picture of that man who was killed—wait, now—wasn't *both* of these men killed in some town around here—what's the name—?"

"Long Piddleton. It's about twenty miles away."

She looked absolutely astonished. "You mean to tell me Mr. Creed was killed there, too? You got a mass murderer running round free as air, and you sit here asking me fool questions?"

They had by now got a full report from the Cambridgeshire police on Creed's career—a career rather swiftly curtailed, according to Superintendent Pratt. "See, there's your regular mumping, and there's the kind of stuff Creed pulled off: he took commissions from certain garages for sending them breakdowns. It's one thing to get repairs on the cheap for yourself—his superiors might have looked the other way if it had been that. Or the free meal, maybe we all do a bit of that. I'd like a pound for every free meal I've accepted from restaurants when I was doing a beat. So with Creed, it wasn't bribery proper, but it was the next thing to. He'd almost got a nice little business going on the side. So you could certainly say he was on dab. Still, they let him 'resign.' Anyway, we've asked his old mates about this present business, and they haven't a clue. Creed was a zero, a blank. Not very good at his job even in the best circumstances. It's unlikely he'd ever have made D.I. anyway. No sign of his knowing these others—Small and Ainsley. His mates never see him anymore, anyway." Pratt's long legs were stuck up on the desk in the Weatherington station. He was still wearing his heavy overcoat and trying to light up an ancient pipe. "Thing is . . ." He sucked in on the stem and struck another match. "Bad press is killing us; the reporters are baying round me like wolves over in Northampton where I spend as much time as possible. For one thing it keeps them there and out of your hair, doesn't it?" He sucked in on his pipe several times and finally got a weak, coal-like glimmer going. "I read everything that crosses my desk, and I swear I can't make head nor tail of this business. What I wonder is whether the victims were chosen at random, or because they made up a pattern?" Pratt scratched the day's growth of beard bristling on his chin with the stem of his pipe. It made a small, rasping noise. "Or were two of them done in to mask the other? The real victim?"

"It has also occurred to me that the real victim might not have been murdered yet."

Pratt blinked his red-rimmed eyes. "Oh, God, that's a lovely thought." His pipe had gone out again. "You're thinking it's going to be someone in the village, is that it?"

"I don't know. It's certainly a possibility."

"The murderer of Small did not come in that cellar door, that's clear. So you've narrowed it down, I think, to just those people at the Load of Mischief that evening."

"Less one, I think it's safe to say: Melrose Plant. Of course, he hasn't an alibi for the times Small and Ainsley were murdered, but it's hard to believe more than one murderer is involved."

Pratt scratched his chin again. "Then we're a lot nearer finding him, if that's the case. Next time that Superintendent Racer rings me up, I shall certainly tell him you've made considerable progress. Excuse me for asking—but has he something particular against you? Seems a trifle waspish where you're concerned."

"Oh, it's just his way," said Jury.

CHAPTER 12

The next morning Jury was sitting at Pluck's battered wooden desk, Wiggins looking over his shoulder. They were studying Darrington's book, *Bent on Murder* and its sequel, the second book, lying side by side on the desk. Jury would run his finger along a line of one, then shift to the other. "There's a tremendous difference in the quality of these two. The style's almost totally different. Or, let's say one seems a clumsy imitation of the style of the other."

Wiggins shook his head. "I don't see it, myself, sir. Of course, I'm not that much of a reader."

Jury closed the books. "I don't think Darrington wrote *Bent on Murder*. I think he was trying to copy the style and botched it in this second book. I think whoever wrote the first book also wrote the third—" Jury pulled another from the stack of four. "*Bent Takes a Holiday*. Yes. Those two were written by the same hand. But not the other two. Darrington must have appropriated two manuscripts and then spaced them out."

"But who do you suppose wrote the two good ones?"

"No idea. It presents the interesting possibility that someone else might have known about this plagiarism. And decided to blackmail Darrington."

"Like Small, you mean? How would Ainsley and Creed come into it, then?"

"They could have been in it together. . . . What I want you to do is ring up London and have them check out the publishing firm where Darrington worked. That's where he could easily have come by the manuscripts." Jury rose and pocketed his cigarettes. "Myself, I'm simply going to put it to him, directly. See what happens."

As Jury was getting into the blue Morris, Melrose Plant pulled up in his Bentley and rolled down the window.

"Where are you off to, Inspector Jury?"

"Oliver Darrington's place."

"Tomorrow is Christmas, you know. And I should like very much to have you dine with me."

"I accept with pleasure, circumstances permitting."

"Fine. Right now I'm on my way to Sidbury to pick up Agatha's present."

"What are you getting her?"

"I thought a pair of matched pistols might be nice. Mother-of-pearl handles, for dressy occasions."

Jury laughed as Plant pulled away, and then turned the Morris toward the Sidbury Road.

It was Darrington this time who answered the door, and started talking the moment he saw Jury. "What in hell is this? About a copy of my book in the hands of this man who was found dead at the Swan?" His eyes blazed. Clearly, he was more concerned with the reading matter of the corpse than with the corpse itself.

"If I might just come in, Mr. Darrington?"

Darrington flung wide the door, and Jury noticed Sheila Hogg in the sitting room looking beautiful, worried, and nervous. He went in and took the seat he had occupied the day before. Oliver glowered over him, and Sheila fidgeted behind the couch opposite, picking at some invisible thread along its back. She was fully dressed this afternoon—a flowered, silk pant dress—but managed still to look undressed. The outlines of her body simply leaped out at one, and that part of Jury's mind not occupied with startling Darrington into some sort of admission took appreciative notice of this. "There are just a few questions I wanted to ask, Mr. Darrington." They still made no move to sit down, so Jury made them wait while he lit a cigarette. "You obviously have got the news already that another man has been murdered, and I was wondering if you could tell me where you were between ten and a little past noon yesterday?"

"Right here. Sheila was with me."

Jury did not see anything in their expressions to belie this, but had never known anyone like the guilty to stare you straight in the eye when they lied. He smiled and said, "Also, I just wanted to return these to you." Jury held out the books. "They're rather interesting, especially in their differences." He observed the same nervous spasms of Sheila's face and hands take hold. "As a matter of fact, I was thinking you might have had a bit of help there." Jury put it so mildly, that even he was surprised when Darrington wheeled on Sheila.

"Bitch!"

"I didn't tell him, Oliver! Honestly!"

His anger died down as quickly as it had arisen and he sighed. "Oh, hell, there's one charade over. You might as well tell him."

As usual, thought Jury, leaving Sheila to carry the can back.

"It was my brother," said Sheila. "He was killed in a motorcycle accident. It was only by accident—when I was going through his things after he died—that I found the letter Oliver had written him about his book. I didn't even know Michael—my brother—had *written* a book, much less that he was trying to get it published. I don't think anyone knew. He was very secretive. Anyway, I went along to Oliver's firm, I suppose with the intention of somehow seeing the book got published as—I guess—a nice memorial. Oliver was the editor on whose desk it had landed. He was very sympathetic and we had lunch and talked about Michael's book, how good it was. Then we had dinner. Then lunch, then dinner, until . . ." Sheila sighed. "Well, I fell for him, which was"—she leveled a deadly glance at Darrington—"his intention, wasn't it, love?"

Darrington merely studied his drink.

"There was another manuscript, *Bent Takes a Holiday,* that I also found amongst the things in Michael's trunk. Oliver read it and said it was just as good as the first. The temptation was too much for him: he could publish the first under his own name and put the other away against a rainy day." Sheila laughed artificially. "And when Oliver writes, it rains, all right."

"Thanks," said Darrington.

"Don't mention it, love," she said, bitterly. Then, to Jury: "There it is. Rotten, nasty—what can I say?"

A nice memorial, thought Jury. Love, he thought sadly. It had involved her in that dishonor and wouldn't even throw in a marriage certificate. He felt sorry for her. "So you kept the second manuscript as a hedge against the possibility of the one you wrote yourself flopping at the book stalls?"

Oliver raised his face. At least he had the grace to be humiliated. "That's right. I'd tried a bit of writing. I thought I could do a fair job, only I couldn't. I'm a rotten writer. When the second book didn't sell and got such bad reviews, I pulled out Hogg's other manuscript and that put my star in the ascendancy again. I thought surely on the next try I could pull it

off. And now . . ." He spread his hands in a futile
gesture. Then he apparently remembered the discussion to hand was not the biggest problem. "Wait a
minute, now, Inspector. What has all this to do with
the man found this morning?"

"You didn't know him?"

Darrington looked angry. "Damn it! Of course I
didn't know him!"

Jury enjoyed what he was about to say, in return
for Oliver's cheap treatment of Sheila. "Funny. He
was an admirer of yours. That book, you know." Jury
pretended a fresh thought had come to him, and
snapped his fingers. "Or perhaps not an admirer, after all. There's always blackmail, you know, as a motive for murder."

Darrington shot out of his chair. "My God! I *didn't*
kill him. I never saw the man before—"

"How do you know that, Mr. Darrington?"

"What?"

"I assume you've not seen him *since* he's been murdered. How do you know you've never seen him,
then?"

"Trying to trap me, aren't you? I suppose my book
in his hands just ties it all up for you, doesn't it?"

Sheila, with more perception than Darrington had
shown, said, "Oh, for God's sake, Oliver. I don't
imagine Inspector Jury thinks three different people
came here to blackmail you, do you, Inspector?"

Oliver looked from one to the other like a child
who wonders if his parents are in collusion against
him. What on earth, wondered Jury, did Sheila see in
the man?

"The book is one thing that suggests you *didn't* kill
him." Jury got up and pocketed his cigarettes. "For
you yourself to leave a clue in the hands of the murdered man, one which points back to you, would be
strange, now, wouldn't it? Only a very daring person

and one with iron composure, not to mention a rather macabre flair, would dare such a thing. And in you, Mr. Darrington, I haven't seen any of those qualities."

Sheila burst out laughing.

CHAPTER 13

Melrose Plant tooled along the Sidbury Road, smiling at the notion that Agatha would be smarting when she realized that *she* was still a suspect, but *he* wasn't. Hardly sporting of Melrose to wriggle out of the vise-like grip of New Scotland Yard that way, while she (after all of her dedicated assistance) was left to struggle alone. That's how Agatha would see it. She would conclude it was all Melrose's fault. Probably a conspiracy between Melrose and Jury.

As long sweeps of sun-starred meadow rolled by him, Melrose slid down in the seat of the Bentley and wondered if he had an unconscious hankering to be a detective, some dark side of his nature that had gone heretofore unsuspected. He entertained himself by reviewing the possible answers to this rash of killings. Had only one of the victims actually been the real object, the other two done in to disguise that? The old red herring gambit. A possibility, of course, but one somewhat undermined by the fact that all three were strangers. Why on earth bring strangers to town to kill them? Why not just kill off instead a couple of superfluous locals?

Melrose looked about him a little guiltily; it really was a rather cold-blooded way of thinking of the village folk. The only things looking back at him were a lamb and a ewe, out there in the fields, slowly chewing. What could they have found to eat in this cold?

It was possible that all of these present murders were only leading up to another, the rather shuddery prospect put forth by Jury. The reason it made his blood run cold was because the first person he thought of as the real mark was Vivian Rivington. All of that money, and so many people wanting it. The darkness that swept over his mind seemed projected in the sign ahead of him, a small one with a black spot, across from the Cock and Bottle, coming up on his left.

Plant lifted his foot from the pedal and slowed to a crawl so that he wouldn't rip out his muffler going over the narrow rise of mounded earth meant to slow down cars for the oncoming turn. It was, appropriately enough, called a "dead man." Something flashed in the strong sunlight as he approached the rise. Bumping over the "dead man" he peered out of his window and saw that the reflection had come from something lying there in the dirt, a bit of glass, probably. Then, suddenly, a picture of what he'd actually seen froze in his mind and he braked so hard he nearly threw himself through the windscreen. He sat there for a few seconds telling himself that the dirt-covered object couldn't have been what he thought it was.

A ring. But had it really been attached to a *hand?*

While Sheila still laughed, Jury was pulling on his coat and leather gloves. "There'll be more questions, Mr. Darrington. For both of you. At the moment, however, I haven't time for them. What I'd like to do is use your telephone if I may, to call my sergeant?"

"It's just through there," said Darrington, indicating the door to the hall. A little of his old, sneering confidence returned when he said, "Then I take it, Inspector Jury, the fact that *Bent on Murder* turned

up in the man's hands is more or less proof that I
had nothing to do with it?"

A bastard to the end, thought Jury. No concern for
Sheila, who had given over probably all of her self-re-
spect so that Darrington might rise in the world. The
bloody fool needed a bit of a shakeup. "What I said
was that it was one indication you didn't do it. But it
by no means lets you off. There's one motive that
only applies to you, Mr. Darrington: publicity. It
would have done wonders for your failing reputation,
wouldn't it? To have *Bent on Murder* on the front
page of the newspapers? Send the sales of all of your
books skyrocketing. So you rid yourself of the black-
mailer, and give yourself a bit of publicity, to boot."

Once again, Darrington went white.

"The phone, Mr. Darrington?"

As if cued for its entrance, the telephone rang.
Sheila, with more self-possession than Darrington,
went to answer it. From the hall she called back, "It's
for you, Inspector."

He thanked her and as he took the receiver and
watched her go back to the drawing room, he hoped
she'd find a better man than Darrington. Though he
certainly hadn't written off Sheila as a suspect. She'd
more guts than her boy friend, that was sure.

"Jury, here," he said, and listened with growing
amazement to the words of Melrose Plant. "Look, Mr.
Plant, just you stay right there. It'll only take me ten
minutes." He slammed down the receiver, dialed the
Long Piddleton station, and thought, as he listened to
the *brr-brr,* that Wiggins or Pluck damned well better
be there. Finally, Pluck answered, and Jury told him
to get hold of the Weatherington station, get the
Scene of Crimes officer, get Appleby, get the whole
crew, and get them over to the Cock and Bottle without delay. There'd been another body found. Poor
Pluck sputtered, stuttered, and finally said, "Yes, sir.

Right away, sir. But there's all these reporters crawling round the station demanding to talk to you. They streamed in from London not a half hour ago."

"Forget the reporters, Sergeant. And don't, for God's sake, tell them a thing about this, or there'll be so many cars on the road to Sidbury I won't be able to get round them."

"Right, sir. But I thought I should just mention," and he lowered his voice, "that Lady Ardry's been talking to these men from the London dailies six-to-the-dozen. And I should tell you that Superintendent Racer has been trying to get onto you for the past hour. Awful mad, he sounded."

"Well, Sergeant, the next time he calls, let Lady Ardry talk to him."

The blue Morris did the thirteen miles from the house to the Cock and Bottle in twenty minutes, calling forth outraged responses from the more sedate drivers, out for a pleasant Christmas Eve drive.

When Jury saw the Cock and Bottle about a quarter of a mile down the road, he swerved over onto the right shoulder and braked just before the rise of mounded earth. He jumped out of the car, not bothering to slam the door, and ran over to the spot where Melrose Plant was kneeling. The rise had been covered with a tarpaulin.

"I didn't try to get the earth off; it's very hard, anyhow. But I assumed you wouldn't want the ground disturbed. I did brush some of the loose stuff off her arm."

"You did the right thing, Mr. Plant." Protruding from the hard, snow-encrusted mound was a hand and arm, about half-way up to the elbow. The nails of the hand were painted an incongruous, bright red, and a large, cheap ring encircled one finger. Jury felt the arm. Stiff as an icicle.

"It was pretty obvious," said Plant, "that whoever belongs to that arm wasn't down there still desperately trying to breathe. So I let it be. I threw the tarpaulin over it because of passing motorists. I didn't imagine you'd want curious passersby to stop. I just stood here and directed them over to the other end of the road. Probably they thought I was the road works man."

Jury couldn't help smiling a bit, even in the circumstances. That suit Plant was wearing was probably not the common uniform of road works men. It did not take long for it to seep into Jury's mind that the "dead man" was right in front of the Cock and Bottle, which sat well back from the road off to their left. Another inn. The papers would love it.

He said to Plant, "You've done a good job. It's as well you didn't try to dig her up. The Scene of Crimes officer would have our heads if anything had been disturbed."

They stood there for another ten minutes, and Jury heard the whine of a siren. Well, at least Pluck had been quick about it. Weatherington was on the other side of Sidbury, about ten miles from the market town. "Mr. Plant, why don't you go up to the inn, there, and soften up the proprietor—do you know him?"

"Not well. I've a kind of nodding acquaintance with him. Fell asleep once at the bar when he was telling me his life. What should I say?"

Jury looked down at the frozen hand as the police car rounded the bend. "Just tell him I'll be up to ask him a few questions."

Dr. Appleby waited, patiently smoking, as the Scene of Crimes officer, a man with a face like a graven image, recorded every detail. The marks of ligature were plainly visible on the victim's neck. And the victim was, as Jury had suspected, one Ruby Judd, lately the vicar's housemaid.

When the police photographer had finished up taking pictures from every angle, Dr. Appleby looked at the chief inspector the way a father sometimes rivets his eyes on a child who has gone off the straight and narrow once too often. Even Jury, who didn't often dodge the eyes of his fellowman, looked away. "Inspector Jury, are you sure you wouldn't like me to wander about the countryside lashed to your side? I seem to be turning up so often at the scene of one of your crimes." Appleby's nicotined fingers lit a fresh cigarette from the butt of the old one.

"Very funny, Appleby. But it is not really 'my' crime, as you so charmingly put it. It is actually someone else's." Jury only wished he hadn't been saddled with a wiseacre of a police surgeon. He suspected Appleby was thoroughly, if perversely, enjoying himself. How often was he called in to treat more than measles or women's complaints or ulcerated stomachs?

Dr. Appleby puffed away, his answer ready: " 'Someone else's', yes. But the question still remains: Whose? The population hereabouts is steadily on the decrease." The doctor flicked ash into the newly dugout "dead man." The corpse, wrapped in a polyethylene sheet to prevent the loss of any items on its person, had been removed to the ambulance. The fingerprint man, the one with the crew cut and the chewing gum and the whistle, had had very little to go on here and was now on his way to the vicarage, for a look at Ruby Judd's room.

"Dr. Appleby, the facts, please."

"I've given them to you three times before, why not just use the old ones—?"

Jury's impatience was growing. "Dr. Appleby—"

Appleby sighed. "Very well. From the condition of the body, I'd say anywhere from three days to a week.

A little difficult to tell—the body's fairly well
preserved. She might as well have been in a frozen
food locker." Appleby lit another cigarette, and Wiggins, who had been taking down the doctor's information in his notebook, took the opportunity to blow
his nose and pull out a cough drop from a fresh
packet. Dr. Appleby picked up his narrative again, in
a droning voice: "Cause of death: strangulation, this
time by a knotted cord of some sort. Possibly a thin
headscarf, possibly a stocking. Hemorrhages on face
and inside eyelids. No other damage done I can see.
But of course, we haven't a pathologist behind every
tree, like you boys in London. Have to do the p.m.
myself. Incidentally, nothing much on the Creed man
that seems helpful, since you know he was killed
somewhere between ten and noon. I certainly
couldn't fix it better than that."

Having supervised the moving of the body to the
ambulance, Appleby snapped up his bag and moved
off. On either side of the road detective constables
were combing the cold meadows for further evidence.
Jury was hoping some sort of bag—a suitcase, perhaps—would turn up in the woods or the meadow
near the Cock and Bottle. He imagined that whoever
murdered her had got her to pack up a bag, probably
under the pretense of a weekend of passion (which
would have meant a man, if that were the case),
knowing that no questions would be asked for at least
a few days. Appleby said there was no sign of "sexual
interference," but he couldn't tell Jury if she were
pregnant until he did the postmortem. It was a cold,
cold trail. But Jury had been right about one thing:
Ruby Judd was no stranger.

When Jury finally ascended the hill to the Cock
and Bottle, he found Melrose Plant seated at the bar
with a half pint of Guinness before him. The beefy-

looking proprietor was leaning across the bar, talking. His name was Keeble, and he was wiping his perspiring face with a bar towel, quite overcome. His wife, however, who had just come out of a door to the right of the bar, was granite-faced and dry-eyed.

Plant offered Jury a cigarette from his gold case and Jury took it gratefully. "What can you tell me about this young woman, Mr. Keeble?"

"Well, as I was just saying to the sergeant, here"—he indicated Wiggins, whose notebook was dutifully opened on the bar, handkerchief beside it— "this Ruby, I hardly ever seen her, except once or twice in the shops, so I can't help much. They been working on that 'dead man' out there in front a long time." Mrs. Keeble put in how bad it was for business, always having the road torn up.

"And when did the road works men finish filling it in?"

Keeble thought hard. "Now just a tic and I'll tell you exact—aye, it was the afternoon of the fifteenth. Tuesday week. I remember because it was the next evening we had this big party to serve dinner to and I was glad it wasn't all dug up out there." He celebrated his part in the horrendous event by drawing off a beer for himself; his wife sniffed her disapproval. "Then one of them come back that night, to finish up. The night of the fifteenth last Tuesday."

Tuesday had been the day Ruby had left, supposedly to visit her family in Weatherington.

Keeble's mention of the dinner party had suddenly made Jury hungry. Jury said, "We could do with a bite. Can you rustle us up something? You're hungry, aren't you, Mr. Plant? And Sergeant Wiggins?" They both nodded.

"We've only got plaice," said Mrs. Keeble.

Plant made a noise in his throat, but Wiggins said, "And chips and peas, if you don't mind."

She looked at all three of them as if they had dragged the body of the girl there themselves, just to discommode her. She also looked as if she were debating whether she could expect Scotland Yard to pay, or whether she was stuck with doing her civic duty. Plant said to her, as she was passing through the kitchen door, "If we could just have a bottle of Bâtard-Montrachet to wash that down?" She stared at him. He added, "Nineteen seventy-one?"

Her mouth set even more firmly. "We ain't got no wine cellar; this ain't the Savoy."

Plant surveyed the room with its plain fixtures. "Odd. I could have sworn . . ."

Mr. Keeble, however, was more interested in their comfort, and said, "How's about a pint of our best bitter, sir? On the house, it is." He lowered his voice, and looked toward the kitchen.

"Kind of you, Mr. Keeble," said Jury. He accepted the pint gratefully and drank off a half.

Plant had left the bar and walked over to the gabled window in front of the inn. He stood there, gazing out. "You can't see the 'dead man' from here, Inspector. My guess is you can't see it from any of the windows, not with that stand of oak."

"Meaning?"

"That roads man wasn't really taking much of a chance of having someone see him from the inn, here. Nor on the road, either. It's really pretty flat; you can see for a good quarter mile either way. There's that bad dip in the road, of course, where the black spot is, but all the same . . ."

"Meaning the workman was not really a workman, I take it? Yes, the ground would have been easy enough to dig up again the night of the fifteenth. And if anyone had seen him, had passed that way, they would have taken him for a worker come back perhaps to finish up something. He could even have safely worked by lantern-light."

"Ready-made grave, just waiting there," said Plant. "A bit of a change of clothes, a cap, and so on, and no one would really have thought much about it."

"There was always the chance that he'd be seen dragging the body from—where? let's say that stand of oak—the short distance to the 'dead man.' But by whom? From here one might see a man working on the road, but if the body were tarpaulined, or covered somehow, it's just too far off to be distinguishable."

"And if he had enough nerve to bring this off, he'd not stick at waving a car round the shoulder, if one happened to pass."

"Or *she*, Mr. Plant."

"I can't believe all this was done by a woman."

"But it's possible. A woman could as easily dress up as a road worker."

"Very well. She could have done."

Mrs. Keeble had banged in from the kitchen with a tray and deposited the food on the table. The three of them took the table against the wall by the cold fireplace where a deal table had been laid out with cutlery, napkins, and three white crockery plates, each with the same portions of fish, potatoes and mushy green peas.

Melrose Plant took one look and shoved his plate away and reclaimed the pint of bitter which Keeble had topped up. Jury looked disconsolately at the fish, fried, he was sure, in one of those batter mixes that comes in paper packets. Only Wiggins seemed to be digging in with relish, pounding the malt bottle on the bottom to shake the vinegar through the tiny holes.

"The wine," said Plant, "will be along any minute. I only hope she remembers to let it breathe."

Wiggins let out something somewhere between a giggle and a snicker. Jury was so unused to hearing Wiggins laugh, he couldn't quite identify the sound. "Incidentally, sir," Wiggins was saying around a mouthful of chips, "Superintendent Racer says you're to call him immediately. I told him you hadn't hardly had a moment to even sit down since you got here, sir." Wiggins was undoubtedly feeling guilty for the morning he had spent in bed, but it seemed to have done him good; it certainly had made him more voluble. He was shoveling in the fish and chips, and scarcely hesitated at all when both Plant and Jury slid their own food onto his plate.

The front door of the Cock and Bottle opened and three men, one of them Superintendent Pratt, came in. Jury could spot reporters a mile away, and sighed.

They were equally adept at spotting the police. Over they came, the photographer clicking pictures right and left at different parts of the saloon bar as if it were a fashion model doing naughty poses for him.

"You'd be Chief Inspector Jury, C.I.D. I'm from the *Weatherington Chronicle*." (Small potatoes, thought Jury, and not hard to shake off.) The other didn't bother identifying himself, just stood with his pad and pencil at the ready. They asked their standard questions and got their standard answers. No, the police hadn't got their man, but investigations were proceeding . . . Jury thought he might have that stamped on his headstone: *Investigations Are Proceeding*. Yes, they'd have something to tell the press in a day or two. One of the reporters made a snide comment about Jury's having his pint at this particular moment, which drew an angry word from Pratt: if they worked half as hard as the chief inspector, they'd not have time to ask damnfool questions. The newspaper crew packed up their gear and left, coattails flying.

Jury introduced Melrose to the superintendent. "It was Mr. Plant here who discovered the body."

"Just imagine," said Melrose, "how Aunt Agatha will take that. It's going to ruin her Christmas."

Just before they left the Cock and Bottle Constable Pluck was before them, proudly displaying a piece of luggage which he set on the table in front of Jury.

It was a dark blue, cheap, vinyl overnight case, the sort usually reserved for cosmetics and nightgowns. A removable plastic tray held plastic bottles and jars. The bottom of the case contained only some fresh undies, a nightgown, and an extra blouse. There were also some gaudy bangled earrings. Jury took out the clothes, looked inside the jars, smelled the bottles. "Nothing else lying about the woods?"

Pluck shook his head. "No, sir. The case was closed, just as you see it. It'd been hid under a pile of wet leaves and twigs and stuff."

"Very good. See if you can stir up the Judd family a bit. I'll want to talk with them this evening, and it may be very late when I get there. But I don't imagine they'll be getting much sleep tonight, anyway."

"I can't understand it," said the vicar, looking even grayer than his years. "Why would anyone want to kill that poor, harmless girl. Couldn't have been more than nineteen or twenty."

"Twenty-four, she was, Mr. Smith. And perhaps not quite so innocent as we might like to believe. The point now is that we may have to go over some of the same ground again; her murder throws altogether a different light on matters." The fingerprint officer was upstairs, the photographers having come and gone, but Jury knew it would be useless. He imagined that when Mrs. Gaunt cleaned, she made a proper job of it, and she had cleaned Ruby's room some days ago.

The fingerprint expert clattered down the stairs, case in hand, saying that there wasn't a print up there worth spitting at, except the same ones everywhere—probably the Gaunt woman's, and a man's—Jury's own, perhaps, when he looked the room over. Were Jury's prints on record? The officer snickered.

"As I told you before, Inspector," said the Reverend Smith. "It was Daphne Murch who got the girl for me. They were good friends, I think. If anyone would know why she left, it might be Daphne." The vicar poured himself a glass of port, offering some to Jury and Wiggins, both of whom refused. Then the vicar leaned back, and Jury assumed he was adjusting his mind to the idea of his housemaid's death. Instead, he said, "The Cock and Bottle: most people assume the word's some sort of corruption of 'cork,' which would make a bit more sense. But it isn't. 'Cock' was a word they used for spigot, the sort which would be found on a keg, you know. So it was really meant to advertise draught beer, with the bottle standing for bottled beer." Then he blushed, apparently realizing this was no time to delve into the lore of tavern art. "To think this is what it was all leading up to, these murders: the murder of that poor girl."

" 'Leading up to'?" said Jury. "No, I think you've got it the wrong way round, Mr. Smith. Ruby was murdered *before* any of the others. I don't mean to say there's no connection, of course." Wiggins had searched out some Players from his coat pocket, rooting among the boxes of lozenges, cough drops and nose drops, and he handed them now to Jury. "Did you ever suspect that Ruby knew something about someone in the village here, something they'd rather not have known?"

"Blackmail? Is *that* what you're suggesting?"

Jury didn't answer.

"No. She chattered a lot, but I didn't always listen.

Though there was a bit of talk—I don't credit gossip, of course—about Ruby and Marshall Trueblood."

"*Marshall Trueblood?*" Jury and Wiggins ex- changed disbelieving glances, and Wiggins nearly choked. Jury said, "Vicar, I don't really think so now, do you? Trueblood's a homosexual."

The vicar, happy to display his worldliness in such matters, said: "But he could be what's called *bi*sexual, Inspector."

That was true enough, and Trueblood did seem to overdo his act. "But you don't know this for a fact?" The vicar shook his head. "And the day Ruby left, she didn't seem especially excited, or anything?" The vicar shook his head again. Since Jury had already spoken to Mrs. Gaunt and found her also ignorant of any unusual behavior on Ruby's part, he supposed he had got out of them all he could get. It would have to do for the moment, at least. Jury rose and Wiggins snapped shut his notebook.

Outside, Jury asked Wiggins if he'd mind going on ahead to Weatherington and preparing the Judds for his visit: no matter how painful this might be for Ruby's parents, he needed to talk with them that eve- ning.

When Jury walked into the saloon bar of the Man with a Load of Mischief, he found Twig in his leather apron polishing up glasses. Wearily he hitched himself up on one of the oak stools and asked for a whiskey. In the beveled mirror he saw only one other customer—a middle-aged woman who seemed to be ticking off likely possibilities on a racing form.

"Where's Mr. Matchett, Twig?"

"He's having drinks in the dining room before din- ner, sir." Jury started to get up. "With Miss Vivian, sir." Jury sat back down again. He stared down at the

amber liquid in the glass. He was a policeman. He
should be in there, asking questions.

He forced himself to pick up his glass and head for
the dining room.

At first he thought it was empty. It was, certainly,
dark—lit only by the red-globed lights that flickered
on the tables and reflected on the walls. Jury was
standing in a deep pool of shadow by the door. Then
he saw them, Simon Matchett and Vivian. They were
nearly hidden by the stone buttress of one of the alcoves. Vivian's profile was present to him, but all he
could see of Matchett was one hand, which now was
lying on Vivian's wrist.

He was really quite close to them, not more than
perhaps twenty feet away. He tried to move his feet
to cover that short distance, to walk up and start
asking questions. But he didn't. At that moment he
knew the meaning of being rooted to the spot.

Now Matchett was leaning toward Vivian, and the
hand which had encircled her wrist reached round to
lie across the back of her chair and across her shoulders.

Jury moved a bit farther into the shadows, slightly
beyond the door, prepared (if need be) to appear to
be just then entering the room in case one of them
should turn and see him.

In the brief moments he had been standing there,
all three of them had been silent as the grave, a *tableau vivant*. Then he caught the tag end of something
Matchett was saying:

". . . where we live, darling."

Jury stood motionless in the shadows, his drink like
a lump in his hand.

". . . couldn't live *here*, Simon. Not any longer.
Not after all of this. And now—even poor Ruby Judd.
My God!" She pulled her sweater closer round her,

helped by Matchett, his hand coming to rest on her shoulder.

"Good Lord, love! No more could I. What you need is to get straight away. *We* need, I should say. It holds too many unpleasant memories for both of us. Vivian, love—" He ran his fingers from the nape of her neck up to her hair and they seemed caught in its tawny strands as if entangled and entrapped. "Ireland. We'll go to Ireland, Viv. It would be perfect for you. Have you ever been to Sligo?" She shook her head, staring down. "Well, we must go—it's right for you, that country. It's so strange how nothing can disturb that tranquility, not even that forever war they go on having. It's still one of the most peaceful spots on earth."

She folded her arms across the table and looked at him deeply. "You seem just a bit too vital for a place like Ireland. Unless you mean to join up with the I.R.A."

His hand had moved from her hair slowly down until one finger was tracing the curve of her cheek. "That's rot. I want peace as much as you do, my dear. I want to sit in a great, damp room, with a roaring fire and a couple of wolfhounds. Look, this place will fetch a very good price, and I can buy something over there with the profits—a pub, maybe. Or become a gun-runner, anything to keep us going—"

There was a brief silence. "I shouldn't really think we'll have to worry too much about being kept."

The hand that had been at her face dropped to her shoulder, then back to the table. "Give it up, Vivian."

"Give what up?"

"The money. Give it to charity or something. You don't need it, and I don't want it, and as far as I can see it's doing nothing but causing misery—at least to me. My Lord, you won't even let me tell anyone about us. You won't even share Christmas day with me!"

She laughed. "Oh, Simon, you're being childish." She enclosed his hand with her own. "I promised Melrose ages ago—"

"He's probably the only man you've ever known you're sure isn't a fortune hunter. If I had half his money you'd marry me tomorrow," he said bitterly.

As he tried to press himself farther into the darkness, Jury had the unreal sensation he made of an audience of one watching a performance in a theater.

"—God knows I don't blame you for the doubts you have," Simon was saying, "not after your dreadful childhood. Frankly, I think you'd be well rid of Isabel."

"I've never heard you talk against Isabel."

"I'm not exactly *against* her, I just think you should be shot of her. She's a reminder of old tragedy. And I'm not so sure but what she doesn't play up to it. You think you owe her too damned much. Darling—you don't owe anyone a bloody thing. If you refuse to marry me, then just go off with me. Live with me. Then your money will be forever beyond my reach—" She was somewhere between laughter and tears, now. "Listen, love. We'll buy up some old wreck of a castle over there. Can you imagine what Ireland will be like for your writing? I won't bother you there. I'll just go off with the damned wolfhounds, or to the pub, or anything—so long as I have you with me. Yeats country. I'll buy you a tower, like Yeats did for his wife. Though I'm glad your name isn't George, I must say." Now she *was* laughing. "What did he write? Something about building with a mill forge—'I build this tower for my wife, George,/And may these images remain/When all is ruin once again.'"

"Beautiful," said Vivian. "But he wasn't really so much in love with her, was he? Wasn't it Maud Gonne he really loved?"

"Sorry. Then it's Maud Gonne you remind me of. Not old George."

She laughed. "How very accommodating of you."

"Maud Gonne. Or Beatrice, perhaps? Or do you remind me of Jane Seymour—wasn't she the only one Henry the Eighth loved?"

"I think so. Certainly one of the few he didn't kill."

"Never mind. Cleopatra, you remind me of—"

"That's going a bit far, isn't it?"

"Not for you. And Dido—ah! Dido, Queen of Carthage. Remember what she said when she first saw Aeneas?"

"I blush to say I don't. Are you casting yourself as Aeneas?"

"Certainly. '*Agnosco veteris vestigia flammae.*' She says—"

" 'I recognize,' " said Jury, looking squarely at Vivian and setting his glass heavily on the table, " 'the vestiges of an old flame.' "

They stared up at him, openmouthed. Then both spoke at once: "Inspector Jury!"

"Sorry, didn't mean to creep up on you like that. You were . . . engrossed."

Vivian gave a little gasping laugh. "Don't apologize! I'm a bit overwhelmed to be in the presence of such learned men. Sit down, do."

Jury pulled out a chair and lit up a cigarette. "Not me. It's just a great line, that's all. What man in his right mind could resist it?"

"Or woman, either, Inspector." She was smiling at him, but he looked away. "It's a beautiful line."

"Well, we haven't much time for beauty, have we, then?" he said somewhat overbriskly, shoving his silverware around. "We seem to have another murder on our hands. You may've heard by now. News travels fast."

He saw Vivian look away quickly, and down at the tablecloth, like a chastened child. "Ruby Judd," was all she said, her voice very small.

"Ruby Judd, yes."

"We were just talking about it," said Matchett.

Oh, weren't you just? thought Jury.

"We were about to have dinner, Inspector. Won't you join us?"

"Yes. Thanks."

Twig came into the dining room and was sent to fetch the salad.

"Isabel went over to the Bicester-Strachans," said Vivian. "I just didn't want to stay home alone." She stared at the stone support behind Matchett's chair, as if across its ancient surface some warning were written. "Maybe we've been expecting it."

"What?" asked Jury, surprised. "That Ruby Judd might be killed?"

"No. But that it would finally be someone in Long Piddleton. Did we really believe these were merely aimless killings?"

"I don't know. Did you?"

She appeared puzzled—understandably, he supposed—by his acid tone. Well, her relationship with Matchett was no business of his, was it? Matchett had poured a generous portion of a white Medoc into the large globe of Vivian's wineglass; Jury himself refused the offer of wine.

Matchett said to Vivian, smiling. "Speak for yourself. I think most of us believed just that—that they were aimless, in a way. But why on earth would someone want to harm Ruby Judd? She'd be the last person I could imagine."

Jury inferred from this, as Twig rolled in the salad

table, that Matchett had an idea of the social fitness
of things: if one is going to do murder, one should
murder the swells and not the peasants.

Twig was arranging the wooden bowl of lettuce
and small dishes and vials of oil. When he began
squeezing lemon juice onto the greens, Matchett got
up, saying, "I'll do that, Twig." Expertly, he dribbled
oil round the bowl and began tossing the contents
with a wooden fork and spoon.

"Where were both of you Tuesday a week ago, in
the evening?"

Matchett went on calmly breaking an egg over the
lettuce, but Vivian looked nervous as she said, "At
home—I can't remember . . . Simon?"

Was Simon her memory, too?

Matchett shook his head. "Can't say off-hand. No,
wait. That would have been two nights before this
chap Small was killed—" He halted the fork and
spoon in midair. "I was here, I remember, all afternoon and evening."

"I must have been at home," said Vivian, uncertainly. "I think Oliver stopped in." Jury noted
Matchett's grimace.

"Don't you ever go off duty, Inspector?" Matchett
grated fresh cheese over the greens and tossed in a
handful of croutons.

"I would do, if only our murderer would do the
same."

Matchett passed over two glass plates of salad.
When Jury sampled it, he found it delicious. There
must not be many men who could discuss a fresh
murder, mix a Caesar salad, and be the intended of
this lovely creature, Vivian Rivington. Whatever he
was, he wasn't Simple Simon.

"Now Daphne, about Ruby Judd."

It was an hour later, and they were sitting at the

same table in the dining room. Matchett had left to
take Vivian Rivington home.

Daphne had wadded up and discarded a whole
pocketful of tissues, from all of her crying since Jury
had told her about Ruby. "You were on friendly
terms with her, weren't you? I understand it was you
who got her the job at the vicarage?" Jury had pulled
the picture from his wallet and placed it between
them on the table. It was a standard, static pose.
Ruby had long, black hair, a pretty, vacuous face.
The other snapshot showed more of her figure, which
was heavily endowed: large breasts pushing at a too-
tight jumper, and well-formed legs. Her mouth was
drawn up in that unflattering expression that comes
of squinting into the sun. The face was half in
shadow.

"Yes, sir. 'Twas me," said Daphne, shoveling damp
curls back from her forehead, which shone from nervous perspiration. Her face was puffy and crimson
from weeping.

"How long had you known her, Daphne?"

"Oh, for years. I knew her in school. We was class-
mates. I come from Weatherington, you know. When
the vicar's housemaid took herself off to get married,
and there was only that Mrs. Gaunt from the village
to do for him—an old poker, she is—I asked him
would he like another girl, as I knew one out of a job
and a very good worker. He said to send her along."
Daphne looked down at her shoes, and added rather
wanly, "I guess I should've thought twice about it, sir.
I mean, sir, with her not bein' the most dependable
person in the world." Then she clapped her hand
over her mouth at having implied some ill of the
dead.

"What do you mean, not dependable?" Jury noticed Twig was making quite a job of polishing the

crystal goblets; he'd been at the same one for five minutes.

Daphne lowered her voice: "Ruby'd been in one or two little scrapes, see."

"What sort?" Jury was fully aware the scrapes were probably sexual, given the rising color in the waitress's face. She seemed unable to find her tongue, so he helped her out: "Was Ruby pregnant?"

"Oh, no, sir. I mean, not to my knowledge. She never told me she was. But . . . well, she had been. Once. Maybe even more than once." Daphne looked almost as if it were she who had trodden the primrose path.

"She had an abortion, is that it? Perhaps more than one?"

Daphne nodded, mutely, casting a surreptitious glance in Twig's direction. But the old Boots had moved down the line of tables, under Jury's stare.

"Sometimes, though, I felt almost sorry for her. What else is a girl to do, if she can't get no help from her family? Ruby's family's a bunch of old sticks. She daren't have told them. When she was little she had an uncle and aunt she was always bein' sent off to live with. Aunt Rosie and Uncle Will, she said. She liked them ever so much more than her mum and dad. I think they just wanted to be rid of her, I do."

"Then you and Ruby were pretty thick?"

Daphne ran a tissue under her nose. "In a way, yes. But the stuff she'd tell me, it was more like by way of teasing me into asking questions, not like she was really confiding in me."

Jury was gratified by this ability of the girl to make such a fine distinction. Most girls would have thought that giggling innuendos were exchanges of confidence.

She went on: "Ruby wasn't walking out with anyone round here I knew of. But she was always drop-

ping hints she'd more'n one fellow she was—"
Daphne blushed and smoothed the skirt of her black
uniform.

"Sleeping with, you mean."

She nodded, apparently finding the phrase less vulgar on the lips of a policeman. "The thing is, Ruby
always acted that way—secretive like. Whether there
was anything in it or not. She wanted to make a big
mystery out of everything. Like, didn't I want to
know where she'd got a new dress, or bag, or bit of
jewelry, or something, as if someone in Long Pidd
was—well—*keeping* her. And she had this gold
bracelet she always wore—always had it on her—my,
but didn't she set great store by that! First it's somebody gave it her, and later on, it's that she found it.
You never knew when Ruby was telling the truth.
Then there was all the stuff she was trying on with
that Mrs. Gaunt. Ruby didn't do her work by half,
the work she was paid to. When she was supposed to
be dusting or cleaning, she'd start chattering to the
vicar, and he'd start in back, and she'd pretend to be
interested, and he'd not realize she wasn't doing her
work—just whisking the feather duster across his desk.
When she was supposed to be sweeping the church,
she'd just sit out there and read a film magazine, or
write in her diary. Sometimes she even lacquered her
nails." Daphne giggled.

"Ruby kept a *diary?* Did you ever see it?"

"Oh, no, sir. She'd hardly be showing it to me, now
would she? Not her bein' so secretive, the way she
was."

Jury made a mental note to have Wiggins question
Mrs. Gaunt on this point.

"One thing Ruby did say that really made me wonder was as how she'd got something on someone in
Long Pidd."

"Those were her words?"

Daphne nodded. "Have you any idea what she might have meant?" Daphne shook her head so decisively the light brown curls bobbed like little corks round the rim of her starched white cap.

"No, sir. I was real curious about what she did mean, and I kept trying to worm it out of her, but the harder I tried, the more she laughed and just kept saying what a surprise it would be, that she had somebody on a piece of string, and wouldn't we all be half surprised?"

Jury sighed. It would be hard, with a girl like Ruby Judd, to separate out the wheat from the chaff. Her "secret" could be anything from seeing one of the local ladies pull down her knickers for the milkman . . . to murder.

Weatherington was a medium-sized town, about twice the size of Sidbury, which was in turn about twice the size of Long Piddleton. They lay equidistant from one another, Sidbury some ten or eleven miles west of Long Piddleton; Weatherington another eleven southwest of Sidbury. The Home Office had set up one of its labs in Weatherington to assist provincial police forces. And there was a small hospital where Appleby had his postmortem room.

Chipped paint was the overall effect of the station, with glossy beige walls. But, then, the place wasn't built for beauty. Jury went through to the charge room, past the switchboard where a grandmotherly lady sat knitting a red wool scarf. In the charge room, the station officer was bent over his book, sitting beneath one of the yellow "No Waiting" notices. Jury often wondered who would want to come to these places just to loiter. He passed counters and cupboards where documents spilled from insides and tops, and men who seemed to be spending most of their time moving the typewriters about, like a team of reporters. He put in a call to Appleby.

"No, she wasn't," said the doctor, when Jury asked him if Ruby Judd had been pregnant when she died. "Doubt she ever would have been. Not the way she was torn up inside. I'd say more than one abortion, certainly. Several years ago."

In a way, Jury was relieved. Had she been pregnant, he might have had to start searching along the lines of the lover who didn't want marriage, disgraced if Ruby had gone blabbing her mouth off. Such an explanation of her death would surely have separated Ruby's murder from the others. The vicar, Jury thought, had got it just the wrong way around: the other murders didn't lead *up* to Ruby's; they must have led *away* from it.

"Thanks, Dr. Appleby. I'm sorry I had to ring you up so late."

"Late? It's only half-ten, man. We small-town boys work the clock round." Appleby snickered and rang off.

Jury went over to a detective constable at the desk. There were at least a dozen men in the station, at this hour. They were only too eager to get in on the show and seemed delighted Jury had turned up. "The superintendent isn't here, is he?"

"No, sir."

"Have you got the report on the Celia Matchett case? The one at that inn in Dartmouth years ago?"

"Yes, sir, if you'll just wait a bit, I'll—"

"No matter. I've got to see the Judd family, so I'll pick it up when I come back." Jury turned to Wiggings, who was getting his notebook and pencils together. "You rang the Judds?" Wiggins nodded. "Let's go, then."

       *   *   *

Mr. and Mrs. Jack Judd lived in Weatherington's newer district, a development of rows of brick bungalows, indistinguishable at night as they probably were even by day. Perhaps a step above the gray council houses on the other side of town, but not a big step. Weatherington held few charms. It had begun as one of those projects, the planned garden-city type, and then somewhere along the line the funds must have dribbled off, or been diverted into other, unaesthetic pockets. The result was an amorphous mass wherein no special style predominated.

In the dark garden-plot in front of the Judd's bungalow, Jury could make out the outlines of decorative additions, probably plaster geese and ducks and rock-nooks, nearly hidden now under snow.

It was a young woman who answered the door. She was a more angular version of Ruby, if Ruby's picture were a good likeness. It must be the sister, thought Jury. "Yes?" Her voice was nasal, and her pretense of not knowing who he was reminded him of Lorraine Bicester-Strachan. Only Miss Judd hadn't quite the air to bring it off.

"Miss Judd, is it?" She nodded, managing to keep her nose—which rose rather high on her thin face anyway—in the air.

"Inspector Richard Jury, Miss, C.I.D. And Detective Sergeant Wiggins." Wiggins tipped his hat. "I believe Sergeant Wiggins rang you that we were coming."

She stood aside. Jury noticed as he and Wiggins walked past into the darkened hall that there wasn't much of the air of the mourner about her. There was no offer, either, to take their coats, so Jury tossed his over the banister.

"In there," was all she said, pointing to a room down the narrow, dark hall to the rear of the house. Probably a back parlor, since the front one was unlit.

Saved up for Sunday tea. A scraggly, tinseled tree stood in one corner of the room, its base surrounded by imitation snow.

In the room at the rear, warmed by an electric fire and night-storage heaters, the Judds sat, incredibly dry-eyed.

Mrs. Judd, a stout woman who scarcely looked up from her knitting when she spoke, and even then made it sound as if Ruby were someone else's daughter, said, "It's terrible to think you work your fingers to the bone for them, and they turn out this way."

It was difficult for Jury to control his temper in the face of such cold-bloodedness. "I doubt your daughter was looking for what she got, Mrs. Judd. I don't think she wanted to end her life in a ditch." He made the description as cold as Mrs. Judd's reception of the news of her daughter's death.

Mr. Judd said nothing; he made guttural sounds in his throat. He was one of those who let his wife do the talking.

"Ever since she was little there's been no controlling Ruby. Only people who could do anything with her was her Aunt Rosie—that's Jack's sister. We'd just pack Ruby off to Devon when we couldn't do nothing with her. Then after she grew up, she was in and out of our lives as if we wasn't even kin to her, much less her mum and dad. Never sent a tad of money home, never paid her keep those months she wasn't working. Living on the cheap with us, she was. Not like our Merriweather, here—" And the mother smiled fondly at the dry stick of a girl reading a film magazine by the electric log. Merriweather smiled primly, then tried to look distressed at the thought of her sister's death. She even had a handkerchief wadded in her hand to catch the tears that didn't fall.

"Our Merry's never given us a sleepless night."

Mrs. Judd rocked, and looked smugly at the girl as her knitting needles clicked away. Judd, in vest and suspenders, finally put in: "Don't go speakin' ill of the dead, Mother. It ain't Christian."

Seldom had Jury seen such indifference to the death of a child. Not death, even, *murder*. None of the Judds showed the least interest in the attendant horrors of their daughter's death. Well, the hell with it. It would make his job easier. No condolences, no soft-spoken and guarded questions to protect ravaged feelings.

"Mrs. Judd, when was the last time you saw your daughter?" Wiggins had taken out his notebook and a box of licorice lozenges. He began to suck and write his shorthand, while Mrs. Judd put by her knitting and looked at the ceiling, thinking over her answer:

"That would have been, let's see, this is Thursday—last Friday week. Yes, I remember, because I was just in from the fishmonger's. Had fresh plaice and I remember remarking to Ruby about it."

"But I thought you said she seldom saw you. That would only have been about two weeks ago. Only a few days before she died. We think she was murdered on the fifteenth."

"Well, that was it, then. But she only stayed the night. Said she'd got to be back on the Saturday, as the vicar needed her for something, she said."

"Why did she come?"

Mrs. Judd shrugged. "Who ever knew with Ruby? Suppose she came to see some boy. She had too many of *them* for her own good, I can tell you. That policeman this afternoon said Ruby's told people she was visiting us when she went off last week. That's a laugh, that is. Gone off with some fellow, she was."

"Apparently not, Mrs. Judd," said Jury, keeping his voice level. But the arrow hit home, at least. She reddened. "She was popular with the men, was she?"

"It don't take much to be popular with men, Inspector." And she looked him up and down as if he ought to know. "Ruby was always out, gadding, those months she was living at home. Now, Merriweather—"

But Jury had no interest in the excellent Merriweather Judd, with her wedge-shaped face and crinkled hairdo. When she caught Jury looking at her, she dabbed at her eyes with the handkerchief.

"Where was Ruby, then, before she came here to live with you? That is, where was her last job?"

"London. Don't ask me doing what. Said she was a hair-stylist's assistant, but where did she ever get the training for that?"

"You don't know her address or who her friends were in London? Or why she came back here?"

Mrs. Judd looked at him as if he were a not very fresh piece of plaice himself. "I told you, because she hadn't got the money to live in her usual high style—"

"Probably she wasn't just a hairdresser's assistant," interrupted Merriweather. "Probably got her money from other sources."

"Are you both hinting that Ruby was a prostitute?"

The effect was electric. Mrs. Judd turned beet-red and dropped her knitting. Merriweather gasped. Even Judd stirred in his chair.

"That's a terrible thing to say about a poor, dead girl!" Mrs. Judd searched a tissue out of her apron pocket. Judd patted her arm.

"I'm sorry, Mrs. Judd." He turned to Merriweather. "It was the remark about the money, Miss; I assumed that's what you meant."

"She just said she was going to be living on Easy Street one of these days. Plenty of money she'd have, she said."

Jury riveted his attention on Merriweather. "When was that?"

The girl wet her finger, turning the page of the

magazine. "When she was here. When Mum said. Last Friday week. She hinted this and that like she always does. I never pay any attention to her."

"What sort of hints?" Jury persisted.

"Oh, like 'I'll be buying my clothes at Liberty's and not Marks and Sparks from now on.' Silly things like that."

"Nothing as to who might be going to give her this money, or why?"

Merriweather only shook her head, her face still on the magazine.

"I understand Ruby kept a diary. Have any of you ever seen it?" Three heads shook in unison.

"I'll just send an officer round tomorrow, then, to look at her room."

"It's been gone over once," said Mrs. Judd. "I should think you lot would have more feeling than to be bothering the poor kin—"

Feeling a sour taste rise in his throat at this blatant hypocrisy, Jury rose quickly. Wiggins got up too, stuffing his pen in the pocket of his shirt. "Your daughter's body will be released to you for the funeral as soon as we get Home Office approval."

Mrs. Judd managed a commendable act there at the end, crying, *Oh, Jack, our poor Ruby.* And Judd saying, *There, there, Mother.*

Merriweather alone forgot to do her part. As she walked them to the door, she was smiling down over a picture of Robert Redford.

On the way back to Long Piddleton Jury slowed for the "dead man," now lit with lanterns beyond the dark Cock and Bottle. He saw once again in his mind's eye the arm of Ruby sticking out from the hardpacked earth. He shivered and ran a hand over his face. Some vagrant thought seemed trying to work its way up from the depths of his mind. What was it?

He was still trying to make it surface as he bumped
the Morris up to the front of the Man with a Load of
Mischief.

Jury fell asleep that night with the folder on the
Matchett murder propped on his chest.

CHAPTER 14

When he awoke on Christmas morning, the folder was on the floor. He retrieved it, and spent a good hour going through the loose pages. What Matchett had told him was here confirmed. Both he and the girl, Harriet Gethvyn-Owen, had alibis—all of those people in the audience. It was the maid, Daisy Trump, who had brought Celia Matchett her tray. Her mistress had called to her to bring it inside (though usually it was left by the door) and put it on the little table just inside the door. So Daisy could testify to having seen Celia Matchett alive then. The cocoa was drugged, and that was one thing the police couldn't understand: why would an ordinary thief drug the cocoa and then come back to rob her office? Why not wait until she was out of it? Jury agreed it made little sense. He looked at the diagram of the office. Desk facing window, where she had been sitting. Door to hall opposite desk. Little squares marking off tables, chairs, bureau.

Jury replaced the papers in the folder. God. Two days ago he had only *two* murders to solve. Here it was Christmas morning, and he had five.

"More coffee, sir?" asked Daphne, hovering at his elbow, waiting to be of service.

"No, thanks. Did Ruby ever say anything about being a hairdresser's assistant in London?"

"Ruby? That's a laugh. She wouldn't do work like that. She had a job, all right. More like posing for— you know, photos."

Jury thought of Sheila Hogg, and her supposed "modeling" job in Soho and wondered. Through these meditations he heard the distant *brr-brr* of the telephone, and in a moment Twig was fetching him.

"Jury, here."

"I'm at the Long Pidd station, sir." Wiggins had begun referring to the village in the affectionate diminutive. The piercing whistle of Pluck's kettle served as background music. "No diary in Ruby's room at home or in the vicarage." Wiggins interrupted himself to thank Pluck for a cuppa. "Now, this Mrs. Gaunt— and isn't she the old flintheart?—said she'd often seen Ruby write in a book. She said it was small and dark red. Didn't she ever get huffy, though, when I asked her if she'd taken a look in it!" Wiggins slurped his tea. "Said she didn't remember when she last saw Ruby writing in it."

"All right. Now, there are a couple of bits of information I want. First of all: William Bicester-Strachan. He was with the War Ministry, so ring up C1 and see if you can get the story on some sort of inquiry at the time he lived in London. Second: have them go through the obits for an accidental death that occurred roughly twenty-two years ago in Scotland—Sutherland, to be exact. James Rivington was the name. I'm particularly interested in the exact time of his accident."

"Very good, sir. Merry Christmas." Wiggins rang off. Jury sat there feeling a little ashamed of himself. He supposed that for a long time he had been underestimating Wiggins, who certainly did his job as long as his health could hold out. Would his poor corpse be clasping a notebook, along with his hand-

kerchief? For years, Jury had been trying to call him
by his first name, but somehow stuck at "Al." Well,
he was always right there with his pen and cough
drops. Jury thought he was probably looking forward
to his Christmas dinner with Constable Pluck and his
family. And Jury was certainly looking forward to his,
with Melrose Plant. And family. But first he'would
have to stop by Darrington's and Marshall Trueblood's.

"That girl, Ruby Judd. She was a real busybody.
No wonder the vicar liked her, she could talk the
teats off a cow. They must have had some lovely old
natters." Sheila Hogg was well into her third gin-
and-tonic by now.

"Where did you run into her, Sheila?" asked Jury.

"In the shops. She was always mooning about me
thinking that she might be invited up to the house to
have a look at the Great Author." She was sitting by
Jury, swinging a silken leg and a foot clad in a velvet
shoe which matched her long skirt. But she was looking at Oliver—and looking, Jury thought, bleak,
despite the sarcasm.

"And did she?" asked Jury. "Get over to the
house?"

"Oh, yes. Several times, she carried my parcels for
me. Went all over the place, oohing and aahing and
peeking behind doors and so forth. Nosy little—well,
she's dead now."

"And you, Mr. Darrington. Did you have anything
to do with Ruby Judd?"

The pause was fractional, but still too long. "No."

"Is that a fact, love?" said Sheila. "Then why is it
she suddenly started coming the heavy over me? You
didn't give her a bit of a feel now and then?"

"God, but you're vulgar, Sheila!"

"Mr. Darrington, it's very important we know as

much as possible about Ruby Judd. Is there anything
you could tell us that would help? For example, did
she ever mention anything to you about anyone in
Long Piddleton that might have been cause for blackmail?"

"I don't know what you're bloody talking about."
He shoved his own nearly empty glass toward Sheila.
"Give me another drink."

"Where were both of you Tuesday week? The
night before the dinner at the Man with a Load of
Mischief?"

Oliver lowered the hand that held the glass, looking at Jury with eyes glazed over either by gin or fear.
"I suppose now you think I killed Ruby Judd, is that
it?"

"I have to check the movements of all of those
people at the inn the night Small was murdered. Obviously, there's a connection."

Sheila's foot seemed to stop in midswing. "Do you
mean to say you think it was one of *us*? Someone at
the Man with a Load of Mischief that night?"

"It's certainly a possibility." Jury looked from
Sheila to Oliver. "Where were you?"

"Together." Oliver drained his glass. "Right here."

Jury looked at Sheila, who merely nodded, her eyes
on Oliver. "You're quite sure of that?" Jury asked.
"Most people can't remember where they were two
nights ago without searching their memories. This
was over a week ago."

Oliver didn't answer. But Sheila did, turning a
somewhat overbright smile on Jury that belied the
grim determination in her tone: "Believe me, sweetie,
I know when Oliver is here." The smile faded as she
looked at Darrington. "And when he's not."

It being Christmas, Trueblood's shop was closed, so
Jury went round to his cottage, situated in the village

square. It was a charming house, cruck-ended, the gracefully curved split oak meeting at the top and straddling the base. On the near end were two well-spaced diamond-paned windows.

Trueblood was just putting the finishing touches to his toilette (could it be called anything else?), preparatory to dining with the Bicester-Strachans.

"Aren't you coming along, old chap? Give you a good opportunity to question us all at once. The *creme de la creme* of Long Pidd. Except for Melrose Plant. He wouldn't be caught dead at one of Lorraine's omnium gatherums." He affixed a knot in his gray silk tie.

"I'm having dinner with Mr. Plant." Jury was looking for a place to sit, but every bit of furniture looked too precious to carry his weight. He finally settled on a plum-velvet love seat. "I take it Mrs. Bicester-Strachan was interested in Mr. Plant?"

" 'Interested in'? Darling, she nearly wrestled him to the floor one night at the Load of Mischief." Trueblood flipped his tie inside his vest, adjusted his perfectly tailored jacket, and fetched a cut crystal decanter, two tulip-shaped sherry glasses, and a bowl of shelled walnuts, which he set before Jury.

"I assume you've heard by now about Ruby Judd."

"God, yes. The one who did the moonlight flit. Pity."

"It wasn't exactly a 'moonlight flit,' as you say. I think she was seduced away by someone. The murderer probably suggested she pack up a bag to make her absence more acceptable. Otherwise, there might have been questions asked."

"The sort that are being asked now, I take it?" Trueblood lit up a small cigar. "And you want to know where I was on the night in question. Whatever night that might have been, say I, innocently."

"Yes. But that's only one question. The other is, What was your relationship with Ruby Judd?"

Trueblood was shocked. "My *'relationship'*? Surely you're jesting." He crossed his beautifully tailored legs and dribbled a bit of ash into a porcelain dish. "Why, if you old dears at the Yard found me in the back streets of Chelsea with a ring in my ear, you'd pull me in before I could get my falsies off."

Jury choked on his sherry. "Oh, come on, now, Mr. Trueblood."

"Call me Marsha. Everyone else does."

Jury hadn't the time for Trueblood's patter. "Were you or were you not sleeping with Ruby Judd?"

"Yes."

Jury still had his mouth open, prepared to override more of Trueblood's jokes. The direct answer threw him off balance.

"But only the once, mind you. Well, she was rather a cute little baggage, but deadly dull. Mindless. Now, look, darling, you're not going to let this get around, are you?" Without the act, Jury realized he might be appealing to women. Trueblood went on: "It would simply *ruin* my reputation. My business would go down the drain. And I've this, you know, *friend* in London who would be heartbroken if he knew I'd been unfaithful. Silly little twit, Ruby was. But what's one to do in a one-eyed village like this except listen to all the argy-bargy between the old crows like Miss Crisp and Agatha. I gather she'll be at Melrose's ruining the festivities. Oh, *do* come to Lorraine's, you'd have so much more fun. There'll be so many more people to accuse—"

"I'm trying to find out just who it was in this village Ruby Judd knew enough about to get herself killed over."

Trueblood looked puzzled. "I'm afraid I don't follow."

"I think she was blackmailing someone."

"Me? That's just like the coppers. Run about in their panda cars looking for the queers to blame the rising crime rate on—"

"As a matter of fact, I *don't* think it was you, but I may take you in anyway just to get some proper answers."

Trueblood lowered the pitch of his voice to a more normal tone. "Oh, very well. I'll try to remember if the girl said anything that might help. She had so little to say one would want to listen to. Stuff about her life, that sort of thing."

"Tell me about that, then."

"I was only laying her, Inspector, not doing her biography. I hardly listened."

Jury wished *someone* had listened to Ruby Judd.

"She did say her mother was an old stick, and her father on the hob but mostly falling off. Gin. Sister spent her nights in front of the goggle-box mooning over American detectives." Trueblood took a swig of sherry and lit another small cigar. "Then there was this aunt and uncle in Devon where she spent most of her ill-trained childhood. Then on and on through odd jobs here and there—"

"Like 'modeling'? Read for that, porno stuff."

"Who, her? I doubt it. Oh, I think she might have tried to rustle up a bit of street-corner business now and again, but she'd have made a poor dirty postcard."

"Where were you on the night of December fifteenth, Tuesday?"

"All by my lonesome, dear. Where were *you?*"

"More goose, sir?"

Ruthven was standing at Jury's elbow, offering an enormous silver platter on which rested the remains of two birds, still in their adornments of cherries and truffles. But it hardly registered on Jury, whose eyes were on Vivian Rivington, seated across the table from him. Her amber hair curled above her gray cashmere sweater, and she looked as if she had materialized out of the mists of Dartmoor or the mysterious moors of Yorkshire's West Riding. If the goose had got up and started quacking across the table, Jury wouldn't have noticed. Her sister, Isabel, had opted for the Bicester-Strachans.

Lady Ardry spoke now. "Not very hungry, hey, Inspector? Perhaps if you'd be up and doing a bit more, you'd have some appetite. As I've been doing."

"Indeed, Aunt? And just what have you been doing?"

"Investigating, my dear Plant. Can't have more of these murders, now can we?" She piled some chestnut stuffing on a split scone and tucked this starchy ensemble into her mouth.

"Oh, I don't know," said Plant. "Perhaps one more. No, thank you, Ruthven."

"I'll have some more," said Agatha. "And speaking of the investigation, have you your alibi ready, Vivian?"

Jury cast Agatha a malevolent look. She had obviously not forgiven him for establishing an alibi for Melrose Plant.

"As a matter of fact," said Vivian, "I've probably less of an alibi than anyone else. Except Simon, perhaps. We were at the Swan when that man was killed." She looked at Jury so unhappily, he had to avert his gaze to the wineglass.

"We're all in the same boat, dear," said Agatha with mock sweetness. "Excepting, of course, for Melrose. Only one in Long Pidd with an alibi." She said it with such snappish truculence, one would have thought Melrose had been printing up alibis in the back room and refusing to hand out copies. She was

wrestling a forkful of food from the drumstick she had
speared from the silver platter, as if she and the bird
were locked in mortal combat. "You needn't snicker,
Inspector. Plant isn't out of the woods, not yet.
Remember you were only with him from eleven-thirty
until noon or so, when I returned."

"But you were with him for three hours prior to
that, Lady Ardry." What the hell was she up to, now?

"You sound as if you were *sorry* Melrose has an
alibi," said Vivian.

"Let's flip for it, Aunt Agatha," said Melrose, taking a coin from his pocket.

"You needn't be frivolous," she said to her nephew.
Then to Vivian: "Certainly, I *would* be glad if Plant
were clear. Only the truth is bound to come out in
the end—"

"Truth? What truth?" asked Jury.

Carefully she put by her knife and fork, giving
them their first rest in the last half hour. Snuggling
her chin on her clasped fingers, elbows on table, she
said, "I mean that I wasn't with you for every minute.
Don't you remember, my dear Plant? I went out to
the kitchen to see to the Christmas pudding. Martha
does like to skimp on the mace . . ."

If Melrose had forgotten, Ruthven hadn't. Although he didn't spill a drop of the wine he was
pouring, he closed his eyes in pain.

"I thought you'd merely gone to use the facilities."
Melrose sighed and asked Ruthven to clear away the
dinner plates. "Anyway, you couldn't have been gone
very long." Reprieves from Agatha were never long,
his tone implied.

Jury watched enviously as Vivian put her hand on
Melrose's, which was twirling the stem of his
wineglass. "Agatha! You should be ashamed!"

"We've all of us got to do our duty, my girl, no
matter how painful an office that may be. We can't go

about protecting our loved ones, merely because we wish to see them as innocent. The moral fiber of Britain was not built upon—"

"Never mind about Britain's moral fiber, Agatha," said Melrose. "Tell me, how did I manage to get to the Swan, kill Creed, then nip back in the short time you were in the kitchen driving Martha crazy?"

Calmly, she buttered a biscuit. "My dear Plant, I hope you don't think *I* have been sitting around working out your crimes for you?"

Jury blinked. He had read several books on formal logic, but Lady Ardry defied them all.

"However," she continued, "since we're speculating, you could have jumped in your Bentley, dashed off—"

Jury couldn't resist. "But, surely, you remember, Lady Ardry, the motor of the car was dead cold. It took us a good five minutes to get it going." Vivian Rivington bestowed upon Jury a beatific smile.

As Agatha's face fell, Melrose said: "Don't give up, Agatha. How about my bike? No, too slow." He seemed to be debating the little problem. Then he snapped his fingers. "My horse! That's it! I could have saddled up old Bouncer, dashed across the meadow to the Swan, dispatched Creed, and back again—zip! like a bunny."

Vivian said, "It would have to be zip! like a bunny, considering your horse."

Melrose shook his head. "Well, there it is, Agatha. It simply won't wash. My alibi stands."

As Agatha gritted her teeth, Ruthven brought in the dessert—a magnificent pudding. He touched a match to its brandy-soaked surface. After he served it, he poured some Madeira into the third wineglass.

When Melrose observed Agatha sitting there glumly, probably working out another way to destroy his alibi, he said to Ruthven: "That small package

up there on the mantel. Hand that over to her la-
dyship, will you?"

Agatha's face brightened as she took the present
and opened it.

Vivian gasped when Agatha drew from the small
box a bracelet of emeralds and rubies. They gleamed,
nearly spurting into small flames themselves when
they caught the candlelight. Agatha thanked Melrose
lavishly, but without a trace of bad conscience for all
she had just been trying to do. She handed the
bracelet to Vivian, who admired it and passed it
across to Jury.

He had not seen the real thing since he was very
young, working the robbery division. He knew now
why rubies were described as "blood red." Suddenly
that missing detail floated into his mind. Rubies.
Ruby. A bracelet. That was it, that image of the wrist
sticking out of the ground. Ruby's wrist, but no
bracelet. *She always wore it, sir, never took it off.*
Daphne's voice came back to him.

Then where was it? His eyes were riveted on the
gems as he passed the bracelet back to Agatha, his
mind still so much on Ruby's naked wrist that he
barely heard Agatha's comment:

"Quite handsome, Melrose. For paste."

The ladies retired to the drawing room, leaving
Jury and Melrose to their port. *Retired* was perhaps
not the most apt description of Lady Ardry's leave-
taking. Vivian finally got her out of the dining room,
but Agatha managed a few assaults on it, coming
back to collect various items that seemed to have
dropped from her person—handkerchiefs, buttons,
and her bracelet, which she had left in an untidy
heap on the table as if its red and green magnificence
were a handful of olives.

When she had gone off with that, Jury said, "That was a very generous gift, Mr. Plant."

"I think she missed the red and green symbolism. Christmas colors. I thought it would be nice." He studied the tip of his cigar, and blew on it to make it burn.

"Excuse me for asking, but what did she give you?"

"Nothing." Plant smiled. "She never does. Says she's saving up for a specially nice gift—something she's been considering for years. Wonder what it is. A new car fitted out by the I.R.A.?"

Jury grinned, and then said, "There are a few ideas I'd like to toss around with you regarding these murders."

"I'm listening."

"Well, what intrigues me is their flamboyance. What sort of mind would think them up?"

"A very cool one. He might be a psychopath under it all, but I'll bet it's well hidden. I agree, though. The killer is being horribly *public* about it all. If you want to kill someone, why not arrange a *private* meeting?"

Jury drew a folded copy of the front page of the *Weatherington Chronicle* from his jacket pocket. "I can give you a good reason, I think." He flicked his finger against the banner: *"Inn Murders Continue."* There was a long account of the murder of Ruby Judd, followed by a review of the Creed murder. "It's the pattern. Either this inn business means something, or it doesn't—"

Melrose Plant blew a smoke ring. "That statement, Inspector, has probably unraveled a million years of philosophical speculation. 'Either it means something, or it doesn't.' "

"Mr. Plant, there are times when I'm happy I'm not your aunt."

"Keep talking as you just did, and I'll soon be unable to tell the difference."

"Mr. Plant, be careful. I could break your alibi."

"You wouldn't."

"If there were more than one murder—? How about that? You're only covered for the Creed murder."

"Let's get back to our theories: now, is the murderer trying to get at something in these inns? What about gold in a press table? Or perhaps Matchett has the original Hogarth sign and doesn't know it—well, that sounds rather improbable. *Or* this inn business is a smoke screen."

"I see you thought of that, too. Also: sometimes the most public way of committing a crime is the most private. The 'purloined letter' idea. You hide something in plain sight. And since the murderer isn't hiding the bodies, well, maybe he's trying to obscure the motive."

"Except for the body of Ruby Judd. There are two variations from the pattern. She was buried and she *wasn't* a stranger."

"It's the variations that are interesting. Although it must have made no difference when the others were discovered, it *did* make a difference in the case of Ruby Judd."

"But why murder Ruby Judd anyway?" Melrose twirled his port glass.

"Perhaps because she knew something about someone in the village."

"Blackmail? Good heavens, what have we all been up to?"

Jury answered this obliquely. "There is some indication that Ruby had something going with Oliver Darrington." Plant looked astonished. "Yes, I think the Judd girl really got around."

"That chubby little farm girl?" Plant shook his head. "Some men have strange tastes."

"Including Marshall Trueblood."

Melrose nearly dropped the port bottle. "You're kidding."

Jury smiled. "Trueblood does seem to be the standing butt of Long Piddleton's jokes, I admit."

"Yes. But I've always felt jokes about another man's race, religion, or sexual persuasion to be in deplorable taste. Those are generally things one can't do much about. Not that I like him. If he walked down the High Street standing on his hands he couldn't be sillier." Melrose shook his head in disbelief. "And Trueblood was actually sleeping with the Judd girl?"

"Only once, he claims. But there are things in Trueblood's past, as there are in Darrington's, that neither one might want known and that Ruby Judd might have found out. Then we have the Bicester-Strachans—"

"I'd plump for Lorraine, myself. She'd murder to protect her holy reputation—"

Agatha popped back into the dining room just then to hear what was going on, her excuse being she needed a drop of brandy for her splitting headache. "Just get me some, won't you Ruthven?"

Ruthven, who had just come in at that moment to clear the sideboard, turned haughtily and said, "My name is pronounced *Rivv'n*, madam. *Rivv'n*, as his lordship has so often told you."

"Then why don't you spell it *Rivv'n*?"

"I do, madam." Ruthven started for the kitchen, tray in hand.

"Well!" Agatha turned to Melrose. "Is that the way you allow your servants to talk? And what aspersions have you been casting on Lorraine Bicester-Strachan?"

Turning round at the kitchen door, Ruthven came

close to shouting, "Madam, it is *Bister-Strawn! Bister-Strawn!*" He wheeled round and went through to the kitchen.

Agatha was openmouthed.

Melrose, who thought he caught a whiff of the old malt on Ruthven's Christmas breath, grinned. "Consider, Agatha: you've been shriven by Ruthven."

She whirled and stomped out.

Plant picked up the topic Agatha had interrupted. "I think Bicester-Strachan himself would be my last choice. That nice, chess-playing old man—"

"I've seen nice, chess-playing old men do strange things before. Then there's Simon Matchett—"

Plant's green eyes gleamed. "Isn't there just! I only wish I knew more about his wife and all that sordid business to toss up to Vivian, the silly girl."

"A bit of prejudice operating there, Mr. Plant?" In more than one case, Jury thought, guiltily. "You're quite dead set against his marrying Miss Rivington, aren't you?"

"You know her. Wouldn't you be?"

Jury chose to study his plate rather than answer directly. "I don't understand why the engagement, if there is one, is so undecided."

"Nor do I. It's Isabel's doing, that so-called engagement. Been pushing them together, though I swear I can't see *why*, not the way Isabel looks at Matchett, and the fact she'd lose out if the purse strings transferred, not to Vivian's hands when she's thirty, but to *his*. Damned puzzling."

"Not if—"

"If what?"

"Nothing. What do you think about that story of the accident to her father?"

"Funny you should ask, because I've often wondered about that. Vivian seems quite convinced that she was a real brat, and that she was continuously fighting with Daddy, and all the rest. I imagine you'd agree it's difficult thinking of her as having been a hellion as a child. Not only that, but she was only—what?—seven or eight when he died. Don't we tend to *bury* the more traumatic incidents of childhood? Yet Vivian paints in all of the details of what happened at that time as if it were yesterday. I'm just wondering, you see"—and Melrose inspected the tip of his cigar before knocking off the ash—"who's been filling in the brush strokes."

"You mean she might have had the picture painted for her by Isabel?"

"Who else is there? They've no relatives left."

"Then there might have been some need for Isabel to convince Vivian of the accident. And that might give Isabel a motive for covering up her past."

"You don't honestly think a woman could have done these murders?"

"You're such a sentimentalist, Mr. Plant."

Jury asked to use the telephone, and Melrose went into the drawing room to join the ladies.

Jury apologized for dragging Constable Pluck from his Christmas dinner, but said he had to speak with Wiggins.

When the voice said, "Yes, sir?" Jury said, "Listen, Wiggins, when you're through dinner, I'd like you to get on to the police in Dartmouth and run down a list of names for me. You'll probably have to go through Central, eventually." Then Jury read off the list, all of them either guests or help at the Goat and Compasses sixteen years before.

Poor Wiggins was not at all happy. "But that's twenty-three names you've given me, Inspector. Those people won't all be around."

"I know. But some of them will be. Perhaps one of them has a good memory." There was a snapping sound in his ear, and then a crunch. Wiggins must be eating a stalk of celery. He mumbled that he'd get onto the list as soon as possible.

As Jury entered the drawing room, Agatha was arranging her skirts within the confines of the openwork calamander chair. Marshall Trueblood would have gone into a swoon, seeing her large frame thus fitted into it. She adjusted her new bracelet and said, "I imagine it was quite dear, wasn't it?" Apparently, she had forgotten her earlier insinuation that the gems weren't real.

"I can tell you exactly what it cost, Agatha—"

"Don't be vulgar, Melrose. It's quite handsome. Of course, it's not *old*, like Marjorie's jewels."

"Who is Marjorie?" asked Jury.

"My mother," said Melrose. "She had a fine collection." He stared up at the ceiling. "I keep them up in the Tower. With the ravens. You can view them for fifty pence, if you like."

"Oh, do stop trying to be funny, my dear Plant. It doesn't suit you."

Vivian rose. "Melrose, it's been a wonderful dinner. But I do have to be going—"

"Good God, why?" asked Melrose, rising also. "You could stick around and help break my alibi—"

"Melrose!" Vivian looked at him as if he were a wayward child.

"But Agatha will need someone's help—"

"Melrose, stop it!" Vivian seemed truly disturbed.

Jury thought she had a way of taking everything a trifle too seriously—not, of course, that these murders weren't serious enough. But clearly Plant was only trying to lighten their load. Perhaps that was the way of it with poets. And policemen. But, no. He could still appreciate Melrose Plant's humor.

"Leaving, are you?" asked Agatha. "Well, I think I must stay for a bit."

"But you trudged up here with Vivian, dear Aunt. Are you going to let her go on her own?"

"I daresay Vivian is old enough to take care of herself," said Agatha, smoothly. "Inspector Jury can give her a ride."

Melrose smiled. "I shouldn't be too saucy with the inspector, Auntie." He was standing in front of his marble fireplace, blowing smoke rings.

Jury helped Vivian into her coat, and Melrose saw them to the door. He said to Jury: "Really, it's hardly sporting for you to take off Vivian and leave me with Agatha."

"I've never been known for my sporting blood, Mr. Plant."

"What can I get for you, Inspector? A drink? Coffee?"

He was quick to let her know this wasn't a social call. "Nothing, thanks. I wanted to ask you a few questions."

She sighed. "Fire away, Inspector. You seem never to go off duty."

At that, Jury bridled: "It's hard to go off duty with four murders."

"Sorry," she said, rubbing her arms, as if the house had grown suddenly cold. "I didn't mean to be flippant about it. It's just . . ." She sat down on the couch and picked up a cigarette box.

Jury sat on the armchair opposite, the coffee table between them. He was almost afraid to get too comfortable. "First of all. I understand you're engaged to Simon Matchett."

Her look, he noticed, as she passed the cigarettes to him, had something in it of a fox run to ground. He lit her cigarette and then his own, hanging on her answer.

"Yes. Yes, I suppose that's true." She rose. "I'm having a drink. I wish you'd join me."

Jury stared at the tiny red coal of his cigarette. "Whiskey."

As she went over to a Welsh dresser and got out glasses and bottles, he looked around the room.

Coming back to him, she said, "About Simon: I'm not really decided." She put the drink in his hand.

He looked at it, wondering if the liquid would turn purple. "You mean you don't know if you're going to marry him? Why not?"

She stood before him, looking off at some distance he couldn't fathom. "Because I don't think I love him."

The furnishings Jury had not really noticed before suddenly began to glow like jewels in the dark. He cleared his throat, wondering if his voice would come out sounding human. "If you don't love him, why marry him? If you don't mind my asking," he added quickly, downing nearly the whole of his drink.

Seated across from him now, Vivian studied her own glass, turning it in her hands like a crystal ball. Then she shrugged, as if reasons were beyond her. "One gets tired of living one's life alone. And he does seem to care for me—"

Jury set down his glass, hard. "What an absolutely insipid reason for marrying."

Her eyes widened. "Well, *really*, Inspector Jury! And what reasons would *you* allow for marrying?"

Jury was out of his chair and over at the window now, staring out at the snow sifting down in the light of the street lamp. "Passion! Besottedness! Sex, if you like. Not being able to keep your hands off someone, or think about anything else!" He turned from the window. " 'Caring'—what a bloody washed-out word *that* is! Haven't you ever felt any of those other things?"

For a moment she just looked at him. "I'm not sure. But apparently you have."

"Never mind about me. How much money do you inherit?"

"A quarter-million pounds, if it's really germane to this discussion." Now her voice had risen several notches.

"Has it never occurred to you Simon Matchett might be a fortune hunter?"

"Of course it has! *Any* man might be!"

"That's absurdly cynical. Plenty of men aren't. Women like you"—and his mind darted to that little picture in the drawer in his flat—"invite disaster. You wrap your vulnerability like a cloak about you and are amazed when someone takes advantage."

"That's hardly cynicism you're describing." Her voice dropped to its normal pitch. "But I must say it's rather poetic."

"Forget the poetry. How well did you know Ruby Judd?"

Her hand went to her forehead. "Good heavens. Talking to you is like trying to grab hold of a whirlwind. You make my head spin."

"Did you know Ruby?"

"Yes, of course. But not well. I used to see her at the vicarage."

"What did you think of her?" As she hesitated, Jury said, "It won't do to stand on false sentiment, Miss Rivington."

"Well, I didn't dislike Ruby. But the way she was always listening in when I was talking with the vicar. The girl was just too curious, that's all. She was always popping in and out. I think Ruby was just a kind of tearaway. I'd heard she's been after most of the men in the village. Oliver. Simon, probably. Even

Marshall Trueblood, if you can believe it. Perhaps Melrose Plant is the only one who escaped." She paused for a moment, then said, "You spoke of fortune hunters." She laughed artifically. "At least I'm sure Melrose isn't."

It was the way she said it. Jury stared blindly at the liquid in his glass, the tiny bit left. Couldn't she have chosen someone else, *anyone* else, to be in love with? Robert Redford, for instance?

"Isabel hates Melrose. I've never been able to discover why."

The reason for that was obvious, if Isabel had Simon in mind for Vivian. But there it was again: Why would Isabel want the money she would most certainly get from Vivian falling into the hands of someone she hadn't any control over, as she apparently had over her stepsister. Unless, of course, she *could* control him. The idea that had taken hold of Jury while talking with Plant made his blood freeze in his veins.

"What difference does it make what your stepsister wants or doesn't want?" he asked.

She answered the question indirectly. "Has anyone told you about my father?" He nodded, and she went on. "It was my fault, you see. I was up on my horse, and he came out to the stables. It was very dark, a moonless night, and he went round behind the horse, and the horse reared up and kicked him." Vivian shrugged stiffly. "He died immediately."

"I'm terribly sorry." Jury thought for a moment. "This happened in the north of Scotland, I understand."

She nodded. "In the Highlands. Sutherland."

"There were just the three of you—you and your father and Isabel?"

"Yes. And an ancient cook. She's dead now."

Vivian was staring into the untouched liquid in her glass as if she might be seeing old faces in a pool.

"How did your sister—stepsister—get on with your father?"

"Not very well. And to tell the truth, I think she's always been angry about not having got more in her own right. From the will, I mean."

"But why should your father have left money to a stepchild he'd only had for—what?—three or four years?"

"That's true, certainly." Vivian took another cigarette from the china box. The first one had turned to a snaky ash in the china tray. She waved her hand, as if to clear away the smoke of the past.

"You were very fond of your father, weren't you?" Still looking down, she nodded. He thought she was close to tears. "According to Isabel, you had got angry with him and run out of the house to the stables, and jumped up on your horse. Do you actually remember doing that?"

She looked puzzled. "Remember? Why, yes. I mean, not exactly."

"It's what you were *told* happened, isn't it? By your—"

"Getting sloshed together?"

Both of them looked around in surprise. Neither had heard Isabel come in. She stood in the doorway among the melting shadows there, looking mysterious and very handsome—if a bit too rich for Jury's blood. Velvet hunter's green pantsuit, Russian amber beads, and that coat of silver mink, which she now had casually hitched over her shoulder. "How are you this evening, Chief Inspector Jury?"

Jury rose and bowed slightly. "Fine, thank you, Miss Rivington."

She walked into the room, tossed the coat on a

chair in a heap, and moved to the Welsh dresser. "Mind if I join you?"

"No, of course not," said Vivian, but without enthusiasm, Jury noticed. Her moral debt to Isabel Rivington seemed to pinch her a bit around the mouth.

Isabel went heavy on the bourbon, splashed some soda into it, and came over to put an arm around Vivian, squeezing her tightly. The gesture struck Jury not so much as affectionate, but proprietary, entrapping. Then she plopped down on the couch, punching the cushions behind her. "You two are certainly pulling long faces. Didn't Melrose feed you properly? You should have come to Lorraine's—quite a spread."

"It was a marvelous dinner," said Vivian a bit snappishly. Jury was glad to see some spirit.

"Simon wasn't very happy at your absence," Isabel added, casually.

Vivian said nothing.

"Unfortunately, the Reverend Denzil Smith was there, so we spent most of the evening listening to stories about priests' holes, and smugglers' holes in coastal inns, and the history of inn signs. These murders have really got him going. And the rest of the time we spent talking about poor old Ruby. It's really dreadful. The vicar said you'd searched the house top to bottom looking for some sort of bracelet. And the girl's diary."

Jury did not reply. He only wished some of these villagers would keep their breath to cool their porridge. Jury looked at his watch. "Thank you for the drink. I must be going."

Vivian walked with him to the door, and as he started down the path toward the Morris, she called, "Wait!" Then she dashed back into the house and returned with a small book which she held out to him.

"I don't know if you like poetry . . . I'd think anyone who quotes Virgil must . . ."

He looked down at the book—a pamphlet whose
cover was thick, dark paper; whose title he couldn't
read in the dark. "I like poetry, yes. This is yours?"

She seemed to be looking all around, everywhere
but at him, clearly embarrassed. "Yes. It's mine. That
was published three or four years ago. It didn't sell
like hotcakes, as you can imagine." When he didn't
answer, she kept on talking, as if trying to fill up the
space between them. "Of course, you don't have time,
I suppose, to read anything but police reports. But
there aren't many poems there, actually. I don't write
all that many. I mean, I find it hard to write even
one . . ."

As her voice trailed off, Jury said. "I'll find the
time."

He spent the night in bed, reading Vivian's poetry.
The poems were certainly not the work of a weak-
minded young woman who lets herself get pushed
about, or who would let herself be talked out of marrying the man she wanted to.

And then he suddenly thought: perhaps the trouble was that Melrose Plant did not want to marry
Vivian Rivington.

The book of poems fell from his hands as he went
to sleep wondering how anyone could not want
Vivian Rivington.

CHAPTER 15

SATURDAY, DECEMBER 26

Sergeant Wiggins told Jury, over a breakfast of sausages, fried eggs, and kippers, that he had rung up the Yard as soon as he'd talked with Jury yesterday and that they'd turned up the addresses of two of the former servants at the Goat and Compasses. "Daisy Trump and Will Smollett, sir. They seem to be the only members of the staff sixteen years ago who're still around. And we've located none of the inn guests as yet. I can try and ring up this Trump woman and Smollett and arrange for you to see them."

"Absolutely," said Jury, helping himself to more kippers. "It was Trump and Rose Smollett who figured most in finding Mrs. Matchett's body."

"Also, I made a few notes here about Mr. Rivington." Wiggins pushed a sheet of paper toward Jury.

Jury read over the half page of neat typing and found the sparse facts there not much addition to what Isabel and Vivian had told him. Except it gave the exact time of the accident, which was what Jury found so interesting.

"Thanks very much, Sergeant. You did a damned good day's work, and I'm sorry I spoiled your Christmas dinner."

Wiggins would rather have a commendation from Jury than a Christmas dinner any time. He smiled, but the smile was cut off abruptly by a coughing fit.

He excused himself to go upstairs and spray his throat.

"Tell Daphne Murch I'd like to see her, will you, on your way?"

Daphne appeared five minutes later, coffeepot in hand. "Were you wanting more coffee, sir?"

"I just wanted to talk with you for a minute, Daphne. Sit down." She did not hesitate at all, having got used to her exalted position as chief witness and friend of Ruby Judd. "Daphne, there are two articles, things that belonged to Ruby, that haven't turned up, and it seems to me they should have: that bracelet, and her diary. Now, you said she never took the bracelet off, right?"

"That's what she said, sir. And it's true—I never seen her without it."

"She wasn't wearing it when we found her."

"Well, that's ever so odd, that is. Especially as she was going somewhere. I mean if she wouldn't take it off to clean and dust, she'd be sure to wear it when she went on a trip, wouldn't she? Maybe the clasp broke, or something. I remember not long ago . . ." Daphne paused and averted her face.

"Yes?"

She coughed nervously. "Oh, it wasn't nothing, I guess. It was up in her room at the vicarage. We'd visit one another. Sometimes she'd come here; sometimes I'd go there. Well we were fooling about—having a pillow fight, actually—and we were really slugging away at each other, so hard Ruby rolled off the bed and right under. That set us laughing fit to kill. I reached down and tried to grab her—just grabbing under the bed—and she held my wrist so hard my bracelet came off. The clasp on it's not very good. Then as I was laughing and trying to get it back, she rolled out from under the bed and said, 'That's funny.' I remember that clear as a bell. 'That's

funny.' Well, she looked like she'd seen a ghost. Or
had some kind of awful shock. She just sat there holding my bracelet and looking like she'd come over
queer. Then she kept looking at *her* bracelet, and she
said, 'I just thought I'd found it,' like she was talking
to herself. I told her to stop acting the fool. She got
up then, but just sat down hard on the bed, and kept
shaking her head. And it wasn't long after that that
she started this business about knowing something,
about having someone on a string."

"What did the bracelet look like?"

"Nothing special. Just a charm bracelet. I do think
the charms were real gold, though. At least, she said
they were, but you never could believe Ruby. I
remember there was one of those little cubes with a
quid inside it. And a tiny horse. And a heart. And
some others I can't remember." She looked at Jury almost fearfully. "You think what's happened to Ruby
had something to do with that bracelet?"

"I wouldn't be at all surprised."

Jury got out of the blue Morris in front of the
Long Piddleton police station and went inside. He
was yanking off his coat when the telephone rang. It
was Detective Sergeant Wiggins.

"I got hold of this Daisy Trump, sir. And also the
Smolletts—or, rather, a cousin who lives next door.
Smollett's away, and the missus died a few years back.
Rosamund, that would be."

Damn it, thought Jury. "What about this other
woman—can I see her?"

"Daisy Trump? Yes. Lives in Robin Hood's Bay.
Up in Yorkshire."

"Get her down here, Sergeant. Wait a minute. You
go up to Robin Hood's Bay—shouldn't take you more
than a few hours. And book a room somewhere for
the Trump woman. My God, is there an inn in the

whole of Northants that a murder's not been done in?
Have we run out altogether?"

Wiggins turned away from the phone and Jury
heard a mumbled conference before the sergeant was
back again. "There's the Bag o' Nails. That's near
Dorking Dean, sir. It's a few miles beyond the Swan."
Wiggins slurped his tea. "Wasn't that the name of
one of the Matchetts' inns?" he asked brightly.

"Yes," said Jury. "It's a fairly common name. Well,
book her in there, and for heaven's sake put a police
guard on the poor woman."

"Yes, sir," said Wiggins. "Superintendent Pratt's
wondering if you could come to Weatherington. He'd
like to go over some details of the case with you."
Wiggins lowered his voice as if London might be listening in. "And Chief Superintendent Racer's been
ringing up in a real state. Is there something I can
tell him the next time he calls?"

"By all means. Wish him a Merry Christmas for
me. Belated, but from the heart." Jury hung up as
Wiggins snickered. No love lost.

Melrose Plant was sitting at the table in the bay
window polishing off a piece of Mrs. Scroggs's veal-
and-egg pie when the door was shoved open and Marshall Trueblood walked in. Trueblood was a person
whom Melrose found he disliked more in the abstract
than in the actual living flesh. On a late winter afternoon over a friendly pint, Trueblood could be an entertaining person.

"Hallo, old bean, mind if I join?" Trueblood was
shaking out his gray cashmere scarf which he draped
over a chair.

"Please do." As Melrose waved his hand toward the
window seat, the door opened again. Smiling, Melrose
added, "Indeed, we might as well make a party of it,
now Her Grace has arrived."

Mrs. Withersby was standing in the doorway, glancing suspiciously around, as if the pub might have changed hands overnight and she could be walking into a nest of thieves and cutthroats.

"Hallo, Withers, old trout," said Trueblood. "Shall you buy this round, or shall I? Let's not haggle now, you're much too generous." Trueblood was counting out some change.

Mrs. Withersby had not put in her teeth today, and when she spoke her mouth caved in toward the back of her head. "Well, if it ain't the owner of the Pansy Palace. Time you bought. I stood the last round, less'n a week past."

"Withers, the last time you ever stood a round was in the ring. What'll it be?"

"Usual," she said, and flopped down beside Melrose, whom she immediately began to upbraid. "Ain't it time you be doin' an honest day's work, me lord?"

Melrose inclined his head politely and offered his gold cigarette case, at the same time pulling back from the onslaught of a combination of gin, garlic, and whichever of her mum's inspired recipes for longevity Mrs. Withersby had been engaging in that day.

"So whatcha doin', me lord, back here in the dark with Pretty Boy, hmm? Hope yer dear auntie don't here of it. Ah! Thank ya, dearie," she continued, changing her tune as Trueblood set her pint in front of her. "Yer a sweetheart, you are, salt of the earth, always did say so. There's others should be as generous." And she cast a malevolent look at Melrose.

"Tell us, Withers," said Trueblood, pleasantly, as he lit up a Balkan Sobranie of bright lavender, "what you think of all the hideous doings in Long Pidd. I hope you've been assisting the police with their inquiries." Trueblood leaned toward her and lowered his voice. "I didn't tell them, of course, that I saw you

crawling down from that wooden beam"—he pointed
toward the window—"on the Fatal Night."

"Piss off, ya pansy! Ya niver seen no sucha thing!"
She drew from her sweater pocket a butt, pinched off
the burned end, and plugged her mouth with the remainder.

She got the butt going, blew the vile smoke in Melrose's face, and said, with pride in her voice, "Flayed
me a skunk this mornin'."

Trueblood, who had taken out a small, silver
penknife, was cleaning his nails. The news did not
seem to perturb him. "Flayed a skunk, you say?"

Mrs. Withersby nodded, beat her empty glass on
the table, looked heavenward and nearly shouted,
"Flayed me a skunk and nailed the carcass to a tree!"
Apparently, she was issuing a warning to whatever
gods were up there. "Me mum always flayed a skunk
when evil was abroad. It keeps off the ghouls—"

The door of the pub swung open once more, and
Lady Ardry appeared, swathed in her Inverness cape.

"Well," said Melrose, "not quite all of them, I see."
He watched as his aunt's eyes peered through the
dark interior and came to rest on their happy band.
What a tableau they must have presented.

She stumped over. "So here you are!"

"Hello, old sweat," said Trueblood, folding up his
little knife and dropping it into his pocket. "Join
us?"

"Yes, do," said Melrose. "Here are your three favorite people in Long Pidd, all foregathered to greet
you." He rose to offer her a chair.

Mrs. Withersby was gumming her greeting when
Lady Ardry, brandishing her stick, nearly decapitated
her. "I must talk with you, Plant." She looked at the
others darkly. "In private."

Trueblood made no move to leave, but simply

drank his bitter. "Have a seat. Withers here has flayed a skunk."

Agatha looked as if she'd gladly drive Trueblood under the table with her stick. "Was looking for you earlier, Mr. Trueblood. Might have known you'd be here imbibing rather than tending to business, and there's your shop standing wide open. Don't you know just anyone could walk in and help himself?"

"True. What'd you help yourself to? Pockets out, now, there's a good girl. Under that cape you could secret my Georgian love seat."

Agatha brandished her stick and Trueblood reared back. "A private word, my dear Plant!"

Melrose yawned. "Oh, why not come along with us to Torquay. We've planned a lovely holiday, and you could make a fourth."

As Agatha banged her stick on the table, Mrs. Withersby jumped up, muttered, and shuffled off.

"Scroggs!" shouted Agatha, as she took Mrs. Withersby's chair, "bring me some of that shooting sherry." But Mrs. Withersby was back.

"If'n it be down this evenin,' if'n it be fell from the tree, then the spell's broke, and the evil's done!" And she slammed her empty pint on the table, this time making Agatha jump.

"What are you raving about, my good woman?"

"Told you," said Trueblood. "About the skunk. We're waiting for it to fall from the tree so's we can all sleep in our beds again."

"Mr. Trueblood," said Agatha with mock sweetness, "you've ten people in your shop all wanting service. Hadn't you better see to them?"

Trueblood drank off his pint and got up lazily. "Never had ten people in my shop in my life. But I can see I'm not wanted. Ta ta." And he took himself off.

"Well, you've managed to clear the table, Agatha. Now what the deuce is it?"

Triumphantly, she announced: "We've found Ruby Judd's bracelet!"

"*What*? And who's 'we'?"

"Myself. And Denzil Smith." She tossed off the Reverend Smith's name so casually that Melrose suspected who had really done the finding.

"They searched that vicarage from top to bottom. Where was it?"

Agatha was overlong in answering. He could visualize some mole in her mind burrowing down for an answer that wouldn't discredit her. "I don't think I should say." Casually, she added: "It was on the premises."

"Meaning, dear Aunt, you don't *know*. The vicar found it, then. He's given it to Inspector Jury?"

"He would do, I'm sure," said Agatha sweetly. "If he could *find* Inspector Jury. He always seems to be darting about the countryside when you need him."

"Have you told anyone else?" Melrose felt uneasy with this discovery floating about the village.

"I? Not *I!* I keep my own counsel. But you know what a gossip Denzil Smith is. I just came from Lorraine's and they'd heard it already." This was said with some irritation; clearly she wished she had got to them first.

Melrose sighed. "Inspector Jury will be the last to know."

"If he'd stay in the village for two minutes running, he might be the first. I've just been to the station. Couldn't get a thing out of Constable Pluck. I've been spending my morning doing what Jury should be doing."

Melrose seriously doubted that, but couldn't resist asking: "And what have you been doing?"

"Systematically questioning the suspects on this

list." She drew from her pocket a bit of paper, wilted like a lettuce leaf, and handed it over to Melrose, at the same time shouting again to Dick Scroggs to bring her sherry and be quick about it. "I've been working my way up the High Street."

Melrose adjusted his glasses and surveyed her list. There were two headings: *Suspects* and *Motives*. "What are all of these *Jealousies* doing under Motives? Who would Vivian Rivington be jealous of? And you've struck Lorraine's name altogether."

"One can see she didn't do it. Ah, here's my sherry." Dick stood over her, waiting to be paid. Melrose dug down for some change.

"Incidentally, we're all going along to the Lord of Mischief for dinner tonight."

Melrose held his glass in one hand, the list in the other. "Who's 'we all'?"

"The Bicester-Strachans. Darrington and that scarlet woman he runs round with. And the light of your life, Vivian." She added slyly: "Simon was at her place when I was there this afternoon."

Melrose ignored this. "How do you know Lorraine wouldn't have been involved in these murders?"

"Breeding, my dear Plant, breeding."

"That explains why her horse wouldn't have done them, but not Lorraine."

Still perusing the list, he noticed his own name was buried among the others, in smaller print, squeezed in between Sheila and Darrington almost as an afterthought. Under Motive was a question mark. "Do you mean you can't think of a motive for me, Aunt?"

She grunted. "Didn't have you down at all, at first. It's that damnable alibi you and Jury trumped up between you."

"I notice, though, that your name is absent."

"Of course, you simpleton. *I* didn't do it."

"But under Trueblood's name you've got *Drugs*. Drugs? What's he to do with drugs?"

She smirked. "My dear Plant. Trueblood *is* in the antiques business, isn't he?"

"I've known that for some time."

"With all of those things he's got coming in from abroad—probably even from Pakistan and Arabia—well, where would *you* secrete hashish or cocaine you wanted to smuggle into the country?"

"I haven't a clue. In my ear?"

"These men who were killed were, what d'ya call them? 'Connections.' Well, it could have been a *gang war*."

"But Creed was a retired policeman." Despite himself, he had to reason with her.

"Exactly, my dear Plant! He was after them, don't you see? The whole dope ring. So Trueblood had to—" And she drew her finger across her throat.

Melrose hated himself for asking. "And Ruby Judd—?"

"A go-between."

"Between who?"

"There's *always* a go-between."

Melrose left it. "Look, Jury must be informed of this bracelet."

Agatha drank off her shooting sherry. "Perhaps Interpol can locate him." She smiled meanly.

Jury sat in the lounge of the Man with a Load of Mischief waiting for Melrose Plant. They had arranged that morning to meet at the Load of Mischief that evening. Jury checked his watch: 8:35.

Jury yawned. *Well, where is he, then?* Looking at his face in the long bar mirror, he saw it distorted by the bronze-tinted glass etched in an elaborate filigree of morning glories and vines. No, he probably really looked that bad. He felt very tired after an afternoon of going over the evidence with Superintendent Pratt.

He also felt sorry for himself, observing the proximity of Vivian Rivington and Simon Matchett at a table in the corner. Near them sat Sheila Hogg and Oliver Darrington, who had been engaged in unfriendly colloquy when he first came in, but who were now putting on smiles for Lorraine Bicester-Strachan and Isabel Rivington. Willie Bicester-Strachan Jury had seen wandering through the rooms, looking for the vicar. He had asked Jury just a few moments ago if he had seen Smith.

Jury heard his name and looked up in the mirror to see Melrose Plant standing behind him. "I—*we*—just got here. Sorry I've been so long, but my dear aunt has been bending my ear for the last hour. She's out in the hall now doing the same to Bicester-Strachan." Plant took the stool beside Jury. "Have you seen Denzil Smith?"

"No, but he's supposed to be here."

Plant seemed concerned. "Look, according to Agatha—"

"Agatha can speak for herself, thank you very much!" She squeezed in between them, shoving Jury aside. "A pink gin, please, Melrose."

As Melrose ordered drinks, he said, "Surprisingly, Inspector, even *I* think you should listen to what my aunt has to say."

Jury noticed that Lady Ardry's ruby-and-emerald bracelet encircled a handsome leather glove. He wondered what had happened to the mittens and felt almost a sense of loss. She regarded him now much as the Queen might have run her eye over some drab of a kitchen girl. "Had you come to *me*, Inspector, I might have been able to give you one or two little ideas."

"I should certainly appreciate your giving them me now, Lady Ardry." Jury tried to look properly abject, and only hoped she would come straight to the point . . . which, of course, she didn't. First she had to arrange a few oddments about her person, the little button on the glove properly seen to, the ratty-looking fox furpiece moved a fraction of an inch, her hair smoothed into no place it seemed to belong. As Melrose put her pink gin in front of her, she was prepared to speak. "This afternoon I paid a visit to the vicar. It was after I'd stopped off at the Rivingtons. And I must say, Melrose, the light of your life Vivian, might be a wee bit more hospitable. If you want *my* opinion, Chief Inspector—"

"And pigs might fly," said Melrose. "Get to the *point*, Agatha."

"You needn't take that tone. There're quite a few little things I discovered during the course of my questioning of suspects that the inspector might pay dear to know." She simpered. Jury kept his countenance and waited patiently. To attempt to hurry her along would only make things worse. "At any rate," she went on, "it's very well to go about ignoring quite obvious things—such as Trueblood's being an antiques dealer—"

"Get to the vicar, Agatha."

"Who's telling this, Melrose?"

He shrugged. "The Ancient Mariner?"

"After my visits to just about everyone on the list—"

"The bracelet, Agatha."

"I'm coming to that."

"Am I to understand this has something to do with the Judd girl's missing bracelet, Lady Ardry?"

"That's the thing I've been trying to tell you, were it not for the constant interruptions of my nephew. I found the brac—"

"*He* found, you mean," corrected Melrose. "You admitted you had nothing to do with the finding."

"Well, *where*, Lady Ardry? We looked the whole house over."

Agatha studied the tips of her shoes. "I'm not sure, but—"

"Oh, hell, Agatha. Smith wouldn't tell you where because he didn't want to have you tell the whole of Long Piddleton."

"That was not the reason." She looked thoughtful. "He didn't want to endanger my life!" Then she looked worried. "Good God, it won't will it?"

Jury felt his scalp prickle. "When did he find it? How long has he known about it?"

"I don't know, precisely. I was with him this morning. He'd been trying to get ahold of you, but you were out gadding—following up wrong leads, no doubt."

"And you actually *saw* this bracelet?"

"Well, naturally!"

"Where is it now?"

"Denzil has secreted it somewhere. He said he was going to put it right back where he found it, it was such a good hiding place. But he wouldn't tell me where." She shoved her pink gin around, sulkily. Then she said, "My whole theory about this whole dreadful catalogue of crimes has to do with Marshall Trueblood's—"

"Marshall Trueblood's what, old twig?" Jury had not seen him come up. Trueblood did not seem at all put out about being talked of behind his back. He smiled happily all around the table. "And listen, love, hadn't you better give back my letter opener before I take it up with the police? You were in the shop alone today, remember?"

Agatha turned red. "I beg your pardon, sir! I want none of your cheap Arabian goods!"

"Oh ho. Not cheap this. Cost me twenty quid, it did. So give it back, will you love." He snapped his fingers several times.

Jury got up from the table and strode over to Bicester-Strachan's group. "Mr. Bicester-Strachan, did the vicar say he was going to be here at some definite time?"

"Yes." Bicester-Strachan took out a big turnip watch. "An hour ago. Eight o'clock sharp, he said."

"Christ," muttered Jury. He rushed back to the table and said, "Mr. Plant, can we use your Bentley?"

They were out of the door before the others could close their gaping mouths.

CHAPTER 16

The knifelike letter opener had been plunged into his chest nearly all the way up to the ivory-carved hilt. The body of Denzil Smith was lying in the middle of the library floor, face up.

Though not a shambles, the library of the vicarage had clearly been searched: books thrown from the now-bare shelves, drawers pulled out, closets opened.

"I don't understand," said Melrose Plant. "If he were after the bracelet, why would the murderer have exposed himself just to retrieve it? Wasn't it only an ordinary charm bracelet to anyone except himself and Ruby Judd?"

"I don't imagine it *was* only to get at the bracelet. Maybe he came for something else: Ruby's diary. One missing article has turned up, and he might have thought the vicar had the other. He certainly couldn't afford to take that chance." Jury went around behind the desk, sat down, and, being careful to use a handkerchief while he did so, called the Weatherington station. He left instructions for Wiggins to come along with the lab crew. Then he called Constable Pluck.

"My God, sir, not another?" Pluck was breathless.

"Yes, another. Now, what I want you to do is get up to the Man with a Load of Mischief straightaway and start getting statements—Simon Matchett, the Bicester-Strachans, Isabel and Vivian Rivington,

Sheila Hogg and Darrington. Also Lady Ardry. Get rid of everyone else."

In a voice that might have been used to discuss a child's serious illness, Pluck said. "I don't know if I can rightly get up there, sir. It's the Morris, see. She's making this funny little pinging noise, I don't—"

"Constable Pluck," said Jury, with charming affability, "you'll have a funny little pinging noise between your ears if you don't get up to the Man with a Load of Mischief immediately. For God's sakes, man! Take anyone's car. Take Miss Crisp's from next door; stop anyone going by in the street—"

At Jury's tone, Pluck must have straightened. Even his voice saluted. "Yes, *sir!*"

Jury banged down the receiver and balled up the bit of paper on which he had doodled a picture of a Morris running into a tree. As he started to toss it in the wastebasket, he noticed a sheet of paper lying half under a piece of lavalike rock that served as a paperweight. Jury pulled it out and looked at what appeared to be disjointed notes made, possibly for a sermon.

"Listen to this," said Jury to Melrose, who was still standing in the middle of the room gazing down at the vicar's body. "Listen, the vicar's made some odd notes here: 'Bacchanals . . . *Hirondelle* . . . God encompasseth us . . .' What on earth do you suppose he means by all that?"

Plant came around the desk and looked down at the paper and shook his head.

"We'll take it along as soon as the fingerprint man goes over it. But, frankly, I certainly haven't a hope of anything turning up by way of fingerprints." He made a survey of everything else on the desk: blotter, ink bottle, pens, a vase of late roses. His eye traveled down the row of open drawers, seeing their contents had been disturbed but not ravaged. There was a squelch of tires outside to the rear of the vicarage, and through the dark pane they could see a flashing blue light, either police car or ambulance. Then the crew from Weatherington came stumbling in, along with Detective Sergeant Wiggins, all of them looking punch-drunk from these constant calls to Long Piddleton. Rain had started and was coming down in sullen, slanting waves, with brief flurries of thunder, like drumrolls from a far-off planet, and spurts of lightning—the perfect night for a murder.

"Who is it this time?" asked Appleby, wearing a smile like a Christmas wreath.

Jury, feeling shabby and guilty about the vicar's death—could he have averted it by being in Long Piddleton instead of Weatherington?—said bleakly, "The Reverend Smith. Denzil Smith. He was vicar of St. Rules."

The police photographer—they always reminded Jury of rather grim-faced tourists—was taking pictures of the corpse from every conceivable angle, bending himself like a contortionist. Jury fingered a cigarette out of his packet and watched the print man with his glass and brush dusting everything from doorknobs to lampshades. One detective constable had stationed himself at the door, one was roaming the upstairs, and one was about to start taking directions in this room from whoever wanted to give them.

When the picture taking was finished, Dr. Appleby bent over the body, and Wiggins stood behind him, notebook in hand. Wiggins looked peaked. And no wonder. Appleby droned on with the details about the manner of death, the condition of the victim— height, weight, years. He put the approximate time as between six and eight that evening. But state of rigor, he said, was not that conclusive. There was a jarring familiarity about everything, as if the same film were being run again and again.

There was another crunch of tires, slamming doors, opening doors, and the stretcher men came in for the removal of the body. They stood mutely at attention waiting for Appleby to give the sign. Appleby finished his cursory examination, and they wrapped the body in a rubber sheet.

When everyone had finished in the library, and the print man had trudged upstairs with a detective sergeant, Appleby lit up. He blew a small smoke ring and said, "I was considering a little cottage here for my retirement. But in the circumstances, I'm not sure it would be a good investment." He snapped up his bag and was at the front door when he turned to tell Jury he would see him. Soon.

"That doctor's got a weird sense of humor," said Melrose.

Jury was back at the desk, plucking the paper up and studying the notes the vicar had made. There had been a smear of ink on his finger, Jury had noticed, and there was a similar smear on the paper.

Car doors outside were opening and slamming shut. Headlights turned the fog yellow as the cars backed up. Wiggins returned and collapsed on the couch, pulling out his handkerchief. Long Piddleton was doing his mythical ailments no good at all. A clap of thunder and a terrified shout from Wiggins made Jury whirl round to see, in a flash of lightning, a shape and a pale face outlined beyond the French window behind the desk. Jury bolted toward the window and then stopped, seeing who it was: "Lady Ardry! What in the *hell*—?"

"Agatha!" exclaimed Melrose.

She stepped inside, dripping buckets of water. "No need for obscenities, Inspector. I've been watching the proceedings."

Jury had had enough. "Wiggins! Slap the cuffs on her!"

Her face went through a selection of random expressions from disbelief to tooth-clattering fear. Wiggins, who had no cuffs and never had, was looking at Jury with wonder.

She found her voice. "Melrose! Tell this crazy policeman he can't—"

Melrose merely lit up a cigar in leisurely fashion. "I'll get you a good solicitor, never fear."

She was about to go for her nephew, when Jury stepped between them. "Very well. We shan't take you in yet. But what were you doing out there?"

"Watching, naturally. I wasn't standing about trying to get a suntan," she snapped.

"I shouldn't take that tone with the inspector, Agatha. *You may have been the last person to see the vicar alive!*"

She gulped and went dead white. She might want to be a witness, but not that much of one. "Well, I followed you. Shortly after you left the inn. Borrowed Matchett's bicycle. Damned unpleasant ride it was, too."

"You stood outside all this time?"

"Got here when that doctor was messing about over the body. I saw it! Trueblood's letter opener! Told you, didn't I?'" Then she must have remembered poor Denzil was a good friend, and she dropped her head in her hands. There were moans.

Jury said to her. "You saw the bracelet here earlier?"

She nodded. "Feel a bit faint. A spot of brandy, perhaps?"

Plant went to get her the drink and Jury sat down opposite her. "Lady Ardry, what was the vicar doing while you were here?"

"Talking to me, naturally."

Jury said impatiently, "I mean, what else?"

"I don't know. Wait a bit. Yes, he was doing his ser-

mon. Trying to make a silk purse out of a sow's ear,
as usual. Some sort of gibberish about church building." She accepted the snifter from Melrose, knocked
back half the drink, wiped her mouth rather inele-
gantly on her new leather glove and looked round
the room bleakly.

Jury produced the paper from the desk. "Does this
look like anything the vicar might have included in
his sermon?"

Agatha got out her glasses, peered closely at the no-
tation on the paper and said, "What's this nonsense?
'God encompasseth us'? Doesn't make sense. Doesn't
sound like Denzil, either. Too religious."

Jury folded the paper and put it in his inside
jacket pocket. "If you saw the bracelet, where was it
then?"

She pointed: "He took it out of the desk drawer."

"And said he was going to put it back in the same
place he found it, is that right?" She nodded. "We've
searched this house top to bottom," said Jury, shaking
his head.

"How about the church?" asked Melrose.

"My God!" said Jury. "Of course—no one thought
of the church. Let's have a look, then." He told Wiggins to stay in the house.

"Stay clear of the dog's side," whispered Agatha as
they made their way up the church walk, she trailing.

"The what?"

"Oh, you know. They always bury a dog underneath unbaptized babies and suicides to keep them
from walking."

"How interesting," said Jury.

Jury had his electric torch, and Plant had got another from the Bentley. The church was damp, very
cold, and lit by spiderwebs of moonlight diffused

through the window traceries. Switching on his torch, Jury let it play over the pews, which ran the length of the nave. Empty squares in the side panelings showed there had once been nameplates—now, democratically, removed. He imagined one of them had been the private pew of Melrose Plant's family. The larger pews were lined with baize or puce. Rows of plainer ones were meant for the farmers and simpler folk, and were unlined.

Since Agatha had no torch and could not get Plant's out of his hand, she held first to one sleeve, then to another. At one point, she caught her heel in the loose, soft carpeting that lay over the brass rubbings and nearly fell. Jury and Plant heaved her up.

"Where the devil are the lights?" asked Jury. No one seemed to know.

They walked down the nave, fanning the aisles with their torches, and Agatha plucking at their sleeves like a blind woman.

There was a rood loft, no doubt rebuilt after the Reformation. A loft staircase had been cut in the masonry. The pulpit was higher than any Jury had ever seen before, one of those eighteenth-century "three-deckers," the pulpit, lectern, and clerk's seat combined in three tiers. A little staircase running up to the pulpit allowed the vicar to ascend.

"I'll just have a look up here," said Jury, mounting the narrow, thin stair. There was a shelf running around the inside of the pulpit, on which were a few books, and he ran his flashlight over them. Only a well-thumbed New Testament, and a Book of Common Prayer.

"Find anything?" asked Melrose.

Jury shook his head, and then noticed the lamp, which was hung over the pulpit on a brass arm. He reached up and pulled the beaded cord. A pool of warm light spread across the pulpit and fanned out through the chancel, where it ended weakly before the altar.

He descended the steps and the three of them walked under the chancel arch, Lady Ardry still plucking at Plant's coat as if the murderer were at that moment breathing heavily in the dark seclusion of one of the unlit aisles. The altar had been freshly decked with flowers for the holiday services. In the dimly lit and damp enclosure, they gave off a fragrance that was heady and exotic. There was a small sacristy in the southeast corner, which opened into the church by a door in the chancel wall. Jury went through it, played his light over the tiny room, and let it stop a moment on the chalice. Perhaps it was his insatiable policeman's curiosity. He walked over to it and drew the napkin off the top.

Inside the cup was a gold charm bracelet.

Quickly, he pulled a handkerchief from his hip pocket, shook it open, and reached into the chalice. He went back out to the altar, where the two others were standing, looking at the altar.

"Goor Lord!" said Agatha when she saw what he was holding.

"In the chalice, if you can believe it."

There was a brief silence as they considered their prize. "But wouldn't it have been found last Sunday?"

"No Communion," said Lady Ardry. "Denzil was always forgetting Communion. Anyway, he'd not have used that. Thought it unsanitary. He used small, silver cups, occasionally."

"You're assuming," said Melrose, "it was Ruby left it there? Before she disappeared?"

"Yes. It was rather clever, really. I think it was a kind of insurance. She knew the bracelet was important, and knew it would eventually be discovered, if she didn't get back to claim it herself. One would almost think she'd a head on her shoulders."

"That," said Lady Ardry, "is doubtful."

When they returned to the Man with a Load of Mischief fifteen minutes later, Jury found that Pluck had managed to arrive and detain the others, and that they were none too happy about it. They were bunched up at the bar: Trueblood, Simon Matchett, the Bicester-Strachans, and Vivian Rivington. Isabel sat alone at the bar drinking a syrupy liqueur. Sheila Hogg, according to Pluck, had left before he got there, apparently in a fit of temper over a flirtation between Darrington and Mrs. Bicester-Strachan.

Jury asked Daphne Murch to bring him cigarettes and read through the statements Pluck had taken down. There was not one of them who could substantiate an alibi for the hour or two before they got to the inn. He seemed to remember Plant's saying that Lady Ardry had been with him during that time, and, if so, she might be clear. But Jury would take a bit of delight in keeping that to himself for a while. As for the others, any one of them could have left the inn here at almost any time without attracting undue attention. It was only a few minutes to the vicarage, and cars were always pulling in and leaving the cobbled courtyard. Jury learned from Pluck's notes that Darrington had driven Lorraine home to get her checkbook. Likely story, that. Sheila Hogg must have thought so too. At one point, Jury remembered Matchett's leaving the lounge bar. And at another, Isabel had been missing. Maybe just to the loo, but, still, there it was. Everyone and no one.

When he looked up from his notes, everyone was staring or fiddling with buttons, or laces, or hair. Jury told Wiggins to go after Sheila Hogg and get a statement from her; he would stay here and follow up on Constable Pluck's notes.

It was Simon Matchett who broke the tension by

saying: "I've a feeling of *déjà vu* about this. One
might think we were all back here the night that man
Small was . . ." But his voice broke over the last
few words.

"How true, Mr. Matchett. And now, if I could see
each of you? Constable Pluck, I think the best place
might be the small room in the front."

"Mr. Bicester-Strachan, I'm sure this is extremely
painful for you. I know you were a very good friend
of the vicar." Bicester-Strachan kept his head averted,
taking out his handkerchief, then stuffing it back in
his pocket. "You were supposed to meet Mr. Smith
here, I believe you said?"

Bicester-Strachan nodded: "Yes. We were to have a
game of draughts after dinner. That is, he wasn't
coming here for dinner, but after he had done his sermon for tomorrow . . ." The voice cracked.

"When did you see him to make these arrangements?"

"Just this afternoon. About two, I suppose it was."
The old man's gaze wandered round the room, as if
he were trying to fix on something to take his mind
off the vicar's death.

"You went outside for a walk—did you leave the
premises?"

"What? Oh, no. Just walked up and down in the
lot. It gets so stuffy in the bar with all the cigarette
smoke. And I was concerned about Denzil." He
looked puzzled. "He's always so prompt." And Bicester-Strachan turned toward the door as if he might
expect the vicar to walk through it, even then.

"Do you recognize this, Mr. Bicester-Strachan?"
Ruby Judd's bracelet was lying on the gate-legged
table, resting on Jury's handkerchief. Bicester-
Strachan shook his head and looked annoyed, as if

Jury really shouldn't be so frivolous as to bring the subject around to jewelry.

"But you knew Mr. Smith had found it this morning."

Bicester-Strachan frowned. "I don't know what you're talking about."

"Didn't the vicar inform you he had found a bracelet belonging to Ruby Judd?"

"Ruby? That poor girl who was . . . yes, I suppose he did. But I didn't think much about it."

Jury thanked him and excused him, thinking the man looked as if he'd aged a good ten years in the course of these two hours.

"Mr. Darrington, you drove Mrs. Bicester-Strachan home for her checkbook, is that right?"

"Yes." Oliver didn't meet his eyes.

"Why did she need it?"

"Why? Good Lord, how should I know?"

"Well, surely, Mr. Bicester-Strachan had money for dinner. Or Matchett would put anything on a chit for any of you, surely."

"Inspector, *I don't know* why Lorraine wanted it."

"Do you recognize that bracelet, Mr. Darrington?"

"It looks vaguely familiar."

An impossible liar, thought Jury. Darrington couldn't keep his eyes from it. "You've seen it before."

Oliver lit up a cigarette, shrugged, and said, "I may have done."

"On Ruby Judd's wrist, perhaps?"

"Possibly."

"According to your statement, you dropped Mrs. Bicester-Strachan at her house, and then went to yours. Why?"

"Why? I wanted some money, that's all."

"Everybody seems short of money tonight. You're

quite sure that you didn't go home with Mrs. Bicester-Strachan?"

"Look here, Inspector! I'm sick of your insinuations—"

"She didn't go home with you?"

"No!"

"I see. Well, that's too bad, in a way. I mean, if she *had* that would have given both of you an alibi, wouldn't it?"

Lorraine Bicester-Strachan pulled her chair as close to Jury as she could get and crossed her silk-stockinged legs. And since her long tweed skirt was buttoned only from the waist to above the knee, it showed a great deal of leg. "No, I've never seen it," she said of the bracelet. "Is it supposed to be mine, found at the scene of the crime?"

Jury was always amazed at the callousness of some people. "Your husband is terribly upset over the death of the vicar. They must have been close friends." She merely flicked the ash from her cigarette over the fireplace fender at that remark. "Of course, it's quite possible friendship—and loyalty—don't mean all that much to you."

"What's that supposed to mean?"

"That information your husband was supposed to have let slip into the wrong hands some time ago. They were your hands, weren't they? Or, at least, your hands passed that information along to someone who was not exactly wearing the Old School Tie."

She might have been sculpted from ice.

"Your lover, right? And also a 'friend' of your husband. And to save your reputation, Mr. Bicester-Strachan let his own go right down the drain. And has continued to do so. *That's* loyalty. Some people even call it love—"

Lorraine leaned toward him suddenly; her hand

flashed out. But Jury merely caught it in midair, almost like a ball, and pushed her back, not overgently, into her seat. "Shall we get back to the present business? Were you bored this evening, Mrs. Bicester-Strachan? Is that why you invited Mr. Darrington home?"

Now she was confused in addition to being furious. There was no way she could tell from Jury's blank expression whether Oliver really had told him anything.

"Well?" asked Jury, amused at the horns of a dilemma on which Darrington and Lorraine found themselves impaled.

"He's lying if he said I went with him." She twisted the diamond circlet of her watchband.

Jury smiled. "I didn't say he said it, Mrs. Bicester-Strachan. I merely made that assumption."

He wanted to laugh at her smugness, at the little half-smile bestowed more upon her own cleverness than upon him. As she walked out, swaying her hips just so, it occurred to him that the idea of Oliver and Lorraine making love in some dark corner was unutterably boring.

Pluck sent in Simon Matchett.

"Ruby Judd's," said Matchett, without hesitation. He rolled his thin cigar in his mouth.

"How are you so sure, Mr. Matchett?"

"Because the girl came over here rather often, to see Daphne. She always wore it."

Jury nodded. "Did you leave the premises this evening? Say, between six and eight?"

"Meaning, have I an alibi? Inspector, I haven't a clue."

Jury asked again, "Did you leave the premises?"

"No. I did go out to check on the electrical box. Something shorted out in the kitchen."

"What time?"

"Around seven, seven-thirty."

"According to this"—Jury indicated Pluck's notes—
"you had gone to Sidbury and got back here at about
six-thirty."

"Yes, as well as I can remember. Shops close there
at six and it takes about half an hour to get back."

"I see." The name of the last shop he had visited
was in the notes. Easy enough to check if he'd been
there. Jury took another tack. "Mr. Matchett, what is
your relation with Isabel Rivington?"

"*Isabel?*"

"Yes. Isabel."

"I don't think I understand you."

"Yes, you do. I get the impression that her feelings
for you are more than friendly. I'm sure you get the
same impression." Jury smiled thinly.

Matchett was a long time in answering. Finally, he
said, "Look, that was all over a long time ago. A *very*
long time ago. At the risk of being less than gallant,
I'll only add, at least for me it's over."

That rather threw Jury. Somehow, he hadn't taken
into consideration that there might have been something in the *past*. It would certainly explain his suspi-
cions about Isabel's feelings for Matchett. "And does
Vivian know about this old liaison?"

"I hope to God not."

Jury glared at him. "A generous thought, Mr.
Matchett."

Isabel Rivington sat across from him, looking ex-
pensively composed. Her deceptively simple dress, of
some coarse, brown material, Jury bet had cost the
earth.

"Where were you, Miss Rivington, before you came
up to the Load of Mischief this evening?" He reached

over and lit a cigarette that she had extracted from a pack she had balanced on the arm of her chair.

"I told Constable Pluck."

He smiled. "I know. Now tell me."

"I went for a walk. Up the High Street. Poked about a bit in the shops. Then I walked up to the Sidbury Road and along the path that goes across the fields."

"Anyone see you?" Isabel did not strike Jury as being much of a walker.

"On the High Street, yes, I imagine so. But not later." As she leaned toward the table to flick ash from her cigarette into the china tray, her eye went to the bracelet. She said nothing, and leaned back.

"Have you seen that bracelet before, Miss Rivington?"

"No. Why?"

"What is your relationship with Mr. Matchett?"

The sudden change of subject startled her. "Simon? What do you mean? We're friends, is all."

Jury made a sound in his throat which he hoped suggested that he didn't believe her, and changed the subject again. It was the question he had been burning to ask her for two days. "Miss Rivington, why have you let Vivian live all of these years with the idea she was responsible for her father's death?"

Mouth open, cigarette frozen in position, she looked as waxen as a dressmaker's dummy. When she spoke, her voice was unnatural, the pitch high and shaky. "I don't know what you mean."

"Come now, Miss Rivington. Assuming it was an accident at all, it was you up on that horse, wasn't it? Not Vivian?"

"She remembered? Vivian remembered?"

Well, he thought, with a sigh of relief, there it was. If she could have maintained more control, she might have swaggered her way through. After all, he had no

proof. "No. She didn't remember. It was just that neither your story nor hers made much sense. And her
story seemed almost learned by rote. From you, I expect. Vivian was obviously very fond of her father,
and if the little girl was anything at all like the
woman, she hardly seems the type to have been always rowing with him. But mainly, there was that description both of you gave of the night in question.
'It was very dark, a moonless night' when she supposedly went out to the stables. Now, she was only
eight, and though it's certainly possible a child of
that age might be up after dark, this is *Sutherland*
we're talking about. I've an artist friend who loves
the Highlands, loves to paint there. Not only because
it's beautiful, but because of the light. He jokes about
being able to stand on a street corner and read a
book at *midnight* because it's still light. It's highly
unlikely a little girl would be all dressed and dashing
about at *midnight.*" Jury drew the typed report on
James Rivington from the folder which he had been
holding. "Time of accident: eleven-fifty P.M. I'm surprised the police didn't make more of that at the
time." He had watched Isabel grow progressively
paler as he talked. "So I came to a couple of different
conclusions: whether or not the horse business was an
'accident' or deliberate on your part, I don't know. I
envision something like this: you're up on the horse,
the horse kicks your stepfather, you rush to your little
sister's room, pull some clothes on her, and bring her
down to the stable. You don't even need to put her
up on the horse. All you had to do was implant the
idea in her mind that she was on it. And over the
years you kept insinuating into her mind a lot of nonsense about the 'fights' she had with Rivington, to
keep her feeling guilty, to keep her under your influ-
ence as much as possible." Jury, who seldom allowed
himself an editorial comment, could not help it now:

"How vile, Miss Rivington. How utterly vile of you. Why did you kill him? That will of his must have been an enormous disappointment to you."

Her mouth was so red against the pallor of her skin, she looked like someone in pretty clown makeup. "What are you going to do?"

"Make a bargain with you. You'll have to tell Vivian—" When she started to protest, he held up his hand. "—Tell her enough of the truth so she won't have to be weighed down under what must be unbearable guilt. Tell her you caused the accident. You may give as your reason for foisting it off on her that if you had had to admit to the authorities you were the one on that horse, they would have had you up for manslaughter. You can put on a big act of having been terrified, et cetera, et cetera. Cry a bit. I'm sure you can manage it. You've been deceiving her for twenty years; I'm sure you can bring off one more deception."

Some of the color had returned to Isabel's face, and much of the old hauteur. "And if I don't? You can't prove one damned thing!"

Jury leaned forward. "That may be. But remember that you've got a lovely, lovely motive for murder, haven't you?"

"That's absurd—"

Jury shook his head. "And if you don't tell her, be damned sure *I* will. And I may leave out that it was an accident."

She shot out of the chair and made for the door.

". . . *And,* Miss Rivington, all I need do is drop a word in somebody's ear around here and you'd be finished."

At the door she whirled round. "That's absolutely unethical. No decent policeman would do such a thing."

"I never claimed to be decent, did I?"

* * *

Vivian sat across from Jury, in a plain rose-wool dress, clasping and unclasping her hands. "I can't believe it. Whoever would want to hurt the vicar? That harmless old man."

"The victims usually *are* harmless. Except to the murderer. Do you recognize this bracelet, Miss Rivington?" And he shoved it toward Vivian.

"That's the one he found."

"You knew about it, then? When did he tell you?"

"Today. This afternoon sometime. I'd just stopped round to the vicarage to chat with him."

Jury's heart sank. "What time was that?"

"Oh, about five. Perhaps later. I'm not—" Her hands went to her face. "Not again. You're not going to tell me I was about when another one's happened."

"I'm not going to tell you anything, no." Jury smiled, but didn't feel like it. Why the hell didn't she stay home and write poetry? He looked at the notes Pluck had made. "Were you at home after that? Between the time you left the vicarage and the time you got here?"

"Yes." Her head was bent over her lap and her hands were pleating her skirt.

"Would you like a brandy, Miss Rivington? Something?" Jury said gently. He ducked his head down a bit, trying to get a peek at her face. From the way her shoulders moved, he judged she was crying—yes, he was sure of it. Automatically, he reached out a hand to her, then jerked it back. He felt utterly bleak, imagining her face—which he couldn't see—all screwed up like a child's. He took out his folded handkerchief and put it in her lap. Then he got up, moved some distance from her over to one of the windows, and went on from there.

"Were you with your sister when you went home?"

Still not looking up, she shook her head. "No. Isabel had gone out."

"And the maid?"

Vivian blew her nose. "Gone, too."

Jury sighed. Worse luck. "Thanks, Miss Rivington. Could I have someone see you home? Constable Pluck?"

She was up now, but still looking down at the floor. She shook her head. The left hand still held his handkerchief, and the right pleated her skirt. She said nothing, and with her head still bent, walked to the door.

"Miss Rivington!"

She turned.

Jury felt wretched. "That's a, ah, pretty dress." *Idiot*, he added, furious with himself.

But she smiled slightly. Finally, she looked up at him, her face so deadly serious, her gemstone eyes so earnest, that he was suddenly terrified she was going to confess to the murders, the whole lot of them.

When she opened her mouth to speak, he very nearly put out his hand to stay her words. "Inspector Jury—"

"It's all right—"

"I'll wash your handkerchief." She turned and walked out of the room.

"Lady A's going to slap the cuffs on me momentarily, Inspector." Marshall Trueblood crossed one leg primly over another. "She's quite convinced I'm the one. Dear me, I wouldn't say boo to a goose. Much less kill the dear old boy."

"When did you last see that letter opener, Mr. Trueblood?"

He studied the ceiling for a moment, then said, "I can't say for sure. A couple of days ago, perhaps."

"Do you often leave the shop unattended?"

"I pop into Scroggs's place, it's only just next door; yes, without locking up."

"So this afternoon, anyone could have walked in and out again, and you'd have been none the wiser?"

"Yes, but why would anyone *want* to? Isn't there something called modus operandi, Inspector? I mean, why a knife, this time? The others were strangled." Trueblood bethought himself. "Forgive me for putting it in just that way."

"Not at all. Indeed, that's perceptive of you, Mr. Trueblood. I would assume the knife might serve the same purpose as did the book by Darrington left at the Swan with Two Necks: it would serve to implicate someone else. Who was in the shop today?"

"Well, Miss Crisp came over from her own sweat shop to see if she could palm off a few cheese-parings on me. I think that woman does business with the tinkers and then tries to tell me—*me*, mind you—the silver's Georgian. Gypsy would be more like it—"

Jury sighed. "If we could just stick to the point, please?"

"Sorry. And then there was a couple from Manchester, leaving trails of coal dust, looking for Art Deco, that ungodly stuff; then Lorraine, looking for Simon Matchett, who she must have been chasing down the High Street, then—I don't know." He lit up a pink cigarette.

"When did you first miss the knife?"

"Letter opener, dear. This afternoon. After Lady A came over to Scroggs's and generally cleared the place out with her inimitable presence."

Jury watched Trueblood's eye travel to the bracelet, look away, and then bend to peer at it. "Where'd you get that awful piece? Isn't that the Judd girl's?"

"You recognize it, then?"

"Yes. Tawdry bangle." He leaned back and clapped

his hand over his mouth in mock horror. "Probably just condemned myself out of my own mouth—well, what with my letter opener in the body of poor old Smith—it's a dead cert, isn't it?" Beneath the bantering tone, he did look a bit ashen.

"There's motive to consider, after all. Is there anything in your past, Mr. Trueblood, you'd prefer not to be made public?"

Trueblood looked genuinely astonished. "Are you kidding, old twig?"

CHAPTER 17

Jury and Plant sat in the bleak dawn of the Long Piddleton station. Jury stared down at the paper which he had taken from the vicar's desk and said, "If it wasn't notes for a sermon, what was it?"

Melrose Plant looked over Jury's shoulder. " 'God encompasseth us.' That doesn't sound like the Reverend Smith. For the first time in my life, I agree with my aunt."

"Then it's a quotation, perhaps. Biblical?"

Plant took up the paper. " 'Hirondelle.' French for 'swallow.' Swallow? Does that mean anything to you?"

Jury shook his head. They sat for a good five minutes looking at the words until Jury threw down his pen in disgust. "I guess I'm just dim. But I can't make it out." He picked up his cigarettes, took one and lit it, saying around the draw, "I'm simply going to assume—though I could be dead wrong—that the murderer might have come to pay a 'friendly' call on Mr. Smith to see if he could get any information out of him. He wanted to find out how much the vicar knew. And that while they talked, it occurred to the vicar that this caller might be guilty of these murders. So he sat quietly at his desk making these notes. Why not simply write down the name of the guilty party? It must have been Smith thought his life was in danger, and that the murderer would certainly have gone about removing anything incriminating from the premises. I think we've been underrating Mr. Smith. And I only hope he hasn't overrated *us*. He was hoping we'd be smart enough to hit on something the murderer couldn't." Jury smoked and thought. "Well, that theory's possible. Anyway, I've nothing to lose by assuming the note meant something. But perhaps quite a bit to lose if I ignore it." He got up and stretched. Then he tossed the paper to Melrose Plant. "There. You can do the *Times* crossword in fifteen minutes. Then you can figure this out."

Plant's reply was interrupted by the *brr-brr* of the telephone.

"Jury here."

"Inspector Jury," said Chief Superintendent Racer with extravagant politeness, "there have been three more murders since you've got there. What've you been doing? Advertising?"

Jury sighed inwardly, and started looking through Pluck's desk drawers for something to eat. He found a package of stale digestive biscuits. "Ah, Superintendent Racer. I was hoping you'd call." He munched a biscuit.

"Oh, weren't you *just*, Jury. *I've called every day since you've been there, lad.* And got no reply—you're chewing in my ear, Jury! Can't you forgo the food and drink long enough to report, lad? A publican, a caterer, that's what you should've been! Well, this tears it, Jury. You can expect me in Northants at noon tomorrow. No, that would be noon *today.* The way I make it out is this, Jury. Today is the twenty-seventh. You got there on the twenty-second. Not counting today, that would average out to approximately two-thirds of a murder for every day you've been there!"

"Yes, sir. I suppose it does rather work out that way. Fractionwise." Jury doodled little replicas of inn signs on Pluck's blotter while Racer went through the litany of punishments which awaited his chief inspector. These ranged from being drawn and quartered, and his head stuck up on Tower Bridge, to being put back together again so that he could be delivered in a wagon to a place of public execution. The superintendent's punishments always leaned toward the medieval.

"Sorry so little progress has been made, sir. But it's difficult enough having *one* murder; remember, I've got four here."

"If you can carry the calf, you can carry the cow, Jury."

"It's doubly difficult, sir, it being Christmas—"

"Christmas? *Christmas?*" Racer made it sound like a new holiday only recently forced into the calendar by Parliament. Then, softly, he continued. "Strange, isn't it, Jury, how sex maniacs are still prowling the woods on Christmas. Did the Ripper stop for Christmas, Jury? Did Crippen?"

Jury took the opportunity. "I don't actually believe Jack the Ripper was in the alleys on Christmas Day, sir. As I remember it—"

Silence. "Are you being funny, Jury?"

"Oh, no. It's hardly a joking matter, is it?"

Another silence. Then Racer snapped. "Expect me there on the noon train. And Briscoe's coming with me, too."

"Very well, then, sir. If you insist." Jury started doodling a tiny engine with a puffing smokestack crashing head-on into another train. Jury was holding the receiver a few inches from his ear, and the strident voice of Racer darted into the room.

"And furthermore, I don't want a bed in any of your roach-ridden pubs or flash houses, either. Get me digs in the best place around—" He dropped his voice "—And try to find one where I won't be throttled in my sleep. With only *you* to protect me,

I'm nervous, lad. And make sure the place has a decent menu and stocks its wine cellar. And, preferably"—the lasciviousness in his voice was palpable— "has a decent-looking wench at the bar."

How about a Hell Fire Club? wondered Jury.

". . . Though I expect in a one-eyed town like that you can't have everything. I'll see you later." Racer slammed down the telephone.

"Yes, sir," said Jury, yawning into the dead receiver. As he dropped it back in place, Plant said:

"Friend of yours?"

"Chief Superintendent Racer. He doesn't care for the way. I'm handling the case. Coming here himself and wants to be put up—at the Savoy, actually. Wants the best place in the village." Jury grinned wickedly.

"Well, look, old chap, I'd be happy to give Ruthven a jingle—"

Jury was shaking his head and moving the phone toward Plant. "I wasn't thinking of Ardry End."

Melrose stopped in the process of lighting a cigar and grinned at Jury through the smoke. "I think I take your meaning." He dialed, waited a longish while, and there came an answering squawk. "Aunt Agatha? Sorry to get you up so early. But Inspector Jury wonders, would you do him a big favor . . . ?"

An hour later they were still going back over the vicar's notes, when Wiggins and Pluck came in, shaking a light dust of snow from their coats. "She's here, sir," said Wiggins. "Daisy Trump."

Pluck broke in: "We've put her up at the Bag o' Nails just outside Dorking Dean. Wouldn't stay at any of the other inns, she wouldn't, and I can't say's I blame her. And we left a local copper with her, you never know what's the next inn'll be hit, now, do you?" Pluck was clearly enjoying his role in all of this.

"Who's Daisy Trump?" asked Plant.

Wiggins was about to answer, and seeing he might be divulging privileged information, shut up like a drawer.

"It's all right, Constable. Mr. Plant's been helping me." Then he turned to Melrose. "Let's go along there, then, to the inn."

"You want *me* to go?"

"Yes, if you wouldn't mind. Wiggins can man the fort, here. And Constable Pluck can drive."

Pluck beamed and saluted.

Miss Trump, according to the waitress who served them their coffee at the Bag o' Nails, had gone up to her room just to have a wash and would be with the gentlemen directly.

"Daisy Trump," said Jury, spooning sugar in his coffee, "worked at the Goat and Compasses. Funny name, that. It's no wonder your aunt can't get our English names straight. *Bister-Strawn* instead of *Bicester-Strachan*, that sort of thing."

Plant smiled. "And *Ruthven, Ruthven, Ruthven*, instead of *Rivv'n*." Plant caught his breath and stared at Jury. "Pluck."

Jury grinned. "Oh, I think even your aunt can say *Pluck*."

Plant was not smiling. He merely said, once again. "Pluck!"

Jury stared at him.

"Get Pluck in here, man!"

Jury was so unused to Plant's giving him orders, that he did as he was bid. In a few moments he was back with the puzzled Constable Pluck in tow.

"Say it again, Pluck!" ordered Melrose, without preamble, his green eyes glittering.

Poor Pluck stood there, bunching his cap in his

hands, like a man just called up for poaching on his lordship's acreage. "Say what, my lord?"

"What you said before. When you and Sergeant Wiggins came into the station. Go on, man, go on!"

Pluck looked at Jury for support. Jury merely shrugged, but said, "You said you'd got Daisy Trump, and . . ." Jury's voice trailed off.

Melrose was nodding. "Right, *and* you put her up—" He was nodding at Pluck, trying to wrench the words out of him.

Pluck scratched his head stupidly. "Yessir. I said we put her up at the Bag o' Nails."

Melrose looked at Jury, but Jury was as blank as Pluck.

"That's it! That's it!" said Plant, closing his eyes and mouthing words silently. Lady Ardry would have pointed this out, no doubt, as the habitual manner of crazy Melrose.

"Yes, that's it! How could I have been so stupid!" Melrose's usually sober face split in a broad grin. "Say it again, Pluck."

"Ah, you mean Bag o' Nails, sir?"

"You hear it, Inspector? It's that it sounds differently when Pluck says it, since his diction—you'll pardon me, Constable—is not quite precise. He slurred it a bit. Come on, Inspector. *'Bag o' Nails.'* "

Jury suddenly clapped his hand to his head. "My God. *Bacchanals!*" He looked at Pluck, who seemed straight out of it, his brow furrowed in puzzlement. Just as well, since Jury didn't want the Town Crier wise to the business. "Constable, go back to the station and tell Sergeant Wiggins to sit by the telephone. I'll probably be calling him."

Pluck saluted, turned smartly, and left.

"And now, Inspector," said Melrose Plant, "the Goat and Compasses. Say that two or three times and slur it."

Jury did so, silently mouthing the words. "God encompasseth us! Matchett. It's Matchett! Those were two of the inns. But what was the third. There's no inn named 'Hirondelle.' "

"Of course not. It's a derivative name, like the others. Good lord, no wonder the vicar thought you might be able to pick up on the message. He'd been talking to us about inn signs. You were right, we did underrate him. How damnably clever."

"And brave. How many people would have that presence of mind?"

"What was the name of Matchett's third inn?"

Jury was already looking through the papers he'd brought with him, the folder on the Matchett case. ". . . Goat and Compasses. Devon, Devon . . . here it is. Well, I'll be damned."

"What's the name?"

"The Iron Devil."

Daisy Trump was in her early fifties or thereabouts—a round little person, like a ball about to bounce away. She could not, she said, imagine what Scotland Yard would want with the likes of her, but she seemed to be regarding all of this as a holiday, with the government paying expenses. Her hair looked newly permed.

"You've lived in Yorkshire how long, Miss Trump?"

"Oh, these ten years, I'd say. Went up there to keep house for my brother after my sister-in-law died, God rest her—"

Jury broke in before the biography got too involved: "You were chambermaid at an inn in Devon, Dartmouth it was—run by a Mr. and Mrs. Matchett, about sixteen years ago, Miss Trump?"

"Aye. Where that awful murder happened. Is that why you wanted to see me? The madam, it was. And they never found who done it, whoever it was broke into her study that night and made off with the money."

"You remember the Smolletts, I expect? She was cook, but I'm not sure just what he did."

"Nothing mostly. Right old layabout was Will Smollett. Rose was my very best friend. Dead now, poor soul." And here a handkerchief was brought out from the sleeve of her dress for a ritual pass at her nose. "Dear Rose. Salt of the earth. That husband of hers just did odd jobs from time to time. Him and that Ansy-the-Pansy." She sniffed.

Jury smiled. "And who was that?"

"Queer as 'a fruitcake, was that one. But him and Smollett was thick as thieves."

Jury remembered nothing in the report of such a person. "What was his name? I mean, besides his adopted one?"

Daisy Trump shrugged. "Andrew, maybe. I don't rightly remember. 'Ansy' we called him. Yes, it must have been Andrew."

"We've been trying to locate Mr. Smollett to see if he might remember anything. I don't suppose you keep in touch—?"

"No more I don't, not since Rosie died. Went to her funeral. They was living somewhere outside London. Crystal Palace, I think." She asked if she might have another cup of tea.

Jury signaled the waitress, and said, "Do you think you could remember the events of that evening? I know it's been a long time, but—"

"Remember? I should say. I only wish I could *forget*, sometimes. What with *me*, mind you, even being suspected. They wanted to know did I drug the poor woman's cocoa. Well, I told them, Mrs. Matchett was always taking them sleeping draughts at night. But it just seemed this evening she'd taken more'n was

usual. It was me always took the tray to the madam's
office of an evening. And then either Rose or me, one
of us, would come and get it. That night it was Rose,
poor thing. And don't think she didn't get a proper
shock, seeing the missus bent over the desk that way.
At first she just thought she'd fallen asleep. But then
she saw how the room'd been messed about. All the
money gone. Though I still say, it was little enough
to kill somebody for. A few hundred quid—"

Jury broke in, saying: "Part of the inn—a courtyard—had been turned into a theater, is that right?
And the room Mrs. Matchett used was just down a
narrow hall from the stage?"

"That's it, sir. I think she always wanted to know
just what Mr. Matchett was up to. I wonder he ever
could have got out from under her eye long enough
to get mixed up with this girl, to tell the truth."

"Harriet Gethvyn-Owen."

"Aye. That was it. Fancy name for a fancy piece of
goods, was that one." Jury smiled. "Much younger'n
him. But he was younger'n the missus, too, I wonder
he married her in the first place. For a soft berth,
maybe."

Jury drew the charm bracelet out of his pocket,
wrapped in the handkerchief. "Did you ever see this,
Miss Trump?"

She took the bracelet, looked it over carefully, then
raised a shocked face to Jury: "Where did you get
this, sir? This here bracelet—it was the madam's.
Stake my life on it, I would. The reason I remember
it so well is, each one of these little charms had some
special meaning, though I don't know what each
stands for. This fox—she liked to ride to hounds. And
this here little cube with the money in it. She had
some kind of bet on with Mr. Matchett, I remember . . ." Daisy was looking at the bracelet in wonder.

"There was a play on that night, wasn't there.

Othello? Mr. Matchett played the lead and the girl—Harriett Gethvyn-Owen—was in it, too. Playing Desdemona?"

"I don't remember which play. Morbid thing it was. But then I'm not quite smart enough for that sort of thing. As I went along with the tray to the madam's office, I could hear him, Mr. Matchett, shouting at one of the other actors."

"Yes. And—?"

"I was about to leave the tray outside, when I noticed the door was open a bit, and Mrs. Matchett asked if that was me, and would I just put the tray inside on the little table by the chair, and so I went in."

"Where was Mrs. Matchett?"

"At her big desk, like always. She thanked me and I left."

"Do you think you could actually close your eyes and envision the room, Miss Trump? And then describe exactly the proceeding as you see it in your mind's eye?"

Obediently, Daisy clasped her eyes shut as if Jury were a stage hypnotist. "She says to me, through the door, that is—'Daisy. Please put the tray on the table by the chair.' Then I goes in, sets down the tray, and she says to me, kind of over her shoulder like—'Thank you.' And I asks her—'Will there be anything else, mum?' She says, 'No, thank you.' Then she goes back to her books. She kept all the money accounts. Clever woman, was the missus. But cold-like. Not like Mr. Matchett, not at all. Ever so nice, he was. Popular with the ladies, and I don't wonder, him being so handsome, and all. That's what bothered her so much. I just know she kept that office there so near to that theater to let him know she was always there. Kept him on a short string, I can tell you. Jealous. I never did see a woman so jealous."

"Who did you believe killed Mrs. Matchett?" asked Jury.

Without hesitation, like a primed pump, she said, "Why, a thief, of course. Just like the police finally said. Got in the window and made off with everything." She lowered her voice. "To tell the truth, I even wondered about that Smollett and Ansy-the-Pansy. Wouldn't have put it past either of them. Though I'd not have mentioned it, not for the world, because of Rose, you see."

"Everyone there at the time seems to have been cleared, though, Miss Trump, including the help."

She only sniffed, still unconvinced.

"But didn't you also suspect her husband, Matchett?"

With admirable frankness, she said, "Of course. Rosie and me heard them fighting over and over again, in the room just over the kitchen. Going on about how he wanted a divorce. She could yell like a banshee when she got going. Well, that was the missus. What was hers was hers, and she meant to keep it, even if it didn't want to be kept. I remember both Rosie and me thought right away when she was killed, 'Well, there he's gone and done it.' But then the police decided that not him nor his girl friend could have done it. What do them French call it? Crime-something?"

"*Crime passionnel,*" said Jury, smiling.

"Lovely word, that is. See, it had to do with the times: she had to be killed between the time I brought her her cocoa and Rose came to collect the tray, when she discovered the poor woman's body. They'd got it down to the minute, nearly. And Mr. Matchett, nor his fancy lady, they couldn't have done it because they were both in this play the whole of that time. And poor Rosie, beside herself, she was—"

Something had turned over in Jury's mind, like the

leaf of an old book. Devon. Dartmouth was in Devon. Could he really have been so blind? Rose. Rosie. Mrs. Rosamund Smollett. Will Smollett. *"Down to see her Aunt Rose and Uncle Will."* Mrs. Judd's words came back to Jury. Will Smollett. William Small. Hardly took much imagination to make that change.

From the folder he took pictures of Small and Ainsley and passed them over to her. "Miss Trump, do you recognize these men?"

She picked up the one of Small and studied it closely. "I should say I do. That's the living image . . . I mean, yes, that's Will. Only he had a mustache." Her eye moved to the second picture. "Dear God in heaven, if it ain't the image of Ansy-the-Pansy. Only he *didn't* have no mustache."

"Not Andrew," said Jury, "Ainsley. 'Ansy' stood for Ainsley."

Daisy was staring at him. " 'Ainsley. *'Ainsley.* That's it. But we was always kidding him about dropping 'is 'aitches. His name was *Hainsley. Rufus Hainsley.* 'Can't you even get your own name straight?' we used to kid him."

Like Smollett simply changing his name to Small, thought Jury.

"But where'd you get these pics, sir?"

Jury didn't answer that. "Did the Smolletts have a niece who stayed with them sometimes?"

"Didn't they ever!" Daisy raised her hands in mock horror. "Ruby. Little Miss Curious, into everything. But there you are: with a mum and dad what shoved her off whenever they'd a mind to, what could you expect from the little beggar?"

Jury held up the bracelet. "She might have stolen this, then?"

"That? Not likely, sir. Mrs. Matchett, she wore it all the time, she did, she was that attached to it. Almost like some women feel about their wedding rings.

Oh, no. Ruby wouldn't lay hands on that. Not unless it was over the madam's dead body."

Daisy Trump left, to be driven in style by the county constabulary back to Yorkshire. Jury sat at the table, his cold coffee pushed to one side, and stared at the diagram of the office Celia Matchett had occupied that fatal night at the Goat and Compasses. Matchett had to have killed his wife; it was his only motive for the present murders. Ergo: this little scene in the office had been staged for an audience of one—Daisy Trump, the only witness to Celia Matchett's still being alive at that moment. But she wasn't alive then, Jury would have bet his badge on it. Ergo: the woman at the desk was not Celia Matchett, but a stand-in. And the only likely prospect for that was the mistress, Harriet Gethvyn-Owen. People see what they expect to see, and Daisy Trump had expected to see Celia. From behind, a certain costume, a wig, perhaps, and the room in shadows.

That still left the problem, seemingly insurmountable, of the alibi. Jury read the police report again. Both Matchett and the Gethvyn-Owen woman were supposed to have been on the stage when Celia Matchett was murdered. There were all of those witnesses—the entire audience. Jury considered the role of Othello. That called for very heavy makeup for the Moor, a good enough disguise for anyone. But had someone else, another actor, taken Matchett's place for that performance that would mean yet another conspirator, and that was even more unlikely. Or was it? Could one of these three men—Ainsley, Creed, Small—have been in on it? Not that way, certainly. There wasn't a big enough one among them and they hardly seemed the type to walk out on a stage. And, anyway, if it were merely a case of having someone take his place on stage, why would it be necessary to have his mistress imitate Celia in her office?

Jury gave it up, totally frustrated. He got up and looked out of the window, to where Melrose Plant was lounging beside the blue Morris, talking with Constable Pluck, who was supposed to have gone back to the station a good half hour ago. Jury sighed and cranked out the window.

"Constable Pluck, would it inconvenience you too much to carry out my orders?" Jury yelled.

"Oh, I have, sir. Been to Long Pidd and back again. I thought you'd be needin' the Morris, sir."

"I see. All right, thanks. And Mr. Plant, would you mind coming in here for a bit? I want to talk with you about something."

Plant detached himself from the car and Pluck and came inside.

Jury ordered up some more coffee, then said, "I want you to put your mind to this. I'm sure Matchett killed his wife at that inn in Devon. But the question is, How the devil did he manage it?"

Jury reviewed all of the facts in the case, ending with, "The snag is, of course, their alibi. They neither of them could—to all appearances—have been near Celia during the time the police fixed for her murder."

"But isn't that done all the time, Inspector? I mean, you kill someone and then stuff them down a well, or something, and have someone else take their place for the crucial time period to fix your alibi?"

Jury shook his head. "Done, yes. Only not here. Celia Matchett *was* alive before the play started. At least half-a-dozen persons saw her, under varying circumstances just before the play. So the problem remains. How could the man be in two places at once?"

Plant was thoughtful. "Well, in a sense, an actor is always in two places at once—"

"I don't follow."

"When did the play start?"

Jury opened the folder: "Eight-thirty, or a few minutes after."

"And when was Celia—or the other woman, that is—seen in the office?"

Jury turned a page and ran his finger down it. "About ten-forty, from what Daisy Trump said."

For a good two or three minutes, Plant was silent, smoking. His green eyes seemed to illumine the dark corner in which they sat. Finally, he said, "The play's the thing, Inspector."

"I beg your pardon? You're not saying you know how he did it?"

"Yes. But I'd rather show you than tell you; I will have to make arrangements, so pardon me whilst I ring up Ruthven." And before Jury could protest, Plant was heading for the telephone.

A half hour later, Pluck deposited Jury at the Long Piddleton station. Wiggins was inside, ministering to himself with nosedrops.

"I'll be at Ardry End, Wiggins."

"Yes, sir. But Chief Superintendent Racer's here—I mean, *was* here. He's gone off with Superintendent Pratt to Weatherington."

"Never mind that. Look, I want you to hop it up to the Man with a Load of Mischief and keep an eye on Matchett. Don't let him out of your sight, but don't let him know it."

Wiggins was astonished. "You mean you suspect him?"

"That's right, Sergeant. And another thing—" Jury broke into a coughing fit. He hoped to God he wasn't catching one of Wiggins's nameless diseases. He blew his nose and went on: "Another thing: when Superintendent Racer returns—if you should happen to forget just where I've gone, well, it's all right, I won't hold it against you."

Wiggins smiled broadly. "I've a rotten memory, sir. But here—" He reached in his pocket and brought out a brand new box of cough drops. "You best take these. Oughtn't to neglect a cough like that, you know." Wiggins was delighted to share his pharmacopoeia with his superior.

Jury tried to give them back: "I don't really need—"

But Wiggins, if sometimes uncertain about matters of police procedure, was not to be toyed with here. "I insist. Put them in your pocket."

Meekly, Jury did as he was bid.

CHAPTER 18

When they walked into the drawing room of Ardry End, Jury was surprised to see both Lady Ardry and Vivian Rivington.

Agatha seemed equally surprised to see Chief Inspector Jury. "So there you are! I suppose you realize that Superintendent Racer—a most unpleasant man, I must say—has been trying to track you down ever since he got here?" She seemed clearly torn between aiding and abetting Racer's cause and being privy to her bit of information. She wheeled on Melrose Plant. "I asked you when you called where he was, Plant, and you said you'd not seen him all day."

"I lied."

"And just where is Superintendent Racer?" asked Jury, wanting to make sure he knew which places to avoid.

"I'm sure *I* don't know. Had his room all nicely done up—always happy to do *my* part—and the dreadful man walked in, took one look around, turned on his heel and marched out. It's no wonder this country's in the mess—"

"Begging your pardon, sir," said Ruthven, after a discreet cough. "But I believe the superintendent is ensconced at the Man with a Load of Mischief, sir. I believe he wanted to be at the scene of the crime." Ruthven seemed not a little thrilled.

"Thank you, Ruthven." Scene of the wine cellar

would be more like it. Matchett had the best one for miles, *and* a superior cook.

"Is Martha ready?" asked Plant. Ruthven nodded. "And you've fixed up the alcove in here, I see. Good, good."

Jury saw then that the alcove at the far end of the room had been fitted up with a curtain, as if it were a tiny stage. The French doors led out to the garden beyond, now layered with snow. But instead of the table and Queen Anne chairs which usually sat in front of this window, a sort of chaise lounge had been moved in and piled with pillows and velvet coverings, so that it resembled a bed.

"What's going on?" asked Jury.

"Don't ask *me*," said Agatha, striking her ample bosom with her fist. "It's one of crazy Melrose's schemes. Always has been theatrical."

"If you'd only stop complaining," said Vivian, "we could get on with this. Though I must admit, I'd like to know what's going on, too."

"Neither of you need to know," said Melrose. "Just play your parts. And now, Inspector, if you will excuse us for just a few moments, I must rehearse my cast."

Ruthven escorted Jury from the room in a way that almost made him feel he was being taken into custody. He was left staring at the pikes and staffs in the hallway. In a few minutes, he saw the woman who he presumed must be Martha, Ruthven's wife, come through the hall and make him a brief curtsy. Then she passed into the drawing room. In another ten minutes, Plant opened the door and beckoned him in.

Plant drew a chair around for Jury, placing it about thirty feet from the curtained alcove. "Now then, Inspector Jury. We are going to present a scene—or part of one—from *Othello*. I shall play that part; Martha is to be Emilia; Vivian will be Desdemona. All right, you have your parts, everyone?"

Truculently, Agatha said, "*You* have parts. All I'm to do is—"

"Don't talk about it; just *do* it," said Melrose.

"I still can't see why I'm not to be Desdemona; after all, Vivian's had no—"

"God! We're not trying out for the Royal Shakespeare Company! It's merely a demonstration for the inspector, here. He has to *see* it. Now, get back there behind that curtain and do as you're told!"

She marched off, sullen. "I've not even got one line to say."

"If I gave you one you'd be saying it all afternoon."

Agatha made a face at Melrose's back, and let the curtain drop in front of her.

Melrose then turned to the cook, Martha. "Now, Martha, all you need do is read those few lines I've checked, and don't worry at all about how you sound." Martha turned beet-red. She must really have felt this to be her stage debut.

"Pretend this area"—Melrose made a sweeping gesture with his hand, standing before the curtain—"is the stage. The curtained recess is Desdemona's bed. Now, Othello has been on stage for some time with Desdemona. There's a lot of talk about the handkerchief, and Iago. Vivian—I mean, Desdemona—is in the bed."

Vivian took her place, lying down rather awkwardly among the pillows and bedclothes, and said, "Kill me tomorrow; let me live tonight!"

"Now, here, the stage direction reads: 'Smothers her.'" And Melrose picked a pillow from the bed and held it a bit above Vivian's face. Then he turned away from the bed, dropping the pillow, and pulled the curtain in front of it. Martha, standing off to the left, having watched the proceeding intently, walked up and pretended to be knocking at an invisible door.

From behind the curtain came a rustling, and a moan: " 'O Lord! Lord! Lord!' " Martha still beat on the door—the thin air—with both hands. Melrose made an elaborate display of looking from Martha to the bed, and recited: " 'What, not dead yet.' " He walked over and pulled the curtain back, where Desdemona lay obscured partially by the disheveled bedclothes and pillows. Melrose stood in front of her, raised the pillow and lowered it, saying, " 'I would not have thee linger in thy pain.' " There came from the bed another thrashing and moaning.

In the meantime, Martha-Emilia was still pretending to hammer on the door with upraised fists. Melrose got up from the bed, where he had been leaning over poor Desdemona, and again closed the bed-curtain. He went to the absent door, pretended to open it, and Martha walked through, reading woodenly; " 'I do beseech you/That I may speak with you, O good my lord!' "

Plant put his hand on her arm. "That's enough, Martha. We've made our point. From here, Inspector, there would have to be one change. In the text, Emilia goes to the bed, and Desdemona says, 'Commend me to my kind lord,' and dies. That would have to be omitted. Because Desdemona"—and Melrose drew back the bed-curtain—"is already dead."

Agatha sat up in the bed, rubbing her throat, and saying, "You did it deliberately, Plant; you nearly killed me, you silly fool—"

Vivian had in the meantime come in through the French window from outside, shivering. "Good lord, Melrose. Next time you want me to do Desdemona, give me a coat. It's freezing."

Jury was momentarily struck dumb. A switch. It

had been a switch—the drugged body of Celia
Matchett put in the bed in place of Harriet Gethvyn-
Owen. Jury applauded.

Melrose bowed and said: "That will be all ladies.
Thank you."

Agatha, who had climbed off the bed and was pulling down her skirts, gaped. "All? *All?* You drag us
over here, make us go through this ridiculous charade,
and then don't explain to us what it's about? Idiot!"

Even Vivian seemed a bit put out. "Yes, really,
Melrose. What *is* it all about?"

It was well she should ask, thought Jury. She didn't
know it, but Melrose Plant might just have saved her
life.

After Plant had got rid of the women, he and Jury
settled down before the fire with whiskey and such
canapes as Martha could muster after her brief brush
with the stage.

"It wouldn't have taken much of an actress to
throw a few words over her shoulder at the maid,"
said Jury.

"No. And I imagine she had on Celia Matchett's
clothes under her costume and the Matchett woman's
hair-do done up under her stage wig. Probably Harriet Gethvyn-Owen made sure the room wasn't well
lit. They had to be sure someone saw 'Celia' alive
whilst the play was in progress. She was actually lying
dead on the stage." Plant lit up a cigar.

"On the stage. God, what nerve—smothering her
right before the eyes of the whole audience."

"Was she drugged, do you think?" said Plant. "And
then brought—by Matchett, I assume—to the curtained recess before the scene was played. There was
a curtain behind the bed, too. That's how Celia got
out and then back in again. When I closed the curtain Vivian (it would have been Harriet) got off the

bed, went out the French door, and Agatha simply got on the bed. Of course, Harriet would have had to *lift* Celia on, dressed in identical costume. But from that distance, amongst the pillows and bed-coverings, and with Othello obscuring the view, no one in the audience would have suspected there were two Desdemonas, would they?"

"Then Gethvyn-Owen goes the few feet to Celia's office, takes off her costume and wig and sits down at the desk," said Jury. "And Daisy comes along, and assumes the woman at the desk is Celia. Then Harriet would have had to go back to the stage-bed, and carry the now-dead Celia to the office. Mrs. Matchett was a small woman, so I guess she could manage it. Anyway, it was only a matter of a few feet. Then Harriet is ready for her curtain-call. My God, what nerve!"

"If she was that cool a customer, it makes one wonder why she didn't just leave her stage-bed, go to the Matchett woman's office, and do her in there. Ever so much simpler," said Melrose.

"Would you? Had you been Harriet? And left your lover with a perfect alibi while you had none? A cold-blooded woman, but not a dumb one, apparently. This way, they are really in it together," said Jury. Then he shrugged. "Of course her killing Celia in the office would still be a possibility, except that four other murders have been done in Long Piddleton to cover up what happened sixteen years ago." Jury leaned forward. "My guess is that Ruby Judd found that bracelet somewhere round that stage-bed. For Simon Matchett, it would be a real facer, wouldn't it? What in hell was his wife's bracelet, the bracelet she always wore, doing on Ruby Judd's arm sixteen years later? He must have guessed where she found it. And he had no way of getting it back. He must have felt in constant danger of her remembering." Jury helped himself to more whiskey. "Then he finds out that

more than one person knows about it. Maybe Ruby
got her Uncle Will in on it by way of getting advice.
Then Will gets in his old friend, Ansy-the-Pansy.
Which of them knew Creed is anybody's guess. So now
we have the presence of the policeman in case
Matchett cuts up rough. Only just imagine: it must
have been like a horrible game of dominoes for him.
First he discovers Ruby's told her uncle, then her
uncle lets him know *he's* told Hainsley, and, perhaps,
Creed. So Matchett had to get Hainsley and Creed
here. He was working against time and he couldn't
leave the village anyway. Since he was an actor it was
probably no trick at all to imitate the voice of Smollett
and lure them here. And it might account for the
weird, public aspect of the killings. It's not that easy
to get rid of one body, much less *four*. He could
hardly walk about the streets of Long Pidd with a
shovel to bury them all. So he does just the opposite—
displays them. What gall. That way, perhaps we'll
think there's a maniac on the loose."

"You think Ruby was blackmailing Matchett herself?"

"More likely sexual blackmail. Maybe she thought
she could get him to marry her. After all, she tried it
on with just about every other man in town, and
Matchett is the most attractive of all. Where was she
going when she left, if not to meet someone? Stupid
girl. Yet she left the bracelet behind. And somewhere,
dammit! that diary!"

"But if they were thinking of blackmailing
Matchett—Small and his friends—well, Matchett has
no money to speak of—oh, stupid of me. Vivian Rivington does, though. Matchett would have to marry
Vivian to get it, don't forget."

"Matchett could have told Ruby that after he'd got
the money, well, then, he'd, ah, get rid of Vivian, and
marry Ruby. Frankly, I think Simon Matchett could

convince any woman of any damned thing he wanted. Like—" Jury paused.

" 'Like'?"

"Like Isabel Rivington, for example."

Plant was silent for a moment. "What do you mean?"

"Well, you wondered, didn't you, why Isabel, so besotted with Matchett herself, would push Vivian at him? To say nothing of losing control of the money herself?"

"You're not suggesting Simon and Isabel have some sort of 'arrangement'? As Simon and Ruby might have had?"

"Yes, of course. Though I doubt we'll ever know the truth of it. But that's what I've always thought."

Melrose looked at Jury for a long moment. "What do you suppose happened to Harriet Gethvyn-Owen?"

Jury considered this, then said. "What I wonder is, what was going to happen to Vivian Rivington?"

They drank their whiskey and sodas and stared at one another, and then at the fire.

CHAPTER 19

Jury drove slowly toward the High Street, heading in the opposite direction from the Man with a Load of Mischief. He was delaying the tiresome, inevitable meeting with Chief Superintendent Racer. Perhaps he could stop at the Jack and Hammer and have Mrs. Scroggs fix him a meal.

When he got to the driveway which led up to the church, he pulled in and parked his car. At least the church was one place he doubted Superintendent Racer would be nosing around, and he wanted some time to think.

The church of St. Rules was as damp and cold as it had been in the early hours of the morning and now it was beginning to get just as dark. As he sat in one of the rear pews, the feeble light of the evening faded from the aisles and the corners even as he watched. He slid down on the hard bench and looked around him—at the arches, the ceiling bosses, the three-tiered pulpit, and the small, black board to one side which held the number of the hymns that the congregation would have sung that morning, had there been a service. The small hymnals were lined up on the narrow shelf that ran the length of the pew in front of him. Jury picked one out, opened it to No. 136, and intoned a few bars of "Onward, Christian Soldiers."

Then feeling a little silly, he closed the book, and looked absently at the cover.

It was stamped in rather worn gold: *Hymns*. It was small, only about five by six or seven inches. Red leather. The voice of Mrs. Gaunt—or was it Daphne?—came back to him. *"I come in and saw her writing. It was in her diary. A little red book."*

It took Jury no more than fifteen minutes, going along behind each pew, pulling out the hymnals and replacing them, before he finally found it: slightly fatter than the hymnals and of a different shade of red, a bit more garish. Easily detected, but only if one were looking for it, since all of the hymnals were partially hidden by the narrow wooden shelf which secured them to the back of the pew. Had one of the parishioners been sitting just there the past Sunday, he would have found it. But there were many more hymnals than villagers to sing from them. Had Ruby left it here as insurance against something, as she might have done with the bracelet? Or had she stuck it in here and simply forgotten it?

On the outside, in the approximate position where the word *Hymnal* was inscribed on the others, was the one word *Diary*, in fading gold cursive. Block letters, dramatically enlarged, graced the first page: RUBY JUDD.

The light had failed completely by now, and he had had to use a torch during his search through the pews. He took the book up to the pulpit, ascending the little ladder, and then pulled the neck of the narrow brass lamp down so that the light would play brightly upon the pages of the book. Most of it, that part covering the early months of the year, was the kind of drivel about boys in Weatherington, or men in Long Piddleton—tradesmen, a salesman; no mention of Trueblood or Darrington—the sort of syrupy

nonsense he would have expected. It was later that
the theme of Simon Matchett began to be sounded,
interspersed with remarks about Trueblood (surprisingly good in bed for a man of his sexual persuasion)
and Darrington (surprisingly bad) . But always it re-
verted to Matchett, who was "ever so handsome"
many times over. *Eyes like the Rydal Water.* Jury
softened at this surprisingly lovely metaphor from the
plodding mind of Ruby Judd. *To think Daphne's got
that, whilst I'm stuck here with the Warden*—Mrs.
Gaunt, no doubt—*and the vicar. Wouldn't they love
to know I'm sitting here writing this whilst I'm supposed to be doing the dusting? Well, I don't get
nearly the pay Daphne does, and all the while working for him, to boot.* Then there were pages
describing her sexual exploits with Darrington, the
part-time boy at the newsagent's, and others, interrupted by comments on the boredom of life in Long Piddleton. Jury flicked forward several pages and found
what he wanted: an account of that pillow-fight with
Daphne. *Rolled off the bed, I did, and when her arm
dangled down, grabbing for me, that bracelet she
wears, tacky thing with a gold cross, it slid off. Suddenly it all come back to me. I was lying under a bed,
and an arm just dangling down and a bracelet. Years
ago, it was.* Was it possible that Ruby, curious little
girl as she was, had actually *crawled under* that stage
bed, and lain there during that performance? She
could actually have been there when Matchett smoth-
ered Celia, and not realized what was happening.
*God!!! Then I remembered sudden-like, what bracelet
this was I found. It was hers, that Mrs. Matchett's,
that got killed. What does it mean???* That was
underlined five times. There was no entry for a
couple of days. Then it seems Ruby had gone to
the Weatherington library and looked back in the
stacks of old newspapers and read it all up: the mur-

der at the Goat and Compasses. But she knew now
that Celia Matchett had been killed in bed, and not
in her office. She remembered with the sudden recollection of the seven-year-old, the vivid feel of that
limp arm.

Now she was spending her time going up to the
Man with a Load of Mischief, still trying to draw Simon Matchett into some sexual overture, despite all
of this. Then she started planning: *Called Uncle Will
today. If he'd remember, anyone would, and at first
he told me I was bonkers—"Ruby you was seven years
old, you don't know what went on." Well, it took me
a long time, but I finally got it over to him that Simon must have done it, must have killed her. Either
him or that girl, Harriet, the paper talked about. I
can remember now how scared I was. That arm.
Ugh!!! And I never told anyone about finding this
bracelet. Thought I'd get in bad trouble.*

The next day: *Uncle Will rung me back and told
me not to do anything, that he was ringing up some
friends of his, some copper. I asked him was he going
to get Simon arrested, and he just kind of laughed. I
kind of got the idea he was talking about getting
money out of Simon. I remember, I told him there
was talk Simon was going to marry this frumpy old
heiress. Pots of money she's got.*

And the next day: *But if he can get money out of
him, why can't I get other things, too?* Jury could almost picture Ruby, her eyes gleaming and her schoolgirl giggle ringing from the church rafters.

There was a lapse of two or three days and then
she wrote: *He was down cellar getting the wine for
the dinner and I just kind of took myself down there
and held out the bracelet and asked him, Didn't he
remember it? He must have, I said, the way he liked
to fiddle it about on my wrist. Then I just up and
told him what I knew. At first I thought he was going*

*to hit me. But he reaches over and pulls me to him
and kisses me!!!!! He said it was too bad, me telling
my uncle, and had I told anyone else? I said, No.
Which wasn't a lie. There was nothing to be done for
it, now, he said, and too bad, for he had always felt
this way about me, but since I was so much younger,
he daren't try nothing. Looked so sad, he did. And
that's when he asked me to go away with him for the
weekend, so's we could work things out. But I'm not
stupid. I said to him he needn't try that on me. He
just wanted to make sure I'd not tell anyone. He
broke open a bottle of champagne and we sat there
and laughed and kissed. I know now he's serious
about me. I'm to pack a bag and say I'm going to
Weatherington so no one will wonder. I just remembered, though, Uncle Will told me to take off this
bracelet and leave it somewhere and not to wear it
anymore and that's all right with me. I'll be wearing
a big diamond soon. I just thought of a marvelous
place to leave the bracelet!! Won't that be a bit of a
giggle??!!*

And the final entry: *Can't write now. Here she
comes.* Mrs. Gaunt, probably. *Must close. MORE TO-
MORROW!!!!*

Ruby must simply have dropped it back into its
little nook, in a row with the hymnals, and picked up
her broom. So the diary was probably just put by,
with the intention of getting it later, and then in her
excitement, she had simply forgotten it.

MORE TOMORROW!!!! Jury read the pathetic
words once again. The silly girl. There had been no
more tomorrows for Ruby Judd. He stood there in
the dark church with the little lamp making a pool of
light on the white pages. So deep was he into the
schoolgirl passion Ruby Judd had felt for Simon
Matchett, that he had only half-heard the heavy, oak
door of the church open and then swish shut.

Jury could not see into the dark vestibule of the church, but he knew Matchett's voice.

"I saw the light from the road and wondered who might be here at this hour. Strange place to find a policeman—in the pulpit."

There was a silence, and some movement, and Jury imagined Matchett was settling himself in one of the rear pews.

"And you, Mr. Matchett? What are *you* doing in church at this hour? Or are innkeepers more religious than policemen?"

"No. But certainly as curious."

There was something unnerving in any circumstances in holding a conversation with a disembodied voice. The only point of light in the church was the puddle cast by the lamp over the pulpit. Jury felt like a jack-lighted deer.

"I suppose the same thing occurred to me as to you, Inspector. If the diary weren't in the vicarage, then possibly the church . . . ? I assume you're not up there reading the Book of Common Prayer?"

"If I were, Mr. Matchett, you'd be by way of having, as they say, 'tipped your hand,' now, wouldn't you?"

A brief laugh floated up through the darkness. "Oh, come now. Your detective sergeant has been like a hound at my heels. Doesn't seem to want me to go anywhere, however hard I may try. No, don't worry. He's quite all right, sleeping by the fire. Hot buttered rum rather liberally laced with sedatives. Now, I think I'd better have that little book, Inspector."

Jury assumed that there was a gun leveled at him. Matchett's confident assumption he would hand over the diary testified to that.

"And if you've a gun, Inspector, suppose you just throw that down here, too. I've never seen one on you, still, one never knows."

Jury didn't carry one. He'd found long ago it was
more dangerous to have one than not to have, in the
main. But there was no point in assuring Matchett of
that. What Jury wanted to do now was to give himself a bit of time to study his predicament. Slightly
out and above this three-tiered pulpit was the rood
loft, perhaps not more than three feet off. "Mr.
Matchett, if you intend to dispatch me—you do intend it?—how can you be so sure no one else knows
you murdered these people?" Jury had no intention
of mentioning Plant, but he needed to keep Matchett
talking.

"Come now, Inspector Jury. Don't try that old trick
on me. Not even your chief superintendent knows
anything. Your sergeant must, but I can take care of
him."

The height and distance of the loft were not great,
though God only knew he was not so agile as he used
to be. "Would you just satisfy my curiosity on one or
two points, Mr. Matchett? Why did you choose to
make such an outlandish display of the bodies? You
could have simply left Hainsley dead in his bed, and
buried Ruby in the wood." Jury knew serial murderers like Matchett were horribly vain. They found
their own cleverness irrisistible. After all, to go to so
much trouble and not to be able to let someone know
how brilliant you are must be torture. At first, he
thought Matchett wasn't going to answer, though. In
these dark and vaulted chambers the tiniest noise was
amplified, and Jury thought he heard the snick of a
safety being drawn back. But he hadn't been wrong
about the murderer's compunction to advertise.

"Surely, you guessed it was the red herring idea, Inspector. The best way to disguise one noise is to make
a bigger one. I hadn't time to be quiet and subtle
about these people, and their, ah, disposal. The Judd
girl, her uncle, and Hainsley, and that policeman

friend of theirs, Creed—all of them were more or less upon me simultaneously. If I couldn't do it quietly, I decided I'd go to the other extreme: make a noise so loud and so bizarre it would be put down to some wild and motiveless murderer. A psychopathic killer."

"Which it was, for a time." Jury didn't much care for the sound of movements, which indicated Matchett was rising and coming down the nave. From the rood loft to the gallery running around the other three sides of the church—that would be no problem. But it would have to be quick.

"Let me ask *you* a question, Inspector Jury. I assume you must have discovered that I murdered my wife. But how on earth—?"

"Stupid of you, Mr. Matchett, to make that assumption. And to confess in the meantime. I've been wondering all along, though, exactly what your commitment to Miss Rivington was?"

Matchett was silent for a moment, and then said, "Which Miss Rivington?"

"I imagine that answers my question." Jury was still gauging distances. "And did Small—I mean Smollett—get the other two here? Or did you?"

"I did. Smollett's voice was easy enough to do after I'd discovered from him he'd told Hainsley and Creed. I simply called them, told them—as Smollett— they'd got to come immediately. I told them to book rooms at the Jack and Hammer and the Swan—well, I couldn't have them all dying at the Man with a Load of Mischief, could I?"

"So you actually got to the Swan, not at eleven, but at ten-thirty. Parked your car in the woods . . . you must have known we'd discover that window. And the tracks."

"Yes, of course. I wanted you to; since I was sitting in the Swan with Vivian at the time of the murder— or near enough—I didn't care *who* you thought came through that window. Outsized boots and a coverall to keep my clothes clean—nothing to it."

Jury wanted to keep him talking. "How did you ever manage to get behind Creed?"

"He thought—rather, I convinced him—that I was merely checking the plumbing. The coverall helped there. And I *am* an actor, Inspector—"

"I've noticed. Why in heaven's name didn't you meet Creed in some *other* place rather than bringing him to Long Piddleton?"

"Well, now, you wouldn't let us leave, would you? What choice had I? And I was beginning to enjoy the inn motif the newspapers had worked up."

"I see." Jury was too busy judging the amount of leverage he'd need to waste emotion on this invisible man in the inky darkness whom he couldn't see. "Does murder get to be a habit after a while?"

"Perhaps. But I really must insist on having that diary, now, Inspector. And if you would be so kind as to move *very slowly* down those pulpit steps—"

"Not much choice, now, have I mate?" Jury suddenly switched off the light and ducked behind the pulpit as the first shot splintered the wood above his head. Then he jumped to its edge and heaved his weight toward the rood loft. The now-total darkness was his only cover and it took every ounce of strength to grasp the edge of the loft. His hands grabbed and held and he dangled momentarily, until his last burst of strength pulled him up and over. Another shot landed in the general direction of the ceiling boss above his head and then there was stillness, which he tried not to break by breathing, though his lungs seemed about to burst. From the loft, he could easily swing over to the gallery—how ironic, Jury thought, that the church resembled a theater—but at the moment his mind was engaged in trying to figure out what sort of gun Matchett had and how many shots were left. Matchett was not fool enough to waste them by continuing to fire into the dark.

Jury heard feet scraping off to the left, and he knew that Matchett must be ascending the rood-loft staircase, which had been cut into the wall off to his left. He made his way, crouching, over to the other end, and jumped from the loft to the gallery on his right just as Matchett reached the top of the stairs, and there was another flash and a shot that Jury could have sworn barely missed his ear. Crouching still, he made his way between the benches, down the gallery, and then stopped. Another silence. Slowly, he took the electric torch from his raincoat pocket, set it on the gallery ledge, flicked it on, and darted down the west side of the gallery while another shot rang out. The torch rolled and crashed into the nave below.

What Jury had felt when he brought out his torch was the inside pocket of his raincoat with the box of cough drops Wiggins had given him. If he could just get the cellophane off without giving away his position—for in the other pocket was the catapult the Double boy had given him. *Bless you, James.* He dislodged a sticky cough drop from the others in the box, placed it in the rubber band, and aimed at the nearest window. There was the *pinging* sound of glass, followed by another shot. He tried to keep up this reflex action on Matchett's part by quickly pulling back the band and aiming another cough-drop missile below, into the nave. He fired into the dark recess and heard a shattering sound. Possibly winged the plaster statuette of the Virgin. Jury prayed. Oh, how he prayed.

But instead of an answering shot, there was the sound of running feet moving down the rood-loft steps and into the nave.

Again, a long silence, and then a light fanning out over the gallery. Jury ducked down.

"I admire your diversionary tactics, Chief Inspector," came the voice from below. "But it was just as unfortunate for you to give up your torch as it was stupid of me not to bring mine. And since it is quite obvious you've no gun, and I still have, don't you think you'd just as well come down now?"

Since Matchett was not about to fritter another shot away, Jury supposed he hadn't much choice. Would he simply shoot Jury when he had him in view? Or would he wait until he made sure he had the diary in hand? Jury hoped he would wait.

"If you'd just step down here into the nave, Inspector? I really must have that diary. And then we can go for a little drive."

Jury stopped sweating for the moment. Between here and a grave in the woods he could surely think of something. "I'm coming down, Matchett."

"Carefully, now, carefully."

Jury walked past the benches to the east side toward the stone steps that Matchett had used a few moments before. Looking down, Jury noticed Matchett was standing about midway in the nave, between the rows of pews. As he passed between the benches he quickly plucked a hymnal from behind its little wooden slat, and held it. Then he descended the steps, and as he reached the bottom, he raised the book above his head, both hands in the air.

"Now, if you'll just bring the diary over here—"

Jury was walking toward him, and Matchett told him to stop when he was about ten feet away. "Close enough, I think—"

At that moment, Jury opened his fingers slightly and the hymnal fell onto the soft carpeting which covered the brass rubbing. They were both standing on it.

"Clumsy," said Matchett.

Jury started to lean down, knowing full well Matchett would stop him.

"Uh-uh, Inspector. Just kick it over here, if you don't mind."

It was what he wanted, and he only hoped he had enough strength left in his leg to do the job. Jury jabbed with his heel against the thin covering, jerking it back toward him and doing it just quickly enough to throw Matchett completely off balance. The last shot exploded, grazing Jury's arm, and then he lunged. It was not a hard job, shouldering Matchett back against the pew, and Jury was so enraged—all of the suppressed anger at this madman coming out now—that the blow to Matchett's jaw and the other to his stomach were simultaneous and quite effective. Matchett crumpled and dropped onto the stone floor between two of the pews.

Jury picked up the hymnal. The diary was still up on the pulpit. He had slipped it under the huge, illuminated Bible while he had been talking to Matchett. He looked down at him now, and wondered about a man who could develop a taste for murder as some men do for oysters. Jury said to his unconscious form: "Mr. Matchett, you are not obliged to say anything unless you wish to do so, but what you say may be put into writing and given in evidence. Understood?"

He turned and walked back up toward the altar and ascended the pulpit once more. He switched on the little light, lifted the Bible, and pulled out Ruby Judd's diary. His arms spread-eagled over the pulpit—very much like a man of the cloth—he looked down at the book which would put an end to Simon Matchett.

Once again he heard the heavy door at the rear swing open and softly smack shut. From the dark

recess of the vestibule came the waspish, sarcastic
voice of none other than Chief Superintendent Racer.

"Finally found your vocation, have you Jury?"

Matchett was taken to the Weatherington station.
He had been "officially" arrested by Racer and his
right-hand man, Inspector Briscowe, who had accom-
panied his superior to Long Piddleton, to "wind
things up," as Racer put it to the reporters late that
night. The very moment the chief superintendent hit
town, the case seemed to solve itself. Racer said none
of this blatantly, but the cause-effect relationship was
not lost on the London reporters.

"The bloody little creep," said Sheila Hogg, who
was, at midnight, pouring Scotch for Jury as if it
came out of a spigot. "He's going to take the damned
credit for this after you did all the work. And nearly
got yourself killed in the bargain. Here." She shoved
a pint-sized glass in Jury's free hand, his other arm
having been bound up by a considerably chastened
Dr. Appleby.

Within an hour of Matchett's arrest, all of Long
Piddleton knew of it—Pluck's work, no doubt. (Jury
had rather enjoyed watching Pluck try to elbow Briscowe out of the photographers' camera range.) Sheila
had veritably dragged Jury back to the house for a
drink. He was to her, certainly, a hero.

In answer to her complaint, Jury said, "Oh, well.
As long as things finally got sorted out, it makes no
difference, does it?"

"And lucky for you they did," said Darrington, jealousy now sparking his usual hostility. "You were
about to come a purler there with me, weren't you?"
Darrington smirked.

Jury raised his eyebrows in mock surprise. "You?
Oh, come now. I never suspected you. I thought that

was clear. You haven't the imagination. Look at Matchett's style. Had he not had that kinky mind, he might have been a writer."

Sheila giggled, half with drink, half with delight. Darrington turned red and got up. "Why the bloody hell don't you just get out? You've made my life a misery ever since you came, and you've no more business here!"

Sheila slammed down her glass. "Neither have I!" She got to her feet a bit unsteadily, and at the same time attempted to assume a regal pose. "Oliver, you are also a creep. I'll send for my things later."

Darrington had resumed his seat and scarcely looked at her. "You're drunk," he said, staring into the depths of his own glass.

Jury put out an arm to steady her as she whirled on Darrington. "I'd rather be drunk, you bloody fool, than be . . . be . . . *unimaginative!* Right, Inspector?"

Although the words got slurred a bit in the saying, and she leaned toward him as if in a wind, Jury agreed with her, absolutely. He even offered her his arm and escorted her from the room.

"He thinks I'm kidding. I'm not. I'll get myself a room at the Scroggses'. Unless . . ." and she looked hopefully up at him from under her thick lashes.

He smiled. "Sorry, love. The Man with a Load of Mischief is off-limits. No more guests." As he helped her on with her coat, he saw that her face was crumpling a bit with disappointment, and he winked at her. "But there's always London. You do go down to London, don't you?"

Her spirits restored, she said, "You bet I do, sweetie!"

As they walked out to the car, Jury saw Darrington silhouetted against the light from the hall. "Sheila? What the bloody hell . . . "

*   *   *

After seeing to it that Sheila was in the motherly
hands of Mrs. Scroggs, Jury made his way, light-
headed, back to the Man with a Load of Mischief. As
he got out of the Morris, he noticed a light downstairs in the saloon bar.

It was Daphne Murch, wringing her hands, waiting
for him to come in. Jury remembered that she must
have been here when they came to gather up
Matchett's things.

She ran over to him and said, "I couldn't believe it,
I couldn't! Mr. Matchett, sir! Him as has always been
so aboveboard, you might say."

"I'm truly sorry, Daphne. You must feel awful."
They were sitting at one of the tables now, where
Daphne had put out tea things, a cuppa being the
true Englishman's cure for everything, from tired feet
to mass murder. Daphne kept shaking her head in
disbelief.

"Listen, Daphne. You've no job, right?"

She was looking very depressed, and Jury added,
"I've some friends in Hampstead Heath." He took
out his small notebook and jotted down the address
and gave it to her. "I don't know if you'd like London—" (from the expression on her face, it was clear
she was thrilled) "—but I assure you they're very good
people, and I happen to know they're looking for a
housemaid." What Jury also knew was that they had
a very presentable young chauffeur. "If you want, I'll
get in touch with them immediately I get back to
London, and . . ."

He was interrupted by Daphne's running round
the table and kissing him. Then she flew from the
room in pink confusion.

CHAPTER 20

MONDAY, DECEMBER 28

When Jury woke the next morning, it was with little recollection that he'd even stumbled upstairs and dropped on the bed. He hadn't undressed. Those drinks at Darrington's, on top of little sleep in the last forty-eight hours, must have been lethal. It was the rather tentative knock on the door which had woken him. To his "come in," Wiggins poked his head around the door.

"I'm really sorry to wake you, sir. But Superintendent Racer's down in the dining room and he's been asking for you for the last hour. I've been putting him off, but I don't think I can much longer." Wiggins's awful remorse at having let Matchett slip from his grasp had been alleviated only by Jury's telling him how he had made use of the cough drops. "If it hadn't been for you, Sergeant—" The implication that Wiggins had just about saved Inspector Jury's life had infused the sergeant with courage. Wiggins was now four-square in the room and saying in no uncertain terms: "To tell the truth, sir, I think it's shameful the way he's been acting. You haven't had any sleep hardly for a week. You work too hard, if you don't mind my saying it. So I told Superintendent Racer I'd call you at a decent hour and not before." Sergeant Wiggins stopped suddenly, as if the words he had spoken might sprout wings and fly off to New Scotland Yard.

"You really told him that?" Jury propped himself up on one elbow and stared at Wiggins.

"Indeed, I did, sir."

"Then all I can say is, you've got a hell of a lot more courage than I, Wiggins."

The sergeant, beaming, left Jury to dress. And Jury noticed he hadn't once pulled out his handkerchief.

"You wanted to see me?" Jury deliberately omitted the *sir*. "Shall I sit down?"

Chief Superintendent Racer was already seated in the dining room, the remains of a lavish breakfast spread in dishes about him: crumbs of scone, bits of buttered egg, bare bones of kipper. Light glinted on his onyx ring as he twirled a freshly lit cigar in his mouth.

"Been catching up on your sleep since you've been in the country? It's a damned good thing this case came to a close when it did, Jury"—Jury noticed there was no mention of who had brought it to a close—"or you'd have had the A.C. down here, never fear."

Daphne Murch, blushing on into the morning, set a silver coffeepot before Jury, smiled broadly, and retreated, unmindful of Superintendent Racer's eyes, fixed on her legs.

"Not a bad little baggage," he said before turning to lean across the table and glare at Jury. His chesterfield coat, which had been swankily draped across his back, cascaded from one shoulder, and he rehitched it. "Jury, although I certainly cannot credit every move you've made in this case, still, we have managed to wrap it up, so there's no hard feelings on my part. I never did think you were a bad policeman, although a bit too popular with the other men for my tastes. That feeling the men under you have about you—all that bloody 'nice chap' business. You've got to make the men *respect* you, Jury. Not *like*. It's not only that. You disobey orders. You were told to call in every day. You didn't. You were told to keep me informed of every move. You didn't. You'll never make superintendent that way, Jury. You've got to know how to deal with the men above and the boys below."

To Jury it sounded like the title of a bad American war film.

"Well, I'm off. You can wind things up here." Racer tossed a handful of change on the table—he wasn't, to give him his due, cheap—and looked round the room. "Not a bad place for such a one-eyed village. Had quite a decent meal last night. There's something to be said for a man who brews his own beer . . ."

If only Jack the Ripper had brewed his own beer, thought Jury, buttering up a piece of cold toast.

"What is it, Wiggins?" snapped Racer.

Sergeant Wiggins had popped up like a cork at their table. "Sergeant Pluck's brought round the car, sir."

"Very well." As Wiggins turned to leave, Racer called him back: "Sergeant, I don't especially care for the tone you used with me this morning—"

Jury's patience had worn thin. "Sergeant Wiggins just about saved my life." At Racer's raised eyebrow, Jury went on: "You've heard of the soldier saved because his old mum insisted he carry a Bible in his breast pocket—?" Jury tossed the box of cough drops on the table.

"And what the hell's *that* in aid of?" asked Racer, shoving the box with a tip of his finger, like a dead mouse.

"Together with a catapult, those cough drops saved me." Jury drank off his coffee and decided to embroider. "Wiggins knew I hadn't a gun. As far as I'm concerned it was pretty quick thinking on his part."

Absolutely delighted with this unexpected and (he suspected) undeserved praise, Wiggins beamed and looked perplexed in turns. He seemed unsure as to how to decipher this runic message Jury had just delivered to his superior.

Racer looked from the one to the other and merely grunted. Then he said, with honeyed venom: "If you don't mind, Inspector Jury, we won't put the public onto the fact Scotland Yard's only got catapults to protect itself with, will we?"

Delaying as long as possible his good-bye to Vivian Rivington, Jury sat in the Long Piddleton police station, shuffling through papers and listening to a mild argument between Pluck and Wiggins. Pluck, upholding the virtues of country living, was scouring the *Times* for the latest rapes, muggings, and murders in London's alleyways, when the door seemed to wrest itself open as if torn by ghostly hands and Lady Ardry walked in. Melrose Plant, looking apologetic, followed her. At the sight of Agatha, Pluck and Wiggins exchanged glances and retreated with tea and newspaper to the outer room.

Lady Ardry shot out her hand like a switchblade and pumped Jury's. "Well, we did it, didn't we, Inspector Jury?" Her earlier rancor had quite vanished in the breeze she had flapped up with her victory flag.

"*We*, dear Aunt?" said Melrose, settling himself in a chair in the corner so that he was behind her and in the shadows. He lit up a cigar with an especially heavenly aroma.

Jury smiled. "Well, whoever did it, Lady Ardry, just let's be glad it's done."

"I just stopped in to ask you to lunch, Inspector, and happened to meet my aunt coming down the street—"

"Lunch?" said Lady Ardry, who was arranging her

cape about her chair like the Coronation robes. "That should be jolly. What time?"

"The invitation, dear Aunt, is for Inspector—"

But she merely flapped her hand over her shoulder. "We've more important matters to discuss than food." She planted both hands firmly on her walking stick. Jury was happy to see the cutoff-fingered mittens back in favor. Clasped about the wrist of one brown mitten was Plant's emerald-and-ruby bracelet. Jury thought its regal splendor had already begun to tarnish.

"Had to be him, didn't it? Matchett. Always thought so. One can tell from the eyes, Inspector. It's always the eyes. Paranoid, quite mad, Matchett's are. Hard and cold . . . Well!" She clapped her hand on the desk. "All I can say is, it's good you were here, Johnny-on-the-spot, instead of that *awful* man, your superintendent. I'm sure you wouldn't care for me to repeat to you the contemptible way the man acted in my house—"

"We certainly wouldn't, Agatha," said Melrose, who was slowly enveiling himself in a shroud of smoke like a kind of translucent armor.

Over her shoulder, she tossed back at him: "All well and good for you to sit up there in Ardry End, lolling about over port and walnuts—"

"Lady Ardry," said Jury, aware he was jeopardizing his newly won popularity, "had it not been for Mr. Plant here, we'd never have got the evidence to put Matchett behind bars."

"Decent of you to say so, my dear Jury, but then you always were a generous, pretty-spoken man—"

Behind her, Plant choked on his cigar.

"But," she continued, "*we* know who did *the work* in this case." She gave him a smarmy smile. "And it wasn't Plant, not much more was it that crazy superintendent, who's been too busy sniffing up to all the girls in the village." She polished one or two of the

emeralds in her bracelet with a mittened hand, then
leaned across and whispered, "I hear he was in the
Jack and Hammer last night, hanging round Nellie
Lickens."

Jury indulged his curiosity. "And who's Nellie
Lickens when she's at home?"

"You know. Ida Lickins's girl. Who keeps the
junkshop. Nellie does for Dick Scroggs now and then,
and no better than she should be—"

"Idle gossip, Agatha."

"Never you mind, Plant. Granted, my own humble
abode isn't Ardry End"—and she turned to sneer in
Plant's direction—"but Superintendent Whoever-he-is
had no right to treat me in that offhand manner.
Walked into my cottage, took one look, and turned
on his heel and walked out. Even had dinner laid on.
Some of my very nice eel stew—you needn't make that
retching noise, Plant—and the man had the audacity
to walk into my kitchen and look in the pot!"

"Terribly sorry, Lady Ardry, if New Scotland Yard
has inconvenienced you in any way—"

"Well, let me tell you, I'm sure I manage to make
my guests quite comfortable. As a matter of fact, I've
just been thinking today of putting up a B and B
sign. I seem to have a knack for that sort of thing—"

"Lovely," said Melrose, through a screen of smoke;
"then our next series could be called 'The Northants.
Tourists Murders.'"

"As a matter of fact, Plant," she threw over her
shoulder, "I wonder you don't do the same. Do you
some good to work for a living."

"Are you suggesting I make Ardry End into a Bed
and Breakfast establishment?"

"Certainly. You'd do a smashing business." From
the way her eyes glittered, Jury was sure she'd just
come upon this quixotic notion. Now she would tilt
at whatever windmills rose in her path. "Twenty-two

sleeping rooms—my heavens!—why didn't we think of it before? With Martha to do the breakfasts and me to take charge—a gold mine!"

"I haven't the time," said Melrose calmly.

"Time? You've nothing *but* time. That University business hardly takes up more than an hour a week. You need something to *do*, Melrose—"

"But I *have* something. I've decided to become a writer." Through tendrils of smoke, Melrose smiled weirdly at Jury. "I'm writing a book."

Nearly overturning her chair, she jumped up. "What on earth are you talking about?"

"Just that, Agatha. I'm writing a book about this whole grisly affair."

"But you can't! That'd be two of us doing it! You know I told you I was writing a kind of semi-documentary. Like that Capote person about those murders in America."

"Not *Ka-put*, for God's sake. *Ca-po-te*. Three syllables, long *O*. Must you slaughter the names of your own countrymen?"

"Never mind. I've got the whole thing plotted out."

"Well, then, you'd better be getting on with it. Or I'll finish before you do."

"Finish! Well, it's not all that easy, you know. You've got to find a publisher. We who scratch away at our desks all day know how difficult this writing game is—"

"I'll simply buy a publisher, then." Melrose kept his eyes clamped on Jury.

"Oh, that's just like you, Plant."

"Isn't it just. I've already got my first chapter done." Melrose tapped the ash from his cigar neatly into the palm of his hand.

She whirled on Jury as if she meant for him to stop this madman in his tracks. Jury only shrugged. "Well, you two can sit here lollygagging all afternoon. I've got to get back to my writing." She raked her walking stick across door and doorjamb in her sudden exit.

"At least," said Melrose, "we're rid of her for the afternoon, Inspector. Time to have a quiet luncheon. That is, if you'll come?" Plant rose, depositing his cigar ash in a tray on the desk.

"I'd be delighted."

Plant extended his hand and Jury rose. "An inappropriate thing to say, in the circumstances," said Melrose, "but I'm sorry it's all over. I seldom meet anyone whose mind does not unravel like an old piece of tatting when life becomes problematical." He drew on his kidskin gloves and patted his cap into place. As he turned to the door, Jury asked:

"Mr. Plant. One question: Why *did* you give up your title?"

"Why?" Plant was thoughtful. "I'll tell you, if I can depend on your not letting it get around." Jury smiled and nodded. Plant lowered his voice to a whisper. "When I put on that capelike gown and that wig, Inspector, I looked exactly like Aunt Agatha." He was out the door. Before he closed it, though, he stuck his head round the corner. "There was a reason. I'll tell you some day. Good-bye, Inspector." He touched his fingers to the brim of his cap in a salute.

As he walked out the door shortly after Plant had left, Jury heard Pluck and Wiggins arguing.

"Now just look here what happened yesterday in Hampstead Heath," said Pluck, slapping his fingers against a page of the *Telegraph*: "Fifteen-year-old girl goes and gets herself assaulted." He tossed the paper aside. "An' you say London's a right old place. Ha! You won't catch me living there." As Jury shut the door, Pluck slurped his tea and added: "Man could get himself killed."

* * *

He had agreed to meet Vivian around noon, and it was close to that now, and he was putting off the meeting. When he saw Marshall Trueblood behind his Regency window, pecking with his finger like a bird against the pane, Jury was glad of the reprieve.

"My dear!" said Trueblood, as Jury walked in the shop. "They told me you were leaving! Listen, you could have pasted my ears to the top of my head when I heard it was Simon! Simon, of all people! I mean, he was so *attractive!* Was he trying to implicate me by taking my letter opener, the rotter?"

"Probably. I doubt he could have taken the vicar by surprise as he did the others and strangled him, anyway."

"My God, I just thought: poor Vivian. What if she had *married* the man?" Trueblood shuddered as he lit up a bright pink cigarette. "So it was Matchett who murdered his wife?"

"It was. He finally admitted to that." Jury looked at his watch and rose. "If you're ever in London, Mr. Trueblood, be sure to look me up."

"I wouldn't *miss* the chance, darling!"

There was a bench on the green, and the square was once again a clear, glistering white, for it had snowed during the night. Jury sat there, staring at the ducks. Then he stared across the square at the dark stone of the Rivington house. He should go over as he had promised. But he just sat there. Finally, he saw the door of the house open, and a figure come out, coated and scarved. She left behind her a very neat set of tracks on the smooth, crisp whiteness, a single line of them as she walked toward him.

As she came round the edge of the pond, he got up. "I thought," she said, smiling, "you were going to come round at eleven. I was watching out the window for you, and then I saw someone sitting over here, and wondered if it could be you." Jury said nothing, and she went on. "Well, I just wanted to thank you for everything."

His mouth felt stiff with the cold. But he finally brought out, "I hope you weren't too . . . downcast by the news, Miss Rivington."

Her eyes went over his face. "Downcast. What a felicitous choice of word. No, not really. I was just horribly shocked. I seem to have surrounded myself with people I couldn't trust." She wrapped her arms about her, warding off cold, and the tip of her overshoe pushed back the snow. "Isabel told me the truth. About what happened to my father." She looked up at him, but Jury did not comment. "She said it was her conscience, that it was weighing very heavily on her. I wonder. After all these years, would one's conscience suddenly begin acting up? You were her conscience, weren't you?" Vivian smiled. Jury stared down at the snow as if daisies might suddenly spring through it, the way things do in timed-release photos. When he didn't say anything, she went on. "There's one thing, though, I must know."

"What's that?" His voice sounded strange to him.

"Simon and Isabel." She had her hands stuffed in the big pockets of her coat now, and her head was bent so low all he could see was the knitted crown of her cap. "Were they lovers?" She raised her head and looked directly at him. "Did they plan on rather unceremoniously disposing of me and then making off— as they say—with the swag?"

She was smiling slightly, but the pain in her eyes went through Jury. It was precisely what Matchett had planned, Jury was certain. He had needed Isabel to push Vivian toward him. The idea of her fiancé and her sister making love and laughing about it behind her back—that must be something of the image she was carrying about in her mind.

"Was that the way it was?" she asked.

"No. You—and the money, I guess—would have satisfied Matchett."

Vivian expelled a long breath, as if she'd been holding it. "I don't know why that would have bothered me so much, now he's been taken in. But it would have." She sighed. "Awful to say, perhaps, but I'm relieved, I think. I mean, at not having to marry him."

" 'Having to'? You never had to."

"Yes. I know."

"I don't think he was the man for you, in any event." Jury looked up at the clouds scudding across the watery blue of the winter sky. "Not your type." He stood there, waiting for God to solve his problem.

"What type, then?"

"Oh, someone more reflective, maybe."

She was silent. Then she asked, "What was that line, the one you quoted? *Agnosco* . . . something?"

"That? '*Agnosco veteris vestigia flammae*: I recognize the vestiges of an old flame.' "

"He must have been something."

"Who? Aeneas?"

"No. The old flame. If not even Aeneas could take his place."

"I think the thing is, maybe he could."

"I wonder." She too turned to look up at the weak blue of the sky. "I think I shall go to France or, better yet, Italy."

Or Mars.

She stood there for a moment longer, looking at him, and then turned back toward her house. "Goodbye. And thank you. How inadequate that sounds." Her hand merely grazed his.

As he watched her walk away, making another neat line of tracks across the unbroken snow, he thought, *You're a real devil with the women, Jury. It's no wonder they all come screaming out of the bushes and tear at your clothes every time you happen to walk by.* From this distance, it was like watching a doll go into a dollhouse and shut the door behind her.

How long he sat there, staring at the ducks, he didn't know. They were bobbing in the warmer water beneath the brown rushes, some of them in pairs, as if even they were better at this sort of thing than was Jury. He was supposed to be at Melrose Plant's for lunch. As he was dragging himself off the bench, he heard a rustle in the bushes behind him and turned just in time to see the top of a mousy brown head disappear below the line of shrubbery.

"All right. Out of there, straight away." Jury used as sinister a tone as possible. "If I once use my trusty Magnum forty-five on you, you'll go round with your stomachs looking like doughnuts."

Giggles. Then slowly the Doubles came forward. The little girl turned her face down to the ground, circumscribing a circle in it with the toe of her old boot.

"Well, James. And James. And why are you on my trail today? Come on—out with it!"

A bird-titter from the girl as she dipped her face as if she meant to wash it in the snow. The boy said, "We heard you was leaving sir. We come to give you this." He pulled from his sagging coat pocket a rather dirty package, wrapped in leftover Christmas paper. It was flat, and tied with a bit of heavily handled ribbon, which once had been white.

"A present? I certainly do thank you." He undid the package and found a piece of cardboard, cut to serve as a kind of crude frame, and against this was glued a picture. It showed a mountainlike projection, covered in deep snow, and off in the distance a dark, amorphous creature, like a poorly focused King Kong. It had come from a magazine. Jury scratched his head.

"It's that Abominable Snow Man," said James, his tongue sticking on *abominable.* "Lives in—what's the name of that place—?" and he looked to his sister for information, but got only a furious shaking of her head. Her lips were, as always, sealed.

"The Himalayas?"

"That's it, sir. Don't it look like him, though?"

Jury scarcely knew how to answer. But he said, "That's quite wonderful, James. Really, it looks exactly like him."

"And just look at them *tracks,* Mr. Jury. That's what I thought you'd like—them tracks. Just think what he could do round here!" And James spread his arms to take in the village green. Then observing the neat lines which Vivian had made coming and going, he said, "Who's been muckin' it up?"

Jury smiled and folded the wrapping paper back round the picture and said. "Your other present just about saved my life." And he related a blow-by-blow account of the confrontation in the church.

Their large eyes nearly swam in their faces at the telling of this marvel.

"Jesus, Mary and Joseph!" said the girl, and quickly clapped her hand to her mouth.

Jury said, "So one good turn deserves another. I thought perhaps you two would like to take a little ride with me—" He pointed to the police car.

"Crikey!" said James. "You mean in that there *police* car?" Totally awed, they looked at one another, and then nodded their heads firmly. Confirmation and reconfirmation.

As Jury bundled them into the car, he noticed how much better he felt. He envisioned the sweeping, untrammeled vistas of Ardry End, glistening, snow-crusted, smoothly white and gently curving.

As the High Street became the Dorking Dean Road, Jury thought, *Oh, what the hell?*

And turned on the siren.

Dear Jury,

You have been gone for three months now and, with only Agatha to keep me company, it seems like three years. Her visits are, however, considerably reduced, owing to her belief we are in a mad race to see which of us will finish his book first. I simply tell her I've done another chapter, and that sends her scurrying home.

Speaking of writers, Darrington has gone off to America to set the course of the American novel back a few hundred years. I was not really surprised when I learned of his plagiarism—you didn't think Pluck's lips would stay sealed on that one, did you? Sheila was glad to be rid of him. She's talking about writing up the whole business of their fraud for the newspapers, even if it means going to gaol herself. The girl has a conscience.

Lorraine ages monthly from her frequent trips to London and mentions dropping in on you. Lock your doors, old chap. Willie has found another companion in the new vicar, a much younger man, but still, vicars always look as if they need to be dusted daily.

Isabel has gone and so has Vivian, but definitely not together. Vivian settled a bit of money on her with the understanding she'd stay out of

her life. Vivian has got herself a villa in Naples.
Aren't you due for a holiday?

I have a dog. I was thinking of getting one,
anyway—one of those sleek ones, like a whippet,
the sort that turns up in drawing-room pictures
of country gentlemen. However, I had cycled out
to the Man with a Load of Mischief one wet afternoon (for sentimental reasons, perhaps—or
does that sound too macabre?) and walked
about. The stables, the eaves, the old sign raining rain, and I wandered back behind the stables
to find—guess who?—Mindy. Matchett's dog,
which he had made no provision for. I can fancy
a man killing five people, but to leave one's dog
stranded is really beneath contempt. At any rate,
I allowed the brute to follow me home, a lengthy
procedure, since Mindy is not very quick, as you
may remember.

Those peculiar children—the Doubles?—visit
me now and again. Heads pop up in the shrubbery at odd moments. The girl I especially admire for her having learnt so young the secret of
truly good conversation: silence. She makes so
few demands on one to sparkle with wit, and so
forth, and we have many an interesting, if one-
sided talk.

May I ask you a favor? If ever you come across
another case—really, I am not particular—and if
you would permit me to be of any help to you,
do. My life here offers little challenge to the
imagination.

There is no more snow.

The heavy embossed stationery was signed, in thick,
black ink, with the one word: PLANT.

Jury bundled the letter back into its envelope and

stuck it up on his mantel like a message left for him by someone who had come and gone. Looking at the little white square of Plant's letter, with the address in small, black figures brought back to him great expanses of crystallized snow, with tracks running through it. Well, as Plant said, there was no more snow. He looked out of his window, gray and dismal with rain.

He plucked his raincoat from its peg behind the door and walked out the door.

Jury also loved the rain.